continued .

D0981750

"Fast-paced but filled with humor and pathos. A powerful, action-packed thriller."
—*Genre Go Round Reviews*

"Benson has brought the series to a new, impressive height—dark, startling, and [with] plenty of shocking surprises. Urban fantasy fans should not miss this fantastic series."
—*SciFiChick.com*

Cat's Claw

"Callie bounces from twist to twist as she explores Benson's richly imagined world, where multiple mythologies blend and the After-life is run as a corporation."
—*Publishers Weekly*

"An entertaining, frenzied fantasy frolic that will have the audience laughing at the chick-lit voice of the heroine, who is willing to go to Heaven on a hellish cause."
—*Genre Go Round Reviews*

"Benson is back with a second helping of her refreshing take on death and Purgatory . . . Callie's offbeat humor and viewpoint guarantee a madcap romp."
—*RT Book Reviews*

Death's Daughter

"Amber Benson does an excellent job of creating strong characters, as well as educating the reader on some great mythology history . . . A fast-paced and very entertaining story."
—*Sacramento Book Review*

"An urban fantasy series featuring a heroine whose macabre humor fits perfectly with her circumstances. Sure to appeal to fans of Tanya Huff's Vicki Nelson series and Charles de Lint's urban fan-tasies."
—*Library Journal*

"A beguiling blend of fantasy and horror . . . Calliope emerges as an authentically original creation . . . The humorous tone never gets in the way of the imaginative weirdness of the supernatural events."
—*Locus*

"In *Death's Daughter*, Benson provides a fun romp that defines the rules of an exciting new universe you'll be chomping at the bit to dive back into time and again. There's action; there's intrigue, redemption, an adorable hell puppy, and even a hot guy or two. What more could you ask for?"
—*Buffyfest*

"Amber Benson writes an amusing, action-packed, chick-lit urban fantasy loaded with more twists and curves than a twist-a-whirl . . . Filled with humor and wit, this is a refreshing, original thriller as double, triple, and nth crossings are the norm."

—*Genre Go Round Reviews*

"With a creative story line as proof, Ms. Benson adds writing to her ever-growing list of talents. Set within an intriguing paranormal world, *Death's Daughter* unfolds a seductive tale of power and deception. A great start to a series that will be easy for readers to get hooked on."

—*Darque Reviews*

"Opens the door on an intriguing, fully thought-out universe, with a likable main character and the potential for mayhem around every corner. It's a lot of fun."

—*Fangoria*

"A lively and funny story packed with nonstop action . . . Benson's flair for combining mythology and pop culture to create laugh-out-loud characters and incidents strongly reminded me of Esther Friesner's *Temping Fate*."

—*The Green Man Review*

"Callie is sarcastic, smart-mouthed, and overwhelmed. I liked her a lot! I found this to be an amusing book from start to finish. It was refreshing to have a lighthearted but still-suspenseful para-normal come on the scene. The mythology and settings were unique and creepy (my favorite) . . . Callie's voice was spot-on for a twenty-four-year-old assistant living in New York who is suddenly dropped into the middle of Hell. I have a feeling this is the start of a series, so I will be eagerly awaiting more adventures of Callie, Clio, and Runt the hellhound."

—*Night Owl Reviews*

"A clever and well-told story . . . It's also a step outside the current paranormal-fantasy rut but with enough elements in common to please fans of that form as well."

—*Critical Mass*

"Amber Benson has created a brash, sassy heroine oozing attitude as she deals with family, business, an angry goddess, zombie armies, and betrayal in this imaginative blend of assorted mythologies. The snappy dialogue keeps pace with the quick pace while providing a fun touch of self-deprecating humor. It should be interesting to see where Benson takes Callie next."

—*Monsters and Critics*

Ace Books by Amber Benson

DEATH'S DAUGHTER
CAT'S CLAW
SERPENT'S STORM
HOW TO BE DEATH
THE GOLDEN AGE OF DEATH

THE WITCHES OF ECHO PARK

The Witches of Echo Park

AMBER BENSON

ACE BOOKS, NEW YORK

THE BERKLEY PUBLISHING GROUP
Published by the Penguin Group
Penguin Group (USA) LLC
375 Hudson Street, New York, New York 10014

USA • Canada • UK • Ireland • Australia • New Zealand • India • South Africa • China

penguin.com

A Penguin Random House Company

This book is an original publication of The Berkley Publishing Group.

Ace Books are published by The Berkley Publishing Group.
ACE and the "A" design are trademarks of Penguin Group (USA) LLC.

Library of Congress Cataloging-in-Publication Data

Benson, Amber, 1977–
The witches of Echo Park / Amber Benson.
pages ; cm. — (The witches of Echo Park ; 1)
ISBN 978-0-425-26867-4 (softcover)
1. Witches—Fiction. 2. Magic—Fiction. I. Title.
PS3602.E685W59 2015
813'.6—dc23
2014035728

PUBLISHING HISTORY
Ace trade paperback edition / January 2015

PRINTED IN THE UNITED STATES OF AMERICA

10 9 8 7 6 5 4 3 2 1

Cover art by Larry Rostant.
Cover design by Diana Kolsky.
Interior text design by Kelly Lipovich.

To all the special women in my life—I treasure your friendships. They get me through my days and inspire me to be a better lady.

Acknowledgments

The witches were born from a sangria-filled lunch with my amazing editor, Ginjer Buchanan. We talked for hours about what my next book would be (I had lots of ideas), but when I mentioned wanting to write about the amazing friendships I had with the women in my life—friendships that were strong and beautiful and enriching—well, Ginjer's eyes lit up and she suggested witches!

A shout-out to the women whose friendships helped to inspire the witches: Liz, Mo, Sarah, Dani, Danielle—Long live AHLA!

Thank you to my debonair agent, Howard Morhaim, who has class in spades and likes to check in and make sure I'm still alive out in Los Angeles. Thanks always to Christopher Golden and the rest of the Goldens—my East Coast family. To everyone at Ace/Roc—you guys have been so wonderful and supportive of all my endeavors . . . Thank you, thank you, thank you!

Another shout-out to the Shamers. I wrote this book under your watchful eye. You guys are the best. And to the Heroine Club ("Kick-ass female protagonists, not drugs," as Nick's wife says)—you guys read the pages and encouraged me to keep on going even when I wanted to pull my hair out. A special singling out to Sarah Kuhn and Jeff Chen—you guys are the best. Sarah, I must've sent you a thousand freaked-out texts over the course of the witches. Thank you for reading the pages a bazillion times and for talking me off the ledge more often than I care to remember. Also, love to Angela and Tim; you guys inspire me every day.

I want to thank my dad, who is hard at work on his own book, and my mom, who is also hard at work on a manuscript. I guess I come by my love of words honestly. Thanks to my aunt Beverly, who feeds me home-cooked meals when I am in the throes of writing and not taking care of myself properly. To my sister, Danielle, who inspired the character Lyse—I love you! And to Breehn, thank you.

And, finally, thanks to the mysterious Echo Park, where all the magic began.

Eleanora

"*It's in the blood.*"

Hessika's voice was low and gravelly as she spoke, her drawn-in Cupid's-bow lips overenunciating each word.

*There was a loud snap as the green pod in Eleanora's hands split into two, three glistening peas falling into the half-filled orange ceramic bowl cradled in her lap. She sat in a weathered rattan rocking chair, her bare legs and arms sticky with the autumnal California heat, the dark blue chambray shirt and jean shorts she'd put on that morning plastered against her pale, freckled skin. She stopped rocking at those words—*It's in the blood—*and turned to look at the woman who was twelve years her elder.*

Hessika sat perched on a rocking chair the twin of Eleanora's, but it looked small and fragile beneath her massive frame. In other, less forgiving times, she would've been drummed out of her home and marginalized to the fringes of society for the way she looked, but now she was just a curiosity, an object of intense fascination for the neighborhood children who liked to loiter at the bottom of her lawn and stare at the giantess as she worked in the garden that was her sanctuary.

Standing six feet, eight inches tall in her stocking feet, Hessika was a female oddity of extreme contradictions: She had the posture and grace of a prima ballerina, but one who thought nothing of squatting barefoot in the dirt to pull the hardiest of weeds from her flower beds. Her garden was as close to a shrine or temple as their kind believed in, and Hessika was its rough master, forcing her enormous hands, joints stiff and swollen from arthritis, to do her bidding there. She alleviated the worst of her pain with a homemade stinging nettle tonic she took twice daily—a recipe she swore by but had never written down. Something Eleanora and the others had only realized upon her death.

The first moment Eleanora had laid eyes on the master of the Echo Park coven, she'd known Hessika was a different creature from any other she'd encountered before.

It was an indefinable thing, this differentness, but Eleanora believed it was due to the impenetrable nature of Hessika's personality. No one would disagree that she was as immovable as a rock when attacked, utterly impervious to the whims or whines or worries of those she did not respect. A true force to be reckoned with, she could bend people to her will with the calming weight of her words and actions but did not manipulate her reality just for the sake of manipulation. As master of their coven, she was also adept at rooting her blood sisters to the earthly plane, reminding them of their obligations to the world they inhabited.

Upon her arrival in Southern California, it was Hessika who'd embraced her like an older sister, hugging Eleanora's thin frame to her massive bosom, so that, embarrassed, Eleanora had blushed scarlet. Then, her body and mind reeling from days of sitting up to sleep in coach on the train from Boston, she'd gone limp in the strange woman's arms and cried like a baby while the whole of Union Station watched.

Instead of chiding the younger woman for her weakness, Hessika had spirited Eleanora back to the bungalow on Curran Street overlooking Elysian Park, settling her down in the tiny, womblike second bedroom and petting the girl's long brown hair until her tears had dried up. Never once did she question Eleanora about the trip, or the heartbreak she'd left behind in Duxbury when she'd hitched a ride into Boston and never looked back—and, for her silent kindness, Eleanora had loved Hessika with a girlish awe that bordered on hero worship.

To that order, it seemed only apropos that Hessika would be the one to foretell her fate.

"The blood?" Eleanora asked, leaning forward in her seat so the rattan bit into the backs of her legs, the bowl suddenly becoming heavier against the tops of her thighs.

"I dreamed of blood," Hessika said, an almost imperceptible lisp giving her Southern-inflected sibilants a soft, misshapen sound.

Hessika continued to work as she spoke, the cracking and voiding of shells into her bowl a staccato counterpoint to the rhythmic rocking of her chair, its runners seesawing along the thick slats of the wooden porch like a ship pitching back and forth on uncertain seas.

Hessika was a Dream Keeper. It was a gift she traced back to the Old Testament stories of Joseph.

Raised in a Primitive Baptist household in Lower Alabama, where the Old Testament had been her parents' rod and staff from which they did not deviate, Hessika didn't subscribe to the tenets of Christianity—though she was not uninterested in its mythologies and practices. The Primitive Baptist predeterminism of her childhood was not unlike her own self-discovered belief that human fate was a tapestry woven long before a person was born: If we were lucky, we might catch a glimpse of the pattern, but we could never change it.

When Hessika spoke of her dreams or interpreted the dreams of others, it was with the authority of someone who was touched by something greater than human knowledge—and those who were targeted in her dream readings quickly learned to listen carefully to her interpolations or else face their futures blind.

It's in the blood.

Hessika's words nibbled at Eleanora's brain, making her heart beat faster as she waited for her friend to say more—but there was only the steady onslaught of peas dropping into a bowl and the creaking of Hessika's rocking chair biting into the old wooden porch.

Day had long faded into inky twilight, the gloaming having come and gone on tiptoe, so Eleanora only now realized the world was dipped in full-scale night. Like looking into the face of a loved one day after day and missing the imperceptible changes as age crept across their features—the slackening of jowls, the pulling at the labial folds around their mouth, the creping of skin beneath their eyes—Eleanora had missed the shifting of Time.

She blamed Hessika. Time was pliant on her friend's front porch, stretching out like warm taffy in the hot summer sun. Here, seconds hung like minutes, minutes like hours, hours like days until Time ceased to have any meaning at all. But Hessika's portent— It's in the blood—*had acted as a catalyst, speeding things up and kicking Eleanora back into the present. She blinked, finding herself aware of her surroundings again, the shrill hum of the nighttime insects like a warm blanket enfolding everything around her.*

Then, without warning, Hessika stopped rocking.

With the silence came the irrational fear that her life, barely in its prime, was about to be cut short. Eleanora had turned twenty-four the previous spring and she'd done almost nothing with herself. She'd only been with one man—someone she did not dare to ever think of again—the event traumatizing at best; she'd never traveled to Europe or learned to play the piano . . . and in this age of free love and drugs, she'd never even smoked marijuana. There was so much she wanted to do, so much she wanted to see and experience—she wasn't ready to shuffle off this mortal coil just yet.

"You understand that these things are not precise," Hessika said, snapping another green pod in two and releasing its contents into the bowl.

Eleanora understood better than she wanted to.

"I do."

Hessika nodded, the moonlight casting a shadow across her angular face, obscuring languid, almond-shaped green eyes wreathed in midnight-black false lashes. She set her bowl of peas aside, making room for it on the small rattan side table by relocating her glass of merlot, then she coaxed a cigarette from a soft pack of Lucky Strikes. She plucked a silver Zippo lighter from her skirt pocket— a gift from a bulldog-faced Marine she'd once bedded—and lit the cigarette.

Eleanora watched as moths dive-bombed the overhead porch light, the frosted-glass globe keeping them from self-immolating against the sixty-watt bulb. She felt like she'd been set adrift upon the ocean, the orange glow from the cigarette's tip and the pale yellow of the porch light the only illumination in what seemed like a sea of night.

Hessika's words came out muddled, the cigarette dangling against her lower lip, perverting the sounds into something Eleanora had to translate before she could pick out any meaning from them:

"I dreamt of a dark time. When our coven was the last to stand against something truly evil."

Hessika paused, the orange coal flaring like fire as she pulled on the cigarette, then removed it from her mouth, cupping it limply in her hand. Around them, the insects wove their songs of longing and attraction like a fine netting, the cacophony of legs rubbing together in a sexual frisson so overpowering it made Eleanora's head ache.

"In that time I was a ghost—a Dream Walker—invisible to you, but you knew I was there, keeping watch. You were a crone then, ma belle, withered and wasted away—I could smell the blood beneath your skin, blood that was flecked with something black and rank."

Eleanora kept her mouth shut, choosing not to interrupt the flow of Hessika's words. Instead, she idly watched the cigarette burn to ash between Hessika's long fingers.

"There was a girl, she liked to wrap her arms around your shoulders, her hands were always covered in dirt"—she stopped to pull on the cigarette again and then release a long trail of smoke from her lips—"and you were preparing her. She was the next in line—and she would help protect something important. Be the last to stand when all the others had fallen."

Eleanora froze as Hessika turned to look at her, their eyes

locking. Without breaking the connection, Hessika took another drag from the cigarette, the stink of ash and phosphorus making Eleanora's nostrils itch. There was a softness around Hessika's eyes—sad eyes, Eleanora had always thought—but the wreath of exhaled smoke around her face made them seem frightening and irisless in the dark.

"She will follow you and you, well . . . it looks as though you're gonna follow me."

Eleanora's throat tightened. She'd been so sure Hessika was about to tell her that she was going to die—it'd happened before, Hessika's words like a magic noose around some young person's throat, inching tighter and tighter until they'd choked the life out of what was once young and gay—but this, this was something else entirely.

"A dream of the future coupled with a dream of death, ma belle," *Hessika added as she reached a long arm across the space separating them and grasped Eleanora's wrist.*

Her touch was at once light and reassuring yet burned within the cold fire of empathy. It was an odd sensation, and not one Eleanora hoped to experience again.

"My dreams are never wrong, ma belle," *Hessika continued. "Remember that. Maybe not precise, but never wrong."*

Now all these years later Hessika's portent had finally come to pass. Eleanora's blood was black with cancer—and there was only one final task left to complete before Death could finally collect its due:

Prepare the girl. For she was next in line.

Lyse

The staccato cadence of the blond stewardess's Midwestern twang slammed into Lyse's head like a sledgehammer, every word a sharpened nail driven into the gray matter of her brain.

Because it was an oversold flight and she'd booked her ticket at the last minute, she hadn't been able to choose her seat—which meant the airline gave her what was available: a middle seat in between an older grandmotherly type on the aisle and a young Hispanic kid two sizes too big for his window seat. The kid had spent the entire preflight ramp-up arguing with the stewardess over the need for a seat belt extender, and at one point Lyse had almost snapped at the stewardess to leave the poor kid alone. Not just because she agreed with the kid, but because she wanted the stewardess to stop talking.

But she knew she stunk like a distillery and was scared of getting kicked off the flight, so she kept her mouth shut, rejoicing internally when the kid finally relented and, grumbling to hide his embarrassment, took the seat belt extender from the triumphant stewardess, clipping it in place.

Lyse wished there were something she could say to make the kid feel better about being humiliated at the hands of a smug stewardess in a pastel blue uniform, but she decided her continued silence was probably a better balm than any fumbling attempts at commiseration.

As the plane took off, Lyse closed her eyes and tried to sleep, but once they were airborne and the *Fasten Seat Belt* sign was turned off, she spent most of the flight trekking back and forth to the toilet in order to dry-heave over the commode. She wasn't sure if the nausea was due to a burgeoning hangover or was just the first sign that she'd given herself a concussion earlier that morning when, in a daring feat of acrobatic prowess, she'd tripped over a barstool and slammed the back of her head into the kitchen countertop, the soft skin of her scalp connecting with the hard stone to elicit a sharp, teeth-grinding *thwack*.

To her surprise, she'd found herself relatively unscathed after what could've been a major trauma: There'd been no blood, no laceration . . . just the budding promise of a painful knot.

After the unexpected call from her great-aunt Eleanora, Lyse had comforted herself by downing most of a bottle of Tito's vodka and passing out with her face mashed up against the cold granite kitchen island. The alcohol, coupled with the horrible dreams she'd had while she slept—dreams that made sure she got no rest—contributed greatly to the accident.

Then, hours later, she'd been frightened awake by the feel of someone's eyes on her back. It was unmistakable, the ungodly sense that a stranger was secretly observing her in this vulnerable moment, and fear ran through her body like an electric current.

She'd crawled off the barstool that'd doubled as her bed, hearing the creak of her bones settling back into place after a long night of immobility. She crossed the hardwood floor on bare feet and got as close to the kitchen window as she dared. She'd never bothered with window treatments—the kitchen was in the rear of the house, and the surrounding shrubbery had seemed thick enough to discourage any prying eyes—but as she squinted out into the pitch-black abyss of her backyard, she found herself wishing for heavy damask drapes, or at the very least those ugly poly-fiber blackout curtains.

Of course, no one was out there. The yard was empty and she was alone, but she had a hard time shaking off the creepy feeling someone had been watching her while she slept. Still groggy, she'd turned away from the window, and that was when she'd tripped over the barstool and almost brained herself.

It was that goddamned phone call. It had thrown her whole life off-kilter.

"I should have called you sooner, but I wasn't sure what to say . . ."

The teasing cadence of Eleanora's dropped New England *r*'s as they'd sounded coming through the phone line slipped inside Lyse's head, a siren's call to something she did not want to think about.

"They've done all the tests, so there's no reason to get a second opinion."

Her great-aunt's words were transient and elliptical, floating in Lyse's memory like gauzy white light through layers of viscous liquid. She wanted to pummel the memory away, but it wouldn't go.

". . . three months, maybe less than that. Cancer. Started in the blood but now it's everywhere."

It was like listening to a song played through an aged and crackling phonograph, vowels and consonants blurring together until they lost their meaning.

"Just . . . stop talking for a minute. Let me process this," Lyse had almost shouted into the phone as she leaned against the potting table. Though it'd been past six in the evening,

the air in The Center of the Whorl, the plant nursery she co-owned with her best friend, Carole, felt thick and damp, still oppressive with the day's heat.

Silence. Then:

"Bear? Are you still there?" Eleanora had used the pet name Lyse had chosen for herself the summer she'd turned fourteen—during those three sweltering months she would answer to no other name: Lyse was dead, long live the Bear.

Without realizing it, her body had responded to the shock by seating her ass on the concrete floor, the metal leg of the potting table pressing into her back, holding her up like the stipe of a cross as she began to cry.

I'm not gonna deal with this right now, Lyse thought, pushing the memories away as she stared at the blank screen embedded in the airline seat in front of her. She had always taken shelter in denial, using sarcasm and disdain to distance herself from pain. Logic predicated that this was a perfectly normal reaction to receiving unexpected and tragic news, but she'd never really been one to go in for logic—emotion was what ruled her day to day.

Which was why she'd chosen the oblivion of alcohol to get her through the worst of her panic. The only person who loved her was dying, and there was absolutely nothing she could do about it. She was going to be alone in the world again. Like when she was thirteen and thought she was an orphan—before Child Services had found Eleanora, who wasn't really Lyse's great-aunt (though that was what she'd asked Lyse to call her) but a distant relative on her mother's side, and Lyse's whole life had changed for the better.

Lyse shut her eyes, the knot in her throat abating slowly—very slowly—as she tried not to think anymore, to make her mind a blank slate. Somewhere in the middle of this losing battle, she must have fallen asleep, because soon she began to dream. The visions in her head were raw and vivid, full of familiar smells and sounds, the colors bright and lurid. She might have believed she was fixed inside a strange alternate reality if some part of her hadn't remembered she was flying forty thousand feet above the surface of the Earth.

In the dream she was a teenager again, walking through her old Echo Park neighborhood. There she moved like a ghost through overgrown gardens and derelict houses, visited dusty bodegas selling Santeria charms alongside bottled Mexican soda and Aqua Net hair spray, and stood on concrete retaining walls where shiny spray-painted tags that resembled Celtic knots sprung up like weeds to mark out rival gang territory.

She could taste the past in her mouth, smell it in the air around her as she wandered the streets and stairways of Laveta Terrace, Baxter, Clinton, and Curran, each stairwell a link to the landlocked hill homes that were built, so oddly, without street access. Sweat-soaked limbs and squeaking sneakers were her only companions as she trudged up and down the roughly curving hill streets.

Instinctively, she knew that the universe, and everything in it, was held together by webbing as fragile and sheer as the translucent filament of a spider's home—that her past and present were inextricably linked and had been since the day she'd come to live with Eleanora.

Echo Park was calling her name. It was time to go home.

She woke up when the captain announced the flight would be landing ten minutes early. She was snotty and bleary-eyed, and it felt as though she hadn't gotten an ounce of rest in days.

She made her way off the airplane without incident, stopping in the ladies' room to splash cold water on her face and stare at her reflection in the mirror. She looked like death warmed over: red-rimmed, bloodshot eyes framed by bruise-purple circles; pale cheeks; lips so chapped they were flaking.

As she left the bathroom and followed the influx of people heading toward the exit, she powered her cell phone on.

It began to make frantic buzzing noises in her hand, and she stared down at the cracked screen, surprised to discover one new voice mail message and two text messages waiting for her. It was barely nine in the morning.

Both texts were from Carole: Where are you? I went by the house—we so NEED to talk about that FYI—but you're MIA, so we can't. And: What the hell, Lyse? Call me!

The voice mail was from Carole, too—in her emotional upheaval, Lyse had forgotten to call her best friend and business partner and tell her she wouldn't be showing up at the nursery that morning. She felt terrible, like she'd breached some kind of best-friend trust by not informing Carole she was leaving town, and why.

As she cruised past security and hit the escalator, she texted Carole back: Eleanora called. Long story, but I'm in LA.

She leaned her weight against the rubber handrail as she pressed *send*, exhausted by this simple task, and then closed her eyes, losing herself in the din of conversation around her.

Lyse felt her mind untethering like a shiny copper penny snaking its way toward the bottom of a detergent-blue swimming pool. The inevitable had happened, and it was as cold and punishing as a lungful of chlorinated water.

"Lyse?"

She opened her eyes and was shocked to find Eleanora waiting for her at the bottom of the curved escalator.

"Eleanora?" she said, and dropped her bag onto the dirty airport floor.

She ran to her great-aunt, flinging her arms around this now-frail creature who'd once been so robust and full of life. She pulled Eleanora in as close as she dared, not wanting to crush her. The two women clung to each other—one a crone at the end of her days, the other a maiden, hale and full of future—and the world around them ceased to exist.

"I've missed you," Eleanora whispered, the sandpaper scratch of her voice tickling Lyse's ear.

"Me, too," Lyse replied, meaning it.

Lost in the midst of this bittersweet moment was the realization that Lyse had not told Eleanora she was coming to Los Angeles.

"They've cut down two more trees, the bastards," Eleanora noted, pointing out the pale brown stumps to Lyse as they rolled her raggedy metal cart down the uneven sidewalk, passing the last remnants of the majestic ficus trees that had once lined Echo Park Avenue. "Who cuts down living things, Lyse—creatures of the Earth that clean the air and give shade to weary travelers?"

The dark green foliage and elegant limbs Lyse had stood under, that had kept her dry from the rain and protected her from the scorching sun during the hottest of the summer months, were gone, replaced by empty dirt plots as barren as newly filled graves.

Lyse knew Eleanora hated backward behavior championed "in the name of progress." A decade earlier, she would have led the protest, taking names and causing heads to roll, but these days, Lyse realized, her great-aunt was too tired to do any damage to the members of the city council.

"I'll say a little prayer when I get home," Eleanora said, patting Lyse's arm as they walked. "Say a few words to send an ill wind their way, the unfeeling idiots."

Lyse had to laugh. Even though she still felt that gnawing hollow in her middle, it was amazing how easily her fears could be dispelled by her great-aunt's blunt New England sensibility.

"I wish all you had to do was ask God to kick their asses," Lyse replied, running a hand through her chunky bangs so they stuck up like porcupine quills in the heat. Her thick, dark hair grew so fast her bangs were forever in need of a trim, and she was constantly having to shove them out of her eyes.

Southern California was dry—the antithesis of Athens, Georgia, where she lived now, which was humidity city. She wished she'd remembered this fact and brought some heavy-duty lotion with her. Her skin was already beginning to feel dry and cracked. Besides, she was exhausted, and the lack of sleep contributed to the icky "too tight in her own skin" feeling she was having.

"You look tired," Eleanora said, as if she were privy to Lyse's thoughts. "You didn't need to walk down here with me."

Lyse shrugged and said offhandedly, "I'll sleep when I'm dead—"

She immediately realized what she'd just said and clapped a hand over her mouth.

Eleanora laughed.

"Don't censor yourself on my account. I've made my peace with Death, Lyse—and that's all anyone can hope to do in these situations."

Lyse nodded, but inside she was still kicking herself for her slip of the tongue.

"But here we are," Eleanora said, turning her cart into the doorway of the tiny neighborhood bodega.

"*Hola*, Eleanora," the birdlike woman behind the cash register sang brightly as Lyse followed Eleanora inside.

Together, they made their way to the back of the store, where the refrigerator case sat humming, cold bottles of red-labeled organic milk stacked neatly inside it.

"*Hola* yourself, Juana," Eleanora replied, raising a skeletal hand in the bird woman's direction as she opened the refrigerator, seeming to pause as she caught sight of her reflection in the glass-fronted case.

Lyse wondered if her great-aunt saw what she saw: sunken cheeks and bruised skin stretched taut over orbital bones. A wraith. The walking dead.

"Is that all today, Eleanora?" Juana asked, the question cutting through Lyse's thoughts like a freshly sharpened knife.

Eleanora had already moved to the checkout. Lyse joined her and was surprised to see an iPad on the Formica countertop instead of a more traditional cash register. It was a surreal hint of technology in an otherwise old-fashioned setting.

"That's all," Eleanora said, retrieving a five-dollar bill from her wallet as Juana tapped the price into the iPad screen. "And you remember Lyse, my grandniece?"

Juana smiled, her face taking on a beatific glow. "Of course. It's been a long time. But yes."

Juana was right. It *had* been a long time, Lyse realized. At least five years since she'd last been home to visit. For some reason, Eleanora had always made the biyearly trek to see Lyse in Georgia, but never the other way around.

Setting the brown paper–wrapped jar of milk inside the basket of her metal rolling cart, Eleanora headed for the door.

"See you in a few days," she called back to Juana, the *whoosh* of the air curtain above the entrance ruffling her short gray hair as she stepped outside.

"Little one," Juana said, just as Lyse turned to follow Eleanora out the door. "Wait a moment."

Lyse nodded, uncertain as to what the birdlike woman wanted. She watched as Juana stepped away from the counter, then picked her way through to the back of the store, disappearing into the stockroom. Through the plate-glass window, Lyse kept one eye on Eleanora, who was standing on the sidewalk, adjusting her Windbreaker.

"Here. For you."

Juana was back, thrusting a cylindrical brown-wrapped package into her hands.

"I don't—" Lyse started to say, but Juana shook her head.

"It's a gift. Burn it in the house."

She smiled at Lyse, her tan skin surprisingly soft and wrinkled under the fluorescent lighting.

"Thank you," Lyse said.

The package felt awkward in her hands as she left the bodega and stepped out into the heat of the day.

"What did she give you?" Eleanora asked, her sharp eyes glued to the package.

"Don't know," Lyse said, shaking her head. "She said to burn it."

"Hmmph," Eleanora replied as they continued up Echo Park Avenue, the cart rattling softly as it hit each crack in the sidewalk, the sound lulling in its consistency.

Lyse began to unwrap the package, peeling away the stiff brown paper to reveal the contents nestled inside.

"Interesting," she said, as she pulled out the long, cylindrical saint's candle, its smooth glass surface etched with the blue outline of a young woman in a headscarf. A small child sat upon the woman's lap, its head bowed under the weight of a spiked crown.

"Mother of the Virgin Mary," Eleanora said, glancing over at the candle.

"You mean Saint Anne?" Lyse murmured, reading the thick block lettering just below the image. "She was the mother of the Virgin Mary? I didn't know that."

"She's also the patroness of unmarried women," Eleanora snorted. "I think Juana's trying to tell you something."

Lyse groaned.

"Great."

Eleanora smiled as she took Lyse's arm, leaning on her as they walked.

"Watch out, or you'll end up an old spinster like me."

"You're not that old," Lyse said, then paused—because this made her think of other things . . . like the fact that Eleanora was too young to be dying.

"You're sweet," Eleanora said, patting Lyse's hand.

They walked on in silence after that, the sun bright above them, Lyse enjoying the exotic smell of the Spanish jasmine that clung from the gates and fences of the houses on Echo Park Avenue.

"Well, should I burn it tonight, then?" Lyse asked suddenly, holding the candle up, surprised at how heavy it felt in her hand.

"Yes, burn it," Eleanora said, her voice strangely earnest. "Burn it down until there's nothing left."

They reached the front entrance to the old bungalow on Curran, the house Lyse had called home the whole of her teenage years, and Eleanora pulled a set of keys from the pocket of her red Windbreaker—even in the heat, her great-aunt professed to being cold.

"I have some business to take care of," Eleanora said, tucking the keys into Lyse's hand, their warmth making her palm sweat. "Go inside and take a nap—you look beat."

Lyse didn't argue with her great-aunt. She suddenly felt so exhausted she could hardly keep her eyes open. Impulsively, she leaned over and kissed Eleanora's powdery cheek.

"We need to talk when you get back," Lyse said, as a yawn escaped her lips.

"Yes, we do," her great-aunt agreed. "There's so much to discuss—and so little time left to us."

"Please, don't say it like that. I can't bear it," Lyse said, pushing back a wave of panic at the thought of her great-aunt's approaching death. "I just . . . We'll talk when you get back, okay? About doctors and second opinions . . ."

Eleanora nodded as Lyse trailed off.

"Sleep as much as you can, Bear. I need you at your sharpest tonight."

Lyse gave her great-aunt a funny look.

"What does that mean?"

"It's nothing terrible," Eleanora said, offering Lyse the handle of the metal rolling cart. "It's good, actually. And I promise we'll talk about it more when I get back."

With a forced smile, Lyse took the cart, dragging it with her up the stairs. At the top, she turned back around, but Eleanora was already hurrying down the street, her Windbreaker flashing bloodred in the sparkling light.

From her perch high atop Eleanora's patio stairs, Lyse was able to look out over Curran Street, at the bungalows and Craftsman homes, the foliage and greenery that peeked out from every garden. Being home after so long made her feel like a teenager again.

I'd forgotten how glorious this place is, she thought—then shivered when something wet landed on the tip of her nose.

Inexplicably, her first thought was *blood*, but when she looked up at the once-blue sky, she saw it was now a foreboding steel gray—and the splash of wetness was merely a drop of rain. She laughed at her own morbid imagination, then yawned as she rolled the cart toward the front door of Eleanora's bungalow.

Sleep sounded like the greatest thing in the world.

Devandra

D evandra Montrose woke from an oddly restless slumber knowing that Eleanora was going to call on her. This meant she would definitely do her receiving in the kitchen, where it was more comfortable, and where she could enjoy the aroma of freshly baking candied gingerbread (for her younger daughter's school bake sale) while she met with the master of the Echo Park coven—of which Dev was a member.

Usually when she was going to do a reading, she set up shop in the converted garage, aka The Mucho Man Cave, that her partner, Freddy, used to host their popular Echo Park Weekend Bar—and the occasional weeknight poker game for his crew of guy friends—but today was different. Today would be about coven business, and, with its cedar-lined walls and industrial-grade forest-green carpeting that stank of peanuts, cigar smoke, and stale beer, The Mucho Man Cave was not the most appropriate setting for that.

Besides, The Mucho Man Cave always seemed a little sad during the week when there were no neighbors crowding around its homemade tiki bar, sipping cold beer as they discussed neighborhood gossip and flirted with one another.

Of course, the old garage always perked up when Dev used it for one of her readings, her saints' candles and burnished iron censer of smoky sandalwood incense giving the space a rich honey glow and transforming it from a part-time bar and den of poker-playing iniquity into a mysterious world of magical tarot. Though there was always a faint tinge of stale beer underneath the earthy sandalwood, if you knew to smell for it.

Well, if she'd guessed correctly, then The Mucho Man Cave was safe from her machinations today. Eleanora was already more than well acquainted with the spirit world and would have no need for the trappings of the trade, the things she normally employed to make her clientele feel as though they were magically slipping beyond the veil.

But first there were two children to get to school, a client to consult with on strawberry icing, and a dog that needed a walk before Dev was finally free to get out her well-worn Rider-Waites—the slick yellow cards and their whimsical figures more appealing to her than some of the darker, edgier decks—and prepare herself mentally for the surprise reading.

Everyone knew face value was not what you got with tarot cards. Intuition was the name of the game when it came to fortune-telling—Dev's specialty—and either you were born with the chops or you weren't. Nothing analytical or logical about what she did; it was all in the old gut.

Though her children swore up and down that Dev possessed untold psychic abilities, she was not gifted with telepathy, clairvoyance, or any of the other psychic phenomena they ascribed to her. Not that she let them in on this secret. She needed all the help she could get raising two wily, intelligent little girls—and allowing them to believe their mother had eyes in the back of her head could only help her cause. Sadly, divination was her only gift—which meant she was forced to use good old-fashioned logic to make educated guesses about everything else. In point of fact, she expected her visitor was going to be Eleanora Eames, not because she'd had any portent-bearing dreams but because Eleanora had called Dev's number twice the day before, refusing to leave a message on either attempt. She assumed her friend was well aware of the caller ID feature and just didn't give a damn about leaving hang-ups on people's answering machines—which made Dev think a lecture on the finer points of twenty-first-century telephone etiquette might be in order.

While she waited for her visitor to arrive, Dev set a battered copper kettle on the front eye of the white porcelain O'Keefe and Merritt stove and turned the flame to high, spooning Russian tea into two of her favorite lapis-blue earthenware mugs. The day before, in an attempt to get herself into an autumnal mood, she'd made the first batch of the family favorite fall/winter tea, but now the little potbellied jar full of sugar, Tang, cinnamon, clove, and instant tea mixture sat on the butcher-block countertop looking lost and forlorn in its spot between the aluminum mixer and a vintage owl-shaped cookie jar.

Maybe she wasn't getting the spooky October vibe yet because the house still felt light and airy from its summer incarnation. Spying the row of beige seashells up on the windowsill above the kitchen sink, the ones the girls had collected during a family trip to Laguna Beach in June, Dev decided clearing out the summer bits and bobs would go a long way to getting her into a fall state of mind. Tonight when Freddy got home from work, she'd ask him to drag down the boxes of autumn-themed decorations from the attic, so she could get the house ready for Halloween. She knew her daughters, Marji and Ginny, would fall all over themselves to help her turn the house over—and Freddy was always down for getting into the spooky spirit, setting up a life-size replica of a human skeleton (bought at the yard sale of one of their neighbors, who was a retired biology professor) to sit at the tiki bar and scare the guests who frequented The Mucho Man Cave.

She would personally oversee the hanging of the Halloween pièce de résistance: her great-great-grandmother Lucretia's mourning wreath.

When placed above the mantelpiece of the sitting room fireplace, the horseshoe-shaped wreath—mounted to a disc of muted mother-of-pearl and set behind glass—was a real showstopper. Fashioned by Lucretia's daughters when she died in 1891, it was an eerie sight: one large six-petal flower and four smaller three-petal flowers intricately woven from the strands of Lucretia's own famous raven hair.

Over the years, the mourning wreath had been handed down through the Montrose family from eldest daughter to eldest daughter—with Dev being the latest in the line of succession. When Dev's older daughter, Marjoram, came of age at eighteen, the wreath would pass into her keeping and Dev would no longer be responsible for it. Though she'd be sad to see it go—handling the memento mori always gave her a visceral thrill—she was proud of the keepsake's lineage and pleased that her daughter would be part of the long line of women who'd looked after it.

Startled by the near-simultaneous *yip* of the teakettle and the ring of the doorbell, Dev turned off the gas and trundled over to the mudroom, gratified to see Eleanora's silhouette shifting behind the café-curtained window. She'd been right about the identity of her visitor.

"I thought you might be dropping by," Dev said, holding the back door open so her friend could enter.

There was a *whoosh* as the wind tried to follow Eleanora inside, but Dev closed the door firmly behind them, leaving the wind no recourse but to bang the storm door open and shut in protest.

"Wicked wind. Just started up out of the blue as I was walking over," Eleanora said, shrugging off her scarlet

Windbreaker and hanging it up on one of the wooden pegs that protruded from the beadboard wall.

Dev frowned as a sense of dread so palpable she could taste it washed over her. The short strawberry-blond hairs on the back of her neck prickled to life, and her legs felt unreliable beneath her as the room began to spin. She leaned against the wall, using it to hold herself up, her stomach lurching. She bit her lip hard, the abruptness of the pain taking the edge off her nausea, but even when she closed her eyes, the spinning sensation continued.

Get hold of yourself, she thought, tasting blood on her tongue. *You control your body, not the other way around.*

Mustering her strength, she pushed the bad feeling away and forced her eyes open. As she did, she found her gaze settling on Eleanora's scarlet Windbreaker where it hung twisted on its peg in between the shiny primary yellow of Marji and Ginny's raincoats.

"I see you already have the cards out," she heard Eleanora saying as she strode past Dev into the kitchen.

As soon as Eleanora crossed the threshold separating the mudroom from the rest of the house, the hum of ambient noise dropped out, replaced by a weighty silence interrupted only by the rise and fall of Dev's own shallow breathing. A halo of darkness encircled her peripheral vision, limiting her view until all she could see was the scarlet of Eleanora's Windbreaker, so deep and red and pulsing with life it resembled the ragged flesh of a still-beating heart. Confused, she tried to tear her eyes away from the sight, but her gaze merely slid down to the jacket's cuff. There she spied a single droplet of glistening liquid, suspended from the cuff's edge like a translucent red jewel.

Dev watched as it grew in size, liquid from the sodden jacket sluicing down like dozens of small tributaries heading toward the ocean, feeding the droplet until it was so heavy that gravity couldn't hold it anymore, and it plummeted to Earth.

Strange, Dev thought, her eyes free now to drift over to the window, *I didn't realize it was raining.*

But it *wasn't* raining—at least not yet. Outside, the sky had grown gray and swollen with the *promise* of rain, but this promise had not yet been kept.

It's in the blood.

The phrase resonated in her brain, unbidden, and she shivered.

She returned her gaze to the nylon Windbreaker but was unsurprised to find it no longer nestled in between the shiny yellow raincoats. In its place, a scarlet arc of arterial blood had been splashed across the mudroom wall, the viscous liquid dripping down the beadboard and onto the floor, where it pooled in a thick circle. Dev swallowed, her mouth dry as old bone, but she didn't panic, just lifted her eyes from the circle of dark liquid on the floor and once more saw the twisted folds of Eleanora's now-dry Windbreaker.

She blinked—sure her eyes were playing tricks on her . . . or were they? She shuddered, realizing the vision for what it was: an omen of very, very bad things to come.

"Are you all right?"

Eleanora's voice startled Dev, and she jumped.

"I just saw . . ." she said, her words trailing off as she turned around to face the older woman, who was standing in the doorway, leaning her gaunt body against the polished white doorframe.

"What did you see?" Eleanora asked, her bloodless lips compressed into a thin line.

"I . . ." Dev began, but faltered as her words failed her. She shrugged helplessly. "I don't know. It was . . . bad, whatever it was. Blood—"

"You saw blood?" Eleanora asked, and Dev nodded.

"Blood, on the wall, by the kids' raincoats. I felt it, too, inside me—and this phrase keeps repeating in my head: *It's in the blood.*"

Eleanora took a deep breath and visibly relaxed.

"What?" Dev asked. "What does it mean?"

"I've told Lyse that I'm dying, and she's come home. That's what you were seeing. The die is cast."

"I'm glad you've done it," Dev said. "Does she know anything about us yet, about the coven—"

"Not a thing," Eleanora said. "I've kept all of it from her for so long that it feels strange to finally tell her. I wanted to give her the freedom to go live her own life for as long as I could, but now I need her. The time has come for Lyse to learn who and what we are. I've already spoken to Arrabelle and we'll perform the induction ritual tonight. She's going to let the others know."

Dev was surprised.

"Tonight?"

"We're running out of time, Devandra." Eleanora sighed. "You read Marie-Faith's last letter. You know what it means. Why she sent Daniela to us. Things are speeding up and when I die, you will need the fifth. You'll need Lyse's help."

"Yes, of course," Dev said. "Freddy has a poker game tonight, but I'll see if he can feed the girls first . . ."

"It's not a question of *if*, Devandra," Eleanora said, "but *when*. Those who betrayed Marie-Faith *will* come after us and anyone else who stands in their way. They want what we are protecting, and they will do anything to get it."

As if this answered everything and left no need for further explanation, Eleanora turned on her heel and made her way back to the kitchen. Dev stood alone in the mudroom pondering her friend's last words. She knew Eleanora was right—even if she didn't want to believe it.

It's in the blood.

The phrase sang in her brain again, and Dev found herself repeating it under her breath as she returned to the kitchen, where she found Eleanora standing by the stove, looking expectantly at the teakettle.

"The kettle's hot. Shall I pour us a cup?"

"I'll do it," Dev said, taking the kettle and adding hot water to the mugs before transferring them to the table. "Hope Russian tea is all right?"

"Fine," Eleanora said, carefully settling herself into one of the yellow linen spindle-backed chairs and gently resting her bony elbows on the damask tablecloth.

Dev opened a cabinet and took down a tin of homemade sugar cookies, setting the tin along with two chipped blue plates onto the table. Then she took her seat opposite Eleanora.

She's lost more weight, Dev thought as she watched Eleanora retrieve a cookie—a heart-shaped one with white icing—and hold it in her palm, surveying it. She doubted her friend would eat it. These days Eleanora's appetite was small to the point of being nonexistent, but at least she made a show of trying to eat. It meant she was still fighting the good fight.

"Stop looking at me like that," Eleanora said, raising a silvery eyebrow. "I'm not one of those old cats you keep. I'm not gonna go disappearing under the house just because my appetite's a bit off."

"You're the most blunt person I've ever known," Dev replied. "And how would you know what I was thinking, anyway?"

"Oh, I know exactly what you're thinking. You're an open book as far as I'm concerned," Eleanora said, taking a tentative sip of her tea. "And I may be dying, but I'm not ready to be fitted for my coffin *just* yet. Lots of things to do before then."

"Well, I wouldn't dream of burying an old bitch before her time," Dev said, grinning at the tartness of her words. Eleanora always brought out her snarky side. One of the things she enjoyed best about their relationship.

"You may think you have a calling for the cards, Devandra, but this is where your true talent lies," Eleanora said, indicating the tea and iced sugar cookies.

Eleanora was right. Dev definitely wasn't your traditional fortune-teller—as evidenced by the fact that she didn't make her living sowing the seeds of fate but by running a small wedding cake business out of her backyard guesthouse/bakery.

"Don't tell Freddy and the kids," Dev said, laughing. "They think I'm Carrie come to life."

"Ha!" Eleanora cackled, setting her tea down. "I bet they do. I bet they do."

Eleanora was a fan of Dev's daughters, Marji and Ginny, and never acted put upon (like a few others Dev could name) when Dev told anecdotes about her family life. For their part, the girls loved their prickly old Great-Auntie E dearly. They were forever asking to visit Great-Auntie E's magic house where "the big goldfish" lived. The koi pond and red-lacquered wooden footbridge that spanned it made up the vast majority of Eleanora's front yard, along with a well-tended garden filled with fruit and vegetables the whole year long. All these things together meant her house was a lightning rod for the neighborhood children, including Dev's girls.

"Speaking of the cards," Dev said, picking up the deck from the table, her touch instantly warming the cards.

"Let's not speak of them. Let's let them speak to us," Eleanora replied.

"Isn't that what we always do?" Dev said, and then, more circumspect: "And would you like a straight reading? See what the cards say of their own volition, or are we shaping things by asking a few questions?"

"Only one question," Eleanora said, and with a press of her thumb, she broke her cookie into pieces, shards of iced sugar and flour skidding across her plate.

"A simple five-card spread should be pretty elucidating," Dev said, and began to separate out the Major Arcana from the rest of the deck, shuffling only these cards before setting them on the table in front of Eleanora.

"Do you have the question in your mind?" Dev asked.

Eleanora nodded, the light hitting her head in such a way that Dev could see pale pink scalp through the thinning salt and pepper of her friend's pixie cut—a haircut that should only have worked on a younger woman but somehow suited her better than long hair ever had. Dev wanted to cry at her frailness. But since death was not something Dev enjoyed thinking about, she quickly turned to the task at hand:

"Okeydoke, now hold the question in the front of your mind and think of a number between one and twenty-two—"

"Wait," Eleanora said, holding up her hand for Dev to stop. "Don't you want to know my question?"

Dev pursed her lips.

"There's no need—"

"But I *want* to tell you," Eleanora said, reaching over and squeezing Dev's wrist. "Is that a better way of saying that I trust you and that your input is important to me?"

The statement startled Dev. Eleanora had never shared anything so intimate with her before—and especially nothing about their own relationship.

"I know I get tetchy and short-tempered, but I don't want you to think it ever has anything to do with you personally. You know that, don't you?"

"I, well . . ." Dev said, not sure what she felt.

"Arrabelle tells me I'm too hard on you, that I expect too much," Eleanora continued. "If I get impatient, it's only because I feel safe with you. That the love I feel for you and the rest of our blood sisters transcends friendship. That you are *family* to me."

Dev was too stunned to say a word, but she did feel her eyes getting moist. "Oh, stop it," she said, trying not to get so overemotional that she scared Eleanora away. "You've got me tearing up like a baby."

"I didn't mean . . . I just wanted you to know before—" Eleanora began, stricken.

"Stop, it's lovely," Dev said, waving Eleanora's words away. "Now tell me your question before I really start sobbing."

Eleanora nodded, looking a tad uncomfortable with Dev's excess of emotion. She took a long breath, as if she were nervous about saying the words out loud.

"Will Lyse succeed me as master of the Echo Park coven? Is she the next in line, as Hessika foretold?"

Dev froze, her hands reaching for the cards. Hessika had been the Echo Park coven's last Dream Keeper, and upon her death, there hadn't been another to fill her place. The art of Dream Keeping was a dying one—and soon it would be as though the talent had never existed, at all. Not a single Dream Keeper had been born during the last fifty years, and the few who remained were long past their prime.

But what a Dream Keeper dreamed was law, and if Hessika had written of this succession in the coven's Dream Journal, then Lyse *would* follow Eleanora. No matter how hard Arrabelle and the others protested it.

"But I thought Arrabelle . . . ?" Dev asked before she could stop herself.

Eleanora shook her head. "It was never Arrabelle. Whatever she thought, the right was never hers."

Dev tried to remove her own personal feelings from the next question, but Arrabelle was her friend and no matter what Eleanora said now, the others had always taken it for granted that Arrabelle would be the one to succeed her.

"Why was it never hers? She's always been the one you relied on most—"

"I don't make the rules—but I am compelled to follow them," Eleanora said, before adding more pointedly: "Just as you are."

Continuing down this line of questioning was moot. Dev would just have to see what the cards had to say.

"A number, please," Dev said. "Whatever first comes to mind."

"Seven," Eleanora replied, without hesitation.

Dev counted out seven cards and placed The Fool—one of her favorites—into the first position of the spread. There was something poignant about the naïveté of The Fool's golden face, the way the sun hung above him, without judgment, even though it could see how precariously close its charge stood to the cliff's edge.

"The Fool, eh?" Eleanora murmured to herself. Then she said to Dev: "The cards have a will of their own today."

"What do you mean?" Dev said, furrowing her brow.

"I don't think you're interested in my question, are you?" Eleanora said to the cards. She looked at Dev and continued, "The Fool is not Lyse, and they know that I know this."

"How can you—we've barely begun," Dev said, her palms already slick with sweat.

"I wanted to know about Hessika's dreams. I wanted the cards to confirm them. That's not what's happening here."

"I believe you," Dev said. "Shall we continue?"

Eleanora nodded, eyes locked on The Fool, whose borders blended with the yellow of the tablecloth, so the card appeared printed onto the lemon damask.

"Another number, please."

"Seven," Eleanora said.

Six cards were disregarded before Dev came to the seventh, which she flipped over to reveal The Devil. She knew this wasn't a reference to the literal Devil, but the instinctual repulsion she felt whenever this card cropped up in one of her readings was hard to ignore.

"Another number—" Dev said.

"Seven," Eleanora replied, interrupting Dev. "And seven again for the fourth card."

Dev stayed her hand, uncertain.

"Are you sure?"

Eleanora nodded with vigor, but the action seemed to

wear her out and she rested her head in the crook of her left arm, breathing heavily.

"Just read the cards," Eleanora said, her voice hard. "There's something strange going on here and I need you to do as I ask."

Dev didn't appreciate being snapped at, but Eleanora looked so pathetic, her pale cream blouse barely concealing her excavated collarbones and sharpened shoulder blades, that Dev let it pass without argument. Flipping over Eleanora's next card, she set The Hierophant down on the table above The Fool and The Devil.

"Hmm," Eleanora murmured, then watched as Dev drew the last of the chosen cards.

"The Magician," Dev said, holding up this fourth card for Eleanora to see before laying it down on the table beneath the other three cards.

As seen from above, the cards now formed a truncated Christian cross, but one that held an empty space in its middle. This was where Dev would place the final card: a card Eleanora hadn't consciously chosen but was a synthesis of the other four—and would be the card upon which the rest of the spread depended.

In her head, Dev totaled the number values for The Fool, The Devil, The Heirophant, and The Magician, and with this knowledge laid down the fifth and final card of the spread:

The World.

Eleanora seemed to glean the spread's meaning instinctively, shaking her head as if she could hardly believe the audacity of the cards. Dev, on the other hand, had barely processed what she was seeing, let alone come to any conclusions.

"Well, now, isn't that the darnedest thing," Eleanora said, slapping the top of the table with the heel of her hand before shaking her head one more time in disbelief: "Looks as though someone has hijacked my spread."

She sat back in her chair, her sharp eyes scanning the

kitchen, looking—it seemed to Dev—for something . . . or *someone.*

"We're not alone," Eleanora said suddenly, her eyes returning to Dev's face. "Do you feel it? Someone else is here. They won't show themselves to me, but they're here."

Dev shivered. The Victorian was old and drafty, but that wasn't what she was feeling. Eleanora was right. There was something else in the kitchen with them.

Without warning, the light outside shifted, and the room dipped into shadow. Underneath Dev's hands, the table began to shake.

"Earthquake," Dev said, starting to stand up—but the tremors ceased before she was fully on her feet.

Almost as abruptly as it had disappeared, sunlight flooded the kitchen again, and the room returned to normal.

"She's left," Eleanora said, a secret smile playing across her taut lips. "She didn't want to be seen."

And Dev realized she was right: Whatever spirit had been there was gone.

"Tell me what the cards say, Devandra."

The older woman's dark eyes bored into her own, and Dev shivered.

"Only the Innocent stands in the way of the Devil's dominion over the World," she began, staring down at the cards, "and the Teacher will be the one whose balance decides all of our fates."

Dev looked up, and from the smile playing on Eleanora's lips, it was clear the master of the Echo Park coven was well pleased with her hijacked reading.

Lyse

Lyse lit the Saint Anne candle with a match she'd found in the kitchen, the flame flaring to life beneath her fingertips. The glowing wick cast flickering shadows across the white walls of the hallway as she headed toward her old bedroom. Outside, the sky had grown even darker, and the light that came in through the windows was a dusky shade of charcoal gray, giving the glow from Saint Anne a surreal quality—as if Lyse were a ghost moving through the murky underworld, the candle her only touchstone to human reality.

Lyse stood in the doorway for a few moments, her eyes scanning the room's contents. It was the first time Lyse had been back in her old bedroom in years, and she felt all the awkwardness and angst of adolescence fighting to recapture her—as if they didn't realize she was an adult now and relatively immune to them.

She crossed to the solid oak dresser, the heavy piece of furniture pressed up against the wall by the half-open bedroom window. Outside, she could see that the heavens were threatening to open, and soon rivulets of water would condense against the windowpane like teardrops.

She grimaced as she caught sight of her reflection in the "dead mirror" hanging across the room. She'd given the antique wall mirror this name because once upon a time, magazine tearaways of Vivien Leigh and River Phoenix had been nestled in between the silvered glass and wooden frame, the dead keeping Lyse company during the long, dark purgatory of her adolescence.

After a moment, she looked away from her reflection, absently picking at the forgotten tchotchkes still littering the top of the dresser, the detritus of her teenage years gathering dust: the June bug preserved in pale green glass, the tiny porcelain ballerina fixing her bun, the steel artist's rendering of a skeletal hand.

She sighed and walked over to the edge of the antique brass three-quarter bed, its brown duvet cover still spotted with pale stains from her one attempt at bleaching her hair. She set Saint Anne down on the small side table next to the bed, careful not to get it too close to the lamp and its pale yellow shade.

No house fires needed, thank you very much, she thought.

She was overtired from her trip and totally hungover. The stress and alcohol might have blotted out her feelings for a little while, but now the fear and worry were returning with a vengeance—and she felt unsettled by an odd feeling that'd been growing inside her ever since she'd gotten Eleanora's call. The only way she could describe it was like someone was keeping tabs on her, biding their time until they could pluck her like a ripe fruit.

Paranoia is a sign of exhaustion, right? she thought. *I'm just so damn tired, I can't think straight.*

She lay down across the mattress, stretching out like a cat, her head sinking into the welcoming heft of the overstuffed pillow. Above her was the Cure poster she'd taped to the ceiling when she was fifteen, the carnival of pink-and-orange-swirled Tim Burton–esque lettering spelling out the word *Lullaby*. She stared up at the poster as the candlelight from Saint Anne made squiggly shadows dance across the ceiling.

She felt her eyelids grow heavy with exhaustion, her body tingling as sleep fought to overwhelm her, until finally she gave up and let her eyes close. She began to drift, and, before she was even aware she'd fallen, she was dreaming—

It seemed impossible she could've ever forgotten the nightmare she'd had all throughout her adolescence, but not once since she left Echo Park had the dream come to her. In the recesses of her mind, it was a faded thing. Like an upholstered chair left in view of a window until it became threadbare and bleached from time and sunlight, and was banished to the attic.

The dream never varied: It was October—Indian summer—but windy and chilly and crisp once the sun had set. It was a few minutes before the witching hour, but how she knew this was unclear—though she didn't question it.

She was in a clearing in the woods, a place she'd never been in real life, but during the dream it felt familiar, and she intuitively sensed it was a safe place, consecrated to protect those in search of sanctuary from the darkness—just thinking the word *darkness* left her numb and scared. It was more frightening than any spoken word had a right to be.

She looked up and saw the pumpkin-orange harvest moon sitting low on the horizon, a runny egg yolk melting into the dusky, cloud-filled sky just above the tree line. Outside the clearing—where it was definitely not safe—the tree trunks grew in a dense pack, their shadows crisscrossing one another in the moonlight.

She heard the crunch of dead leaves under fast-moving feet, the sound echoing in the air and overpowering the hollow rustle of the wind as it streaked through the naked tree branches. The sound intensified—whatever was out there in the darkness was getting closer—and the temperature dropped in response, turning the air arctic. A chorus of dead leaves somersaulted across the ground, the wind blowing them helter-skelter until they disappeared inside the shadows, their desiccated brown bodies smashed into smithereens by unseen feet.

The crushing footfalls gained speed as the thing—she knew it wasn't human—crashed through the underbrush, moving faster and faster as it closed the distance between them, its breathing ragged. It was running now, moving at an inhuman speed, snarling toward her, its movements building to a heart-throbbing crescendo that stopped just shy of the edge of the clearing. Whatever had come tonight was afraid to cross the boundary the tree line had created.

And then the creature burst through the boundary line, the protective spell broken. The beast, all smoke and darkness and dread, descended on her, ripping at her torso and burying its cold teeth into her gut with feral intent, tearing away the flesh from her body in bloody chunks—

—and she woke up.

Only she was not in her old bedroom anymore. She was in her great-aunt's room, but Eleanora wasn't there. Instead, she saw Saint Anne, the woman from the candle, but then the image dissolved and another woman—a giantess, really—stood at the foot of the long, quilt-covered bed. She was smiling down at Lyse, whose body lay on top of the mattress, stiff as a board, hands crossed over her chest.

But Lyse wasn't in the body on the bed. She was a spirit, and she drifted by the door, close to the doorjamb, gazing at the scene: the giant woman at the foot of the bed and her own body there on the mattress, lying in state.

"Am I dead?" she asked, but the woman shook her head, and Lyse looked closer and could see that yes, the woman was right—the body on the bed was still breathing, the gentle rise and fall of its chest marking it among the living.

"Not dead, *ma belle*, merely dreaming."

The woman smiled then, and suddenly she held a smoldering cigarette in her hand. She took a long puff, then released the smoke so it poured from her nostrils like steam.

"Ah, I miss that," she said, indicating the smoke wrapping in curlicues around her head.

"Who are you?" Lyse asked, once she'd understood her body was okay.

"Humans call us ghosts, but Dream Walker is the name we witches give to souls who do not move on to the next plane after death. I am one of those who chose to stay on Earth after my passing. To help those that I've loved."

"Wait, *witches?*" Lyse said, almost spitting out the word.

"Eleanora never spoke about me or the coven to you," the woman said, "but once, a long time ago, we were very close."

Lyse felt her spirit float away from the door and come to hover next to the giantess.

"There is so little time, *ma belle*. So very little time," the woman continued. "It's coming. It'll arrive unheralded, and only you will know it for its true self. The coven will need your strength then—"

"The coven?" she said, interrupting the giant woman. "What're you talking about?"

On the bed, the body grew restless. It opened its mouth and screamed, but the sound couldn't be heard here in this dream world.

"Damn," the woman said, puffing away on her cigarette, though the ash tip never seemed to grow, "you sure channeled Elsa Lanchester with that scream, baby."

"I don't understand—"

The body on the bed opened its eyes, twisting and turning as it struggled with unseen hands.

"The time's coming for that," the woman said. "All will be revealed soon."

She exhaled a plume of gray-green smoke, like something you would expect from the bellows of a dragon, and this time the smoke didn't dissipate; it filled the room—

—and Lyse was looking at the candle. The flame had gone out while she slept, and a plume of smoke rose from the extinguished wick.

She inhaled sharply as she stared at the face of Saint Anne—and the single tear that slid down the picture's cheek. Lyse crawled over to the candle and, ignoring her fear, pushed her face close to the glass, then sat back, smiling at her own idiocy. Upon closer inspection, it was apparent that what looked like a tear from farther away was actually a dollop of hot wax that'd somehow slipped over the edge and wound its way down the outside of the glass.

The dream—or whatever it was—had left a bitter taste in her mouth, and the crying candle was just a symptom of this. Now she understood why she didn't come back to Echo Park often: Things were always a little wonky at Eleanora's house. She'd just assumed this was because she was a teenager and everything seemed dramatic when your hormones were racing out of control, but she was in her twenties now and the same things were happening again. Strange dreams that were more lucid than any of the ones she'd ever had in Georgia: crying candles, giantesses, and witches . . . It was all just too much to deal with. Especially when her focus should be on Eleanora's illness, on making sure there weren't any other treatment options, that there wasn't a way to stave the disease off or at least stop it from being a death sentence.

A neighborhood dog let out an anxious howl, the unexpected sound reverberating through her old bedroom with enough intensity to make it feel like the animal was standing right outside her window. She scurried backward like a crab, slamming the meat of her palm into the thick brass bed frame, and pain ratcheted up her wrist.

Dammit, she mouthed—then froze as she felt someone's gaze riveted on her back. It was unmistakable, this uncanny feeling of one's privacy being invaded, of having someone unwittingly observe you in an intimate moment. She was not alone, and the knowledge ran through her body like an electric current.

"Who's here?" Lyse heard herself saying, never having felt so unnerved in Eleanora's house before.

No reply.

"Okay, I'm gone," Lyse said—as if there were someone in the room listening to her. "You've spooked me enough for one day."

She jumped off the bed and quickly made for the door. She wanted outside and fast.

The paranoia was back.

Lyse pulled the hood of the shawl she'd grabbed from the kitchen up and over her dark hair, shoving her bangs out of the way so she could see where she was going. It had started drizzling outside, but the dark clouds seemed to be abating. It looked as though she was going to have a nice, sane walk down to the bottom of Echo Park Avenue and across Sunset to Echo Park Lake.

She'd decided that taking a walk was the perfect antidote to being scared all alone up in Eleanora's house. It felt like the specter of death had taken up residence in the bungalow on Curran, and the less time spent there without Eleanora, the better. Besides, she knew it would be good to get outside and clear her head, then make a much-needed call to Carole, whom she should've phoned hours ago.

Instead, she'd procrastinated, telling herself the cell reception was terrible up in the hills, that she'd call Carole later—but she knew this was bullshit; she could've just used Eleanora's landline. The truth was she didn't want to talk to anyone, wasn't interested in regurgitating the events that'd led to her wandering the hills of Echo Park on this wet October afternoon, unable to shake off the horrible dream and the weird feeling of being watched.

How could I have forgotten it? she wondered, remembering the dream that'd dogged her for the entirety of her adolescence.

Not the part with the *giantess*—that was new—but the sacred grove, the creature wanting to eat her, so it could taste her death on its tongue . . . this dream had recurred night after night for weeks at a time when she was a teenager. It had wreaked havoc on her sleep, exhausted her so she fell asleep during classes at school. More than anything, she'd hated the sense of vulnerability she felt when she was in the dream. It reminded her too much of the time after her parents' deaths.

Nope, not going there, Lyse thought, not wanting to think about her parents' double funeral, of her standing alone at the grave site wishing she had joined them.

Survivor's guilt, her therapist had called it—the one Eleanora insisted Lyse see when she was fifteen and the nightmares had been at their worst. *Because you lived and your parents died.*

Removing her cell phone from her pocket, she ignored the old texts and messages and dialed Carole's number.

She hadn't realized it before, but she really needed to hear her best friend's voice. Maybe then she could find the strength to pull herself together and be strong for Eleanora.

"Holy my God, where the hell are you?" Carole said before Lyse could even open her mouth.

No *hello*s or *how are you*s from Carole. Her best friend always got right to the point.

"I'm in Los Angeles—"

"Bemo ate a box of crayons from his toy box last night and we ended up at the emergency room—"

"Wait, *what* happened?" Lyse said without missing a beat. She was used to Carole's habit of changing the subject on a dime. "Is he okay?"

"Gonna be pooping rainbows, but otherwise he's great. He thought it was hysterical. I did not," Carole said. "You listen to my message? I doubt it because you sound way too composed. Someone broke into your place this morning—it's not a mess, but your computer's gone."

Lyse stopped in the middle of the sidewalk, the neighborhood sounds—car engines, trash cans being dragged up driveways, the chatter of children playing behind gated yards—growing louder as her sense of reality flipped upside down.

"No, I didn't," Lyse said, finally. "Listen to the message, I mean. Damn, you're kidding me . . ."

Through the phone line, she could hear Carole shaking her head.

"I don't kid about that kinda stuff, baby."

"Fuck."

"Yeah, *fuck* is right," Carole echoed, but she whispered the word *fuck*. Carole was a single mom whose little one, Bemo, had big ears and a nasty habit of repeating whatever he heard adults say. "I'm on it. The police came—but your neighbor got hit, too, so they think it's hopheads looking for stuff to sell for drugs. Now, why are you in L.A.? What's up with Eleanora?"

Carole knew Eleanora from her great-aunt's visits to Athens. Eleanora adored Bemo, and he was just as smitten with her.

"It's bad," Lyse said, and her throat tightened. "Really bad."

"Hmm," Carole said.

"She's dying," Lyse said, and swallowed hard. "I haven't gotten into the specifics, but apparently there's nothing they can do."

"Oh, babe, I'm so sorry," Carole said—and the pity in her best friend's voice almost broke Lyse.

For the first time in years, she wished she had a smoke. "I want a cigarette."

"No, you don't," Carole said—a hard edge to her words.

Carole had given up smoking when she'd unexpectedly gotten pregnant with Bemo. Then she'd threatened to ban

Lyse from the delivery room unless she quit, too. Bemo was a toddler now and Lyse had never regretted the decision . . . until today.

"What's up with leaving all the lights on at the nursery?" Carole continued, changing the subject again. "You just can't do that, Bear. Overhead is expensive enough as it is without you adding to it. You can leave on the necessary-to-plant-life lights. Everything else, no."

After Bemo was born, Carole decided she was sick of working for other people, and she persuaded Lyse to leave their jobs at one of the local nurseries and open The Center of the Whorl together.

Carole was the business brains behind the outfit, and Lyse had the magic touch with the plants. So far, they'd done pretty well for themselves, but when you owned and worked your own business, you were always waiting for the other shoe to drop. Especially where finances were concerned.

"Yeah, I was in a bit of a daze when I left . . . Eleanora called me while I was still at work."

There was a break in the conversation—as if Carole were waiting for Lyse to say more, and when nothing came she said softly:

"You okay, Bear? Other than Eleanora and the house? 'Cause you sound weird."

Lyse was dying to tell Carole about the strange things she'd been experiencing, but she knew they'd just sound ridiculous, and Carole was nothing if not pragmatic.

Lyse pulled off the hood of the shawl, letting it bunch around the back of her neck and shoulders. The drizzle had stopped, and the crisp, clean smell of growing things filled her nostrils. She took a deep breath, enjoying the earthy smell.

"Uhm, yeah, I'm okay . . ."

"What are you gonna do?" Carole asked, using her *I'm a mother, so don't bullshit me* tone. "How long are you gonna be out there?"

"I don't know," Lyse said, running her hand along the front of a tall redwood fence while she walked. "I guess I'll talk to her doctors, see if there's anything she hasn't told me. Figure out what I can do to make her happy while she's . . . you know."

"Damn, Bear."

An older man was leaning against his chain-link fence, watching Lyse as she talked. It made her feel exposed, standing there on the sidewalk, so she decided to walk faster.

"I don't want to talk about it anymore," Lyse said. "Talking about it just makes me want to cry—and I don't want to do that right now. Tell me about the house, okay?"

"Sure thing," Carole said—the last bit of *thing* cut off by a loud screech on Carole's end of the line. *"Bemo, no! I said no cookie right now—"*

Lyse couldn't help but smile. The thought of Bemo— Carole's ridiculously adorable hellion of a three-year-old— standing in the middle of the kitchen, hands on hips, shaking his auburn curls, and demanding his mama's attention was just too damn wonderful.

"I miss Beams already," Lyse said, feeling an ache in her heart the size and shape of Carole's toddler.

"You want him? I'll put the little monster on a plane to Los Angeles right now."

She knew Carole was only teasing. Bemo was the greatest thing that'd ever happened to her best friend, and she would never let him out of her sight. Still, the thought of Bemo hanging out with Eleanora was, like, the best thing ever.

"I'll take him," Lyse said. "Eleanora would love to have him come stay."

"Yeah, he is pretty damn adorable," Carole said, and Lyse could hear the pride in her friend's voice.

"He's the best," Lyse agreed, wishing she were back in Athens with Carole and Bemo instead of hiding out in Los Angeles. In many ways, Carole and her son were as much a part of her family as Eleanora was. She'd been there holding Carole's hand when Bemo was born, so if that didn't count for something, she didn't know what did.

"Here, take the cookie. I need quiet while I talk to Bear," Carole said to Bemo. "Jeez Louise, that kid has *energy*! Okay, so where were we?"

"Do I need to do anything about the house?"

"They broke a window, but I've got a glazier coming," her friend replied, and Lyse could hear the strain in Carole's voice as she hoisted Bemo onto her hip. "Beams and I can go over there tonight and start putting it back together for you."

"You wouldn't mind?" Lyse asked, surprised to find herself standing in front of a tiny modern glass-and-metal coffee bar that definitely hadn't been there when Lyse was growing up.

"Of course. It's my job to help my best friend out," Carole said. "And please send my love to Eleanora, okay?"

"I will," Lyse said, peering around the row of hedges separating the coffee bar from the local elementary school. "I just wish she were a little easier to reach. It's difficult to really break through to her."

"She raised you, and she loves you," Carole said.

"I know."

There was nothing to add. Carole had called it: Eleanora loved her and she loved Eleanora. Lyse just needed to hold on to that and let it help her through the messed-up times.

"Hey, I need to run, but thank you. For letting me know what's going on," Lyse said. "Am I terrible? I just can't even think about what's happening back there right now. And you can handle the nursery on your own for a while?"

"I can run the place blindfolded, Bear," Carole said, and Lyse could hear Bemo screeching to be let down. "Plus— and I didn't want to say anything until I knew for sure— but Frank is gonna come and stay with us while his place is being renovated. He says it'll help him learn to be a proper dad, and I'm willing to let him try."

Bemo's dad, Frank, was in the picture, but he spent time with Bemo only when he felt like it—which she knew upset Carole. This was a big step forward where Frank was concerned, and she really hoped it didn't end badly.

"I think that's great," Lyse said, the smell of coffee hitting her in the face. "If you trust Frank, so do I."

"He's gonna be on Mr. Mom duty—even if he doesn't know it yet," Carole said, mischievously.

"You're so funny."

"And that's why you love me—*Bemo! Stop harassing the cat!*" Carole obviously had her hands full. "Gotta go, too, Bear. Love you."

"Love you. And Beams!" Lyse said, cradling the cell phone to her ear; she could hear Bemo laughing maniacally in the background as the line went dead in her hand.

She slid the cell phone back into her pocket and decided she needed some caffeine after that interaction. She'd have a latte or something, sit there and let her brain process the fact that someone had broken into her place . . . because that was just *insane*. There wasn't anything in her place worth stealing. No money, no high-end electronics . . . She didn't even own a television—

"Penny for your thoughts, pretty lady."

The voice came from behind her, a rich and commanding male baritone. Surprised, she jumped like a cornered cat, whirling around to find the most captivating man she'd ever seen standing on the sidewalk, grinning down at her.

Lyse

"Sorry, I didn't mean to frighten you," the man said, looking anything but contrite.

"I was just a little lost," Lyse replied, embarrassed by the way she'd initially responded to him. "In my head. I do that. Take a walk in there and get lost."

The man laughed, throwing back his honey-blond head, so all she could see were straight white teeth and pale pink lips stretching into a wide grin. Even when he was done laughing, the smile stayed in place, and she didn't know if she was supposed to be offended or pleased that the man found her babbling hilarious.

"You look concerned," he said, feigning seriousness—though there was still a twinkle in his blue eyes.

"Well, I don't know if you were laughing *at* me or *with* me—"

"Both," he said, grinning again.

She realized he had sexy eyes, pale blue irises flecked with gold, the skin around them cross-hatched with tiny lines from laughing too much. There was something else interesting about them, too. The pupils were very large, even in the daylight, and Lyse remembered reading somewhere that dilated pupils made a person more attractive.

Whether this was really true or not seemed inconsequential—because it wasn't just his eyes that drew her to him; it was his whole vibe. The way he carried himself, the calm confidence exuding from his lean body. This was a man who knew who he was and what he wanted—and, if she wasn't careful, Lyse was going to end up on his "wanted" list.

Trying to distract herself, she looked past him to the covered patio. Here, people sat scattered around small chrome patio tables drinking coffee, working on their laptops, or chatting. Behind the patio and through the building's plate-glass front wall, Lyse could see the interior of the coffee bar, the line snaking around the front of the register as a couple of young baristas filled orders.

"You going inside?" the man asked, scratching the side of his nose with a curled finger, the sleeve of his green flannel shirt slipping down to expose the vivid black-and-purple edges of an octopus tentacle ringing his wrist.

The tattoo reached out from inside the folds of his sleeve, and Lyse was certain if she was ever so lucky as to see him without his shirt on, there would be even more octopus to discover.

The man saw Lyse noticing his tattoo and gave her a languid smile.

"That's Clyde," he said. "Wanna see the rest of him?"

Without meaning to, she found herself nodding, and suddenly he was stripping off the flannel—a weathered wife-beater kept things chaste—and turning his forearm toward her, so she could see Clyde the octopus in the flesh.

"Incredible," she said, and, without realizing what she was doing, found herself reaching out to touch him.

She yanked her hand back but continued to marvel at the beautifully rendered piece of art. It was all swirling tentacles, rounded body, and haunting amber eyes, the vertically slit pupils reminding Lyse of a cat's eyes. Clyde wasn't alone on the man's skin. His arms and torso, at least what she could see of them around the wifebeater, were covered in intricate nautical-themed ink, his body a misguided mash note to the sea.

She felt strangely vulnerable standing in the middle of the sidewalk with this man. She wasn't just looking at his tattoos. She was sharing something intimate with him, speaking a wordless language that was all about context, made up of tentative, shared looks and shyly averted eyes—and then before she could really process everything, the show was over. He was pulling his flannel back on and buttoning it into place.

"I love it," Lyse said. "Clyde's gorgeous."

"Appreciate that," he said, taking a green knit cap out of his back pocket and pulling it down over his head, a few naughty strands of blond hair poking out. "So what's your deal? You live around here?"

Lyse wanted to say that yes, she lived here. That this was *her* neighborhood, and *he* was the interloper—but nostalgia didn't make her the owner of a place. Just because her most poignant memories were made here didn't mean Echo Park belonged to her.

"I used to live here. Up the street, actually," Lyse found herself saying. "But I haven't been back in ages."

The man nodded.

"It's a special place," he said. "You feel it in your bones. When you belong somewhere. From the moment I set foot here, I knew it's where I was meant to be. Sounds stupid. Don't know why I'm telling you this . . ."

He seemed embarrassed by his words, as if he'd unconsciously divulged too much information about himself.

The funny thing was that she understood completely. He'd described the exact same feeling she'd had standing on Eleanora's front porch one wet afternoon twelve years ago, hope burning in her heart like a precious flame. She remembered shaking like a leaf, terrified she'd have to go back to the children's home—just the memory of the place with its urine stink and unwashed-body smell made her feel ill—but then she'd looked up into Eleanora's wise granite face and realized she was home.

Home.

The word caromed around inside her head.

"Where did you just go?" he asked, grinning at her. *The man couldn't stop smiling, could he?*

He was right. She'd been a million miles away and hadn't even realized it. Now it was Lyse's turn to be embarrassed.

"Sorry," she said, looking down at her hands, at the bitten cuticles and ragged nails.

"It's a charming quality," he said. "I'm Weir. By the way."

"That's a very sexy name you got there, Weir," Lyse said, looking up at him through lowered lashes, surprised by her own flirtatiousness.

"Oh . . . yeah?" he said, and blinked, taken aback—no, not taken aback . . . *flustered.* She'd thrown him off his game.

"Sorry," she squeaked, embarrassed again. "I don't normally flirt so unabashedly. So, let's start over. I'm Lyse. And I'll be on my best behavior from now on."

"Nice to meet you, *Lyse,* who will be on her best behavior from now on," Weir said, nodding as if he liked the feel of her name on his tongue.

She brushed her bangs out of her eyes, annoyed with them for getting in the way *and* for making her feel like an awkward teenage girl all over again.

"Well . . ." Lyse said, and let the word linger.

"Well . . . I'm gonna go inside," he said, and lifted his arm, indicating she should go ahead of him. "After you?"

She shook her head.

"Maybe in a minute," she said, quirking her eyebrow in the coffee bar's direction. "Is the coffee good?"

"Well, I think so, but I'm biased."

"Why's that?" she asked, teasing. "You own the place or something?"

He shook his head, more blond hair falling out from beneath his knit cap.

"Nah, just roast the beans they make their coffee with," he said, grinning. "A man's gotta eat, and roasting coffee is the way I do it."

Then, when she didn't make a move toward the coffee bar, he shook his head and went through the gap in the hedges without her.

"See you around, Lyse?" he asked, turning back to look at her.

She shrugged.

"Maybe," she called after him.

"I hope so," he said, and then she watched him cross the patio, admiring the confident way he carried himself—and she might've checked out his butt a little, too, just because she could.

He paused halfway across the patio to talk to a teenage girl who was sitting at one of the tables holding a sketch pad in her lap, a bright pink scarf wrapped around her long neck.

The girl looked up from the sketch pad, smiling at Weir as he talked, though she remained strangely quiet. Lyse felt a stab of envy. The girl was gorgeous, and obviously a favorite of her new friend.

She was tall and willowy, her long legs tucked up underneath her as she reached for her coffee, delicately sipping from the lip of her mug. As Weir continued to talk, the girl's thick reddish-brown hair fell forward, gentle curls framing her face before slipping down her back in thick waves.

Lyse was too far away to hear what Weir was saying, but suddenly the girl's golden-brown gaze had turned in her direction, the dark almond eyes sliding over Lyse, cataloging her.

Lyse smiled back at the girl, trying to defuse the awkwardness she felt at being examined like a bug under a microscope, but the girl only blinked back at her, long lashes floating like butterfly wings as they brushed the tops of her cheeks. Lyse's smile froze as the girl cocked her head, brows furrowing, before returning her attention back to Weir.

Odd, Lyse thought as she watched Weir wave good-bye to the girl, then open the heavy metal door to the coffee bar and go inside.

She decided she didn't really want a latte anymore. She felt out of sorts, and the thought of dealing with Weir again was off-putting. He was obviously a ladies' man, and she was just another pretty lady to play with. She turned on her heel, starting to move away from the patio entrance, but stopped when she felt a gentle tap on her shoulder.

It was the teenage girl—and Lyse had been right. She was tall. Well over six feet with a coltish quality about the way she moved, as though she weren't quite comfortable in her own skin. Up close the girl's beauty was less formed, more immature, like standing in front of an Impressionist's work and seeing the chaotic slap of brushstrokes that from far away resolve into lush landscapes and intricate human forms. Lyse noticed the smattering of light-red freckles on the bridge of the girl's sharp nose, the pimple on the girl's chin, the chapped lips. They were tiny flaws, barely worth mentioning, but somehow they made the girl seem more human and less like an alien creature from the planet Supermodel.

The girl stood there, hands twisting together in front of her waist, eyes skittering here and there: anywhere but Lyse's face.

A shy one, Lyse thought, feeling for the girl.

She'd been a shy kid, too. It was only in college, when she'd finally found a group of friends she trusted, that she blossomed and stopped giving a shit about what other people thought of her.

"Hi," Lyse said, breaking the silence.

The girl blushed, her golden cheeks flushing a deep

pink, and then she held up her right hand, producing a slender pointer finger. Like a magician in the middle of a silent stage show, she was telling Lyse to hold on.

Lyse nodded, and the girl took off, returning a moment later with her pad. She pulled a pencil from her back pocket and began to write, her brow furrowed in concentration. When she was done, she brandished the pad in front of her:

I'm Lizbeth. Are you the Bear?

Lyse was surprised by the use of her pet name, and she must've made a funny face because before she realized what was happening, the girl was abruptly retracting the pad, embarrassment flaming her cheeks again.

"No, don't run away," Lyse said, reaching for the girl's arm to stop her from leaving—she was curious to find out how this kid knew who she was. "You're right. I'm Bear, but no one here calls me that except my great-aunt."

The girl nodded, held up a finger. After a few seconds of scribbling, she flipped over the sketch pad again:

She said you were coming home today.

Obviously the *she* being referenced was Eleanora—who else could it be? Lyse's thoughts froze as something about the exchange with the girl hit a bull's-eye deep inside her unconscious mind, illuminating something she'd been too dazed to put together earlier that morning: *If she hadn't told Eleanora she was coming home, how had her great-aunt known to pick her up at the airport?*

The thought was unsettling.

"Who are you?" Lyse whispered, taking a step back.

The girl reached for Lyse's hand, her long fingers fluttering like frightened birds, but Lyse jerked her hand out of the girl's reach.

"Don't touch me," Lyse said, still backing away. "I don't know you and you're freaking me out."

The girl wrote on the sketch pad, her pencil working furiously:

Please, don't be upset. I don't want to freak you out.

"This is the oddest conversation I've ever had," Lyse murmured, and the girl smiled, nodding in agreement—but then she was back, writing on her pad again.

"Look, it was, uh, nice to meet you, but I gotta go," Lyse said—and she took off before the girl could finish writing out her last thought.

It was a graceless exit, and she wasn't proud of herself for it, but she needed a break from all the weirdness.

As she continued down Echo Park Avenue toward the little bodega, she tried to keep her mind clear, concentrating, instead, on the loud slap of her heels as they beat against the rough sidewalk. But *not* thinking was an almost impossible task. Try as she might, she couldn't stop the bizarre, half-formed thoughts from running through her head.

The girl stood by the hedge, waiting until Lyse finally disappeared from view. She was confused by the lukewarm reception she'd received from the one person she assumed would understand everything.

With a silent sigh, she flipped over the last page she'd used in her pad, but not before scratching out what was written there:

Don't be scared of the tall lady from your dream.
She visits me, too.

Eleanora

Eleanora was relieved when she saw the turnoff for Curran looming ahead of her, the rectangular street sign faded and half hanging from its cylindrical post. The sun was high above her in the sky, which meant there was still plenty of time to sit Lyse down and explain everything—God help her—before they went into the sacred grove to begin the induction ceremony.

Eleanora was finally going to come clean to her grandniece. She'd spent years skirting around the fact that she was a clairvoyant and the master of a coven, but that time was over. She'd stayed quiet, hiding her abilities—she could see and talk to ghosts, or Dream Walkers, as she called them—because she didn't think Lyse was ready for the information, nor did she want to burden her grandniece. Now she felt both excited and terrified to share her secrets—and she wished she possessed a crystal ball, so she could see exactly how Lyse would react to the news.

She hoped her grandniece would be open to joining them, but there was just no way to tell. From Hessika's portent,

Eleanora assumed that Lyse's love of plants meant she would join Arrabelle in the herbalist's trade. Eleanora seriously doubted Lyse even knew her talent *was* a talent—because most herbalists just thought they had a green thumb. They had no idea magic might be involved.

She realized it was asking a lot of Lyse to give up her plant nursery in Georgia, but she hoped her grandniece could build something similar in Echo Park. Still, becoming a member of the coven required sacrifice, and Eleanora had never regretted the choices she'd made—and therefore she didn't feel guilty about asking Lyse to do the same. To give oneself over to the greater good was a sacrifice well worth making. It had given Eleanora's miserable life purpose, had brought her blood sisters and given her the greatest gift of all: Lyse.

She was selfish about her memories, about the sheer joy and love she'd experienced because Lyse had belonged to her. She'd never expected to fall in love—didn't think it was possible even—but it'd happened all the same. The gaunt, dark-haired child she'd found standing on her porch one wet afternoon had, with a single gaze, stolen her heart.

Eleanora remembered the haunted look in Lyse's blue eyes as the girl had stared up at her. This was a child who'd endured misery and had accepted that her life would only contain more of the same. Eleanora had vowed then and there to place this child's needs above her own. She was going to love Lyse with the fierceness of everything she possessed.

Back then she'd seen it as an easy thing, this loving, but somehow, when she wasn't paying attention, it had transformed into something else. It was only now, as death approached and the future remained uncertain, that she realized Lyse would be the greatest gift she left the world.

She felt her breath get away from her. She was winded, the uphill climb harder than she'd expected. She stopped on the sidewalk in front of her neighbor—and blood sister—Daniela's house, leaning against the short wooden fence to catch her breath. She peered past the hedges, curious to see if Daniela was home, but all the lights were off inside, and Daniela's two black cats, Verity and Veracity, were lounging on the wooden front porch—one in a wicker chaise longue, the other sprawled across the porch's top step, belly exposed to the sky.

With its weather-blistered siding and warped wraparound porch, Daniela's house was no longer a showplace, but once upon a time—before Hessika's tenure on Curran, even—the Zeke Title House had been magnificent. A converted artist's bungalow, it'd seen its heyday in the 1920s when Title, an art dealer and rare-book seller, played host to stylish salons with the crème de la crème of Los Angeles's bohemian set.

Even a house falls prey to age, Eleanora mused, her heart rate finally slowing down to normal as she enjoyed the feel of being static.

But static wasn't in the cards.

As soon as the cats sensed Eleanora's presence, they both looked up expectantly, two sets of sea-green eyes focused in her direction. Verity, who was missing half her tail from a run-in with a neighborhood dog, stood up and stretched, arching her back so her shiny black fur stood on end. She jumped down from her perch on the chaise longue and trotted across the lawn toward the wooden gate that separated the yard from the sidewalk.

"Hello there, little one," Eleanora said, as Verity collapsed onto her belly and slithered underneath the gate like a garden snake, emerging on the other side to rub her lithe body against Eleanora's ankles.

Eleanora knelt down and picked up the purring feline, burying her nose in Verity's dark fur.

"I'm not trying to slut-shame you, Verity, but *come on.* I've been gone ten minutes!"

Daniela stood behind Eleanora, holding a brown bag in her gloved hands, the green glass neck of a wine bottle protruding from inside.

"She was just keeping an old lady company," Eleanora said, marveling, as always, at Daniela's choice of hair color: Today, her Louise Brooks bob was bright pink with violet streaks.

Verity squirmed out of Eleanora's arms and joined her sister, who'd come running as soon as she'd heard Daniela's voice. Together, they began to twine around their mistress's legs like a caduceus, nipping at Daniela's suede ankle boots in order to get her attention.

"We'll go inside in a minute, girls," Daniela said, placing one hand on her hip, the other still holding the paper bag. She grinned at Eleanora. "They are such fierce little bitches. And so damn needy."

Eleanora laughed, wrapping her arms around herself as a sudden chill racked her body.

It was true. The cats were obsessed with their mistress—to the extent that if anything ever happened to Daniela, they'd haunt her grave for weeks on end, mourning their mistress until, finally, they'd just curl up in front of her headstone and die.

"I promised Arrabelle I'd bring a bottle for *after* the induction ceremony," Daniela said, switching the paper bag over to the crook of her other arm. "She left me a bitchy voice mail about drinking all her reds last time—and hey, you, I saw your grandniece leaving your place earlier. I'd love to have her sit for me if she'd be down."

"She's not for you, naughty girl," Eleanora said, used to Daniela's ways after the last six months of having her for a neighbor and blood sister. "You know very well that once she's your blood sister there can't be any hanky-panky."

"Aw, where's the fun in having a hot blood sister if you can't—" Daniela began as she took a playful swat at Eleanora's arm.

The instant Daniela's gloved hand touched Eleanora's sleeve, the paper bag fell from her grasp, the wine bottle shattering on the sidewalk, ruby red liquid spreading across the pale concrete like blood. Spooked by the loud sound, the cats took off for parts unknown, leaving Eleanora alone to watch Daniela stiffen, eyes glazing over as her whole body began to vibrate like a tuning fork.

As much as Eleanora wanted to go to her, she knew when to leave well enough alone. Touching Daniela now would only make things worse.

The turquoise leather gloves the girl was wearing should've protected her, but things were stirring in the ether around them, charging the air with electricity, so Eleanora wasn't surprised when strange, seemingly impossible things were born into existence.

"Daniela?" Eleanora said, every instinct begging her to touch the ill girl. "Can you hear me?"

No response.

Being an empath was a dangerous business. No one in their right mind would choose it for themselves. A trick of fate bestowed at birth, this ability to touch someone and "feel" into the emotional core of their being came with a high price: a heightened sensitivity, one that overloaded the brain's circuitry and caused tiny, destructive seizures that slowly chipped away at the brain, until eventually their combined effects created massive and irreversible damage.

Until her recent death, Marie-Faith Altonelli—Daniela's mother—had been a close friend, and so Eleanora knew of Daniela's limitations. The gloves (because touch was the conduit through which Daniela's talent lay) gave the girl a fighting chance at having a normal life. Only twice a year did her blood sister duties compel Daniela to remove them. Otherwise, they stayed on her hands at all times . . . even when she slept.

"Two sisters. The Teacher and the Innocent. Your Saint Anne watches over them so long as you are alive." Daniela's eyes were pitch-black, as though the pupil had swallowed the irises whole. *"You fear once you are gone that nothing can stop The Flood."*

Eleanora stared, her skin pimpling with gooseflesh. It

was no fun to have someone delve into your inner mind's domain.

"The Flood is coming, sister," Daniela whispered—and now she spoke in a reedy voice straight out of Eleanora's past, a voice that froze the blood solid in her veins. *"The Flood is coming and you won't be there to stop it."*

Eleanora felt her heart flutter, not gently, but as though it were being torn asunder.

"No," she rasped, collapsing against the fence and tearing the sleeve of her scarlet Windbreaker as she tried to hold on to the wooden post.

Pinpricks of black danced around her peripheral vision as she fought back the panic clawing its way up her throat. It felt like a vise had tightened around her heart and was squeezing it to death. No, she couldn't, she *wouldn't* die like this. There was too much at stake, too much that had to be settled before she could go.

"Hessika!" Eleanora gasped, reaching out to the ghost of her long-dead friend.

Instantly, she was enveloped in warmth as Hessika's shade appeared before her. She felt the ghost's energy infusing with her own, a trickle of heat that began at the top of her head and oozed its way down the rest of her until she was floating away, the pain receding as though it'd never been. Eleanora closed her eyes, relief washing over her.

Thank you, she thought. *Thank you for the respite, my old friend.*

Though she knew the ghost's energy wouldn't last forever.

Eleanora set both palms flat on the gold Formica kitchen countertop and rested her weight against the cabinet. She closed her eyes and took two deep breaths.

She'd left Daniela recuperating on her front porch, both black cats curled around their mistress's legs like silent, watchful sphinxes. Unlike traditional spirit channelers, empaths were often awake and aware while they worked, so the first two questions on Daniela's mind—once she could speak coherently—had been: *What the hell just happened to me?* To which Eleanora explained that Daniela's body had been used as a vessel to channel a restless spirit. And then: *Who in the hell was I channeling?*

Eleanora had neglected to answer the second question. Not out of ignorance or spite, but because the answer was just too painful.

She opened a cabinet and began pushing aside the ridiculous orange prescription pill bottles the oncologist had prescribed for her—pills that she refused to take—then plucked a tiny glass bottle of cannabis tincture from the back and set it on the counter. At her blood sisters' urgings, she'd done the first round of chemo—she'd been all right with that; it was fighting, and fighting was something she knew about—but once the doctors realized it wasn't working and had started prescribing chemically manufactured crap to "make her comfortable," she'd said *fuck you* to Western medicine. Now she just took herbal remedies Arrabelle made for her and medical marijuana—she had a doctor-prescribed card so she could shop at one of her local dispensaries—and that was it.

If she was going to die, she was going to do it on her terms.

She extracted a dropper full of liquid from the tiny bottle, then released the tincture under her tongue, where it was quickly absorbed into her bloodstream. After a few moments, she felt herself relax, and the blissful freedom of intoxication gradually commandeered her senses.

She knew she was stoned because she could feel it in her ears, and then the silly grin—the one that always accompanied the ear thing—began to spread across her face. She closed her eyes, just for a moment, and when she opened them again, she was sitting on the kitchen floor in front of the sink, head back against the cabinets, smiling like an idiot.

She felt better than she had in hours . . .

Clunk.

Clunk.

Clunk.

Eleanora sat on the bed, the star-patterned quilt that once belonged to her mother and was now hers wrapped around her shoulders like a shawl. She flipped through the pages of her mother's Bible, holding the treasured artifact in her lap as she devoured its contents. When she heard the first clunk *at the bottom of the stair, she panicked and with a shaking hand shoved the old book underneath her pillow. She reached for her knitting where it sat on the table beside the bed and clutched the long needles in her hand. This was the work she was supposed to be doing but had set aside in favor of reading.*

It felt as though she were made for reading, the way the words rolled around on her tongue like candy. She didn't see why this simple, glorious act was considered sinful in her grandmother's eyes. Especially when what she was reading was the blueprint of Christianity itself.

She dropped her stitch, biting her lower lip in unconscious punishment. Her nerves were her worst enemy, she thought, as she absentmindedly scratched her calf with her fingernails. She realized she was digging her nails into her skin, almost drawing blood, and stopped herself. The itchy feeling was starting all over her body, and she willed herself to relax, to slow her breathing down, to stop her heart from racing, to stop itching. These were the tells of her fear, and her grandmother could read every one. She took a few deep breaths, her inhalations becoming a funeral dirge set to the clunking beat of her grandmother's metal brace thumping up the stairs.

The house and stairway were built before the turn of the century when people were smaller and, seemingly, required less space. The clearance of the long and narrow stairwell was so low that only her grandmother didn't have to stoop to climb it. The stairway shot straight up, and if you wanted to make it to the top, you were forced to hold on to the railings, using them to drag yourself up, one step at a time.

Her grandmother was pulling her twisted foot, along with its corrective metal brace, behind her, which meant it would take her just that much longer to reach Eleanora's room. Precious extra time she'd use to collect herself and pretend she'd been knitting instead of reading.

Though she already knew their number by heart, had counted those stairs in her nightmares—both the dreaming and the waking ones—she still kept a running tally of them in her head as her grandmother climbed. Thirteen steps—the Devil's number, her grandmother would say—and each stair ascended was one stair closer to the landing leading to Eleanora's room.

She shivered. As always, she wondered how someone so small and wizened could possess the power to cow her so deftly. Her grandmother saw the Devil in everything, and this fanatical obsession, born out of righteousness, gave rise to her all-consuming crusade against Lucifer, the Fallen Angel.

No one would ever suspect the odd things that occurred in their house. The strange rituals her grandmother made her endure in order to stay free from the Devil's clutches. To the outside world, everything appeared completely normal:

Eleanora attended school like a normal thirteen-year-old; she and her grandmother went to the First Lutheran Church every Sunday come rain, snow, or shine, and her grandmother was involved in a number of charitable church activities.

Everyone in the community called her grandmother a saint. The way she cared for her invalid husband, who, after suffering a massive stroke, was unable to care for himself or even leave his bed. Eleanora and her grandmother did everything for Papa, feeding and changing him, making sure he didn't get bedsores—her grandmother even massaged his arms and legs to keep them from atrophying. It was arduous work, but Eleanora didn't mind. She loved her papa and spent each day after school telling him funny stories about the kids from school, or things she "saw"—

"Wipe that smile off your face, sister."

She was thinking so hard she'd lost her count. Now she wasn't prepared—and one had to be vigilant in this house. Otherwise, there would be hell to pay.

She set her knitting down, but the ball of yarn fell off the bed and tumbled across the floor. She didn't dare leave it. That would be messy and a sin against God—the Lord abhorred anything being out of place. With the quilt still wrapped around her shoulders, she climbed off the bed and retrieved the yarn ball, the material soft in her hand.

Her grandmother stood in the doorway watching her.

"What were you doing up here?" her grandmother asked.

It was a straightforward enough question, but it sent adrenaline racing through her body.

"I was just knitting, Mimi."

She balled her free hand, hidden underneath the folds of the quilt, into a fist, her fingernails digging into the callused skin of her palm. She hated the way her hands felt, dry and cracked and rough. Hours spent washing clothes in the wringer washer, scrubbing the floors on her hands and knees; she was forever toiling, a servant in her own home.

It was for her own good, her grandmother said. Idle hands are the Devil's playthings and cleanliness is next to godliness.

"Really, I was."

Eleanora could see straightaway her grandmother didn't believe her. She didn't know why she bothered to rebel. She was always caught for her indiscretions, like reading when she was supposed to be knitting, or humming when she knew work should be done in silence. Her grandmother's intuition was uncanny, and if Eleanora hadn't known magic was the Devil's work, she'd have said the woman was a witch.

"Lying is a sin, Eleanora."

"I'm not lying—"

"Repent and God will be lenient on you."

She stood there on the bare wooden floor, wrapped up tight in the quilt.

"I didn't lie, Mimi!"

The brace on her grandmother's leg didn't slow the old woman

down. She was at the bed, yanking the pillow away, before Elea-
nora knew what was happening. She held Eleanora's old Bible
aloft—as if it were a burning piece of brimstone straight from hell.

"Liar!" her grandmother intoned, waving the Bible in the air.
Its cover flapped back and forth like a broken shutter in the wind.

"No, don't hurt it!" Eleanora screamed, crawling across the
bed, the quilt forgotten on the floor where she'd been standing.

Her grandmother was quick, stepping away so Eleanora couldn't
reach the book.

"It's Mama's!" Eleanora cried, tears streaming down her
cheeks. "Please, please don't hurt it!"

Jaw set, her grandmother locked her fiery gray eyes on her face.

"The Harlot's Bible. I should destroy it right here and now," her
grandmother spat at her. "It will only lead you into temptation."

"No!" Eleanora cried, collapsing on the bed. "Please, Mimi, don't."

She was hysterical. She had no control over herself. She lay on the
bed, flailing about like a small child having a temper tantrum.

"The Devil's in you, sister," her grandmother said, still hold-
ing the Bible out of Eleanora's reach.

It was an old ritual and Eleanora knew her part well.

"Yes, Mimi," she cried, in between hiccupping sobs. "The Dev-
il's got my foot."

Her grandmother sighed, shaking her head.

"I knew it, sister. I just knew it."

Eleanora sat up, long hair tangling around her shoulders, and
choked back another sob.

"Mimi?"

Her grandmother had softened now. They were on well-trod
ground. Things could proceed as usual from here.

"Yes, sister?"

Eleanora brushed her hair out of her eyes and rubbed her fists
against her wet cheeks, swiping at the tears.

"I need a cleansing."

Her grandmother closed her eyes, the hand with the Bible in it
dropping to her side.

"Praise Jesus."

She opened her eyes, smiling down at her granddaughter. Then she offered Eleanora her free hand. Eleanora took the proffered thing, a claw of a hand, really, knuckles swollen with arthritis, and long nails warped and yellowing. She climbed off the bed— the covers disheveled where she'd lain on them—and let her grandmother lead her toward the stairs.

The Bible, her mother's Bible, was the lure. It and the star quilt were her prized possessions. She would do anything her grandmother said, so long as nothing happened to them.

The afternoon was starting to fade, but still a few rays of sunlight streamed through the windows as she followed her grandmother down the stairs. She held on to the handrail, her teeth chattering with nervousness as she descended. She stared at the back of her grandmother's neck, at the loose strands of gray hair that'd fallen out of her bun and then stuck to her neck, held there by sweat.

There was only one bathroom in the house, and she and her grandmother shared it, each taking their turn in the mornings. Her grandfather had added the addition when Eleanora's mother was a child, so the floor wasn't even with the rest of the house. You had to take a giant step down in order to reach its plain tile floor.

She took a deep breath, then followed her grandmother down into the cramped room.

"Sit down, sister," her grandmother said, indicating the white porcelain toilet.

Eleanora did as she was told, watching as her grandmother set the Bible down on the side of the pedestal sink. She relaxed, knowing the Bible was safe . . . for now.

Her grandmother rolled up the sleeves of her loose cotton blouse and began filling the claw-foot tub.

"Take off your clothes."

Eleanora stood and began to disrobe, unbuttoning her dress and pulling it over her head. She folded it neatly, placing it on the sink beside the Bible, then did the same for her slip and underwear. She was a late bloomer with no breasts to speak of. Some of the other girls in her class made fun of her for it, but frankly she didn't care. To her grandmother, women's bodies were sinful and led to temptation. She was glad she didn't have breasts yet, that her grandmother couldn't use them against her.

When she was finally naked, she knelt down on the floor beside her grandmother, and thus began the "laying on of hands."

"Send the Devil out of this sinful girl, Lord. Rip Lucifer's hands from this girl's soul, keep her safe and part of your flock," her grandmother said, each word overenunciated. "In Jesus' name, amen."

They rose together.

"I'm ready, Mimi," she said, trying hard to hide the quaver in her voice.

Her grandmother turned off the tap and, in the silence that followed, Eleanora could hear the delicate plosh *of the water as it settled in the tub, steam rising in thick waves from its surface.*

She took her grandmother's extended hand and stepped over the lip of the tub, sliding her foot into the near-scalding water. It burned, the pain radiating up her calf, making her eyes water. She closed them and bit her lip to keep from crying. Mimi always made sure the water was just hot enough to hurt but not to cause any serious burns.

"Go on now, sister."

Her foot made contact with the bottom of the tub, and somehow the porcelain was hotter than the water. She wanted to pull her foot back, but this would cause all kinds of trouble. Instead, she put all her weight on the scalded foot, then lifted the other one over the edge of the tub. The pain was excruciating as her toes broke the surface tension of the water, then drifted down to meet their mates at the bottom of the tub.

She stood there, holding her grandmother's hand, legs submerged to the tops of her calves. She looked down and saw that underneath the shifting surface of the water, her skin had begun to turn bright pink. She looked back at her grandmother, who nodded, and then Eleanora held her breath and sat down in the tub.

Her body involuntarily tried to jerk away from the heat, but her grandmother was already there, pushing her backward. The skin on her back screamed as it hit the water, and she resisted, twisting like a hooked fish in her grandmother's hands.

"In Jesus' name, cleanse this child, cleanse her dirty, sinful soul . . . In Jesus' name, save this wretched girl from her sinful ways, release her from temptation . . ."

It went on like this, her grandmother holding her under the water, so she couldn't breathe, air bubbles rising from her nose as she tried to keep her eyes shut, to block the water from scorching her eyeballs. The liquid separated them, muffling her grandmother's words, but Eleanora knew them by heart. She didn't need to hear them.

She held her breath for as long as she could, but then she began to panic, unable to raise herself from out of her grandmother's killing embrace. The need for air was overwhelming. She tried to kick out at her grandmother, but she was getting weaker, the fight inside her disappearing along with whatever oxygen was left in her lungs.

She didn't want to die, but then the realization hit that with death came release and a chance to see her mama again for real, and she changed her mind. She let go, giving in to the blackness as it draped itself around her . . .

She was still sitting on the kitchen floor. It was drizzling outside and the light was fading, casting a burnished orange glow as it congealed in pools around her calves. The rest of her body was in shadow, blocked by the sink she was propped up against.

Her grandmother's voice was exactly as Eleanora remembered it. Slow and reedy—it had sounded no different coming out of Daniela's mouth earlier that afternoon.

She tried not to think about Mimi, about the atrocities she'd endured at her grandmother's hand, but now all those miserable years filled her head. To combat them, she felt an overarching urge to hold her mother's Bible in her hands. She got to her knees, but a sense of vertigo kept her from climbing to her feet. Instead, she began to crawl across the kitchen floor, the linoleum cushioning her palms and knees.

The Bible was in the living room bookcase, on the bottom shelf in between a set of outdated World Books and the *Larousse Encyclopedia of Mythology*. She pulled it out, settling it in her lap, then leaned back, her head and neck pressed against the wooden wainscoting.

She opened the book to the first page, and written along the corner of the cover, in her mama's curling cursive writing, was a name:

May Louella Eames

Her mother.

Underneath it, in the same swirling cursive, there was another name, and a date:

Eleanora Davenport Eames—b. January 9th, 1944

Davenport was her father's last name. Her mother had been unmarried when Eleanora was conceived but had still seen fit to give the baby its father's name—despite the fact that the mighty Davenport family would not lay claim to the child.

The bastards, Eleanora thought.

There were more names in the Bible, but she didn't concern herself with those for the moment. Instead, she ran her fingers across her mama's flowery cursive, as close as she could get to actually touching the woman who was now only a memory, a ghost from Eleanora's childhood.

She sat there in the fading afternoon light for a long while, fingers gently caressing their names: *May* and *Eleanora*—twined together forever in the pages of an old Bible.

Lyse

M ind still reeling from her strange encounter with the mute girl outside the coffee shop, Lyse returned to the house with two bottles of red wine from the bodega wrapped up in a brown paper bag. She didn't know what possessed her to buy them, but the urge had been overwhelming. Now she set them down on the kitchen table and shrugged out of her great-aunt's shawl, hanging it up on a peg by the back door.

"Eleanora?" she called, flipping on more lights as she left the kitchen and walked through the bungalow. "Are you here? I'm back!"

She turned on the lights in the living room, and though the space was devoid of human life, she took a moment to stand in the doorway, admiring it. With its vaulted ceiling, many windows, and three oblong skylights cut into the dry-wall overhead, the room possessed an airy, open quality that made it the centerpiece of the bungalow. As a teenager, she'd spent many an afternoon sprawled out on the hardwood floor, her homework spread all around her as she daydreamed about making out with *this* movie star or *that* famous musician.

She smiled, thinking how her adolescent fantasy life had been so much more exciting than her real life. Setting thoughts of sexy rock stars aside, she let her mind drift back to Eleanora. She didn't know how it was possible to live under the same roof as another human being and not know everything there was to know about them—yet Eleanora seemed to have all sorts of secrets: odd facets to her personality, friendships Lyse knew nothing about . . . And then there was the whole thing with the airport this morning: How *had* Eleanora known when she'd be arriving at LAX?

Lyse figured there had to be a logical explanation for Eleanora's appearance that morning, but no matter how hard she tried to piece it together, the answer eluded her.

Lyse turned off the overhead light, plunging the living room into darkness again, and continued her search.

As she moved down the unlit hall that led to the bedrooms, she felt the night burrowing in around the house, trying to swallow her up. She'd never thought of Eleanora's bungalow as spooky before, but being here alone in the back of the house was kind of unsettling. Even as her eyes adjusted to the lack of light, she still had trouble seeing what was ahead of her. Shadows loomed in the distance, their humanoid shapes startling her—and she actually stopped dead in her tracks at one point, sure she'd seen something nasty skitter across the hall in front of her. After a minute spent frozen in place, staring blindly ahead into the darkness, she decided whatever she'd thought she'd seen was gone, or had never existed at all.

She navigated her way down the rest of the hallway without incident, until she found herself standing in front of Eleanora's bedroom. She rapped her knuckles gently against the polished wood grain of the door and waited.

No answer.

After a minute of hemming and hawing, she tried again.

Still no answer.

Well, she thought, standing in an abyss of uncertainty, fist poised to knock again. *Do I just open the damn door, or do I stand here like an idiot because I'm too scared of what I might find inside?*

Imagination was a strange thing. It could play amazing tricks on a normally sane person.

As she waited outside the threshold of her great-aunt's bedroom, Lyse's mind was dizzy with possibilities—some good and some horrifying. Would she open the door to find her great-aunt resting peacefully on the bed, or would she discover a corpse—

Stop thinking this ridiculous shit, she yelled inside her head. *You're being an* idiot.

The last twenty-four hours had been overwhelming: Eleanora's call, almost no sleep, a break-in at her house in Athens, the bizarre afternoon nightmare, and the nutty teenager at the coffee place . . . Now her great-aunt was probably lying dead on a bed, and Lyse was too chickenshit to go in and find out.

Schrödinger's cat.

The words came unbidden, the phrase from a Quantum Physics for Artists course she'd taken in college. She'd chosen it thinking it would be an easy way to fulfill one of her science requirements but instead found herself really enjoying the theories the professor presented to the class. One of the thought experiments they'd discussed was Schrödinger's cat: Put a cat in a sealed box with a decaying radioactive particle, and the cat was both alive and dead at the same time—until you opened the box, and then all bets were off.

This shouldn't have given her courage, but for some strange reason it kind of did.

"Okay, let's do this," she murmured under her breath, and pushed open the door.

There was a groan of hinges giving way, and then she was inside. The room was pitch-black. She couldn't see two feet in front of her. She felt around the wall until she found the switch plate and flipped it on, bathing Eleanora's bedroom in incandescent light.

The bed. There was someone in it. A lump where a body was curled into a fetal position.

"Eleanora?" Lyse said, taking a tentative step farther into the room.

"Eleanora?"

She spoke louder this time but still got no response. She took another step.

"Eleanora? I'm not trying to scare you, but I'm coming in the room . . ."

She grasped the edge of the star-patterned quilt covering Eleanora's bed and yanked it back in one swift movement to find . . . *nothing*. No body, no corpse, no skeleton—just a pile of bunched-up blankets on top of the mattress. *That* was her lump. Something touched her shoulder, startling her, and she screamed.

It took Lyse a moment to understand that the hand belonged to Eleanora.

"What the *hell*?" she shrieked, terrifying her great-aunt, who was holding on to the wall for support, her breathing labored as she watched Lyse cycle through rage, anger, and shame in the space of a few seconds.

"What is *wrong* with you?" Eleanora sputtered, waving a shaking finger in Lyse's direction.

"You scared me," Lyse said, beginning to feel really stupid for letting her imagination work her up into such a hysterical frenzy. "It was dark and I thought someone was in the bed, and you were gone . . ."

Lyse felt the tears starting. She didn't want to cry, but she'd been so keyed up that a good cry was probably the best way to calm her down.

Eleanora squinted at her grandniece, seeming to decide that maybe Lyse was justified in screaming at her, after all. She offered Lyse her hand and guided the two of them over to the bed, settling Lyse, then herself, down on the edge of the mattress.

"Oh my God, you scared the bejesus outta me," Lyse groaned as she rested an arm around Eleanora's frail shoulder, hiccupping back tears. "I looked all around the house, but you weren't answering me, and then I opened the door, and I thought—"

"You thought I was dead," Eleanora finished, with a snort.

"No, that's not true," Lyse said, lying through her teeth.

"I don't know why everyone wants to put me in my grave before my time," Eleanora said, sighing. "I'm not dead yet, thank God."

Lyse hiccupped up another sob, then sighed.

"I don't want you to die."

She spat the words out, as if saying them fast enough would magically keep Eleanora alive forever.

"But everybody dies, Bear," Eleanora said, removing Lyse's arm from her shoulder. "That's the price of being alive."

"Well, I don't want you to have to pay it."

Eleanora laughed.

"I don't mind, actually," she said after a few moments of silence. "Death isn't the end, Bear. I know it for a fact."

Lyse stared back at her. They'd never discussed Eleanora's religious views before, and she was surprised to discover that she'd expected her great-aunt to be an atheist, or at the very least agnostic. Eleanora's avowal that life went on after death was an odd pill to swallow.

"There is more in this world than what we can touch, see, hear, taste, and smell, Lyse," Eleanora continued. "Which is a lovely way of segueing into another topic, one I've wanted to discuss with you before but was too cowardly to do so."

Lyse's mouth went dry as a desert, the lack of saliva forcing the smooth muscles in her throat to contract painfully against one another as she tried to swallow. She didn't know what her great-aunt was going to say to her, but it couldn't be good.

"Don't look so scared," Eleanora said gently. "I promised

you earlier that there were things to talk about, and they weren't bad."

Lyse nodded but didn't trust herself to speak.

"I guess the way to do this is to just rip the Band-Aid off," Eleanora murmured, looking up at Lyse. She smiled, and Lyse was sure the gesture was meant to convey calm, but it did the opposite. Now Lyse was *sure* something terrible was in the offing.

"Don't give me those sad eyes," Eleanora said, looking put upon for the first time since Lyse had gotten home. "You had that same look on your face the first time you asked me to take you to the store to buy maxipads. It's really not that bad."

Lyse didn't think she'd ever felt terrified *and* mortified at the same time. It was a brand-new experience.

"Just tell me," Lyse said finally, the words sticking in her dry throat.

"Okay, I'll just tell you," Eleanora agreed. "Oh lord, this is gonna sound nuts, but here goes." She took Lyse's hand and gave it a gentle squeeze. "Lyse, I'm a witch."

"Are you high?" It was out of her mouth before Lyse could stop herself.

Eleanora raised one pale silver eyebrow.

"As a matter of fact, I am."

Lyse pushed off the bed, stumbling to her feet, and then she began to pace. Whatever she'd been expecting, it was certainly not this.

"What does this mean?" Lyse said, trying to wrap her mind around what Eleanora had just told her. "Are you, like, a Wiccan or something? Do you like to go burn effigies out in the woods, or dance naked under the stars, or do sexual-healing spells, or whatever?"

Eleanora let out a loud guffaw.

"My goodness, do you have an imagination—"

"*I'm* the one with an imagination?" Lyse said, incredulously. "You're the one who just called herself a witch."

Eleanora shrugged and leaned back against the tangle of bedsheets Lyse had mistaken for a body.

"It's nothing like you think. *Witch* isn't even what we prefer to call ourselves. I use the term because it's the easiest way to explain—"

"Go on, then. Explain."

Eleanora nodded in acknowledgment. Yes, she did indeed have much to explain.

"Do you ever feel like there's something different about this place?" She waved her arm to include the bungalow, herself, and possibly the whole of Echo Park.

"Maybe. Yes. I don't know."

Lyse was feeling very confused.

"It's because this area, all of Echo Park, in fact, rests on a *flow line*. We're sitting on a confluence of energies—psychic and magnetic, just to name two—and this is what gives us the magic—"

"O-kay," Lyse murmured, but now the bedroom was starting to feel claustrophobic, the walls pressing in on her like a slow-moving trash compactor.

"There are covens everywhere, in cities all across the world where the flow lines converge, connecting everyone and everything. All energy, all matter . . . it's the same, Lyse. Nothing can ever be destroyed. It only changes form."

Lyse pulled out the wood-backed chair from Eleanora's dressing table and sat down heavily.

"Now you're starting to sound like my physics professor—"

Eleanora grinned. "Science and magic are very much the same thing. The 'magic' stuff is only called that because science doesn't have an explanation for it yet."

"So, why now? Are you telling me this because you're dying?" Lyse asked, standing up again. There was just something about sitting still that she couldn't handle. She needed to feel her legs working, her body moving.

"Yes and no. Yes, you need to know because I'm dying,

and even if I weren't dying, I need to ask you to promise me something. So you'd have found out either way."

"A promise," Lyse said, holding on to the only sane part of the conversation. "What do you need me to do for you?"

Eleanora sat up, leaving the tangled bedsheets even more misshapen. She hoisted herself onto her feet and stretched.

"My back and hips aren't what they used to be," she confided. "Just a sad old lady these days, Bear."

The day Eleanora had realized guilt was Lyse's chief weakness, she'd become a master at brandishing it like a cudgel. Lyse hated that she could be so easily manipulated, but time and time again, when the right heartstrings were strategically plucked, she found herself acting the part of a complete and total pushover.

Like right now—she was cooped up in this tiny bedroom, emotionally trapped by guilt until Eleanora decided to let her go.

"No shit, Sherlock," Lyse said, angry at Eleanora for being so frail, and mad at herself for not being able to run away. "Please sit down, you're gonna wear yourself out."

But Eleanora was already shuffling over to the small closet in the corner of the room. She knelt down in front of the doorway and began to pull out pairs of shoes.

"What're you doing?" Lyse asked, kneeling down beside her great-aunt.

"Getting something," Eleanora said. "What's it look like I'm doing?"

Making a mess, Lyse thought, but kept that to herself.

Once she'd cleared out the shoes, Eleanora began to run her hands along the dusty flooring, fingers gliding across the slick hardwood.

"Aha," she said, finding what she was searching for. There was an almost imperceptible *click*, and then a section of the wooden floor popped up to reveal a hidden space beneath the closet. "Gotcha!"

Eleanora retrieved an oilskin-wrapped square and held it up to the light. A sheen of pale dust covered the package. Obviously, this thing had been down there for a long time.

"I've memorized every word that was written in here," Eleanora said, beginning to unwrap the oilskin, and Lyse realized it was actually an old jacket. A child's jacket. "I was around for the last third of it; the rest I can only imagine."

"A book?" Lyse asked when Eleanora placed the thing into her hands.

"Not a book," Eleanora said, shaking her head. She reached across Lyse and slipped open the cover. "A Dream Journal. There are four of them."

Three more books sat on the oilskin jacket, each one as thick and well worn as the one in Lyse's hands. They weren't physically large, but there was something weighted about them, as if they contained all the mysteries of the universe inside their pages.

The cover of the one in Lyse's hand was made of firm and unbendable cardboard, a pen-and-ink illustration of a snake eating itself etched onto its plain beige front. She touched the nearly translucent paper inside, tracing the fine blue lines that banded the page like muted veins, and was surprised by how soft the paper felt beneath her fingertips.

She flipped to the next page and frowned. The Dream Journal was empty.

"I don't understand," she started to say, but Eleanora held up a hand.

"It's a Dream Journal, Bear," she said, smiling. "You can only read it in your dreams."

This was too much. Witches, flow lines, Dream Journals . . . Lyse decided that Eleanora was off her rocker. Too many pain meds had made her demented. She set the Dream Journal back with the others on the oilskin jacket and crawled to her feet.

"Well, thank you for sharing them with me," she said,

rubbing her hands together to slough off the dust. "I think they're beautiful. Even if they're empty."

Eleanora did not reply. She continued to sit on the floor, surrounded by the Dream Journals.

"I'm gonna go to my room and change, and then why don't you let me take you somewhere nice for dinner?" Lyse added, staring down at her great-aunt. "Any place in the neighborhood you've wanted to try? Any place that—"

"The promise."

Lyse took a deep breath, then nodded.

"Yes."

"It's very, very important. And not just to me. Say that you'll do it."

"Well, what is it, then?" Lyse asked, unnerved by the intensity of Eleanora's stare. It was electric.

"Promise me you'll do it. No matter what."

"I'm not promising to do something without knowing what it is first—"

"I'm dying," Eleanora said, and the energy drained out of her. She looked like a tired old woman again. "This is my dying wish. That you make me this promise."

Lyse wanted to scream. She was being manipulated, and not even subtly.

"Eleanora—"

"Just promise me—" Eleanora implored, raising her hands together in front of her as if she were praying.

"I can't—"

"Please, Bear, please just promise."

"I—"

"Please!"

Lyse pushed back on her heels, spinning around, so she wouldn't have to look at Eleanora anymore.

"All right, all right! Fine, I *promise*," she cried, just wanting the onslaught of begging to stop.

Aside from her own breathing, there wasn't a sound in

the room. She turned to find Eleanora sitting on the bed. This shocked Lyse because she hadn't heard her great-aunt get up from the floor.

"How did you—" Lyse began.

"You promised," Eleanora said, ignoring Lyse's question. "My blood sisters and I hold you to this promise."

A chill ran through Lyse's body. All of a sudden, this promise was starting to sound ominous.

"Yes, I promised," Lyse said, frowning. "You can hold me to it. Even though you totally manipulated me into it."

Eleanora smiled, her body relaxing for the first time since she'd picked Lyse up at the airport.

"Are you gonna tell me what it is that I blindly promised?" Lyse asked when she realized Eleanora wasn't going to be more forthcoming.

"I want you to take my place in the coven. I want you to become a blood sister."

Humor her. She's dying. She wants you to be a blood whatever, then do it. Who's it gonna hurt?

No one, Lyse thought.

Once Lyse had made the promise, she'd watched a steely sense of determination overtake Eleanora. Even though Lyse was starving, her great-aunt didn't want to go out to eat, nor did she want to stay in and make dinner. Nope, Eleanora wanted to do some kind of weird ceremony out in the woods, and she wasn't taking *no* for an answer.

"Uhm, I don't think this is such a good idea," Lyse said, as she watched Eleanora pull a hand-knit poncho over her head.

She remembered this poncho from adolescence. With its detailing of furry brown llamas around the collar, it'd always been one of Eleanora's favorites.

"And what do you know about it?" Eleanora asked, handing

Lyse the same shawl she'd borrowed earlier in the afternoon. "I think it's a very good idea."

Lyse frowned.

"Jeez Louise, don't get snippy with me."

Eleanora headed for the back door.

"Don't forget the wine," she called over her shoulder as she stepped outside. She had insisted they walk, despite the cold and drizzle.

Lyse threw on the shawl, then settled the wine bottles into a cloth bag she'd found in the pantry. She could feel her stomach rumbling and wished food were on the agenda.

"Lock the door behind you!" Eleanora yelled back at her, halfway across the wraparound patio that led to the front deck.

"Already doing it," Lyse said as she turned the pin in the doorknob, the door locking in place behind her.

The outdoor security lights popped on as Lyse jogged to catch up with her great-aunt. Eleanora walked quickly, and Lyse had a hard time matching her focused stride.

"We have to pick someone up along the way," Eleanora said as they took the footbridge over the koi pond and made their way to the sidewalk.

"Sure, whatever," Lyse said, already regretting her decision to give in to her great-aunt's bizarre request.

The bag of wine was heavy, its thin canvas strap cutting into her shoulder as they walked.

"Slow down, please," Lyse said—every time she hit a bump in the sidewalk or picked up any extra speed, the bottles clattered together, their velocity slamming them hard against her hip bone. They were going uphill, too, which only made her burden heavier.

Eleanora ignored her pleas. She'd set a pace she liked and wasn't gonna slow down for anyone.

"We should've just driven," Lyse huffed, struggling to keep the hood of the shawl from sliding down over her face.

She hadn't noticed it before, but the fabric smelled like Dreft laundry soap, and this was somehow comforting to her.

Once again, Eleanora ignored her.

"Earth to Eleanora?" Lyse said.

"Sorry," Eleanora said. "I was just in the middle of a conversation."

"Excuse me?" Lyse said. *A conversation? What was Eleanora talking about?*

"I was speaking to my friend Hessika. She says hello, by the way."

Lyse wasn't sure how to respond. Then she realized she'd already committed to this insanity, so she might as well make the best of it.

"Hi, Hessika," Lyse said to Eleanora's invisible "friend."

"Oh, she's gone now, Bear," Eleanora scolded, as if *Lyse* were the crazy one.

"Sorry. My bad."

"I'm the clairvoyant," Eleanora said, just tossing this piece of info out like she was talking about the weather, or something else equally mundane. "So I'm the only one who can see the Dream Walkers, anyway."

Lyse didn't dignify this with an answer. Instead, she let her mind drift off into the dusky arms of the evening, enjoying the porch lights burning like torches against the darkness, the scent of night-blooming jasmine filling her nose with its heady bouquet. She missed the ubiquitous hum of the cicadas, though the longer she'd lived in the South, the easier it had become to tune them out. She wondered if she would forget their songs entirely if she ever left Athens for good.

After a few minutes of silent walking, Lyse decided a change of subject was in order.

"How'd you know what flight I was on?" She was worried Eleanora would insist it was magic.

Eleanora shrugged.

"Got a call from the bank's fraud department. Seems they

were worried about a charge someone made on our joint credit account," Eleanora said with a sly smile. "I assured them the charge wasn't a mistake. I assumed—after the poor way you handled my news—you might have decided to come out here to check up on me."

"Shit," Lyse said, shaking her head—she'd totally forgotten Eleanora was the cosigner on her emergency credit card. The card she'd used to book the plane ticket because her debit account was down to its last five hundred dollars—not nearly enough to cover the last-minute nine-hundred-dollar one-way flight.

"With a little wheedling, the nice woman from the bank gave me the details of the transaction," Eleanora added, enjoying the look of awe on Lyse's face.

"You're a piece of work," Lyse said finally, shaking her head in disbelief.

Eleanora stopped walking and turned to look at Lyse.

"I didn't know you would actually get on the plane. I *hoped* you would come soon, but I didn't know."

She smiled as she gave Lyse's cheek a soft pat.

"I'm glad you're here—more so than I can say. Now, let's get up there before they call out a search party," Eleanora said, walking markedly slower now, letting Lyse set the pace.

"So where are we picking this person up?" Lyse asked.

"Arrabelle's house. Arrabelle's one of my blood sisters and the herbalist for our coven. Gives me all those nasty tonics and potions to take," Eleanora said, shrugging. "Anyway, *she's* up at the sacred grove, which is really no more than a clearing that the coven consecrated decades ago. She's pre-paring everything we'll need for tonight. But her apprentice is back at her house, and that's whom we're picking up. She's a teenager and I didn't want her walking through Elysian Park at night by herself."

"Okay," Lyse said, trying to digest all the information Eleanora was telling her.

"And, boy, if I haven't shown you all the nasty stuff Arrabelle makes me take, believe me, in the morning you're going to smell 'em."

"That bad, eh?" Lyse asked.

"Worse," Eleanora cackled. "Like drinking horse piss, only ten times fouler."

Lyse laughed, relaxing now that they were having a proper conversation.

"Arrabelle was the one who made me see a real doctor. She forced my hand. I'd still be ignoring all of this"—she waved her hands around her body—"if I could. She's just awful. You'll hate her on sight."

She winked at Lyse to let her know she was just kidding, but Lyse was keenly aware of how stubborn Eleanora was. If this Arrabelle person had forced her great-aunt to do something against her will, then she must be a real ball-buster.

"I believe it," Lyse said. "You never listen to anyone."

"Ha," Eleanora said. "Speak for yourself. I had to kick you in the behind all the way to Athens, Georgia. You'd have holed up in that room of yours until doomsday if I'd let you."

"What are you talking about?" Lyse said, confused by this turn in the conversation.

"You didn't want to leave Echo Park. You weren't going to go to college . . ."

"That's not true," Lyse said, coming to a stop in the middle of the sidewalk. "I wanted to go to school."

Eleanora slowed down but didn't stop.

"I put you on the plane with a bottle of Pepto-Bismol in your hand. You were a mess."

"I was nervous—"

"You cried and said you didn't want to go," Eleanora said, laughing.

This wasn't at all how Lyse remembered it. She'd wanted to go to college, wanted to get her life started.

"Fuck you," Lyse said. "That's not how it happened—and stop laughing. It's not funny."

Eleanora stopped and put her hands on her hips.

"Don't say *fuck you* to me. That's not how I talk to you," Eleanora replied, sounding more like her old self again. "I expect you to treat me with a little more respect than that. Especially when you're a guest in my house."

Lyse glared back at her, steeling herself for a fight.

"Then don't make up stuff about me."

"I'm not making anything up," Eleanora said, exasperated. "You wanted to stay here with me. I wanted you to go out and explore the world, see some things before—"

"Before what?" Lyse asked.

Eleanora shook her head.

"So you *made* me go to Georgia," Lyse continued, her voice shooting up an octave. "Because why? Because you're a witch or something? I don't understand."

"Because I knew that you were going to follow in my footsteps one day and I wanted to give you a chance to know freedom first—"

"You're nuts," Lyse said, pushing past Eleanora and storming up the hill.

"You don't even know where you're going," Eleanora yelled after her.

"So what!" Lyse yelled back at her. "It's not like you really want me here with you, anyway—I'm just some prodigal child come home to do your bidding! Apparently you couldn't wait to get rid of me before."

Where the hell did that come from? Lyse thought, surprised by the vehemence in her words.

Hot tears cut a path down her cheeks, and she wiped them away with the back of her hand, quickening her pace as the wine bottles frantically banged into her lower back.

I don't need this shit. I just want to go home, she thought—but then this raised the question: Where was her home?

Was it here in Echo Park with Eleanora, or was it in Athens, where she'd already built a life for herself?

Confused was not the word for how she felt. It was worse than that. It was like two different people were trapped inside the same body, both wanting to lead entirely different lives. And as much as she thought of herself as an independent thinker, a woman who did what she wanted and listened only to her own heart, it was hard for her to admit that in this moment, she was completely without a compass.

"Lyse, wait!" Eleanora called after her.

The guilt she felt for antagonizing Eleanora took away the energy propelling her forward, and she stopped, standing in the middle of the sidewalk, breathing heavily.

It took Eleanora a few moments to catch up, but when she did she grabbed Lyse's upper arm.

"Don't you dare," Eleanora said, eyes flashing. "Don't you dare say I don't want you. For God's sake, that's *all* I want."

Eleanora started to cry, and Lyse felt terrible.

"Don't cry," Lyse pleaded. "Please."

Eleanora just shook her head, the sobs coming from deep within her chest.

"I've always wanted you. I've had my failings as your parent. I admit that. But you were the best thing that ever happened to me. I couldn't have asked for a better kid."

Now Lyse was crying, too—and then they were laughing and crying together, holding on to each other.

"We're silly old things, aren't we?" Eleanora said, tears glistening in the wrinkles around her eyes.

"Pretty silly," Lyse said, grinning back at her.

A security light winked on above them, bathing them in an orangey glow.

"You think someone's trying to tell us something?" Eleanora asked.

Lyse snorted.

"Yeah. They're saying: Stop blubbering in my driveway."

"Well, thankfully, Arrabelle's is only a few houses up the way," Eleanora said.

Holding hands like schoolgirls, they took their time climbing the hill, each one careful not to rush the other. When they reached its crest, Eleanora raised a hand to point out Arrabelle's place—a rough-hewn redwood frame clad in towering sheets of glass.

"*This* is your friend's house?" Lyse asked, staring up at what she could only term as *log cabin* meets *industrial modern*.

Eleanora nodded.

"Pretty impressive, isn't it?"

"To say the least," Lyse replied.

"Arrabelle comes from a very wealthy family. You'll see when you meet her. She's fancy."

To Lyse's surprise, Eleanora reached for her hand again.

"Shall we?" Eleanora said, nodding toward the house.

"After you."

Lyse followed Eleanora up the winding driveway, eyes on the massive front door.

Eleanora rang the bell, and a moment later the porch light came on. With the front entrance illuminated, Lyse could see carvings in the wooden door: abstract patterns and strange symbols that seemed familiar—though she couldn't place them.

She opened her mouth to ask Eleanora about the carvings, but then the door creaked open. Standing in the doorway staring at them was the teenage girl from the coffee shop.

And that was when Eleanora fainted.

Arrabelle

A high-pitched howl tore through the calm, and Arrabelle shivered, trying to shake off the unsettled feeling the sound sparked. She froze in place, the unwieldy bag of ash twisting in her hand, and waited for the feeling to pass.

But it didn't.

Instead, it grew larger, unfurling inside her until she was unable to stop herself from looking over her shoulder, eyes darting into the dark recesses of the woods that surrounded the clearing. She saw nothing. No creature standing in the shadows waiting to devour her.

Rigid with anticipation, she waited a few minutes to see if the sound would come again, but there was only the rasp of her own breath as the tension slowly began to ooze out of her body. She reminded herself she was in the woods, that she was trespassing on the habitat of woodland animals, so of course she would hear their comings and goings. There was absolutely nothing to be frightened of.

"Just a dog," she murmured to reassure herself, but the eerie sensation that had sneaked up her arms and the back of her neck would not be assuaged by mere words. Because fear—being honest with herself, that was what this was—is instinctual.

Arrabelle was far too old to give a shit about fear. She'd lived too long, seen too much, dealt with too many idiots *not* to have learned how to laugh in its face. She did what she wanted . . . even if it turned out to be difficult, danger-ous, or otherwise ill advised—and she *hated* anyone telling her no or trying to dictate what she could and couldn't do.

She had an independent spirit, and that meant she wanted to call her own shots. Fearless. That was how she liked to think of herself.

Fearless and curious.

She was interested in absolutely everything, and this innate curiosity seemed to know no bounds. Especially when it came to the human body and medicine. This was due to both nurture *and* nature, her father being a thoracic surgeon and single dad who'd raised his daughter on his own in the urban wilds of San Francisco. Sure, there'd been a parade of clueless nannies to make sure she was fed, clothed, and sent off to school on time—not that any of them checked to make sure she actually *stayed* in class—but she hardly remembered any of their faces; they were just phantoms passing through her life.

In her memories, it was always just her and her dad.

He may have worked long hours at the hospital, but the time he did spend with her was full of love, acceptance, and amazing stories about his work. She loved listening to him talk about the surgeries he performed, and their dinner table conversation was often so rich with talk of blood and entrails that it put most guests off a second visit.

Time alone without her father was spent exploring the old Victorian row house they lived in: A hoarder's paradise, it was filled with an assortment of strange anthropological artifacts and a library full of bizarre medical tomes whose diagrams gave Arrabelle a keen insight into the secret workings of the human body. Many of these items were in her house now, left to her care after her father's passing. Being surrounded by them made his loss feel less sharp.

She shivered.

It was starting to get really chilly out. Arrabelle could feel the cold settling into her bones, burrowing deep inside her. She wished she hadn't told Devandra she could come at eight—she'd felt guilty and relented because Dev had sounded so sad about not getting to tuck her daughters into bed. But my God, wasn't that what fathers were for? Shouldn't Freddy have to bear some of the burden for their care?

Arrabelle honestly didn't see the point in having children. She was perfectly happy on her own. She couldn't imagine being tied down like Dev. The idea terrified her. She wondered if her own father had ever felt this way. Looking back now, she couldn't pinpoint even a *moment* in her childhood when her father hadn't seemed happy to have her around, so maybe she was just a selfish bitch who liked her independence too much.

She laughed at this. Not because it was funny, but because it was closer to the truth than she cared to admit. And because she was still feeling a little spooked at being out in the woods alone.

"Done." She spoke the word aloud just to push back the darkness.

Pleased with her own handiwork, she stood up and wiped the ash from her hands, staining the sides of her coveralls. Then she surveyed the eternal circle she'd cast within the circumference of the clearing.

The coven may have called it *eternal*, but to Arrabelle it just looked like a plain old circle. Creating one was a time-consuming aspect of the ritual process—in fact, Arrabelle and Lizbeth had spent the early-morning hours drinking coffee and burning cedar planks in order to get the right consistency of ash—but it was necessary. All covens used it to create a protective energy barrier around themselves before they began any spell. It kept the good stuff in . . . and the *bad* stuff out.

Not that any of them were worried that the bad things would find them here. The clearing was hidden deep within the heart of Elysian Park, away from the miles of walking paths, the police academy, and Dodger Stadium—but not too far from the Dragon, an outcropping of rocks painted to resemble a large blue-eyed reptile whose scales were made of spray-painted pictures and gang tags. The clearing was actually no more than a little glen surrounded by a grove of eucalyptus trees, their green leaves whispering softly whenever they were tickled by the wind.

But there were protective wards around it. Burlap sachets were filled with herbs, stones, ash, and pieces of precious metal—all blessed and imbued with coven magic—and buried deep within the Earth, tucked in around the roots of the trees to create a warded circle around them. Very rarely a weary but well-intentioned hiker would chance upon the clearing, and the infusion of magic buried there would leave them lighter and happier creatures. But, try as they might, none of them ever found the clearing twice.

It was here the coven met to maintain their rituals—rituals carried out all around the world by a multitude of covens, creating a unified power that kept the Earth in balance. And when the balance was subverted, when covens were destroyed—like in the Dark Ages when the blood sisters, or "witches" as the world called them, were routed out of their homes and burned at the stake—terrible things like civil war and genocide occurred. Even Mother Nature got in on the act, conjuring droughts, wild fires, murderous heat waves and cold fronts, earthquakes, and floods.

Arrabelle opened a canvas bag full of thick white tallow candles and began to lay them out in front of her. She needed ten: four at each compass point inside the circle, five for each member of the coven, and one for the initiate—

Another howl rent the air, and this one was closer. Much closer. Arrabelle looked up, her brown eyes searching the woods, but there was only the quiet rustle of the trees and the hiss of the still-damp grass as the wind danced across it.

"Anyone out there?"

She heard the *crunch* of something treading across the grass, flattening the blades with heavy feet. This new sound startled her, immediately shifting all of her senses into high gear. She knew how vulnerable and exposed she was alone in the woods, totally on display to whatever creature was lurking in the trees, so she went on the defensive, picking up one of the white candles in case she had to lob it at a stray dog . . . or worse.

If she stayed put, she'd be safe within the confines of the circle—but then she realized that her blood sisters had to cross the woods to get to her, and who knew what the hell was out there, watching them. She slid her cell phone out of her coveralls pocket and punched in Dev's number.

A moment later she heard the opening strains to the title song from *The Sound of Music.*

"Dammit, Dev, tell me that is *not* the ringtone you use for me!" Arrabelle called out, scowling into the darkness.

"Sorry!" Dev replied, stepping through the circle of euca-lyptus as she pushed back the hood of her cloak, exposing her head to the cool night air. She'd taken the long strands of her thick strawberry-blond hair and plaited them, the braids falling like burnished rope over either shoulder.

"You're the one who looks like the Swiss Miss," Arrabelle said in a teasing tone—instantly feeling better now that she wasn't alone. "I should Julie Andrews *you* on *my* phone."

"The girls got into my phone and changed my ring-tones," Dev said apologetically, "and I don't know how to change them back."

She knelt beside Arrabelle, holding up the hem of her long skirts to keep them from getting damp, and picked up four of the candles.

"Let me help you," she continued. "Two will get things done faster than one."

"I never say no to that," Arrabelle replied, looking up at the night sky as the clouds overhead began to shift, bathing the clearing in beams of opalescent moonlight.

"Did you hear the howling?" Dev asked, as she set a candle for each of the cardinal directions. "I think it's someone's dog over on Park. I came in that way and it was really loud."

Arrabelle nodded as though this were just a passing topic of conversation. She didn't tell Dev how badly the dog's cries had unsettled her.

"—people just leave them out all night," Dev continued. "That's why they cry. Locked up in a fenced-in backyard—"

"Yup," Arrabelle said, chiming in at the appropriate moments. Her brain was distracted, wanting a logical explanation for what she'd experienced.

In the end, she chose to believe Dev's theory about neighborhood dogs trapped behind fences. It was easier and less frightening than the alternative.

"Eleanora came for a reading this afternoon—"

Arrabelle nodded.

"I know. She told me."

Dev had finished placing the candles and was standing in the center of the eternal circle, at loose ends.

"Don't look like that," Arrabelle said, as she caught the expression on Dev's face. "I know what you're worried about, and it's fine."

Dev looked relieved.

"She told you?"

"She didn't have to," Arrabelle said. "I just knew."

She knew because Eleanora hadn't asked her. She'd waited for the day when Eleanora came to her. Told her that she would be the next in line . . . and it never happened. Eleanora's silence had been more than enough to assure her she was being passed over in favor of someone else.

She'd heard nothing until today—when Eleanora called to ask her to prepare for tonight's induction ceremony.

"I asked her why—" Dev began, but Arrabelle waved her off.

"It's fine. I don't have a problem with it," Arrabelle said. "I trust Eleanora. She's my blood sister, and the master of my coven."

Of course, this was all bullshit. Arrabelle had been *pissed*. It was true she did trust Eleanora and had faith in the will of the Dream Journals, but it'd still hurt like a son of a bitch to be passed over. At the moment, it was a wound she didn't dare pick at for fear it would start gushing blood, so she changed the subject.

"Will you hand me the rucksack?"

Dev turned in place, looking for Arrabelle's bag.

"It's just by cardinal north—"

"Got it," Dev, said, grabbing the bag and bringing it over to Arrabelle.

Arrabelle loosened the tie, and the top of the rucksack fell open. Inside was an old plastic thermos, a double-edged iron Athamé with a coal-black handle, and a stone chalice shaped like the curve of a woman's belly.

She removed each of the items from the bag and set them on a piece of flat sandstone almost hidden in the thick grass. She unscrewed the top on the thermos and held it up for Dev to sniff.

"Smells like stinky tea," Dev said, grinning. "Do you remember your induction?"

She looked like a schoolgirl when she said this, her eyes wide in the moonlight.

"The Horned God appeared to me, and he looked just like Freddy," Dev continued, not waiting for Arrabelle's response as she jammed her hands into the pockets of her cloak. "I was worried the Horned God would come as someone else, but, nope, it was Freddy. Not that I ever told him about the ceremony. Can you imagine what he'd think about everything we do?"

Arrabelle could imagine.

"We never talk about this kind of stuff," Dev continued. "Why is that? Being part of a coven should be like having a perpetual slumber party, but it's not."

Arrabelle shrugged.

"Don't know."

"Well, I like sharing with you guys. We're connected in the deepest of ways and I want to feel like we can talk about anything—"

"Had you ever been with anyone other than Freddy back then? When you joined the coven?" Arrabelle asked. She'd long ago learned that the best way to dissemble was to ask someone a question. People loved talking about themselves, and it got you out of the hot seat.

"Sure, I mean, yes, there was someone else. A guy from school," Dev said, beginning to fidget. "That was why I thought it might not be Freddy. That I'd do the ritual and see this other guy's face instead."

Arrabelle stopped what she was doing and looked over at Dev. Dev was a notorious story repeater, telling the same stories over and over again, ad infinitum, until you could barely stand to be around her, but Arrabelle had never heard this particular one before. And since it obviously made her uncomfortable, it garnered Arrabelle's undivided attention.

"You thought this guy was your true love?"

Arrabelle could tell Dev was nervous, her skirt swishing from side to side as she rocked back and forth on her feet.

"I didn't know. Maybe," Dev said. "I thought maybe he was. But he wasn't. Thank God."

"Who was this guy?" Arrabelle asked, teasing her. "You obviously still carry a little torch for him—"

"I really don't—"

"I think you do," Arrabelle shot back.

"I'm happy with things as they are with Freddy. I love him and he loves me. We have two great girls, we're happy—"

"Happy about what?"

Arrabelle and Dev turned to find Daniela stepping into the clearing. She shrugged off her leather jacket, dropping it onto the grass before continuing over to them.

"God, that walk makes me sweat. What did I interrupt?"

"Nothing," Dev said, shaking her head. "Just talking."

Arrabelle thought Dev was happy to have an excuse to end the conversation.

"Well, some fucked-up shit happened today, ladies," Daniela said, sitting down in the grass and leaning back on her elbows.

"What happened?" Dev asked.

"I touched Eleanora. *With my gloves on*"—she'd caught Arrabelle's disapproving look—"and had an episode, or whatever you want to call it."

Dev gasped, covering her mouth with a dainty hand, but Arrabelle remained silent.

"That's not supposed to happen," Dev said, dropping her hand.

"What can I tell you?" Daniela replied, shrugging her shoulders and sitting up. "But the fucked-up part is that it wasn't normal. I didn't just sense Eleanora's feelings—it was like someone else was using me, my body, to communicate."

"Who was it?"

Daniela glanced over at Arrabelle and shrugged again.

"No idea," she said. "But whoever it was said some eerie shit about two sisters and Saint Anne."

She stopped talking and stared down at her gloved

hands. Arrabelle got the impression there was more to the story, but Daniela was keeping her mouth shut.

"That's so weird," Dev said. "And so not good for you. Are you okay?"

"Fine," Daniela said—with a shake of her head for emphasis.

"What else?" Arrabelle asked, her tone even but forceful. She knew Daniela was being squirrelly, and since she'd only joined the coven a few months earlier—when Arrabelle's mentor, Dezzie, died—Arrabelle didn't one hundred percent trust this blood sister yet.

"I don't like the tone of your voice," Daniela said, crawling onto her knees.

"What tone?" Arrabelle asked, lightly, trying not to set Daniela off.

At just over five feet tall, Daniela was by far the smallest member of the coven, but she had a temper that made her unpredictable.

"Don't think you can fuck with me, Arrabelle. I don't intimidate easy," Daniela said, calm and rational—for now.

Forever the peacemaker, Dev waded into the argument.

"Please, let's not—"

But she was interrupted by another of those awful howls, a sibling to the ones Arrabelle and Dev had heard earlier.

"I think someone just walked over my grave," Dev said, looking out into the darkness as her whole body shivered involuntarily.

"That was no fenced-in mutt," Arrabelle said.

"I don't know what the hell that was," Daniela said, "but I'm glad we're here in this circle and it's not."

No sooner were the words out of Daniela's mouth than a belligerent squawking echoed throughout the glen.

"Oh my God," Dev cried, as three large crows dive-bombed them like shiny-feathered black torpedoes.

The women scrambled out of the way, trying not to get hit by the bodies.

After the siege had ended and they had a moment to collect themselves, Arrabelle reached out with the toe of her sneaker and poked at one of the bodies. The crow didn't move.

"Dead," she said.

She looked heavenward, but there was nothing to see.

Not even a cloud in the sky.

Lizbeth

"Help me," the girl with the dark hair and striking blue eyes almost yelled at Lizbeth from the doorway.

It was Lyse, Eleanora's grandniece. The girl she'd embarrassed herself in front of at the coffee bar. The lady from her dreams had promised her that Lyse would be her friend, but things had not at all gone according to plan during their first encounter.

"Please," Lyse said through gritted teeth.

Eleanora was heavier than she appeared, and it was obvious Lyse couldn't hold up the limp body on her own. If Lizbeth didn't help her soon, Lyse was going to lose her grip—and, to make matters worse, she had a canvas bag of wine over one shoulder, weighing her down.

"Thank God," Lyse said as Lizbeth reached out and slid her arms around Eleanora's slender waist, taking most of the weight for herself. Which wasn't a big deal since she was much bigger than Lyse, and probably a whole lot stronger.

Together, they dragged Eleanora inside. As they struggled, Lizbeth kept her gaze on Lyse, watching as the other woman stepped across the threshold into the house, her neck straining from the physical effort of lifting the deadweight. They carried Eleanora through the dark living room, the glass bottles of wine in Lyse's bag slamming against each other in earnest. When they stepped into the warmth of the kitchen, the light seemed to rouse Eleanora from her stupor, and her eyelids fluttered open.

"What're . . . you . . ." Eleanora murmured, looking around wildly. *"Put me . . . down."*

Eleanora's voice was weak, but she was getting her strength back. She fought them as they settled her onto one of the kitchen table benches, pushing roughly at their hands, and generally behaving like a grumpy old monster with sharp claws and teeth.

Now that Eleanora appeared to be all right, Lizbeth wanted to disappear. She could feel the prickly sensation, the one she got whenever she was upset. That reminded her so much of the times *before*—no, she wasn't going to think about it. Too easy for the prickly feeling to take over, if she let her mind go there. She squeezed her eyes shut, praying the bad mojo would go away.

She knew Lyse could handle things with Eleanora. Maybe she should go back to the living room, grab her coat and bag, sneak home. Weir would be annoyed with her—he thought he was getting the house to himself for the night—but she didn't care.

She just wanted to escape.

"Hey, you know I can still see you when you're closing your eyes," Lyse said. "I really appreciate your help. Thank you."

Lizbeth cracked open an eye and caught Lyse's apologetic smile—and the smile changed everything. After that, Lizbeth was perfectly happy to stay exactly where she was.

There was a bump and then the sound of claws skittering on porcelain as Arrabelle's adorable gray Cornish Rex kitten,

Curiosity, fell into the empty kitchen sink, drenching herself under the running tap. Lizbeth grinned and picked up the kitten, setting her down on the rustic clay tile floor. The kitten stared up at her with saucer eyes and meowed—a tiny little pipsqueak of a sound—and then she began to lick her wet front paws. After a moment, she sauntered off, probably looking for a place to hide out while she dried off.

Curiosity was obsessed with the kitchen faucet, and she'd been sitting on the countertop watching and waiting for Lizbeth to turn her back so she could stick her white-stockinged paw into the cold stream of water. Only this time she'd gotten more than she'd bargained for.

"Poor little guy," Lyse said, resting her hand under her chin. "He's all wet."

Lizbeth wanted to correct her: *He* was actually a *she*.

"Lizbeth is an apprentice herbalist, Lyse," Eleanora said, turning to her grandniece and smiling. "And I think she spends more time with that kitten than Arrabelle does."

Lizbeth smiled because it was the truth. Sometimes she *did* feel like Curiosity was more her cat than Arrabelle's.

"So you're an apprentice," Lyse said from her seat beside Eleanora at the kitchen table. "You didn't write anything about that at the coffee place."

Lizbeth blushed, embarrassed by the way she'd behaved that afternoon. All she'd wanted to do at the coffee bar was reassure Lyse that everything was going to be okay, that the giant lady from their dreams was one of the good guys. Instead, she'd botched it, freaking Lyse out and making a big fat mess out of the whole thing.

"You went to Burn?" Eleanora asked Lyse, surprised.

"That little coffee place on Echo Park? Yeah. But I didn't go in," Lyse said. "I just met Lizbeth outside on my walk to the bodega."

"Hmm," Eleanora said, picking up the mug of pumpkin soup Lizbeth had heated up for her and taking a sip.

"I liked the look of the place," Lyse said to Lizbeth. "You'll have to take me back there sometime."

She likes me, Lizbeth thought. *She thinks I'm weird, too, but that's okay.*

"I'm so sorry I've held us up," Eleanora said, frowning into her mug. "I think it's just the valerian root Arrabelle's been giving me. It makes me dizzy—but we should go now—"

Eleanora started to stand up, but Lyse touched her arm.

"Hey, we're not going anywhere until you finish what's in that cup," Lyse said, frowning at her great-aunt—although the color was already starting to come back to Eleanora's cheeks. "So you'd better get to it."

Lizbeth was sorry Eleanora had gotten woozy, but she didn't mind the respite she'd gotten because of it. It'd given her time to finish the kale, avocado, and pumpkin salad they were supposed to have after the ceremony. She was behind in making dinner because Arrabelle had had her grinding turmeric and ginger all afternoon for a tincture.

As Arrabelle liked to say, their kitchen was more than just the hearth of the home where dinner was made. It was a magical place where the plants and herbs of the Earth were distilled into special tonics and brews that lifted spirits and healed bodies.

"So what's being an apprentice like?" Lyse began, then caught herself. "I mean do you like it?"

Yes-or-no questions were always best for Lizbeth, and she appreciated Lyse's polite rephrasing of the question. She nodded, her eyes roving across the room as if to say, *How can anyone not like working in this place?*

What she *didn't* say was that sometimes she felt like Arrabelle's maid. She cooked some of Arrabelle's meals (so Arrabelle would remember to eat), did laundry on occasion, and tried to keep the place clean (Arrabelle picked up after herself, but she *never* dusted)—all while *also* helping with the preparations for the herbal tinctures, pills, and tonics they made. Making the herbal remedies could be tedious and difficult at times, but she really loved learning about the different plants and their uses—it was just doing the grunt work around the house that bored her.

Lyse raised an eyebrow, and Lizbeth thought the other woman might've intuited that there was a little bit of job dissatisfaction behind the simple nod.

"Was that hearth original to the house?" Lyse asked, looking around the room.

Lizbeth shook her head.

Arrabelle had put in the sandstone hearth—which took up the entirety of the back wall—and the clay tile flooring when she'd bought the house.

"The place was a teardown when Arrabelle got ahold of it," Eleanora said, answering for Lizbeth. "She redid it from the ground up."

"Wow," Lyse said.

"I was with her when she bought this thing," Eleanora said, thumping the top of the long, rectangular pine table where she and Lyse were sitting, its golden wood scored with innumerable gashes and burns—collateral damage from years of Arrabelle mixing potions and preparing poultices on it. "And those guys."

Eleanora pointed to the two huge antique Chinese apothecary cabinets standing sentry on either side of the walk-in hearth.

"Boy, did they cost her a fortune," Eleanora added.

There was an insistent *meow* at Lyse's feet.

"Little lovey thing," Lyse whispered, picking up the kitten and setting it in her lap to ruffle the short, curly fur on top of its head.

Curiosity was in kitten heaven with all the attention. Lizbeth could hear her purring from across the room.

While Eleanora and Lyse were distracted, Lizbeth went to the nearest apothecary cabinet and collected an opaque brown bottle from one of its many drawers. It was a nettle and milk thistle concoction that Arrabelle called Energize. She took the bottle of Energize with her to the sink and retrieved a glass from the drying rack, filling it with cold water. She used the dropper to extract a few drops of the tincture and added them to the glass of water. Then she placed it on the table in front of Eleanora.

"I don't want to drink this—" Eleanora protested.

"Drink it," Lyse said.

Eleanora sighed, resigned to her fate, and did as she was told, her throat working as she gulped it down in one swallow.

"Nasty," she said, making a face as she let out a massive burp. "Excuse me."

Lizbeth grinned.

"God, that burp smelled like piss," Lyse said, wrinkling her nose.

"That's because that concoction tasted like piss," Eleanora said, standing up. "Okay, I think I'm ready to go now."

"Shouldn't we just stay here and forget this thing?" Lyse asked, trying to catch Lizbeth's eye. "Don't you think that's a good idea?"

Lizbeth knew better than to get into a battle of wills with Eleanora—besides, she didn't think anything Lyse could say would stop her great-aunt from dragging them to Elysian Park.

"Nope," Eleanora said, slipping on her poncho. "Terrible idea. Sitting here playing with that cat is not on the agenda for tonight."

Lyse sighed, picked up her shawl, and draped it over her shoulders. She moved to grab the canvas bag of wine they'd brought with them, but Eleanora shook her head.

"Leave them here," Eleanora said. "We're coming back for dinner after."

"You're the boss," Lyse said, rolling her eyes—mostly for

Lizbeth's benefit—before setting the wine down on the table.

Eleanora was already heading for the back door, but Lyse held up a hand.

"If we're going to go traipsing off into the woods, I think I need a bathroom first."

Eleanora pointed toward the living room. "It's in there somewhere."

"Uh, thanks for being so specific with your directions," Lyse said dryly.

Lizbeth curled her index finger, gesturing for Lyse to follow her. She could feel Lyse's gaze on her back as they rounded the corner and passed the plate-glass wall of windows overlooking the city, the squeak of their rubber-soled shoes echoing off the living room's soaring post-and-beam ceiling. She suddenly remembered the lights being off when she'd opened the front door, and decided it would be neat to show her new friend all the nifty things in Arrabelle's collection.

Lyse blinked as the overhead lights came on.

"Whoa," she said, eyes wide as she caught sight of Arrabelle's museum-quality art collection. "This is incredible."

Lizbeth nodded and flashed Lyse a quick smile—she really wanted Lyse to know she liked her. It was an important thing to get across.

At least, it was important to the lady in her dreams, who said Lyse was the one she could trust, that Lyse would look after Lizbeth once Eleanora was gone. Lizbeth really wanted to talk to Lyse about the lady, but how did you write something like that out in words?

It was tough not being able to open your mouth and just tell someone how you felt. And as much as she was grateful for her sketch pad, it wasn't enough.

"This place is like an art gallery," Lyse said, coming to stand beside Lizbeth so that together they could stare at the walls, every inch festooned with West African ceremonial masks.

Lizbeth remembered the first time she'd come to Arrabelle's house, how awestruck she'd been by the masks. The round, beseeching eyes that begged you to take them down from the wall and slip them over your own face. Some of them were less friendly or actually radiated an evilness that frightened Lizbeth. Those bore horrific scowls, slitted eyes, jagged teeth, and pointed tongues, and they wanted only to be left alone. Others were more animal than human: predator cats, hyenas, antelope—and all of them, like preening birds, jockeyed for your attention.

The masks were handmade spirit totems, hewn from the earth and then fashioned by human hands into physical representations of grief, joy, anger, fear, and more. They were a rainbow of human emotion, trapped in wood and displayed for all to see, their jewel tones offset by the twinkling lights of downtown Los Angeles.

It was an impressive room, but impossible to take in all at once—even if you were prepared for it.

Lyse had moved closer to study one of the masks.

"I have no words," Lyse said, shaking her head. "But, damn, this would freak me out if I had to walk through here to get a glass of water at three A.M."

Lizbeth had been prey to similar thoughts about the spookiness factor of Arrabelle's masks—especially when she stayed late into the night, helping Arrabelle with some of the more difficult distillations.

"I wish we could have an actual conversation," Lyse said softly. She'd stepped closer to Lizbeth, speaking in a low voice so what she was saying would stay between them. "Can you just nod or shake your head if I ask you a couple of questions?"

Lizbeth sensed the prickly feeling returning, but she tried to ignore it. She smiled at Lyse and nodded.

"Eleanora," Lyse began. "She believes she's some kind of witch. That this nature walk into Elysian Park is so we can conduct a ritual of some kind . . . Did you know this?"

Lizbeth realized Lyse had no idea who or what they were. This was shocking to her—how could Eleanora not have told Lyse anything about herself? It didn't make any sense.

"Did you know that she thinks she's a witch?" Lyse repeated.

Lizbeth nodded slowly, eyes drifting down to look at her feet.

Lyse took this in, her body tense as she nervously shifted back and forth on the balls of her feet.

"*O-kay.*"

Lizbeth waited for the next question, and for a moment it seemed like there wasn't going to be one, but then Lyse asked: "Has this been going on a long time? This delusion my great-aunt is having?"

Lizbeth didn't know how to answer. It'd been going on for as long as Lizbeth had known Eleanora, *but* it wasn't a delusion. So she nodded first—

"Okay—"

And then she shook her head.

This only served to confuse Lyse.

"Wait, what? I don't understand."

Lizbeth shrugged, not sure how to get across what she wanted to say with just a shake or two of her head.

"Wait, wait . . ." Lyse said, her eyes sparking with an idea. "Do you mean, yes, this has been going on a long time?"

Lizbeth nodded vigorously, her long hair falling across her face.

"And that, no, it's not a delusion?"

Once again, Lizbeth shook her head with vigor. It was nice to feel like she'd made herself understood. It was the hardest part of being what she was, the idea that no one really knew what she was thinking. It was sweet relief to be able to communicate with Lyse.

"So, if you're saying it's not a delusion, then what is it?"

Lizbeth frowned to remind Lyse this wasn't a yes-or-no question.

"Sorry," Lyse said. "This is hard. Like surreal *Jeopardy!* or something."

An amused grin spread across Lizbeth's face, mirrored by Lyse's own smile.

"Let's try that again," Lyse said. "Eleanora thinks she's a witch. Do *you* think she's one?"

The smile disappeared as Lizbeth nodded.

Lyse shook her head as she took this in.

"I don't believe in witches."

Lizbeth raised her gaze to meet Lyse's eyes.

"I'm just gonna play along with this because I promised her I would . . . and because she's dying," Lyse continued. "And I owe her one for taking me in when I was a kid. After my parents died."

Lizbeth understood the pain she heard buried underneath Lyse's words. Loss, bereavement, being alone . . . all those things Lizbeth knew well. She wished she could say, *Yeah, I get it. We're the same. I know how it feels to be lost*—but she couldn't. Instead, she reached out and took Lyse's hand.

Lyse stared down at their clasped fingers.

"It's okay," she said, giving Lizbeth's fingers a gentle squeeze before releasing them. "It was a long time ago."

Lizbeth knew Lyse was wrong: Time might heal a body's wounds, but it could do nothing for the misshapen scars those wounds left behind.

"All right," Lyse said, stepping away from Lizbeth and twisting her head so she could look around the room. "Take me to this bathroom I've heard so much about."

Lizbeth grinned, then ushered Lyse away from the living room. She led them down a long hallway that opened up onto a spacious sitting room decorated in tasteful shades of pale cream and beige, overhead track lighting giving the space a soft yellow glow.

Lizbeth pointed to a door in the back corner of the room. Beside it was a desk that held a metal sculpture of a dancer caught midleap, its body twisted backward in flight. Beside the sculpture sat a brown corded telephone.

"Wait," Lyse said, and Lizbeth, who'd been planning a quiet getaway, was forced to turn back. "Okay, you have to stop looking at me like you're a scared little baby animal. You're making me feel awful."

Lizbeth nodded and tried to relax her face, so she seemed less "scared baby animal."

"I think we got off on the wrong foot earlier, and I wanted to apologize. You just freaked me out a little, and I wasn't the nicest to you, so I'm sorry."

She offered Lizbeth her hand.

Lizbeth stared at it.

"Just take it," Lyse said, offering Lizbeth an encouraging smile.

Lizbeth was tentative in her approach, meeting Lyse halfway. She was unused to shaking hands and squeezed Lyse's fingers too hard.

"Ow! Okay, okay," Lyse said, laughing. "I need that hand."

Lizbeth dropped Lyse's hand, embarrassed all over again.

"So, are we cool?" Lyse asked, massaging the fingers Lizbeth had just crunched.

Lizbeth gave Lyse a shy smile.

"Good," Lyse said. "Now, go keep an eye on Eleanora for me. That way I can actually pee without worrying."

Lizbeth nodded, and then, hair flying behind her, she left the sitting room at a gallop. She felt more settled, and the prickly feeling was almost gone. She floated down the hallway with a wide grin on her face, pleased that Lyse seemed to trust her.

Curiosity was sitting in the middle of the living room, waiting for her. Lizbeth stopped so the kitten could bump into her ankle, rubbing her face against Lizbeth's jeans.

Hi, kitty, Lizbeth thought as she dropped to her knees, picking the squirming kitten up and letting it nuzzle her chin.

She imagined the kitten answering back with: *Hi to you, too, Lizbeth. You smell like magic. I want to eat you.*

Lizbeth grinned, liking the made-up personality she'd given the kitten—this wasn't their first conversation, actually. She talked to Curiosity almost every day.

Hey, you don't want to eat me, Lizbeth thought, as she stroked the soft spots behind the kitten's ears. *I'm your friend.*

In her head, Lizbeth heard the kitten say, *You're nobody's friend.*

Unsettled, she set the kitten back down on the floor and wandered back to the kitchen to wait for Lyse.

Lyse

Walking through the dark streets of Echo Park after they'd left the safety of Arrabelle's house behind them, the streetlights and pregnant moon their only means of illumination, Lyse recalled how, as a teenager, she'd dreamed of the original bohemians and radicals of Echo Park. Not just daydreams, but convoluted, lucid things that woke her up on the hottest nights of the summer to find the covers bunched at her feet, her heart beating in time with her shallow breaths. She would lie there, listening to the birds chirping out their night songs, the sound carrying through windows left wide and screenless to let out the pervasive heat and take advantage of the unpredictable crosswinds.

She dreamed of nights spent dancing around a devilish bonfire lit by the Semi Tropics Spiritualists—a long-disbanded camp of bohemians and psychic enthusiasts who'd resided not far from where Eleanora's house stood. Fever dreams of old Echo Park that made her want to be alive sixty years earlier, when the neighborhood was nicknamed Red Hill because of all the political radicals and artists that populated its lush hills, their tiny bungalows hidden within the tangle of wooded greenery high above Sunset Boulevard.

She'd been a teenage girl full of nostalgia for a time that wasn't her own. But all that changed the minute she slipped the noose of adolescence and left Echo Park behind her for college. She'd lost the magic of adolescence in favor of more adult pursuits. She'd found a few good friends—like Carole—who seemed to understand her, and she was happy.

Her time in Echo Park became a hazy dream, a faded photograph pinned to the sheets of a forgotten photo album.

Walking these streets brought that world back to her with a vengeance. As they got closer to Elysian Park, more memories began to resurface, filling her head with a sense of nostalgia so strong that her heart ached.

They passed a funny little cottage Lyse remembered from her teenage wanderings, and she was surprised to find it hadn't changed a bit. Peeling brown wood, stained-glass front windows, and wind chimes hanging like luscious grapes from the porch rafters, their hollow bodies tinkling wildly as the wind pushed them to and fro.

Night-blooming jasmine grew all over these hills, woven into trellises, snaking over metal and wooden fences alike, permeating the air with its creamy, almost tropical scent. Nature was still alive in Echo Park, concrete and drywall and brick mixed together with trees and wild animals and the smell of living things.

They took the rolling hills at a brisker pace than she'd have liked. She'd have preferred to linger and marinate in thoughts of the past, *and* she was worried about Eleanora wearing herself out, her great-aunt moving too fast when she should've been taking her time.

But this wasn't Lyse's journey. She was just a spectator, following Eleanora and Lizbeth as they led her deeper into the hills, past the houses and streetlights, and into the heart of Elysian Park.

"This is really far," Lyse said, out of breath as they crested a sloping hill.

"Not too much longer," Eleanora said, stepping off the marked trail and cutting into the trees.

"Where are you going?"

"It's just through these trees," Eleanora said, pointing off into the thicket of greenery.

Lyse sighed, aware nothing she could say would dissuade her great-aunt when she had her mind set on doing something. When they were still back at Arrabelle's house, before the epic hike into the heart of darkness, she'd tried to get Eleanora to go home—but she'd been shot down. Her great-aunt was stubborn, determined to do what she liked even when it wasn't healthy for her.

"I'm dying," Eleanora had said. "There's nothing bad a hike in the woods can do to me anymore."

Lyse had no argument for that, though she'd already decided she was going to force Eleanora to get a second, or third, or fourth doctor's opinion—she didn't care how many it took. She remembered that Carole's brother had gone to Sloan-Kettering when he'd been diagnosed with lymphoma. She was gonna call him in the morning and get his doctor's name and number. There had to be more cutting-edge stuff a specialized place could be doing for Eleanora.

Plus, she was worried about her great-aunt's state of mind. Maybe a psychiatrist should be on the docket, too. This whole game about witches and blood sisters and rituals was clearly some kind of psychotic delusion. Eleanora had gotten mixed up with a group of well-meaning (probably) Earth mother Wiccan ladies and, in her demented state, had decided their Earth magic stuff was for real.

And she didn't even want to think about the weird conversation Eleanora had been having on the way to Arrabelle's house. The one with the "Dream Walker" called Hessika.

"Just through here," Eleanora said, her voice low.

The perfume of night-blooming jasmine gave way to the sharp scent of eucalyptus, and Lyse looked up to find herself in the middle of a stand of trees.

"Come on, slowpoke," Eleanora called back to Lyse. "Pick up the pace."

Lizbeth had Eleanora's arm, and the two of them were moving away from her through a gap in the trees. Lyse shook her head, not wanting to follow, but knowing it wasn't a choice. She pushed on, keeping Eleanora and Lizbeth in her sight line.

This is ridiculous, she thought. *It's pitch-black out. We're in the middle of nowhere . . .*

She realized belatedly that Eleanora and Lizbeth were no longer ahead of her.

Shit.

"Eleanora!"

The quiet *whoosh* of the wind through the eucalyptus leaves was her only answer.

"Dammit," she murmured, annoyed with herself for losing track of the others.

The fog was beginning to roll in—or maybe it'd been there the whole time and Lyse just hadn't noticed it. *No, that's not right,* she thought. *There was no fog before. The night was clear.*

An eardrum-shattering *howl* cut through the stygian night, and Lyse took an involuntary step back. The shawl she was wearing wasn't warm enough. It let the cold leak in, chilling Lyse down to her very marrow. She began to walk again, faster than before, moving through the dense stand of unending eucalyptus trees. It was getting colder, and the fog was thicker the farther she ran—because she was running now—her brain thrumming with the need to escape.

"Eleanora!" she screamed into the night, the eucalyptus smell cloying in her throat and nose.

No response.

"Oh shit!" she shrieked, stopping her forward momentum and beginning to backpedal as terror gripped her heart.

Crouched in the fog ahead of her was a feral dog, its muscles tensed to attack. She didn't dare turn her back on the beast, afraid it would pounce if she took her eyes off of it. She slowed down, not wanting to trip over anything in her haste to get away. All she had going for her was that she was bigger than it. If she ended up on the ground, she could imagine the nasty creature using it as an excuse to attack.

"Shoo!" she hissed at the dog. *"Get away from here!"*

Out of the corner of her eye, she saw a fallen branch lying on the ground a few feet away and she started inching toward it.

She slowly bent down to pick up the branch, and the dog snarled at her. She froze, the makeshift weapon a few inches from her grasp.

"Get away!" she yelled, trying to sound as confident as she could, and then in one sweeping movement, she grabbed the branch and swung it out in front of her, brandishing it like a sword.

The dog attacked, racing at her with almost supernatural speed. She didn't flinch, just aimed the branch, and the moment the dog was in range, she swung it like a bat. She missed but was able to sidestep out of the dog's way before it could sink its teeth into her.

The beast turned around and went for her again, but this time she hit it square in the face with as much force as she could manage. The dog gave a pathetic whimper and veered off course, steering itself away from another wallop with the branch.

"Stay away from me, or I'll do it again!" Lyse cried, adrenaline pumping through her body. She felt glorious and sick to her stomach at the same time.

It wasn't light enough to see if she'd drawn blood, but the dog's whimper gave Lyse a clue that she'd scored a direct hit.

"Go home, or back to wherever you came from!" Lyse yelled, swinging the branch around to further dissuade the dog from attacking.

"Need a little help?"

Lyse wheeled around. Behind her stood a tiny slip of a woman in a sexy sweatshirt cut strategically to hang off one shoulder—and though it was hard to tell for sure in the moonlight, Lyse was pretty sure the woman had pink hair.

"I think I've got this—" Lyse started to say, but the dog chose that moment to take another run at her.

"*Go,*" the woman said, stepping in front of Lyse as the dog pounced.

Lyse did as she was told, taking off into the trees. Tree branches sliced into her as she ran, but she didn't dare stop. She wanted to put as much space as possible between herself and the dog.

Behind her, she heard a snarl and then a soft *yip* of surrender, the sound fading into the night. Out of breath, she stopped and leaned against the trunk of an old eucalyptus tree. She took a shuddering gulp of air and realized she'd been holding her breath. She let the branch fall to her side and felt her body shake with relief . . . and the aftereffects of a heavy adrenaline surge.

She didn't know what else to do, so she started walking again. It didn't take long for the fog to clear and the trees to thin out, and soon she found herself stepping through a gap between the foliage.

She gasped . . . and stared into the clearing from her nightmare.

"Lyse," Eleanora said, running over to her grandniece and grabbing her wrist. She was trembling.

"My nightmare," Lyse whispered, patting her great-aunt's arm as she pushed away an overflow of emotion. "It's real."

"Are you okay?" Eleanora said, with an intensity that was frightening. "You were right behind us, and then it was like you'd vanished. I was so worried—"

"I'm fine," Lyse murmured, wanting to reassure Eleanora, even if she had to lie to do it. "There was a stray dog, but it's fine."

She gritted her teeth, channeling all her energy into putting on a happy face. Eleanora didn't need her to fall apart right now.

She slid her arms around her great-aunt's shoulders, hugging the older woman to her. The trembling in Eleanora's body worsened, and Lyse wondered if this was going to become a constant thing—if so, it was even more upsetting than her great-aunt's appearance, which was bad enough, all fragile eggshell skin revealing the bones beneath the flesh.

Dammit, Eleanora was really dying. Any idiot could see it—and *she* was the delusional one if she thought a second opinion would change that.

"I'm glad you're here now," Eleanora said, peeling away from Lyse's embrace.

She'd never been one for prolonged touching, was forever pulling out of hugs too soon, nodding instead of shaking hands. It was an aspect of Eleanora's personality that drove Lyse crazy. Now Lyse was just happy for *any* morsel of affection from her great-aunt.

"This place," Lyse said, the words spilling from her lips. "I know it. I've dreamed of it. For years and years it's haunted me—"

"I didn't know," Eleanora said. "Why didn't you ever tell me?"

"What was there to tell?" Lyse said. "I had nightmares. I didn't know they were actually about a real place."

Eleanora sighed and rubbed at her chin, her fingers splaying across the lower part of her face like wings. She began to nod, turning Lyse's words over in her mind.

"*I* should've known," she said. "I'm the master of this coven and it's my business to be on top of these things. Besides, I know now that I should've told you everything:

about myself, about my ability . . . about the coven. It wasn't fair to keep things from you."

"Why?" Lyse asked. Ever since Eleanora had begun talking about witches and magic and covens, Lyse had wondered why her great-aunt had kept this information from her. "Did you think I couldn't handle it? Or was it that I wasn't good enough to tell—"

"No, you were always good enough for anything," Eleanora said, interrupting her. "That's a ridiculous thing to say. You were just young. I didn't want to burden you—"

"Lizbeth is a goddamned kid!" Lyse yelled, pointing in Lizbeth's direction. The younger girl shied away, embarrassed at being singled out. "She's a teenager. I was her age. That's a bullshit argument."

"You're right. I've been thoughtless," Eleanora said, spinning off in another direction, one Lyse hadn't expected.

"What are you talking about?" Lyse wanted to shake her great-aunt.

"I wanted you to have a normal life," Eleanora said, sighing. "Even if it was just for a little while. I didn't want you to be like me. To only know sacrifice . . ."

"Why would you say something like that?" Lyse said. "That's all I wanted. To be like you. You're wise and strong and I love you—"

Eleanora didn't seem to know how to respond. She shrugged.

"You don't know what I've done in my life, Bear. The terrible—but necessary—choices I've made. If you did, you wouldn't want to follow in my footsteps."

Lyse let her eyes flare with disbelief.

"Then tell me. Let me make my own decisions. Stop trying to protect me or keep me in the dark."

"I don't want to fight with you, Bear," Eleanora said, exasperated. "Please, can we just table this conversation for another time? There's so much we have to do tonight—"

"No," Lyse said. "I'll do anything you want. I'll join whatever club you need me to join. Do whatever 'ritual' you want me to do. But *only* if you talk to me right now. Because tomorrow may be too late—"

She stopped, trying to collect herself and failing miserably.

"Because . . ." She began to cry. "Because you could be dead tomorrow."

"Not unless you plan on murdering me in my sleep," Eleanora said with a snort.

Lyse shook her head, Eleanora's sarcasm killing her tears.

"Fine, don't be serious. I don't care. Just tell me what's going on here. Why have I been dreaming about this place?"

"The coven is your destiny. It always has been. That's why it infiltrated your dreams. The part of you that belongs to the coven wanted to be known," Eleanora said, and sighed. "As to what's going on here . . . I think that's pretty easy to figure out. I'm dying—as you've so succinctly pointed out—and I need you to take my place. I need you to be me. It's as simple as that."

Eleanora pointed behind her—and for the first time, Lyse realized she was standing in a circle within the clearing. A circle someone had drawn with ash or black chalk, she wasn't sure which—and it was quartered by white candles, their flames guttering as the wind whipped across them. Two women, each markedly different from the other, stood in the middle of the circle.

"Lyse, I'm not the only one who needs you," Eleanora said, and smiled. "Meet the rest of my blood sisters."

One was smiling at her, and the other was watching her with a studied gaze that bordered on surliness. The smiling one was the first to step forward.

"This is Devandra."

"Hi, Lyse," Devandra said. "It's so lovely to meet you— and you can call me Dev, if you like. Everyone else does."

Lyse immediately liked the woman with the long strawberry-blond hair plaited on either side of her head. There was a safe, maternal feeling about her presence. Like she had a whole lot of love inside her that couldn't help but shine out of her face like a beacon.

Lyse held out her hand, but Dev only laughed at her.

"We do hugs around here."

She pulled Lyse to her, the scent of her vanilla-spiced perfume making Lyse feel about ten years old.

"I'm Daniela."

Lyse turned to find the tiny woman who'd come to her rescue out in the woods. Her cheeks were flushed from the cold, but the streaks of pink on her otherwise pale face only made her look more beautiful.

"Excuse me if I don't hug you or shake your hand," Daniela continued, coming up to join them, her large expressive eyes thoughtful as she took in Lyse's disheveled appearance. "I have a little condition that precludes me getting too close to anyone."

"Uhm, sure," Lyse said, nodding. "And thank you for your help out there."

"Of course."

She shot Lyse a lazy, snaggle-toothed grin. One Lyse recognized. She was well aware of the hungry look a person got in their eyes when they were attracted to you. In fact, she'd experienced it earlier in the afternoon with the guy at the coffee bar—Weir—who'd looked at Lyse in much the same way Daniela was looking at her now.

"Arrabelle," the last woman said, stomping over to Lyse, hand extended.

An Amazon in jean coveralls, Arrabelle was a statuesque woman with smooth dark skin and a fierce expression in her dark eyes. She almost crushed Lyse's hand when she shook it.

"It's getting close," Arrabelle said, releasing Lyse's hand. "I think we should begin.

Eleanora nodded to the others.

"And so shall it be."

All around her, the women began to undress.

"Uhm, what're you doing?" Lyse whispered to Eleanora, an embarrassed smile plastered on her face.

Eleanora had already dropped her poncho and slipped off her shoes.

"It's part of the ritual," she said, starting to take off her shirt. "There's nothing to be ashamed of here. You're with your sisters-to-be."

"You want *me* to take off *my* clothes in front of a bunch of strangers?" Lyse said, incredulous. "I hope there's nothing about the word *no* that you don't understand, because *no*."

"Is it too cold for you?" Dev asked, folding her clothes into a neat pile and setting them on the grass just outside the ash circle. "Sometimes I leave my socks on and that helps my feet stay warm."

"It's not because I'm cold," Lyse said, turning to her great-aunt. "Although it is frickin' cold out here, *Eleanora*. Do you want to get sick?"

Eleanora shrugged, her breasts pale and flaccid in the moonlight now that her shirt and bra were off.

"I already told you that nothing in these woods is gonna get me before the cancer does."

Lyse threw up her hands.

"Fine. Get pneumonia. I'm not taking care of your ass when you do."

From across the circle, Daniela, who was buck naked except for the gloves on her hands (and totally shaved *everywhere*, Lyse couldn't help noticing) called out, "I'll take care of your glorious ass, Eleanora," and everyone giggled. Except for Lyse. Who didn't think stepping into an all-nude version of *The Twilight Zone* was very funny at all.

"Well, I'm not doing it," Lyse said, crossing her arms over her chest. "I mean, I'll *do* your ritual, but I'm keeping my clothes on."

"Stop being a pussy," Eleanora said, naked as the day she was born, "and take off your clothes."

She was starting to feel like the odd man out—even Lizbeth had removed her clothes and was setting them on the grass next to Dev's pile.

"Oh, Jesus, fine," Lyse said, exasperated, and started tugging off her shoes.

She took off the shawl, then pulled her shirt over her head, releasing all of her trapped body heat in one move.

"Shit, it's cold," she said, shivering.

"Socks are okay," Dev said, smiling, "and they help."

Even in the moonlight, Lyse could see the stretch marks tracing along the line of Dev's hips and breasts, and the cesarean scar that ran along the curve of her belly. Her body may not have been supermodel fit, but it was as beautiful and inviting as any Lyse had ever seen.

"Socks," Lyse said, shrugging out of her pants and folding them with her shirt and the shawl. "I'll give it a try."

She took a deep breath and reached up to unhook her bra. Her breasts were fine, but nothing to write home about compared to Dev and Arrabelle. She dropped the bra on top of her pile of clothes and shucked off her underwear. As Dev suggested, she left her socks on.

"I bet Daniela ten bucks you wouldn't do it," Arrabelle said to Lyse, hands on her hips. "Guess I was wrong."

"Hey, when in Rome, right?" Lyse said, wishing she could stand there as confidently as Arrabelle. The woman seemed completely at home without any clothes on, her sleek swimmer's body trim and muscular, and devoid of fat.

Only Lizbeth seemed as awkward about her nudity as Lyse felt. The younger girl was sitting on the grass, knees curled up to her chest, long hair draped around her shoulders. When she caught Lyse looking in her direction, she grinned widely and shrugged.

"The cardinal candles have been lit," Eleanora said,

gathering the other women to her with her words. "We cast out anything unwanted from the circle."

"*We cast out anything unwanted from the circle,*" the others intoned.

"And we draw together our power here in this protected circle . . ."

"*And we draw together our power here in this protected circle . . .*"

". . . with the promise it shall only be used in good works," Eleanora finished.

"*. . . with the promise it shall only be used in good works,*" they all repeated.

The four candles—*the cardinal candles*, Lyse thought, filing it away in her memory for later—guttered as a blast of icy wind crossed the clearing.

"Light the remaining candles, Arrabelle," Eleanora said.

Arrabelle knelt down in front of a small stone altar resting in the grass. Lyse would have tripped over the thing before she saw it hidden there. With a long wooden match, Arrabelle lit five more candles and passed them out to the others.

Only Lyse was without a candle when she was through.

"We welcome you into the realm of the sisters, may my blood be her blood," Eleanora intoned—and that was when Lyse saw the knife and chalice in her great-aunt's hand.

She almost reached out and knocked the knife away, instinct telling her that any ritual involving something so sharp and frightening could not be good. But before she could say a word, Eleanora had sliced open the tip of her own left index finger, releasing some of the blood into the chalice. She passed the knife and chalice to Arrabelle, who sliced open her index finger and intoned: "May my blood be her blood."

Lyse relaxed—let these ladies donate a few drops of blood to the chalice. So long as this was all the knife was being used for, she wasn't too worried.

Daniela was next.

"May my blood be her blood," she said, and then a few drops from her index finger went into the chalice.

And so it went for both Dev and Lizbeth—only when it was Lizbeth's turn, the girl closed her eyes and mouthed the words. Finally, the chalice and knife made their way to Lyse. She took them from Lizbeth, the stone chalice cold in her hands. The knife was light as a feather, its black handle warm to the touch.

"So I just . . . do it?" Lyse asked.

She didn't know what to believe anymore. Part of her thought Eleanora and her "blood sisters" were crazy. Everyone knew there was no such thing as magic. That people couldn't see and talk to ghosts . . . but then there was the dream. The clearing she'd never been to but had dreamed about night after night for years. This was the stuff that was hard to just explain away. It felt wrong to discount all the strangeness she'd felt growing up in Eleanora's house. To not listen to the voice inside her head. The one telling her to take a leap of faith and see where it all led.

"Yes," Eleanora said, and nodded. "You just do it."

"Here goes nothing," Lyse said, and pressed the tip of the blade into the fleshy pad of her finger. "May my blood be your blood."

She didn't know what possessed her to change the wording, but somehow it felt right.

Eleanora took the chalice from Lyse's hands.

"The sacred potion, please," Eleanora said—then she waited as Arrabelle retrieved a plastic thermos from behind the stone altar.

Arrabelle uncapped it and poured its contents into the chalice. There was a *hiss* and then a finger of steam rose up from within the curve of the stone.

"It's ready," Arrabelle said. Eleanora took a small sip from the chalice and passed it to Arrabelle. Arrabelle did the same and passed it to Dev.

It made its way around the circle, and finally Lyse was forced to take the proffered chalice from Lizbeth's out-stretched hands. She stared down at the liquid contents, pretty sure she was gonna have to take more than the small sip the others had taken.

"All of it?" Lyse asked.

"All of it," Eleanora replied.

Lyse took a deep breath, plugged her nose with the fingers of her right hand, and gulped the nasty-tasting brew down in one swallow.

The drink made Lyse feel funny. Her eyes began to focus in on strange things. Like the fact that Daniela was totally naked except for a pair of turquoise leather gloves. Lyse began to wonder if Daniela was germophobic, or maybe it was just an odd psychological quirk.

Actually, there was something kind of weird about each of the women here tonight: Arrabelle and her museum house, the mute Lizbeth, Daniela's gloves . . . only Devandra seemed normal—but who knew what weird stuff she had back at *her* house.

It was interesting that Eleanora had befriended such a disparate group of women. When Lyse was a teenager, she remembered Eleanora having friends, most of them her great-aunt's age or older. Eleanora had kept Lyse separate from them, but Lyse had been aware of their existence. Now she wondered, what had happened to those other ladies? Had they died, or retired, or moved away to other climes? And if so, why had Eleanora replaced them with these other, *younger* women?

It was very, very *straaaaaaaaaaaaannnnnggggeeee.*

The word elongated in her head, and it was such an odd sound that she began to laugh.

"Lyse?"

She heard her name and looked up to find all the eyes in the circle—and some that weren't in the circle—fixed on her. She must have really been out of it because she hadn't noticed the thread of the conversation being pulled in her direction.

"Uh-huh?" she said, but the word came out as gibberish.

She reached up and touched her ears—nothing wrong there—then her face. Her fingers slid across her cheeks, chin, mouth, and nose. Her skin felt tight in places, loose in others, like she was pushing her fingers into a marshmallow.

"Are you all right?" Eleanora asked, but her words sounded as if they were being filtered through the ocean.

Lyse opened her mouth, but the world began to seesaw back and forth, and she had to close her eyes to keep the vertigo at bay.

"Lyse?" Arrabelle was at her side, lifting her eyelids, checking her pupils to see if they were dilated.

Arrabelle's face began to blur and twist, all her features swimming together into a dark blob. Lyse felt light as air, and before she knew it, she was floating away. She held out her hands, hoping someone would catch her before she disappeared, but she was moving too quickly, floating higher and higher above the clearing as the others gathered around her, watching as Arrabelle eased Lyse's naked body onto the grass.

Coherent thought left her as her brain winked off like a television screen, the picture irising in until it was only a tiny black dot.

Then that was gone, too.

Lyse

*L*yse opened her eyes, the absolute darkness gradually receding from view until she could make out the tenor of her new surroundings. Above her, the honeyed glow of the full moon held the night at bay, and she was able to look around, surprised to find she was standing in the middle of a newly shorn wheat field. She raised her hands, and the feeling of dissociation from her body was gone—

"This way," a voice said from behind her, its cadence warm and feminine, and she was dragged out of her thoughts.

The idea that this place was real became unimpeachable when she felt a hand on her back, fingers pressing against bare flesh, and she looked down to find she was still naked, though the body she saw didn't belong to her. The breasts were too large, the waist and hips too small, and there was a dark mound of curling pubic hair where her own body had been waxed into a thin strip. The air, fragrant with wood smoke, was pleasantly warm, and so despite her nudity, she didn't feel cold.

Fingers were at her waist again, gently urging her forward, and she turned to find a handsome woman in a flowing purple robe standing behind her. The woman wore her hair pulled back away from her face, a garland of intricately woven lavender and heather *encircling her head like a crown, and though her long hair was still thick and blond, her face was crosshatched with delicate lines.*

Youth was no longer hers.

"It's time," the woman said, and smiled warmly.

Lyse felt her feet begin to move of their own volition, heard the crunch of freshly scythed wheat stalks as she trod upon them.

The old woman chose not to accompany Lyse as she crossed the field, but she didn't feel alone—nor was she scared. Instead, her body was filled with a sense of anticipation, her breasts softly bouncing as she walked, the nipples hard with excitement. The body she inhabited was looking forward to the experience that lay ahead.

At the edge of the field, where the human-cultivated wheat crop ended, there stood a raised wooden platform shrouded in fog. She approached cautiously, stepping up onto it, her bare feet pressing against the smoothness of the wooden boards, excitement rippling through her flesh like tiny shock waves. She stood there for a moment, uncertain as to what was supposed to happen next, but then the fog lifted like a velvet curtain parting, and she saw that the platform was actually the beginning of a long boardwalk—one that switched back through a shallow marshland swarming with cattails and bulrushes before disappearing into darkness.

She took a tentative step, and as if her footfall had conjured them, two floating orbs sparked to life farther down the path. Like streetlights on a bridge, they illuminated just the next section of walkway, so she wouldn't miss a step. She moved quickly, wanting to discover the light's source, but her curiosity only grew when she found no magic at work: just two flickering tallow candles, each one placed upon a tall metal spike set into the marshy water on either side of the boardwalk.

More candles winked to life ahead of her, and she wondered if someone was using the cover of darkness to obscure their movements, to stop her from discovering their identity as they lit the candles. Continuing down the boardwalk, she heard the crack of wooden boards shifting under her weight, and more lights flared into being, the candles guiding her way.

She walked for a long time—until the excitement finally gave way to exhaustion—and then she abruptly ran out of walkway. To her surprise, she found a wooden sailboat waiting for her at the end of the boardwalk, its mainsail tied in place as it bobbed up and down like a cork on the surface of the water.

The ship was made of golden timber, its rigging shimmering in the moonlight, and at first it appeared to be unoccupied—but then a man emerged from belowdecks, coming to stand on the bow, his head and shoulders hidden within the long shadows cast by the tall wooden mast. Even in the darkness, she felt his eyes on her, devouring her breasts and belly as his gaze raked across her naked body.

The man on the boat knelt, turning away so she couldn't see what he was doing, and when he stood again, he was holding a hurricane lamp in his hand, the smoky, glass-shrouded light bestowing angles and planes to a face previously obscured by shadow.

She gasped, not because she was frightened, but because the man was not fully a man. He was a giant stag—or, at least, the mask he wore made him look like one. Curving, majestic antlers sprung from the sides of his head like small trees, bulging brown eyes as clear as glass stared back at her; only the lower half of his face was visible below the mask, framing a full, sensuous mouth and a strong, square jaw.

She began to tremble as her body instinctively reacted to what it knew was coming: This man/beast was about to mount her like an animal.

She took a step back, and the man sensed the time was ripe to pluck her. He jumped from the ship, shortening the distance between them in a few strides, and then he was holding her, trapping her body within the confines of his solid, muscular arms. He crushed her nakedness against him, and she could feel the hardness of his manhood pressing into her belly through the thin cotton of his pants. He found her lips with his own—and she thought he was going to crush them, too—but instead he brushed his mouth across hers in a gentle caress.

Trailing soft kisses down to the hollow of her throat, he followed the curve of her collarbone in one direction, then the other, *tongue flicking snakelike across her skin as he tasted her. He reached down with both hands and cupped her ass, squeezing it as he pulled her up onto her tippy-toes, positioning her pubic bone in line with his cock. He moaned as he squeezed her against him, and she jumped up, her legs sliding around his waist as the tip of him pulsed against her through his pants, his erection rock hard.*

She yielded to him, her body relaxing as she opened her mouth, letting him slip his warm tongue inside. He tasted sweet and salty, and she loved it. Her own tongue began to chase his, and as she ground herself against him, he moaned against her mouth. She could feel the wetness between her legs soaking the cotton of his pants, and she wanted him inside her, fucking her.

He swung her around, her body cradled against him, and she nuzzled her face into the warmth of his neck, smelling the cinnamon spice of his bare skin as he carried her over the threshold of his ship and belowdecks.

The ship's galley was neat as a pin, but he carried her right past it and into his bedroom. Gently, he placed her down on the bed, then stepped back so he could admire his prize. The room was small and unadorned, but the glow of a dozen flickering candles bathed the room in golden light.

Now she knew who'd been leaving the candles for her to follow.

She leaned back, her head and neck cushioned by a mound of feather pillows, and smiled, slowly spreading her legs wide, beckoning him to her without words. She wondered if he would take her with the mask on? She hoped he would—there was something erotic about not knowing the identity of one's lover.

She was used to worrying about protection, but this wasn't a real encounter—it wasn't even her own body, for God's sake—so she decided she didn't need to ask the mystery man if he had a condom.

He watched her writhe on the bed, her hips moving in small, sensual circles, letting him know how badly she wanted him inside her. She ran her fingers across her nipples and they grew swollen and hard beneath her fingertips. She arched her back and moaned, hating him for making her wait so long, for making her silently beg him to touch her.

He did not smile as he stepped out of his pants, but she moaned again when she saw how big and hard he was. He was as eager to be inside her as she was to be filled by him. He unbuttoned his shirt but did not remove it, the solid muscle of his chest gleaming in the candlelight. He was gorgeous, all lean muscle and sculpted six-pack, his chest covered in tufts of golden fur that encircled his nipples before trailing down his abdomen. He was glorious and solid and oh so male, and she was dying with need. She arched her hips and bit her lip, feeling so wanton she could hardly stand it.

He knelt down in front of the bed, placing a large hand on each of her thighs, then pressing them into the mattress. He put his lips to the wetness between her legs, and she began to tremble as he ran his tongue across her clit. She thrashed against him—every flick of his tongue driving her insane—but he held her in place, pinned to the bed, so he could have his way with her. He raised his head, the mask making him look garish and almost frightening in the candlelight, but she didn't care. She just wanted him to stop teasing her with his tongue and put an end to the ache between her legs.

He pulled his mouth away and sat back on his heels, admiring her. He seemed to enjoy her little cries of frustration.

"Please, please don't stop," she moaned, but the voice wasn't hers—and it startled her.

Before she could start overthinking things, he was on top of her, easily slipping his swollen cock into the wet cleft between her legs. He was so hard she could feel every inch of him as he thrust into her, and she cried out, digging her nails into his back as the sensation of his cock sliding in and out of her brought her to the edge.

He grunted and pulled out, the loss of him so exquisite it was like a slap in the face. She opened her eyes and stared up at him, surprised by the grin on his lips. Grabbing her around the waist, he flipped her onto her stomach, and she squealed as he lifted her onto her hands and knees, taking her from behind.

Her body was slick with sweat as he pumped into her, her large breasts swinging like pendulums. Not pausing once in his thrusting, he licked his fingers and reached around to rub her clit. She gritted her teeth as his movements grew frantic, and she ground herself against him, urging him to go faster. He began to fuck her harder, sliding in and out of her, her pussy opening to him like a flower. He thrust deeply into the center of her, and she came, giving a strangled cry at the sheer agony of her orgasm.

It was unlike anything she'd ever felt before—it went on and on, waves of pleasure flooding through her—and all the while, he was still moving inside her, still rubbing her clit to increase the intensity of her climax.

The way she was writhing and moaning beneath him proved too much, and he bit into her shoulder to stop himself from crying out. He shuddered as he spilled his seed, the intensity of his orgasm matching her own. Spent, he finally pulled out of her.

She lay there panting until he grabbed her around the waist and hauled her onto his lap, holding her tight against him. She could feel the rapid beat of his heart, and she opened her eyes, a smile curling her lips. She was warm and satiated. She never wanted this night to end.

"Who are you?" she asked.

In answer, her mystery lover reached up and undid the ties at the back of his mask. As the antlers fell away, the smell of sex turned sour in her nostrils.

Weir.

"What the—" Lyse said as she sat bolt upright in the grass, five worried faces encircling her.

Then she threw up.

The retching didn't last long—there was barely anything in her stomach—and when she was done, she felt as though she'd swum up from the depths of the sea and was seeing land for the first time. Reality felt heightened, but there was clarity, too. She'd touched something unreal, and somehow it made her *more* real.

Dev handed her a handkerchief.

"Thank you," Lyse said, dabbing at her mouth.

She gazed at the five—now clothed—women surrounding her, studying their faces for some sign of recognition, some idea that they possessed insight into the surreal, dreamlike reality she'd just experienced—and what she found in their combined expressions was enough to tell her they knew exactly what'd happened to her. Or some version of it.

"What did you do to me?" Lyse asked, as she climbed to her knees and then unsteadily to her feet. "What did I just drink?"

Eleanora nervously clasped and unclasped her hands, and Lyse could tell her great-aunt was trying to find the right words. Lizbeth had fetched her clothes, and Lyse began to slip her underwear on, her hands shaking. She felt woozy, like everything was coming at her through a fog.

"Ayahuasca." This was Arrabelle.

"You drugged me?" Lyse asked as she buttoned her jeans.

"If you drink this, it will settle your mind, calm you down," Arrabelle said, holding out a plastic cup for Lyse to take.

"No way," Lyse said, backing away from her. "I don't want my mind settled and I don't want anything you've touched. I want to know why I was in somebody else's body."

"Induction ceremony," Daniela said. "It's a metaphorical mating with the Horned God, and your initiation into our coven."

"Uh, not so metaphorical," Lyse said, blushing.

"Looks like it was pretty hot stuff," Dev said, giggling. "Did you see his face?"

Now Lyse's cheeks were on fire.

"I think she did," Arrabelle said, raising an eyebrow.

"That's beside the point," Lyse said. "What I want to know is whose body I was in."

Eleanora patted her arm.

"It's just a representation of the Mother. You embody her when you mate with the Horned God. It's nothing to worry about."

"Nothing to worry about? How can you say that? This whole thing is insane," Lyse said, shaking her head.

"Why don't we make a fire, and then we can discuss what needs discussing," Eleanora said—and at her words, Lizbeth, who'd been sitting in the grass watching their exchange with a worried face, got up and took off into the woods.

"Where's she going?" Lyse asked, thinking about the stray dog she'd encountered out there.

Daniela must've had the same thought, because she said, "I'll go with her," and disappeared through a gap in the trees.

"Please take this," Arrabelle said, offering the plastic cup again. "After what you've just been through, I suggest you drink it."

It wasn't a suggestion.

Lyse sighed and took it, placing its edge to her lips. It smelled of lemon, ginger, and a touch of something loamy— as if some of the ingredients had been freshly dug from the dirt.

Lizbeth and Daniela each returned with an armful of twigs and dead branches, and Lizbeth went to work starting the fire.

"Isn't it illegal to burn stuff outdoors?" Lyse asked.

"We have special dispensation from the fire department," Eleanora said. "Religious grounds."

Lyse wasn't sure she believed her great-aunt but decided not to argue.

"I need a cigarette," Daniela said, patting the pockets of her pants.

"Why can't you just smoke normal cigarettes?" Arrabelle asked, frowning.

"You love the smell of my cloves," Daniela said to Arrabelle, grinning as she lit up and took a drag.

She caught Lyse watching her intently.

"I see you looking. Want one?" she asked, offering Lyse the pack.

Lyse started to shake her head no, then changed her mind.

Like the embrace of a longtime lover you enjoyed hooking up with but hated making chitchat with after the deed, clove cigarettes were both familiar to Lyse and hard to turn down—even though she knew she'd pay for it later.

"Yes, I do."

Lyse took the pack and fished out one of the long brown cigarettes.

"That was my last match," Daniela said, "but you can light yours off mine."

"Works for me," Lyse said, taking Daniela's proffered cigarette and using it to light her own.

"Just don't let Eleanora say I'm corrupting you," Daniela joked.

"Oh, I won't," Lyse murmured, lighting up.

The cloves were stronger than she remembered and burned her throat. She coughed, the smoke searing her lungs.

"I don't really smoke anymore. Just when I'm super-stressed . . ."

She trailed off as she took another drag, feeling lightheaded.

Lizbeth had the fire going now, and the warmth from the flames licked at the backs of Lyse's legs, shooing away the cold.

"Let's sit," Daniela said, pinching off the end of her cigarette and returning what hadn't been smoked to the pack.

Lyse, who'd only gotten down a few puffs, did the same. She handed the butt to Daniela.

"Sorry," Lyse said. "I just needed like two puffs."

"Totally got it," Daniela replied, giving Lyse a wink. "Waste not, want not."

Lyse's butt went back into the pack, too.

She followed Daniela over to the fire and sat down,

pulling her knees up to her chest. Eleanora came and sat down on the grass beside her, so close Lyse could feel her great-aunt's body trembling. She reached out a hand and laid it on Eleanora's forearm, her fingers pale white against her great-aunt's poncho.

"I know this is a lot to process," Eleanora said. "And I appreciate you bearing with me."

"'S'okay," Lyse said. "I just want you to explain this to me. Because as much as I don't want to believe the stuff you're saying . . . well, I'm starting to believe it."

Out of the corner of her eye, Lyse saw Lizbeth get up from her spot next to Arrabelle and crawl around the edge of the fire. She plopped down beside Lyse and curled up into a little ball, resting her head on Lyse's arm. It was like being cuddled by a giant child.

"I showed you the Dream Journals for a reason," Eleanora said. "You know where they are and how to access them."

"Yes, the books with no writing in them," Lyse said, tapping her temple with a finger. "I remember."

"Oh, there's writing in them," Arrabelle said, the firelight casting deep shadows across her face. "Only you can't see it except when you're in a dream state."

Dev nodded.

"It's true. Only a Dream Keeper can read them in the waking reality, and since there aren't many of those left, well . . ."

"Why? What happened to the Dream Keepers?" Lyse asked, confused.

"No one knows," Daniela said. "But one hasn't been born in over fifty years. My mother was one of the last."

"And who was your mother?"

"The great and powerful Marie-Faith Altonelli," Eleanora said, speaking for Daniela. "I say *great and powerful* because she held the Dream Keeper's seat on the Greater Council for almost a quarter of a century—"

Across from them, Daniela was staring into the flames, her eyes a million miles away.

"—and until her death six months ago, she was also one of my greatest friends."

It blew Lyse's mind that there was so much about Eleanora she didn't know.

"Are they ever going to fill her seat?" Arrabelle asked.

"I don't know," Eleanora said thoughtfully.

This turn in the conversation caught Daniela's attention, and she looked up to glare at Arrabelle.

"And who would you have take her place?" Daniela asked, her voice a low growl. "Of the Dream Keepers left, most are senile old bats who can't even remember their own name. You want one of them dictating how the covens are managed?"

"That's not what I'm saying—" Arrabelle snapped back.

"There's already been a huge battle over who should take the seat, and it's created a lot of bad blood between the different factions of our world," Dev said to Lyse, to clarify.

"And I thought human politics were bad," Lyse replied.

"Tell me about it." Dev grinned before continuing. "Every coven used to have a Dream Keeper. They see the future in their dreams—though I don't mean that literally. Their dreams only imply what will be, and even then the interpretation is up to the Dreamer."

"But their dreams have always influenced how the covens operated, and it gives them a lot of power," Arrabelle added. "There's been a lot of resentment toward them, and then when the old Dream Keepers started dying off, and no new ones were born to take their place—"

"It's why a lot of people want my mother's seat abolished altogether," Daniela said. "Because the reign of the Dream Keepers is dead."

Lyse wasn't sure how all of this pertained to her, other than she was now a member of this strange coven and the others wanted her to understand its inner workings. Right now she was tired and was just enjoying the heat of the firelight and the lulling murmur of conversation.

Beside her, Eleanora sighed, shifting on her hip bones.

"You're exhausted. I'm exhausted," Lyse said. "Maybe we should call it a night—"

"I think Lyse is right," Dev said, looking at Eleanora. "You're worn-out, and it's not like we don't have time for the rest of the stuff now that the ritual's been performed—"

"Wait, what other stuff?" Lyse asked—it'd already been a full evening, and she couldn't imagine what else there was left to discuss.

"Oh lord, you didn't tell her, did you?" Arrabelle said with a sigh.

"No, I didn't," Eleanora snapped. "I didn't want to overwhelm her."

"Too late for that," Daniela said, wrapping her arms around her knees and rocking back and forth. "I think Lyse has officially reached her saturation point."

Eleanora looked over at Daniela gratefully.

"Yes, you're all correct. I am tired, and we can talk again tomorrow." She turned to Arrabelle. "I think home is the only place I'm going right now. Shall we take a rain check on dinner? We left some wine at your place. Drink up in my honor."

Arrabelle nodded.

"I just might."

"Lizbeth?" Lyse said, nudging the sleeping teenager awake. "Time to get up."

The girl rubbed her eyes and grinned dreamily at Lyse, a secret smile playing on her lips.

"We should close the circle," Eleanora said, picking up a white candle and lighting it from the flames of the fire.

The others did the same, including Lyse, who figured: *Why the hell not?*

"This is a pretty simple one," Dev whispered. She'd come to stand beside Lyse when they'd each lit their candle. "You won't have any trouble with this stuff when you do it. It's easy peasy."

Lyse gave her an uncertain smile and nodded.

"Close the circle and put to sleep all that was created by our work here tonight," Eleanora intoned, and blew out her candle.

"Close the circle," the others repeated before blowing out their own candles.

The small campfire had burned down to embers, but they didn't have to worry about putting it out. The heavens chose that moment to open, letting forth a torrent of rain. They left the clearing at a run, trying not to get soaked— and for the entire walk home, Lyse couldn't help but wonder what Lizbeth had been dreaming about.

Lyse

After getting soaked in the rain, the hot shower was magnificent, waking up her worn-out muscles and making her feel like she was among the living again. She stayed in the bathroom longer then she intended, enjoying the warm prickle of water on her dry skin and the steam that filled the bathroom and fogged the mirror over the sink. But when the cold began to cut into the warm, she knew it was her cue to get out. She dunked her face under the spray one final time, shivering as the last of the hot water filtered through the showerhead. She got out and toweled herself dry, feeling revitalized, even though she'd barely slept in more than twenty-four hours.

"Ow!" she cried when the thick terry-cloth towel brushed against the lump on her head. The one she'd gotten when she'd almost brained herself on her kitchen countertop that morning.

It seemed like all of that had happened decades before, and in another life.

She sat down on the edge of the tub, brushing her wet

and tousled bangs out of her eyes, and parted her hair. Then she rubbed away some of the condensation on the mirror with a hand towel and took a look.

She found the red welt easily and probed it with her fingers. There was no blood, so she left it alone.

. . . and she cried out, digging her nails into his back . . .

She was struck by the memory of her imaginary tryst with Weir—or the Horned God; she didn't know which because they were fused together in her mind. She felt his phantom hands all over her body, caressing and kissing her skin, knowing exactly how to touch her in just the right ways. Making it impossible for her to think straight.

Standing there in her towel, she didn't think she'd ever been more attracted to a man in her life. And what made it all the more interesting was they hadn't actually had sex.

She'd slept with him in a drugged-out fantasy, his giant arms wrapping around her middle, hugging her tightly to his chest, but only in her mind—and she'd felt safe there, enveloped in his scent and warmth. Weir was the antithesis of the wussy, metrosexual men she usually dated: masculine, solid, deliberate, knew exactly what he wanted, and didn't seem afraid to take it when he saw it.

She even loved his tattoos . . . loved the indigo octopus tentacles as they pulsed along with the movements of the muscles under his skin—

Stop it. You hardly know this guy. The ritual made you feel close to him, that's all. You'll see him again and he'll be like a stranger to you.

She opened the bathroom cabinet and took out a bottle of lotion, slathering it all over herself, trying not to imagine that they were Weir's hands running up her body, not her own.

She finished drying off and threw on some sweats. Then she left the bathroom door open so the steam could evaporate. As she walked down the hallway, she heard Eleanora talking to herself in the kitchen and decided to check in on her.

Eleanora was standing in the middle of the kitchen, looking confused.

"I thought I put my pot tincture away after I used it, but it's gone," Eleanora said, throwing up her hands in resignation. "I guess it got up and walked off on its own."

She waited, her head cocked, as if she were listening to someone, and then she laughed.

"Don't be ridiculous. I did not go through that whole bottle in two days—"

"Maybe you put it in another cabinet?" Lyse asked, deciding not to mention the fact she'd just caught Eleanora talking to herself.

Eleanora looked up, surprised to find Lyse standing in the doorway.

"I suppose I could've put it somewhere else."

Lyse opened the refrigerator to get a soda.

"This what you're looking for?" She held up a small glass bottle she'd found on the top shelf wedged in between two soda cans.

Eleanora clapped her palms together happily.

"That's it! You're a genius!"

She plucked the bottle from Lyse's hands and ran to the cabinet to grab a glass. Lyse shook her head and went back to scouring the fridge. She remembered she hadn't had any dinner, and she was starving. She pulled out a pie pan with one slice of quiche left in it and carried the whole thing to the kitchen table.

"Good, I'm glad you're eating that. I was gonna throw it out tomorrow," Eleanora said, turning to face Lyse, who was leaning back in her chair, eating the crumbly quiche with her hands. She wore a blissful expression on her face as she stuffed the last bite into her mouth.

"What?" she said, raising her head, eyes glazed over from too much food, too fast.

Eleanora wore an amused expression.

"Nothing. Just enjoying you being here," Eleanora said. "That's all."

"Enjoying me eating all your leftovers, don't you mean?" Lyse said, grinning.

"That's it," Eleanora agreed. "That's the only reason I like having you here. To eat me out of house and home."

Lyse rubbed her belly and sighed.

"That was delicious."

She closed her eyes and felt sleep tickling her brain. She was excited to go to her old room and crawl into bed. Maybe tomorrow she'd wake up and go through her old clothes, the ones she hadn't wanted to take to Georgia when she left for school. They were still hanging up in the closet. She could take a look at them, see if anything still fit or was at all salvageable.

"I wanted you to have something."

She opened her eyes. Eleanora was sitting across from her, a small leather-bound journal in her hands.

"What is it?" Lyse asked, watching as Eleanora nervously played with the journal's cover.

"It's my personal diary," she said, an earnest expression on her face.

"Like all your girly teenage hopes and dreams," Lyse said, grinning.

She expected Eleanora to respond with some pithy rejoinder, but her great-aunt only stared down at her gnarled hands.

"Come on," Lyse said, sitting up so she could poke Eleanora's hand with her finger. "You're supposed to laugh at that."

"Nothing to laugh about," Eleanora said, not looking up. "This is serious business to me."

Lyse sat back in her chair and sighed.

"Fine, I'm sorry," she said. "I didn't mean to make fun of your diary. I was just teasing you."

"Why don't you bring your chair around here by me?" Eleanora said, patting the spot beside her.

Lyse did as she was told, dragging her chair around the table until they were sitting side by side.

"That better?" Lyse asked.

Eleanora nodded.

"I want to give you a story," Eleanora said, her voice dropping to a whisper. "It's not a particularly happy story, but it's mine and I want you to have it."

The sound of Eleanora's voice was like a drumbeat in Lyse's head, the repetition of syllable and sound weaving together like the incantation of a spell. Lyse yawned, her tired mind yearning for the oblivion of sleep, and that was when she felt the lightest of touches on her wrist.

Eleanora leaned in, her words a hush in Lyse's ear: *"My grandmother Mimi knew that no matter what she did, the Devil had my foot, and she was powerless to stop him from taking me . . ."*

And then Lyse began to dream.

. . . and because she "loved" me—a word that even now sounds unbelievable to my ears—she did something she thought might save me, unhooking the Devil's claws from my soul once and for all.

Of course, I didn't understand any of this until I was long gone from Massachusetts, far away from everything and everyone I'd ever known, my childhood and adolescence a dusty memory locked up tight inside my mind.

My mama had powers, and so did her mother before her— though Mimi did everything she could to excise that part of herself, while my mama was her opposite. My mama reveled in her special abilities: magical powers that, as a nurse, she used to heal the hopelessly sick and to deliver new life safely into the world, when without her help both the mother and infant would've been lost.

While Mimi hated what she was and stuffed her powers deep down inside her until they were dead and (mostly) buried, my mama embraced her calling. She left home at seventeen to become a nurse, and when the Japanese bombed Pearl Harbor, she joined the

Nurse Corps and was stationed in a military field hospital in Italy until she found herself pregnant with me and was discharged.

My existence, you see, was due to pure happenstance:

A wounded young man from Mama's small town in Massachusetts came under her care. He was a year younger than she, but they'd known each other tangentially in school, had friends in common, spent time at the same adolescent haunts. Their shared history, and the intimacy of war, brought them together in a way that could've never happened back home. My mama was poor and my father, James Davenport, was from one of the wealthiest families the town of Duxbury had ever produced.

I was made one frightening night when screaming bombs lit up the sky like the Fourth of July, and everywhere men went off to battle and died like pigs at slaughter. My parents' coupling was quick and unplanned—two terrified human beings clinging to one another in order to remind themselves they were still alive—but it was enough to conceive me. Sadly, my father was sent back to fight shortly thereafter and died never knowing of my existence.

How do I know all this? Did my mama tell me these stories?

Yes and no; in her lifetime she did not get the chance to whisper her stories to me, her only daughter. I did not get to sit at her feet and hear them fall from her lips like precious jewels—because one cold winter morning, on her way back from Mass General after a long overnight shift in the maternity ward, Mama's car skidded on black ice and hit a tree.

For all her magical healing powers, my mama could not heal herself.

Yet I know these things. Know them because of a quirk in my nature, passed down to me through all the Eames women who came before me. I am a blood sister and my gift is clairvoyance. Since I was a small child, I could see ghosts and talk to them. Even visit scenes from their life, experiencing them as if they were my own memories. I was there, observing in spirit, the night my parents created me. And I knelt beside my mama as she lay on the icy road, blood streaming from her mouth as she took her last breath and used it to murmur my name.

This was my crime. Speaking and fraternizing with the dead. This was why Mimi believed the Devil had my foot, and why she enlisted deluded, fanatical men to save my everlasting soul—and it's also the beginning of how I came to live in Echo Park in the bungalow on Curran Street overlooking Elysian Park, and how you came to join me, changing my life forever.

I wanted to tell you this story, Lyse. One I have never told to anyone, at least, in all its parts, because I think it will explain how important the coven is to me, and why I want to ensure it lives on through you, the only other human being, besides my mama, that I have ever truly loved.

It was getting worse. Harder to control. Eleanora didn't have to wish for it anymore. It just sprung itself on her at will—and if she happened to be washing the dishes, well, if there was a dish in her hand it was done for.

"Papa," Eleanora said, taking the frail old man's hand in her own and giving it a squeeze. "The things I see are getting worse."

She called her psychic talents "seeing" because it was easier than explaining what they really were.

Papa hardly ever opened his eyes anymore, staying asleep for longer and longer stretches of time until Eleanora was afraid he would just stop waking all together.

Not that she blamed him. Imprisoned in his body, trapped in a dreary existence offering no respite save death, why did he choose to keep going? She didn't understand, but she knew he must have his reasons.

At least his room was nice, and he could listen to the radio whenever he liked. Mimi kept the station turned to the Jesus Hour, but whenever her grandmother was out, Eleanora would change it, turning it to a classical station Papa liked. No one had ever told her what Papa liked to listen to, but sometimes when she was "seeing," she observed him as a much younger man—and that was how she knew he loved Bach and Beethoven.

"Papa?" She said his name again, and this time he squeezed her hand back. It was so slight a movement anyone else wouldn't have felt it, but Eleanora had been ministering to her papa practically all her life, and she knew what each flicker of his eyelid, each twitch of his hand meant.

"I saw Mama again. She was just beautiful. You must've been so proud of her."

Another squeeze. This one stronger. Her mama, May, had been Papa's favorite. A real daddy's girl, Mimi said.

"She was as big as a house—with me inside her, and she just glowed."

This elicited a twitch of his eyelids.

"I visit her a lot in my mind, Papa. She doesn't always know I'm there, but I can see everything."

Eleanora loved talking to her grandfather. She knew he didn't judge her, and he would never ever, under any circumstances, repeat what she said to him because he hadn't spoken a word since Eleanora was a child—but that wasn't the only reason. Before he'd gotten ill, he'd kept Mimi at bay, acting as Eleanora's protector when she was too small to look after herself.

It scared Eleanora to think of what Mimi would do if she realized how much "seeing" went on inside her head. She'd already endured so many scalding baths in her lifetime that just the thought of getting in a full tub made her skin burn.

"Let's put something better on the radio," Eleanora said as she got up from the hard-backed wooden chair she'd pulled up next to Papa's bed and went over to the radio, fiddling with the knob until she found the classical music he liked.

There was static, and then the opening bassoon solo of Igor Stravinsky's *The Rite of Spring* exploded out of the beige Bakelite radio's tinny speakers, sweeping Eleanora into another world. She pirouetted away from the dresser, where the radio always sat, and skipped back to the bed. She was surprised to find Papa's eyes wide open, bloodshot sclera and bright blue irises fixed on her.

"What is it, Papa?" she asked, as the rest of the orchestra swelled to join the bassoon in a frenetic cacophony of sound.

Papa's eyes drifted away from her, over to the plain wooden dresser, and he began to blink furiously, eyeballs glued to the radio.

"Do you want me to turn it off?" she asked starting to move back toward the dresser, but the blinking stopped. "No? Then what?"

More intense blinking, and his right hand began to twitch.

"Wait," she said, understanding dawning. "You want me to turn it up, don't you?"

Eyes and hand relaxed, almost as though they were sighing with relief. Eleanora smiled, then went over and turned up the volume, the chaotic music filling the room.

That was when she noticed the tear. It hung from the fringe of Papa's right eyelash. He blinked, and the tear dropped down the side of his weathered cheek, getting lost inside the folds of his nightshirt.

"Oh, Papa," Eleanora said, rushing back to his side to grasp his hand and squeeze the soft flesh of his fingers. "Please don't cry."

It happened so infrequently, she almost forgot it was possible, but every now and then Papa would just lie there crying. There was never a specific reason she could discern. After a while, she decided it must be something he was thinking about, a thought or memory she didn't have access to and therefore couldn't understand.

It was awful to watch him cry because there were no sounds or movements to accompany the tears. She was used to her own crying jags, silent sobbing that shook her body and made her head hurt. Sometimes, when she couldn't contain herself, she'd press her face into her pillow and scream, the sound muffled by the pillowcase and the delicate down feathers.

"What is it, Papa? I wish you could just tell me," she said, hating that there was nothing she could do to help him.

The music had calmed, a false lull before the chaos began again, and she sighed, letting the music enfold them both.

"I wish you could talk to me, Papa," she said, her voice low and melancholy.

His fingers twitched against her palm, and she knew he was trying to tell her he wished he could talk to her, too. The music danced around them, loud enough that if Mimi came home, she'd throw a fit and complain, saying, *What will the neighbors think about all this heathen music playing in our house?*

Eleanora didn't think there was anything heathen about beautiful music, but what did she know? As far as Mimi was concerned, everything Eleanora liked came from the Devil—especially the "seeing."

I wish I could take Papa with me, so he could visit with Mama again, she thought, the idea absurd, but then something inside her told her that no, it wasn't absurd—maybe she *could* take Papa with her.

She didn't know why she'd never thought of this before. It seemed like such a simple, perfect idea.

"Would you like to go on a trip with me?" she asked the old man. "Come with me to see my mama again?"

He blinked rapidly, fingers twitching inside the cocoon of her hand.

He wants to go, she thought as a fiery curiosity began to gestate in her belly. *Can I really do it?*

She'd never tried to take anyone with her before—it wasn't as though there was anyone to take. No one outside Mimi and Papa knew about the visions, and she'd always been too terrified to share them with anyone else. Now she wondered how she could do it. How could she bring Papa along with her into the ghostly world of her "seeing"?

"I'm gonna try, Papa," she said, smiling down at him, her words tinged with excitement.

She closed her eyes, still holding tight to her grandfather's hand, and focused on what she wanted to do. She pushed away any worries—like that Mimi would come home early from her Ladies' Auxiliary church meeting—and let her mind's eye wander.

"I want to see Mama," she said aloud, putting her "want" out into the universe . . .

". . . *where is this?*" Papa asked.

He was standing beside her, fingers laced between hers, but he wasn't the papa of now. He was the papa of before—before the stroke that silenced him and kept him trapped inside his head.

Instead of answering him, she took a moment to look around, unsure of when or where they were. All she could see was that they were outside in a field of summer daisies, the sun beating down as the wind navigated its way through the sea of white and yellow flowers with a soft hush. She turned her head, but all she saw behind her were more daisies.

"*I don't know, Papa,*" she said, finally. "*I've never been here before.*"

"*It's so beautiful,*" Papa said, lifting his free hand to shield his eyes from the sun.

He was a handsome man, and Eleanora saw that she resembled him more than she'd ever realized. New Englanders, both of them, cut from the same hunk of granite, sharing the same hawkish nose and flinty eyes, the same stern set of the mouth. Even though his hair was salt and pepper to her brown, and his skin wrinkled with age to her smooth, unblemished complexion—anyone who saw them together would know the same blood flowed between them.

"*May?*" Papa said, and he squeezed Eleanora's hand so hard she could feel her knuckles crack.

She followed his gaze, but all she could see ahead of her was an unending field of flowers.

"*Where's Mama?*" Eleanora asked, struggling to see.

He pointed into the distance.

"She's right there," he said. "Can't you see her?"

But no matter how much she squinted, her mama did not appear to her.

"I'm sorry, Papa," she said, shaking her head. "I just don't see anything."

Papa tried to drop her hand, but Eleanora held tight to him, an alarm sounding in her head as she realized she didn't know what would happen if she lost hold of him in this place.

Don't let him go! *she thought, holding fast to his fingers while he fought to break her grip.* Whatever you do, don't let him go!

"Sister," he said, sounding both disappointed in her and frantic to escape. "You gotta release me."

"No," she said, though her own hands were becoming slick with sweat, making the task of keeping him as futile as holding back the crash of the sea with a plastic bucket.

He stopped struggling and turned so he could look her right in the eye.

"Sister," he said, his voice firm. "You've done right bringing me here, but now you have to let me go."

"No," she said, shaking her head violently.

"You've got to, sweetheart," he said, eyes overflowing with love. "I know it. You know it. She knows it."

He looked back into the distance. To the place where her mama—whom she could not see—stood, waiting for him.

Finally, she understood where they were.

"Papa, I don't want you to go," she said. "Please, don't leave without me."

He shook his head.

"It's not your time, sister."

She didn't want to believe it, but she knew he was telling her the truth. She threw herself into her papa's arms, and he hugged her back fiercely.

"Good-bye, Papa," she whispered. "Tell Mama I love her. As always."

Then she let him go . . .

She knew he was gone before she even opened her eyes.

The Rite of Spring was long over, and something else had taken its place, but her heart was broken, and that was all she could think about. In a daze, she got up and walked over to the radio, turning it off.

"The Devil has your foot, sister."

Mimi stood in the doorway watching her, eyes flat and devoid of emotion.

"Mimi?" she asked, her mind bleary with exhaustion.

"The Devil has your foot, sister, and that's not all," Mimi said. She shook her head and walked out of the room, the thump of her metal brace jarring in the silence.

Eleanora returned to her papa's bedside, the hardness of the wooden chair biting into her back and shoulders as she sat down again—as if she needed reminding of what reality she was inhabiting. She looked over at her papa. His face was still, the light of life extinguished from his eyes.

I have done something good, she thought. *And there will be hell to pay for it.*

The man arrived a week after they buried Papa.

Eleanora was in the kitchen fixing dinner when the knock came. She set down the knife she'd been using to chop spinach and wiped flecks of green onto the white apron tied around her waist. She pulled the clip from her hair, running her fingers through the tangles and smoothing down the wild bits before pinning everything back into place.

"Mimi?" she called as she left the warm kitchen behind her, walking through the living room and heading for the front door.

There was no response from her grandmother, but she hadn't really expected one. Since Papa died, Mimi had been frozen in grief—silent, even, where the Devil was concerned—but Eleanora knew this was only the calm before the storm. Things were brewing behind her grandmother's rigid façade, and Eleanora was already making secret plans to escape the house before things became unbearable. Besides, she wanted to travel, to see strange new places and meet people who were wholly different from the people she grew up with in Duxbury—and none of that would ever happen if she allowed Mimi to continue to control her.

Her papa's death had not been easy for Eleanora, but it'd brought with it the realization that there was no reason for her to stay in Massachusetts anymore. With him gone, she was free of her human bondage.

"Yes?" Eleanora said, as she opened the front door—unaware that this singular action was the beginning of the storm she'd been anticipating.

"Is this the Eames residence?" a man asked, taking off his black fedora and holding it between his hands, revealing a close-cropped head of blond hair.

He wore a light wool jacket over his dark gray suit, and brown horn-rimmed glasses perched back on the bridge of his nose—but the conservative attire and thick glasses did nothing to mask how incredibly handsome he was.

"It is," Eleanora said, blushing. "How may I help you?"

He ran the brim of his hat between his fingers and gave her a warm smile.

"You must be Eleanora. I'm a friend of your grandmother's. From church."

It was such an absurd idea—this man being friends with Mimi—that Eleanora almost laughed. Instead, she nodded politely and invited him in. The man followed her through the doorway and into the sitting room, where she indicated he should take a seat on the couch.

"Is Mimi expecting you, Mr. . . . ?" She let the question mark linger, wanting him to know she thought him a bit rude for not giving her his name.

"Mitchell R. Davis," the man said, bowing his head in greeting.

"Nice to meet you, Mitchell R. Davis," Eleanora replied. "I'll let Mimi know you're here."

She turned to go fetch her grandmother but went only a few steps before she felt a hand on her shoulder.

"Yes—" she started to say, but then a handkerchief covered her mouth.

She struggled against her attacker, a sickly sweet smell filling her nostrils, and the world faded slowly, painfully, to black.

Love is a four-letter word that can be as evil as any curse.

The terrible things done out of love—because the end somehow justifies the means—are innumerable to count.

Had Mimi done this to her out of love?

This was the question most often on Eleanora's mind, pondered without answer over the many weeks of her incarceration.

She once asked Mitchell (after hours spent in his company, she'd come to call him by his first name) if a person could love someone to death. He'd laughed but then proceeded to answer her question with the utmost seriousness:

"Human beings are fallible. They try to live as God would have them live, but they can only fail at this because of their imperfection. Man is made in the image of God. He is of God, but not a God."

Mitchell was in his shirtsleeves. It was his turn to stay with her, to watch and see what incarnation the Devil would take. She hated the other men and would cry when they came to stay in the room with her. Their eyes were forever staring, waiting to see what evilness inside her they could testify to having witnessed.

Only Mitchell she could tolerate. In him, she saw something

redeemable, and, unlike the others, he wasn't afraid to talk to her. This was the reason they hadn't broken her yet, though she didn't want them to know this. Having Mitchell was her saving grace.

"So, that's a yes, then?" Eleanora said, swallowing back the bile always lingering at the back of her throat.

She'd vomited so many times in the past few weeks she couldn't keep count. Fear was the main culprit, and when they'd tried to baptize her . . . that'd been the worst. Getting baptized was too similar to Mimi's scalding baths, and she'd clawed at the men like an animal when they'd tried to force her under the water. This they took as another sign she was in Lucifer's thrall.

She protested her innocence, begged them to let her go, but to no avail; she was trapped—and, after a while, it seemed as if anything she did or said was proof of her possession, so she became mute.

Except with Mitchell.

"I don't know if there's a correct answer to the question," Mitchell said, as he took out a cigarette and slid it between his lips.

Under different circumstances, she would have still found him attractive, but locked in a tiny, cell-like room whose walls and floor were colder than ice, and where she only had one meager woolen blanket to keep her warm? Here she was immune to his charm.

"I'm not possessed," she said, fingernails digging into the flesh of her upper arms. The scratching was becoming obsessive. She did it constantly and unconsciously, her tormentors documenting the red welts she brought up on her arms and legs as visible signs of her demonic possession.

It was strange that where they saw evil, she saw a way to cope with an untenable situation.

She spoke to Mitchell of her innocence as often as possible. She didn't know if he believed her or not, but she felt better when she did it. Of course, this lasted only a few hours, and then the hysteria was back, threatening to overwhelm her.

"Can you prove it?" he asked.

She sat up on her elbows, the metal cot she'd been lying on squeaking under her weight. There was a large, wooden cross nailed high up on the wall, but the cot was the sole piece of furniture in the room.

"Are you serious?" she asked.

This was his first-ever deviation from the norm. Usually, he responded to her protestations of innocence with, "That's not for me to judge." Now he was asking her for proof— and she felt her heart lift with hope for the first time since her incarceration began.

"Deadly so," he replied. "I want to hear why you think you aren't possessed."

She sat up on her knees, toes pressing into the spongy mattress of the cot, until she could feel the outline of the coiled metal springs underneath her. She assumed Mitchell's interest wasn't real, that it was some kind of trap, some new way of testing her. Still, it was also a chance to say her piece.

"What happens to me isn't the work of Lucifer—"

Mitchell stood up and began to pace, the lit cigarette smoking in his hand.

"You say that, but what about your grandfather?" he said, shaking his head. "His death had all the hallmarks of the Devil's work."

Eleanora was determined not to cry. She was tired of these men—stupid, ignorant men—being able to wrest so much emotion out of her. If she could learn to keep her feelings under control, to treat them as she'd learned to treat Mimi, then maybe she could survive this.

"Papa died," Eleanora said. "I was holding his hand when he passed. That had nothing to do with the Devil."

Mitchell moved closer to her, his chiseled face showing nothing of what he truly felt. He knelt down beside her and offered her a drag from his cigarette. She wondered if this was a trick to manipulate her, to create some kind of false bond between them.

"I don't smoke," she said, waving the cigarette away.

He grinned up at her.

"Good for you. It's a nasty habit."

"You wanted proof," she said, crawling over to the edge of the bed so her bare knees were clearly in his view. "I can show you, but you have to take my hand and close your eyes."

He shook his head.

"I don't think so."

She reached down and raised the hem of her nightgown, revealing a slice of one pale white thigh. Mitchell stared at her exposed leg and swallowed, hard.

"Are you trying to tempt me?" he asked.

"If that's what it takes to get you to help me," she said, as frankly as she could manage. "And I'm a virgin."

He sat back on his heels, and she could see his faith warring with his libido. She prayed his libido would win out. He lifted his hand, and in the sickly yellow overhead light she could see it was shaking. It hung there for a moment, uncertainty playing across his face like a frenetic concerto, and so she did the only thing she could to sway things in her favor.

She took his trembling fingers in her hand and guided them toward her mouth, gently pressing his hand against her lips, kissing his knuckles.

"My grandmother hates me. That's why I'm here," she said, leading his hand to her cheek and letting him stroke her face with the pads of his fingertips. "That's my proof."

To his bafflement, she lowered his fingers toward the delicate flesh of her inner thighs, then firmly pushed his hand between her legs.

"Lord, please, help me," he moaned, dropping his cigarette and reaching for her.

Eleanora

The weight of Mitchell's body pushed Eleanora back onto the cot. His fingers were rough, unused to dealing with the delicate parts of a girl, and her body stiffened as his fingernails scraped against her skin. She forced herself to relax. She was inexperienced, but she knew she couldn't let him sense her fear, or this would all be for nothing.

"I think I love you," he whispered in her ear—as if saying those words made everything all right—and then he slipped her white cotton panties down from her hips, pressing himself against her.

He was still fully dressed, his gray twill pants scratching against her bare skin. As nervous as she was, the itch of the twill on her skin was unbearable, and she wanted the pants off—couldn't bear the itchiness—and she gritted her teeth to stop herself from speaking. He pulled on his zipper, undid the button, and yanked them down himself. He was wearing white briefs, but she could feel the hard part of him through the softness of the fabric, and the strangeness of being so close to an almost-naked man made her stop breathing for a moment.

He planted his lips on hers, and she forced herself to remain calm, to be pliant as he kissed her. She closed her eyes—then, ever practical, decided it was better to see what was going to happen to her rather than to be a coward about it.

She tried to participate in the experience by kissing the side of his face but pulled away because his cheek was so scratchy. Like the twill pants, anything rough that touched her skin set her teeth on edge and made her start itching.

"You're so beautiful," he moaned in her ear. "From the first moment I saw you, I wanted you."

From the moment you kidnapped me, she thought, but pushed it away.

She couldn't think like that if she wanted him to help her. She needed to give over to him, to entice him however she could—even if there was something abrasive about him that reminded her of sandpaper.

"You were so handsome," she whispered back to him. "When you came to the door. I wanted you, too."

She felt sick the moment the lie left her mouth. She realized then that this was a terrible mistake.

"Oh, Eleanora," he whispered into her throat, kissing the tender flesh there.

She felt him take off one of his shoes and heard it clatter to the concrete floor, where the other shoe quickly followed, the sound echoing in the windowless room. He yanked at his underwear until they were awkwardly bunched around his ankles, then stopped kissing her long enough to remove them and his pants altogether.

"That's better," he murmured into her ear as she felt the length of his naked body pressing against her.

He slid his fingers underneath the thin cotton of her nightdress, touching her with clumsy hands.

Against her will, she cried out, heat burning between her legs as her own traitorous body responded to his touch.

This is a mistake and I've let it go too far, she thought as the bile rose in her throat.

"I want you," he said, his voice almost a growl.

She tried to open her mouth. To tell him to stop, but she was scared. Afraid that telling him no would only make her time in this place worse. She wanted out, and maybe letting him do this to her would make that happen. Maybe the best thing she could do was to just close her eyes and let what would be . . . *be.*

He leaned down to kiss her, his lips parting hers, so he could taste the sweetness of her mouth. She breathed against him, her own lips moving instinctively.

He reached down, grasping himself, and she cried out as a white-hot pain shot through her middle, and she felt something snap. Going into shock from the pain and fear, she began to dissociate from her body, floating up and over their combined flesh, eyes pinned to Mitchell's back as he moved on top of her. She searched out her own face and was surprised to find calm eyes staring back at her.

She blinked and the image reversed. Now she was back in her body, staring up at an empty ceiling.

Reconnected to herself again, she felt a deep ache inside her. She wanted to scream, to push him off, and she grabbed him around the shoulders, scratching her nails into the soft skin of his back as she tried to make the pain stop. Her actions had the opposite effect, seeming to drive him to distraction, and the pain only became more intense. She stared at him, his eyes almost black with desire, and prayed this awful moment in her life would be over soon.

As if he'd read her mind, he bit his lip and squeezed his eyes shut tight, his body shuddering against her.

"Unh . . . unh . . ." he moaned in between gasps—then fell limply onto her chest, his breathing ragged.

She wanted him off her body. He was deadweight crushing

her, making it hard to breathe. She pushed at him, but he was so much bigger than her that she couldn't budge him.

"Please," she whispered. "Can't. Breathe. Get off."

"Oh," he said, his voice sated and dreamy. He kissed her lips before she could turn her head away, then climbed off her.

The door to her room was thrown open, and angry voices filled the air. Mitchell shot to his feet, grabbing his pants from the floor to cover his nakedness. She didn't get up from the mattress, just lay there, limp and ashamed and in pain, hating herself for what she'd just done. She heard Mitchell protesting with a loud, hysterical voice, and then she closed her eyes.

It hadn't been worth it. She was never getting out of there.

She woke up the first time underwater. Eyes bulging from lack of oxygen, she screamed, but no one could hear her, the sound muffled by the water.

She woke up the second time in a hospital bed, all kinds of tubes and sensors protruding from and attached to her body. She reached up and tried to yank them out, but a loud beeping from one of the machines brought in a cadre of nurses. One of them held up a long, evil-looking syringe.

She screamed, and the nurse descended on her, jamming the needle into the fleshy part of her upper arm. She continued to struggle for a few more seconds, but then the drugs took effect and, sedated, she drifted back to sleep.

She woke up for the third and final time still in the hospital bed. She calmly opened her eyes and took in the strange new environment without comment. It was either that or get stabbed with another needle.

The first thing she noticed was a bouquet of white daisies sitting on the nightstand to her right. The flowers looked fresh. Like someone had only just sent them, knowing somehow that she was about to wake up.

"Well, look who's back in the land of the living." It was a new nurse, or at least Eleanora didn't recognize her.

The nurse smiled pleasantly from the doorway and, noticing Eleanora's gaze fixed on the bouquet, came into the room, retrieving the card nestled inside the flowers.

She leaned over the bed and placed the small, square card in Eleanora's hands.

"Here ya go," the nurse said, continuing to smile down at her.

"Thank you." Eleanora's voice was cracked from disuse. "How long have I been here?"

The nurse, a plain-faced woman with short blond hair, thought for a moment, then said, "Two weeks, I believe."

It was a staggering amount of time.

"Oh," Eleanora replied—and she felt lost, like something was missing inside her.

The nurse patted her arm, then began to busy herself changing Eleanora's bedclothes. She watched the woman work for a few moments, then turned her attention to the card. Flipping it over in her hands, she found nothing written on the white envelope. With trembling fingers, she unsealed it and discovered a handwritten note and a newspaper clipping nestled inside.

She set the newspaper clipping aside and went for the letter first, a creased fifty-dollar bill falling into her lap as she unfolded the cream-colored stationery.

She read the note through once and then immediately reread it.

"From your sweetheart?" the nurse asked.

Eleanora jumped, so intent on the letter she'd forgotten the nurse was even there.

"Uhm, yes, my sweetheart, yes."

But the letter and flowers had come from a complete stranger.

The letter read:

My Dearest Eleanora,

I saw the enclosed Los Angeles Times *clipping about the atrocities perpetrated against you, and knew you were the one I'd dreamed about. There is a place for you in California, if you want it. Use the money I've included with this letter and buy a train ticket to Los Angeles.*

There are sisters waiting for you.

I'll know when you are coming.

Your friend,
Hessika

Eleanora waited until the nurse was gone to unfold the newspaper clipping Hessika had sent her.

It was about a botched exorcism attempted by a group of lay pastors in Massachusetts. The article said the girl, Eleanora Eames, had almost died—Eleanora began to shake as she realized how close those men had actually come to killing her.

Of course, the article did not name Eleanora's tormentors, but her high school yearbook picture was right at the top of the clipping.

She read on and saw that as of the writing of the piece, the pastors had not been charged for the crime—and Eleanora doubted they ever would be.

The newspaper article should have made her feel ashamed, but it didn't. She was tired of being a victim. She'd experienced enough pain for one lifetime, and she was done with letting bad things destroy her. She wasn't going to allow anyone—not Mimi, not Mitchell, not those horrible men—to make her feel bad about herself ever again. She was in control of her life now, and no one was going to touch her heart.

She slipped everything—the letter, the money, and the clipping—back into the envelope and set it on the night-stand beside her bed. At least now she knew where she was going.

She just needed to do a few things before she disappeared.

There was no one home when Eleanora let herself into the house. Mimi didn't lock her doors, didn't feel the need to in such a small town where everyone knew everyone else and your neighbors looked out for you, as you did for them.

She closed the back door, and the screen slammed loudly against the doorframe. There was a dish in the drying rack and a glass in the sink, but otherwise the kitchen was spotless.

As she crossed the room, she heard the squeak of the lino-leum underneath her feet, and it made her sad to think this would be the last time she was ever in this room. She touched the top of the worn wooden table, remembering mornings spent with Mimi and Papa, eating oatmeal with brown sugar and a dollop of peanut butter. While they ate, Papa would tell her stories about when he was a little boy growing up in Boston—before he met Mimi and married her and came to live in Duxbury.

Papa had so many stories. Many were about his best friend, Ignatius. How they were like brothers and spent time at each other's houses getting up to all kinds of trou-ble. The stories made Eleanora wish she had a sibling, or a best friend.

She remembered making dinner with Mimi each night. Eleanora chopping the vegetables while Mimi did the heavy lifting, the two of them working in quiet synchronicity to get the job done.

Mimi making Eleanora's birthday cake each year. Yellow cake with chocolate icing, and Eleanora allowed to lick the icing bowl clean—the only time anything so decadent was tolerated in their house.

These were the memories she wanted to keep with her, the good things from her childhood and adolescence that needed to be tucked away for remembering. The bad things could be lost forever, burned up and forgotten.

She passed through the living room on her way to the back stairs and realized the whole house smelled like Mimi's pungent homemade lemon-beeswax wood polish. She used the banister to pull herself up the sloped stairway, ascending each step as quickly as she could. She didn't want to be tempted to stay and wait for Mimi to come home. Better—and safer—to get out before her grandmother returned.

Besides, what could she say to the woman who'd raised her: *Why did you do this to me? Why did you let me almost die?*

She doubted if Mimi even understood the magnitude of what she'd done—and she'd never have to answer for it because she hadn't actually physically committed the crime.

Eleanora shrieked as she opened the door to her bedroom and found Mimi sitting on her bed, waiting for her.

Her Mimi looked shriveled, a husk of her former self. The flesh below her cheekbones had collapsed in on itself, and her jowls were slack. Heavy bags pulled at the skin below her eyes, dragging down her lower eyelids and exposing their raw pink interior.

After taking a moment to calm herself, Eleanora said, "You look awful."

Mimi stared back at her, then said, "You should never have been born."

"I don't think that's true," Eleanora said, standing her ground.

She could see her mama's star quilt resting on the seat of the rocking chair by the window, but her mama's Bible—the only other thing she'd come to take—wasn't on her bedside table.

"And what would you know about it?" Mimi asked.

"I know that you're just like me," Eleanora said. "You have powers, too."

Mimi pointed a gnarled, arthritic finger at Eleanora, her arm shaking with rage.

"Don't you dare say that about me, sister. Don't you dare!"

Eleanora advanced on the older woman. For the first time in her life, she was going to let Mimi know exactly what was on her mind.

"I let you abuse me. I let you tell me I was possessed by the Devil. All because you were too cowardly to admit there's something special about us—"

Mimi shook her head, not wanting to listen.

"—no, no, no . . . you don't understand, sister—"

Eleanora grabbed Mimi's wrist and shook it.

"Listen to me, goddammit!" she screamed.

"I won't hear the Devil's words from your mouth—"

Enraged, Eleanora snapped, slapping Mimi across the face. All she wanted was for her grandmother to shut up.

"You . . ." Mimi whispered, shock written across her face.

"I'm sorry I hit you," Eleanora said—but that was a lie. She wasn't sorry. It felt good to finally have the upper hand for the first time in their relationship. "I am not the Devil and I don't consort with him. I never have—and you know this."

She waited for Mimi to respond, but the old woman continued to rub her cheek, massaging the spot where Eleanora had slapped her.

"Mimi?" Eleanora said.

"I never touched you," Mimi whispered. "In all the years I raised you, I never laid a hand on you."

Eleanora gritted her teeth. Mimi was insane. That was

the only explanation. How else could she sit there and say what was so obviously untrue?

"You boiled me like a Cape Cod lobster, Mimi," Eleanora cried.

"I was saving you," Mimi said, unshed tears in the corners of her eyes. "I did it to make sure you were in heaven with me, child."

Eleanora shook her head.

"No, Mimi—"

"Yes," Mimi interrupted her. "Don't tell me my own mind, sister."

The truth of Mimi's words sank Eleanora's heart like a stone, and she fell onto her knees, the long skirt she wore swirling around her. She stayed on the floor, her body shaking as she was overwhelmed by emotion. The years of suffering washed over her like acid, stripping away the flesh until there was nothing left but bone.

It was true, then. All this torture was because Mimi loved her.

"I believe you, Mimi," Eleanora whispered. "And I forgive you for the evil you did to me—but I will never forget. I can't stay here with you anymore."

"I know that, sister," Mimi said, nodding. "Neither of us will see another New England winter."

It was an odd thing to say, but Eleanora let it pass.

"Why do you hate our gifts so much, Mimi?" she asked, closing her eyes to keep from weeping.

"You don't know what I know, sister. If you did, you wouldn't ask me that question. You wouldn't dare . . ."

Mimi's voice trailed away and Eleanora opened her eyes.

She was alone in the room. Mimi had gone.

She sat up, her knees creaking as gravity, unseen, pressed down on her—and there, as if by magic, she found her mama's Bible on the bed, propped up against her pillow. She picked the book up, feeling its heft in her hands, then walked over to the closet. She took down a small valise—something she'd been given in childhood by her mama but had never used, and placed the Bible and some clothes inside the stiff leather case. She added the star quilt to the top and closed the lid, unsurprised by how few possessions she owned.

Holding on to the valise's metal handle, she went back downstairs. She was tempted to leave right there and then, but something drew her to the tiny room off the back of the kitchen: Mimi's bedroom.

Her grandmother had lived within the confines of an almost monastic cell. There was a twin bed with a white lace coverlet, a nightstand and bedside light, and a rocking chair turned so it faced the window. A polished oak armoire in the corner of the room contained the meager contents of Mimi's wardrobe.

The stench hit Eleanora as soon as she opened the door, the foul smell of released bowels and decomposing meat filling her nostrils. The smell of death had been contained by the closed bedroom door and masked by the pungent lemon wood polish—but now it was free.

She fell back against the doorframe, tears running down her cheeks as she sobbed into her hand, fingers pressed against her mouth and nose. She didn't know how long she stood there, staring at the corpse, but when she was aware of herself again, she wiped her face and walked over to the bed.

Mimi lay on her back, arms crossed over her chest—and all Eleanora could think was that the woman had even died in an orderly fashion.

She reached out and closed Mimi's eyes, lowering the lids with her fingers, then leaned down and kissed the old woman tenderly on the forehead.

"I hope you and Papa and Mama are happy together in heaven," Eleanora whispered.

And she truly hoped to God they were.

She left the house, closing the door behind her, and

never looked back. Valise in hand, she walked down the road for a bit, the sun beating down on her thin shoulders, her body gaunt from its time in the hospital.

After a few minutes, a battered red pickup truck came down the road, passed her by, then slowed down and pulled to a stop on the shoulder. She ran to the truck and threw open the passenger door, climbing inside.

"Thank you, sir," Eleanora said as she settled the valise at her feet.

"Where you headed, then?" the man asked, pulling at the tab of his overalls so he could scratch his chest.

"I'm going to California," she said, which earned her a raised eyebrow. "But I'd be much obliged if you could take me as far as Boston."

He grinned at her, his ancient face grizzled with stubble, and pulled at the brim of his cap.

"Well, now, Boston I can do you."

She felt the gears rattling under her feet as he released the clutch, and then they were off.

Eleanora stared out the window as they drove, but her eyes were not focused on anything she saw. Her gaze was turned inward.

I will not cry, she thought as she remembered Mimi's body lying on the bed, so pathetic and alone in death . . . and in life.

Why did her love have to be so cruel?

I will not cry, Eleanora thought.

I will not cry.

I. Will. Not. Cry.

Lyse

Lyse woke up on the living room couch, hot tears running down her cheeks. She wiped them away and sat up, her head fuzzy from dreaming. Someone—probably Eleanora—had lit a fire behind the mesh screen of the fireplace, the last embers glowing bright orange before fading into a smoky ash. Lyse stared into the dying coals, her mind awash with images from Eleanora's young adulthood. Her great-aunt's personality quirks made so much sense in light of what Lyse had just discovered about her. She'd gleaned pieces of Eleanora's unhappy past from things said in passing, but she would never have guessed the truth.

She stood up and walked over to the window, staring at her reflection in the glass. Her hair was disheveled, her mouth turning down at the corners. She looked emotionally beaten, her eyes shadowed by exhaustion. She was more than ready for bed, but still her brain kept spinning.

She moved away from the window, feeling listless and unsettled by Eleanora's story. Like she'd intruded on something private that wasn't hers to see.

What am I supposed to do? Lyse wondered, sitting down on the couch again. *What does she expect from me?*

It was the strange immediacy of Eleanora's story that bothered her. She'd never experienced a memory that wasn't her own—and that was what this felt like. Like she'd been right there with Eleanora, experiencing everything Eleanora experienced while it was happening—even though she'd never been to Duxbury, never seen the house where her great-aunt grew up, never met Mimi or Papa. How could she? They'd been dead long before she was born.

And there was something about the story, some small detail that didn't sit right with Lyse. She couldn't put her finger on it yet, but there was something off about what she'd seen. She looked down and realized she'd been compulsively rubbing her hands together as though trying to keep them warm.

The old clock on the mantel chimed once, the sound making Lyse jump. As tired as she was, she knew she wasn't going to be able to sleep—her mind was too keyed up—and she really didn't want to moon around the bungalow, waiting for the sun to come up.

When in doubt, go outside, she thought.

She could sit on the deck and look at the stars, or get some bread from the kitchen and feed the fish in the koi pond. Eleanora's carp were huge, ancient creatures that trolled the bottom of the pond all day long, looking for food. At thirteen, Lyse had been fascinated by how friendly and aware they seemed whenever she fed them. Like they were sentient blobs of color that only magically turned into fish whenever the smell of food was in the air.

She looked down at her nightclothes and decided that she wanted to get dressed. If she wasn't going to sleep, maybe she could feed the fish, then go for a walk. It would be like old times, Lyse wandering the Echo Park hills while everyone else was sleeping. Back then she'd been a lonely kid, going to school elsewhere in the city, an expensive Westside private academy paid for out of the money left to her when her parents died. A social pariah, she was teased and tormented by the other children. She'd learned to ignore the pain of not fitting in, spending her time roaming the hills or hiding out in her bedroom—safe under Eleanora's roof.

She went to the kitchen first and grabbed a slice of bread from the refrigerator, then tiptoed back to her room, not wanting to wake her great-aunt.

The clothes she'd worn earlier in the day were still in a wet pile on the floor. She stepped over them as she shucked off her sweatpants and slipped on a pair of jeans from her overnight bag. She stuffed her long hair into a ponytail, ignored the makeup in her purse, and dug out a red hoodie from the closet. She put it on, reveling in how comfortable and warm it made her feel.

Then she headed outside. No cell phone or wallet. Just a ratty old hoodie, a slice of bread, and her thoughts.

Leaving the warmth and safety of Eleanora's house, Lyse stepped out into the chilly, gray October night. She left the outside lights off, the moonlight making them unnecessary, and crossed the expansive deck. She wandered out onto the arched, wooden bridge overlooking the koi pond and took a seat, letting her feet swing over the side.

She felt like a kid, the pain of childhood nostalgia sharp in her bones. She ached to be young and innocent but still have all the knowledge she'd won as an adult.

The scent of autumn leaves blew in with the wind, reminding Lyse how much she loved the fall. Even in California—which boasted no real seasons, just unrelenting heat and moderate cold—there was still a crispness in the October air.

Thinking about the seasons made her realize that she didn't know when she'd be going back to Georgia. This stuff with the coven was bizarre, and whether she believed in it or not, she'd promised Eleanora she'd be a part of it. Which meant she was gonna put a smile on her face and just go with it until Eleanora wasn't there to see what she did anymore.

After that, well, she didn't think she'd be staying in Echo Park and hanging out with a witches' coven. Not with a house in Georgia and a nursery to run.

She'd called Eleanora and the others "witches," but they didn't seem to like that word. *Blood sister* was what Lyse had heard them call one another over and over again during the course of the evening.

Lyse supposed she was a blood sister now, too. She'd performed a sex ritual and tasted everyone's blood—and she *still* didn't know if magic really existed, or what it was the coven actually *did* . . .

She began to laugh as she realized how ridiculous the whole thing was. She got even more tickled as she tried to imagine herself explaining the antler-man-sex-fantasy to Carole: *Yes, Carole, can you imagine? The size of his penis* was *in direct proportion to the size of his antlers!*

Lyse snorted at the thought.

Feeling lighter than she had in days, she took a deep breath and let it out slowly, shaking off any bad vibes. She took the bread out of the pocket of her hoodie and began to drop small pieces into the koi pond. It was a joy to watch the giant carp rise to the surface in order to search out the food. When the slice was gone, she stood up and stretched, zipping up the hoodie to keep out the cold.

"Night, fish," she said, and offered them an abrupt wave.

It was time to go exploring.

She left the bungalow behind her and plunged into the darkness, not really paying attention to where she was going. She just wanted to see where her feet would take her.

It was good to move without thought, to release her brain and body and let the wind caress her face as she strolled through the night. Even though she hadn't been up some of the streets in years, it didn't seem to matter. Echo Park welcomed her back unconditionally.

Up in the hills there was enough space between the streetlights that as she walked she felt like a ghost flickering in and out of existence. This thought spooked her and she started to jog, wanting to stay in motion so nothing could touch her.

Maybe she was just trying to outrun herself, but soon she was flying down one of the hills, pumping her legs to the rhythmic beating of her heart. She didn't want to think about Eleanora's death. Didn't want to deal with what she'd seen and heard of Eleanora's past. Didn't want to entertain the idea that she might be something more than just a normal human being. And most important, there might be a magical world she knew nothing about.

Lost in her thoughts, she didn't notice the deep fissure in the sidewalk until the toe of her shoe snagged its lip, pitching her forward. She landed on something sharp, cold metal slicing through her thick denim jeans and into the fat of her calf.

At first she only felt a throbbing numbness and thought maybe it was just a scratch. But when she scooted her leg out in front of her, the illumination from the overhead streetlight was bright enough for her to see that the pant leg of her jeans was soaked in blood. Through a rip in the denim fabric, she spied a two-inch-long flap of skin folded over to reveal the subcutaneous fat beneath it.

She looked for whatever she'd cut herself on and was surprised to discover that it was only a small piece of bloodied metal sitting a few inches from her right foot. On its own, it didn't appear to be dangerous, but with the momentum from her fall, it'd really sliced and diced her.

Despite the cold, she unzipped her jacket and slipped out of it. Looping the red cotton hoodie around her calf, she tied the sleeves together to create a makeshift tourniquet that would hopefully put enough pressure on the wound to stop the bleeding.

The rattle of a car engine caught her attention, and a pair of headlights crisscrossed the sidewalk, illuminating her in their bright yellow glare. The light was intense, and her eyes began to water, forcing her to shield her face with her hand. Part of her worried the car would stop and some homicidal maniac would get out and chop her into little pieces. But her rational mind knew help meant a lot less walking on an injured leg, and this was what finally compelled her to raise her hand above her head and wave.

She was annoyed when the ancient Volvo station wagon didn't slow down—she was sure the driver had seen her— but then its right signal light came on, and it pulled into the next driveway.

Too dangerous to stop in the middle of such a steep hill, Lyse thought. *Smart driver.*

In the chilly night air, the station wagon steamed and hissed like a steed pawing the ground, waiting for its rider to dismount. From her vantage point on the ground, she could only hear the driver's-side door opening, but in the gap between the undercarriage of the car and the sidewalk, she saw a pair of black men's boots hit the sidewalk and circle around in her direction.

Over the growl of the car's engine, a voice called out from the darkness: "You okay down there?"

"I'm, uh, a little indisposed . . ." she started to say, but bit back her words when she realized the voice belonged to Weir.

"It's you," he said, tugging off his woolen cap and stuffing it into the pocket of his navy peacoat. A wide grin split his face. "From Burn this afternoon."

"Yep, one and the same," she said, having a hard time looking at him without imagining him naked.

"You never came in," he said, stopping when he reached her side so he could kneel down beside her. He pulled a small flashlight from the pocket of his coat and gave her a mischievous grin. "I thought you'd come in for a drink and I'd at least get to ask you for your number."

She was glad for the dim light. He couldn't see her blushing.

"So what happened here?" he asked, smoothing over a moment that would've been awkward otherwise. "How'd you end up out here in the middle of nowhere with a busted leg?"

"Tripped and fell. Cut myself pretty good," she said, reaching for the sleeves of the hoodie.

He shone the beam of light across her leg, gritting his teeth when he saw the blood soaking the dark denim.

"Well, that's not very good, is it?" He spoke matter-of-factly.

She shook her head.

"I don't think it's as look as it's bad," she said, her words not making sense. Embarrassed, she covered her mouth with her hand. "Wait, not as bad as it looks, sorry, I mean."

It was hard to think straight, and her body was shivering uncontrollably. She wondered if this meant she was going into shock—and, if so, maybe she needed to sit down and put her head between her legs.

"But I'm already sitting," she murmured, and started to lie down on the dirty sidewalk.

"All right," Weir said when he saw what she was doing. "Time to get you in the car."

"My leg hurts," she said matter-of-factly, watching while he retied the hoodie tourniquet. Then, as if she weighed nothing at all, he scooped her up into his arms and carried her over to the car. Her head lolled back against his collarbone, and she turned her face to press her cheek against the warm skin at his neck, catching a whiff of his cologne.

"You smell the same," she murmured into the collar of his jacket. "You feel the same, too."

"Oh, yeah?" he said, amused.

She closed her eyes.

"I'm delirious," she whispered, her lips grazing his throat. "And you're not wearing your antlers."

He laughed out loud.

"I only put those on for special occasions," he teased, shaking his head.

He opened the passenger door and eased her into the front seat. It was warm and toasty, the car heater turned up to high. She closed her eyes and sighed with contentment before remembering she was leaking blood all over his upholstery.

She sat up and grabbed his wrist.

"Put me back on the sidewalk," she demanded. "Blood in your car is a no-no."

"Be quiet and don't worry about it," he said, shutting the door before she could protest further.

She closed her eyes and began to drift. When she came back to consciousness a few moments later, he was in the driver's seat, smiling at her.

"Hey there, out-of-it girl," he said, touching her arm. "Where do you belong?"

"Athens," she murmured, starting to feel a little bit more alert.

"Like the Athens in Greece?" he asked, as he put the car in reverse and backed out of the driveway.

"Like the one in Georgia," she said. "But you only need to take me a few blocks to Curran."

"You staying with someone in the neighborhood?" he asked, curious.

"My great-aunt," she said, as she watched the houses on

Echo Park Avenue rush past her window. "Eleanora Eames. Do you know her?"

"You're Eleanora's kid?" he said, turning his head, so he could get a better look at her.

"You know her?" Lyse asked, surprised.

"Of course I do," he said. "Everyone in the neighborhood knows Eleanora."

"Well, I'm not her kid. I'm her grandniece. I'm visiting for a while."

He gave up trying to look at her as he drove, returning his eyes to the road.

"My sister was talking about you," he said, putting on the turn signal as he approached Curran. "Well, *talking* isn't quite the word. She's got this sketch pad—"

"Wait, Lizbeth is your sister?" Lyse said, and this time it was her turn to be surprised.

"Yeah, I know we don't look anything alike," he said as he pulled up to Eleanora's bungalow. "Half siblings with different mothers."

"Why doesn't she talk?" Lyse blurted out before she could stop herself. "Shit. That was rude. I'm sorry."

He waved off her apology.

"She's had . . . a pretty rough time of it," he said, pulling the Volvo over to the shoulder and putting it in park. "Her mom, Helena, divorced our father when Lizbeth was a baby. When she died, he got custody. He's a real fucking piece of work—a bastard the likes of which you've never seen—and from the beginning he couldn't handle Lizbeth's developmental problems, so he just acted like she didn't exist. Had her institutionalized."

"Jesus," Lyse said, frowning.

"She was seven when he did it," Weir said, "and she really wasn't that bad. She had temper tantrums, couldn't socialize with other kids . . . but she was super-loving . . ."

He paused.

"What happened?"

"She was catatonic when I got her out of there," he continued. "It's taken three years just to get her this functional."

"I'm sorry," Lyse said. "I had no idea."

"How could you?" he replied, shrugging. "Look, Eleanora's
been wonderful to Lizbeth. Invites her over for tea, helped
her get an internship with an herbalist in the neighborhood.
As far as I'm concerned, that woman hung the moon."

"She's got the biggest heart," Lyse said, but she knew
this didn't even begin to cover how amazing Eleanora was.

They sat in silence for a few moments, each lost in their
own thoughts. There was an effortless intimacy between
them, and Lyse felt comfortable with Weir in a way she hadn't
with a man in a long time. She wasn't sure if this was because
he was easy to talk to, or if, in her mind, she'd already had sex
with him, getting some of the awkwardness out of the way.

"Well, I guess this is where I get out."

"Let me help you inside," he said, unbuckling his seat
belt before reaching over to help her with her own. "The
buckle can be a little tricky—"

"Wait, I don't want to go inside," Lyse said, suddenly.

"You don't?"

She shook her head.

"Is that all right?"

"Better than all right," he replied, grinning. "I didn't
want to say good-bye yet."

She blushed, feeling giddy with the high of having a
new crush.

"So, we do need to get that leg disinfected and bandaged—"

"All-night drugstore?" she asked.

"Look, I'm not being forward and I'm not trying to take
advantage of you, but why don't you come back to my place,
and let me put a little bandage on you—"

Lyse cracked up, laughing so hard she was almost crying.

"Oh my God, that was, by far, the most sexual-sounding

non-come-on I've ever heard," she said, gasping for breath in between giggles.

He shook his head, running his fingers through his hair, so bits of blond stuck up every which way.

"I am so sorry," he said. "You're right. That sounded terrible. *Put a little bandage on you* sounds kind of S and M—"

"Totally," Lyse said, still giggling. "But what's *not* okay is that we haven't done this yet."

She leaned over and kissed him lightly on the lips.

"What? You're kidding," he said, pulling back and looking chagrined. "We didn't do that already?"

"Nope."

"No wonder you weren't itching to get out of this car," he said, rolling his eyes heavenward. "Where are my manners?"

He leaned in and kissed her again, wrapping his hand around her neck so he could pull her closer.

The touch of his bare skin on hers was like fire. He must've felt the instant connection, too, because as soon as they pulled apart, he lifted her hand to his lips and gently brushed his mouth across her knuckles.

She swallowed, her body lighting up with attraction.

"Your skin is so soft," he murmured, rubbing the underside of her wrist with a callused thumb.

"I'm soft everywhere," she heard herself whispering back.

The purr of her voice and the intent of the words she'd just spoken shocked her back to reality.

"I'm sorry," she said as she went for the door handle. "I don't know what that was—"

"Wait!" he said, but she already had the door open and was sliding out, careful not to put too much weight on her bad leg.

"Thank you for the ride," she said, and closed the door in his face.

She could hear the Volvo idling behind her as she limped toward the stairs, her eyes on the arched wooden bridge that would take her over the koi pond and back to the safety of Eleanora's deck. She didn't turn around, didn't dare look to see what Weir was doing. She knew if she did, it would all be over: He'd be out of the car and at her side before she could do anything to stop him.

Just let me get up to the deck, she thought. *If I can get to the deck, everything will be okay.*

She couldn't help herself; she turned around.

She saw the car door open, heard his footsteps on the sidewalk, and, as she'd predicted, moments later he was at her side, his strong arms encircling her waist and lifting her into the air.

"Just wait," he said, his lips against her ear. "I'm not going to do anything you don't want me to, but I need you to let me take care of you."

He shook his head and amended: "I need you to let me take care of your leg."

She laughed despite herself. He turned her around to face him, their bodies mere inches apart.

"I'm a gentleman, and I won't take no for an answer."

She was having trouble thinking straight, but this time it wasn't because she was in shock.

"I'm okay," she murmured. "I can take care of myself."

"Nope," he said, tucking an errant strand of dark hair behind her ear. "I can't let you. As a friend, even, I feel like I need to do this for you."

"Please," she whispered.

"I can't," he murmured, running a finger along the line of her jaw, then letting it trail down into the hollow at her throat. "Man, you weren't kidding."

"What?" she said, distracted by his lingering touch.

"You really *are* soft everywhere."

Fuck it, she thought, lifting her chin to look at him.

Their eyes met for a split second before his lips were all over her, tasting her mouth with his tongue, nipping at her lip with his teeth.

Lust kicked *pain* right out of her head, and she threw her arms around his neck, pressing her body down the length of him. He moaned into her mouth, his hands roaming across her back and waist and hips before cupping her ass with both hands.

"This is insane," she growled, as his lips continued to devour her.

"If this is insanity," he murmured into her ear, "then lock me up."

Daniela

Daniela left the moonlight behind as she entered the dimly lit bar. It wasn't an unfair trade—the moon for candlelight and wine—but given her druthers, she'd have asked the wine bar to add a patio, so she could enjoy all three at once, and smoke, too.

The bar was hopping as she weaved through the crowd. She was careful not to get too close to any of the young hipsters and neighborhood cool cats, all here to listen to the three-piece jazz trio that always seemed to be playing whenever she came in for a drink. After her last experience with Eleanora, she didn't dare touch anything human—even with gloved hands.

Eleanora, Daniela thought, and sighed. With her plain-spoken, no-nonsense manner, the master of the Echo Park coven was by far Daniela's favorite blood sister. Eleanora meant what she said, and said what she meant, which Daniela appreciated.

Boy, it's a real bitch she's dying, Daniela thought. *Hits too fucking close to home.*

She'd just lost her mother, and now this whole thing with Eleanora . . . well, it was one of the reasons she wanted a drink—or three—and hadn't gone home after she'd taken both Dev and Lizbeth back to their respective residences. Instead, she'd walked over to Echo Park Lake, braving the drizzle to wander aimlessly around the little park, sitting in one of the playground swings until the rain eased up and the moon came out.

During the day, the lake was overrun with people and Daniela avoided it at all costs. At night, though, when the park was as devoid of life as a graveyard, she would find herself drawn there, eager for the solitude. She could close her eyes and *almost* pretend she was the last person left on Earth—but then a homeless person would amble by with a shopping cart full of glass bottles, or she'd stumble across a horny teenaged couple making out on one of the park benches, and the illusion of solitude would be shattered.

Daniela sidled up to the long, polished wood bar and, staying far away from her nearest neighbor, lifted her chin to get the dreadlocked bartender's attention.

"Lambrusco. Two glasses," she called out, and he went to grab a bottle of the sparkling red wine.

For a tough chick, Daniela loved super-girly drinks. Piña coladas piled high with fruit and topped off with tiny pink umbrellas, sparkling dessert wines so full of sugar they might as well have been candy—if it screamed "Bachelorette Party" or "Girls' Night Out," then Daniela had probably ordered it.

She threw a twenty and a ten down on the bar—which got a big smile from the bartender—and took her drinks over to an empty table in the back of the room. It had an obstructed view of the jazz trio, but Daniela wasn't interested in the music, so it suited her fine.

She draped her leather jacket over the back of her chair, putting a barrier between her damp shirt and the metal crosshatching of the seat back, and sat down. She closed her eyes and sighed, happy to be alone but ensconced within the frenetic energy of an anonymous crowd.

She sipped the first glass of wine, the sweetness fizzing on her tongue, and let her mind relax.

Lyse.

Of course that was where her brain went.

It was hard to see past her physical attraction to Eleanora's grandniece. Those melancholy bedroom eyes peeking out from beneath disheveled black bangs, the winsome face, full lips, and slim body. What drew her to Lyse could not be ignored.

"I wanted to speak to you in private. I hope you don't mind."

Daniela opened her eyes to find Arrabelle standing over her table, beer in hand, dark eyes inscrutable.

"What'd you do? Follow me here?"

Arrabelle shook her head.

"I figured if you weren't here, you'd be at the lake."

Great, she was getting predictable in her wanderings. She was gonna have to mix it up. Stake out another bar or two in the neighborhood—which was a bummer because she really liked this place.

"Don't you know privacy is just an illusion?" Daniela asked. "There's no such thing as a private conversation these days."

Arrabelle raised a manicured eyebrow, then sat down beside Daniela.

"I know that if anyone can hear our conversation over the music, it would be a miracle."

Daniela laughed.

"Touché," she said, leaning closer to Arrabelle.

It was true. The place was loud, but, in Daniela's experience, there were always eyes watching, ears listening.

"So, who the fuck are you?" Arrabelle said, launching in without any preamble.

"Excuse me?" Daniela said, downing the last dregs of wine in her first glass and reaching for her second one.

"You make those awful abstract paintings that you don't sell," Arrabelle said, "and you have no other job that I can see. Yet ten seconds after my blood sister Dezzie dies, you get sent here to join us—like you were being called up from the army reserves or something, by the way—and you can afford to buy the old Zeke Title house? Where the hell does your money come from? Not your mother's estate—everything she had belongs to the Greater Council. Couple that with the way you keep tabs on Eleanora and the rest of us, and it makes me think you're a fucking spy."

"Why did you drag my paintings into this?" Daniela asked, deflecting.

"Because they're terrible and you know it," Arrabelle said, taking a swallow of beer. "And because I was annoyed and felt like being an asshole about something. Look, am I right? Are you a fucking spy or not? You went chasing out of the circle tonight to go protect Lyse. I want to know how you know so much about all the weird shit that's been going on."

"No, I'm not a fucking spy," Daniela said, and finished her glass. "Let's get out of here. I need some fresh air."

She grabbed her leather jacket and headed for the door—away from prying eyes and curious ears. When she paused at the threshold, Arrabelle was hot on her heels.

To the others, Daniela was supposed to be a "normal" member of the coven. Only Eleanora knew her secret. She wasn't just an empath who painted abstract landscapes (paintings that *Daniela* thought were pretty good, actually), participated in coven activities, was pleasant to be around, and, for the most part, did as she was told—but otherwise kept a low profile.

Daniela was embedded in the Echo Park coven for one reason, and one reason alone: to protect the last of the Dream Keepers.

Daniela remembered the day her mother had called her to the Council's apartments in Rome. She'd been vague on the phone, mentioning "a personal matter" they needed to discuss, and that was all.

Marie-Faith was only supposed to stay in Italy for a few weeks, but for some reason the visit lasted more than two months. At the time, Daniela didn't know this was because her mother's life had been threatened—and only later, after her mother's death, did she realize how close she herself had come to being buried in a shallow Roman grave.

But that day, she merely found it strange to be summoned so far for something personal when her mother was going to be returning to the States at any moment.

Daniela had arrived at the Council's apartments in Trastevere, feeling only slightly jet-lagged by the nine-hour flight. She dropped off her overnight bag and, at her mother's behest, joined her for an afternoon constitutional. They walked in silence, each lost in her own thoughts, until they found themselves standing in front of an old ruin, its crumbling façade overrun with feral but friendly cats.

It was here that Marie-Faith handed Daniela a letter:

Dearest Eleanora,

The last Dream Keeper has been born. Unless things change, no others will ever follow her. Hessika was not the only one to dream of her. She came to me as well, and to one other, whom I will not name in this letter, should it find itself delivered into the wrong hands.

   She will find you. She will be no more than a child and will not know who or what she is, but you will. Please keep her safe. She is the last of her kind and could be (can be) the one to save us all—though the dreams are murky where this is concerned.

   I trust you and my daughter above all others. That is why I am sending her to you. Keep each other safe.

   The Flood is coming.

   Beware.

—*M.F.*

"What is this?" Daniela asked after she'd finished reading it.

"Metaphorically, it's the truth . . . and your destiny," Marie-Faith explained, brushing a strand of pink hair behind her daughter's ear. "But literally, it's a letter I'm sending with you to California. I don't trust the post or the telephone, so I've booked you an evening flight to Los Angeles."

Daniela did not understand, so her mother explained further:

At great danger to herself, Marie-Faith had used her standing as a member of the Greater Council to call into being a secret cabal culled from only the most trusted from each discipline—Clairvoyants, Diviners, Dream Keepers, Empaths, and Herbalists—to decide how best to protect a young girl, the only Dream Keeper born within the last fifty years, and the sole thing standing between the covens and the oncoming wrath of The Flood.

"The Flood?" Daniela asked.

"It's an image from my dreams. I've consulted with some of the other Dream Keepers, and, so far, I'm the only one—save Hessika—who's received the message. I think it started with her, she dreamed of it years before, but no one listened then. Now it's stronger and it's going to rush into the others' dreams, breaking over our world like a giant wave."

Her mother's words chilled Daniela to the core.

"Sometimes there's a man riding the crest of this wave," Marie-Faith said, picking up one of the stray cats—a white one with green eyes—and stroking it. "He commands The Flood, encouraging it to overwhelm the world. There's something missing inside him—but I'm never with him long enough to find out what it is. I just know The Flood is coming, and you're one of the few I trust to help stop it. If that can even be done."

The task Daniela's mother laid at her daughter's feet was not an easy one. Daniela was to guard the last of the Dream Keepers—with her life even, if that proved necessary. At the moment, only a handful of people knew of the girl's existence, but once the secret got out, Daniela would need all the help she could get.

The question then became: *Whom could* Daniela *trust?*

"So?" Arrabelle asked, catching up to Daniela on the sidewalk. "You didn't answer the rest of my questions."

Daniela shrugged and kept walking.

"Well?"

"Well, what?" Daniela asked.

Arrabelle sighed, her long legs allowing her to easily keep pace.

"If you're a spy, then you're a pretty shitty one."

Daniela snorted as side by side they headed up the steep incline of Echo Park Avenue.

"So, maybe you're not a spy."

"I'm not a spy," Daniela said, exasperated. "Are you a spy?"

"No," Arrabelle said, "but I don't go skulking around getting into fights with possessed dogs, either."

Shit, Daniela thought, surprised Arrabelle realized the feral dog that attacked Lyse wasn't rabid, but under the control of someone, or something, else. The same was probably true for the dead crows that penetrated the eternal circle—someone trying to breach their coven's protective spells by using an animal host.

"You caught that, eh?" Daniela asked, and Arrabelle nodded.

"I'm an herbalist, not an idiot."

Daniela slowed down.

"These are dark times we're living in," she said to Arrabelle. "I know."

"So if I'm not a spy," Daniela asked. "What am I?"

Arrabelle zipped up her cable-knit sweater and shrugged.

"Don't know," she said, slowing her pace thoughtfully. Daniela slowed hers to match. "But I like you better now. After this walk and talk."

Daniela grinned, liking Arrabelle more, too.

"Thank you for walking back with me," Daniela said, as they reached Curran and made the turn that would lead them to her house.

Across the street at Eleanora's house, all the lights were off, which was a good thing as far as Daniela was concerned. Eleanora and Lyse had both looked like shit warmed over when they'd left the clearing. A good night's sleep would help with that.

"No problem," Arrabelle replied. "Thanks for letting me call you a fucking spy."

There was no handshake or hug good-bye.

"See ya when I see ya," Daniela said, and turned up the walk to her house.

The cats were waiting on the porch, and at the sound of

the gate opening, they both came bounding to meet her. Closing the gate behind her, she knelt to pet them.

"My good girls," she cooed, scratching behind their ears. "Let's go inside and feed you, shall we?"

She stood up and put her key in the dead bolt, turning the lock. She pushed the heavy wooden door open and belatedly realized that she'd neglected to leave a light on that afternoon, so the interior of the house was blanketed in darkness.

"Shit," she said, patting along the wall until her fingers found the light switch. She flipped it on and gasped.

"Oh my God."

She stared at her wrecked living room. Every drawer in the built-in cabinets had been yanked out and smashed into splinters. Papers were fanned out across the floor like discarded ticker tape. The television was busted. The brown leather couches were pushed onto their fronts, the backs slashed to pieces.

And she soon discovered the carnage wasn't limited to the living room. The rest of the house had been violated, too.

She shooed the cats out of the house and closed the door. She wanted to take inventory of the damage without them underfoot—because as much as she loved her babies, they could be real assholes when they were hungry and she wasn't paying enough attention to their needs.

She trooped through the living room, found the kitchen in disorder—dishes, cookware, and packaged stuff from the cabinets tossed into the middle of the kitchen floor, though the refrigerator was untouched—and discovered that the bedroom had been upended, too. Clothes and shoes had been flung across the hardwood, box spring and mattress slashed with a knife.

The bathroom stank of cleaning fluid and crushed bath products. A twelve-pack of toilet paper had been dumped into the half-filled bathtub. Even her art studio had been taken apart: exploded paint tubes, shredded canvas . . . and, the worst, someone had taken oxblood paint and slathered it all over her latest piece.

"Dammit!" Daniela said, wanting to scream, but she settled for kicking a tube of indigo paint across the studio floor instead.

She called the police and, not wanting to contaminate the crime scene, chose not to try to salvage anything yet. She went outside and stood on the porch, the cats surrounding her. She didn't know who was behind the destruction at her place, but she was going to beat the crap out of them.

In a show of frustration, or maybe it was plain old hunger, Verity gently bit Daniela's calf.

"I'm sorry, girls," she said. "I totally forgot. Just give me a second."

She went inside, leaving the cats meowing on the porch, and wove her way through the mess.

Under normal circumstances, she didn't keep all the house lights on at the same time, preferring to turn on lamps as she went, lighting her way as needed. But tonight she felt unsettled and violated, so she left the place lit up like a Christmas tree.

The dry cat food was in the kitchen, stored in a cat-proof plastic container in the cabinet over the refrigerator. This was the only way to keep the girls out of their food. She'd once made the mistake of leaving a giant unopened bag of cat chow in the pantry only to come home to find the kitchen floor littered with kibble.

Stepping over the smashed remains of her favorite dishware—pale blue plates and bowls she'd purchased from a local potter—she dragged the step stool over to the refrigerator and climbed up to the topmost step. She struggled with the cabinet door and ended up taking off her gloves in order to get a good grip on the door pulls. This particular cabinet tended to swell and contract with the heat, making it almost impossible to open.

"Come on," she murmured to the door. Finally, it came unstuck, and she reached inside for the Tupperware container of cat food.

Out of the corner of her eye, she caught a flash of movement.

Shit, no gloves, she thought before she whirled around and slammed her right foot into the chest of a would-be attacker.

Her kick surprised the hell out of him, and he went flying backward into the metal spice rack across from the refrigerator. A lone bottle of cinnamon—sans its top—had survived the first trashing of the kitchen. The impact jostled the bottle forward, tipping its contents out and unleashing a cloud of cinnamon on her masked attacker's head. Sputtering, the man swiped at his face, trying to keep the cinnamon granules out of his eyes. Daniela used the distraction to slam the heel of her boot into his solar plexus.

He hit the spice rack again, releasing another dust cloud of cinnamon, and she played the advantage, landing a kick to his belly.

This time he grabbed her ankle, wrapping his fingers around the top of her boot and twisting her foot, so that she cried out in pain as her ankle made a popping sound. She tried to pull out of her attacker's grip, but she used too much force, and the step stool toppled underneath her. She fell backward and cracked her head against the plastic handle of the refrigerator door.

Stars exploded in her head as she hit the ground, and she fought to stay conscious. Her attacker grabbed her by the ankle again and began to drag her through the house.

The pain in her ankle was exquisite, but she began to flail and kick out with her good foot, landing a blow on the soft underside of her attacker's left knee. His leg went out beneath him and he crumpled forward, releasing his hold on her.

She flipped onto her stomach and began to crawl toward the front door, refusing to look back, eyes focused on her escape exit. But then she sensed him reaching for her and quickly rolled onto her side, lashing out at him with her good foot. He dodged the attack, throwing himself on top of her and wrapping his hands around her throat.

She was being strangled, her airway constricted by the power of his massive hands. She stared up into his green eyes—the only visible part of his face beneath the mask—and searched for some sign of recognition.

And then she remembered.

No gloves.

She reached up, wedging her bare hands underneath the edge of the ski mask until her fingertips found the man's skin. The oncoming seizure hit her with the velocity of a speeding freight train—and just before her brain exploded into a million points of sparkling light, Daniela experienced the most amazing sense of oneness with the universe.

Eleanora

E leanora couldn't sleep.
  Her mouth was dry as a bone, and her brain just wouldn't settle. She rolled onto her side and bunched the covers down around at her feet. She decided she wasn't going to spend the night tossing and turning and crawled out of bed. It was cold in her room, or maybe she just didn't have enough fat left on her bones to keep her warm—whatever the reason, she slipped on her housecoat and wrapped a scarf around her neck, and that seemed to do the trick.

She closed her bedroom door, careful not to slam it—sound carried in this old place, and she didn't want to accidentally wake Lyse—and headed down the long hallway to the kitchen. There was enough moonlight coming in through the kitchen windows that she didn't need to turn on any lights. She opened the refrigerator door, and the interior light cut a slice out of the darkness. She stood there for a moment, trying to remember what she wanted.

Thirsty, she thought, and grabbed a bottle of sparkling water from the top shelf.

Normally, she would just drink straight out of the bottle, but she had company staying, so she plucked a coffee mug from the draining board and filled it with bubbly water. The carbonation tickled the back of her throat. She guzzled down one cup after another without stopping—and this barely quenched her thirst. She started to pour herself a third mugful, but stopped and just drank out of the bottle.

This made her feel naughty, and she grinned as she wiped her mouth, but this happy moment was almost instantly replaced by exhaustion, a feeling ever present within her these days. Bone tired, bone weary, bones too old and weak to keep her standing for much longer, at least figuratively. Nights like this, when she felt her body was too far gone to keep moving, she longed for death. It was like a much-anticipated visitor who'd kept her waiting far too long.

She didn't worry about what came after. She'd seen ghosts—Dream Walkers—her whole life. She knew death wasn't the end. It was the beginning. She did have worries, though. And they weren't for her old bones; they were for Lyse. There was so much the girl needed to learn, and Eleanora knew she wouldn't last long enough to teach her.

She blinked and realized she was standing in front of the open refrigerator door, another unopened bottle of sparkling water in her hand. She didn't even remember finishing the first one. Who knew how long she'd been standing there, letting chilled air escape into the night, aiding and abetting the criminal act of wasting electricity.

Time had a funny knack of getting away from her these days.

It had started with the advent of her illness—the partition between the past and present becoming more and more tenuous until she was afraid the barrier would be breached irreparably. It'd gotten so bad that, at times, Eleanora found it impossible to tell the difference between *then* and *now*, her past overwhelming her so completely she actually felt as though she'd stepped through Alice's look-ing glass.

She returned the second bottle of sparkling water back to its place on the shelf and shut the refrigerator door. She wasn't thirsty anymore.

I want to sleep, she thought, rubbing her tired eyes with the heels of her palms.

She hated taking things to knock herself out, but it didn't seem like there was any other option. Arrabelle had made her a sleeping draught, one she'd avoided using, but tonight seemed like the perfect time to take it on a test run.

She used the same coffee mug to make a cup of hot water in the microwave, then added a spoonful of the powdered sleeping draught to it, mixing everything up. Waiting for it to get cool enough to drink, she took the mug with her and padded down the hall to her bedroom.

Outside, the slam of a car door caught her attention, and she wandered back the way she'd come, curious to see who was parking in front of her house. She expected to find Lyse asleep on the living room couch, but to her surprise there was only a crumpled throw pillow where Lyse had been earlier.

She probably got up and went to bed, Eleanora thought as she pushed back the curtains to peer through the window.

Lyse was standing at the bottom of the front steps, her arms wrapped around the waist of a young man. Beyond them was an idling Volvo station wagon.

Weir.

Not wanting to spy, Eleanora turned away.

She smiled, pleased by this new turn of events. Lyse had always dated intellectually brilliant loudmouths and addicts—bad boys who didn't deserve her time—and Weir was neither of those things. She very much liked Lizbeth's older half brother, and if Lyse was choosing him as a possible partner, then maybe she didn't need to worry so much about the girl's future. Plus, it might help entice Lyse to stay in Echo Park after she died.

Eleanora waited until she heard the Volvo's engine growl to life, and when she looked outside again, Weir, Lyse, and the car were gone.

Now that she couldn't be accused of eavesdropping, she relaxed and stood in front of the window, taking in the spectacular view of downtown. Being at the top of the hill made Eleanora feel as though she were floating over the darkness—and that the other houses dotting the hillside were merely twinkling fairy lights strewn below her.

The sleeping draught wasn't unpleasant, but she took her time finishing it. When she was done, she turned to go, but something, a flash of light from Daniela's place, drew her eye. She walked over to another window, one that had a better view of next door, and gasped: An intruder was in Daniela's house.

Her heart rate quickened, and she only had to take a few steps before she realized the fuzziness in her head was an effect of the sleeping potion.

"Not now," she murmured, fighting the drowsiness as she scurried out of the living room and down the hallway.

She made it to her bedroom, pausing for a moment at the door to catch her breath, then proceeded to the closet. She sat down heavily, the floor seeming to rise up to meet her instead of the other way around. She found the plain cardboard shoe box tucked into the back of the closet and threw open the lid. Inside, nestled between a pair of leather sandals, were a small-caliber handgun and a box of bullets.

She loaded three bullets into the empty chamber and clicked off the safety. Using the end of the bed to drag herself to her feet, she weaved her way across the bedroom and headed for the front door.

She knew she looked a sight—a woozy old woman in a white nightgown and polyester print bathrobe running through the streets in the middle of the night, waving a gun in the air like an overzealous cowboy. She could only imagine the notice in the *Eastsider* newsblog the next morning: "Crazy Old Lady in Ratty Housecoat on Rampage in Echo Park!"

She made it to Daniela's house without killing herself, the night air reviving her a little, and found the cats on the front porch yowling like little demons as they scratched at the front door.

"I'm here," Eleanora said, stepping over their squirming bodies with her bare feet. "Don't worry."

She slipped her finger around the trigger and shook her head, trying to clear the cobwebs from her brain.

She threw open the front door.

"Take your hands off her," Eleanora yelled, leveling the gun at the masked man who was crouched over Daniela's writhing body.

He looked up, surprised by her arrival—and by the entrance of the cats, who shot past Eleanora's legs, claws extended like the deadly weapons they were.

"Verity, Veracity, get back," Eleanora cried.

The cats ignored her, hissing, yowling, attacking, and batting at the man with everything they were worth. The man caught Verity by the neck, and the cat began to thrash in his arms.

"You hurt those cats and so help me, I'll blow your brains out," Eleanora said as she aimed the gun at the man's head, meaning every word.

Her tone seemed to give the man pause, and finally he released the cat. He dropped his hands to his sides, letting the cats swat at him.

"I'm glad you can listen," Eleanora said, keeping the gun trained on the man's face. "Now get off her. Slowly. And they'll leave you alone."

The man did as he was told, scooting far away from Daniela. As Eleanora had predicted, the cats left him alone, protectively curling their bodies around their mistress.

Verity continued to send the man dangerous glares, letting him know she'd kill him if she could.

"Now I want you to tell me who you are and what you're doing here," Eleanora said. "Or I'll use this gun."

She was serious. The man had tried to kill Daniela, and if she hadn't seen the slight rise and fall of the younger woman's chest, she'd have thought he'd succeeded.

He refused to answer.

"I've used it before," she said, adrenaline pumping through her. "And I'm not afraid to use it again."

The sound of police sirens echoed in the distance. The man's eyes locked on Eleanora, and he slowly began to rise to his feet.

"Sit down," she said, her gun hand trembling.

The stupid sleeping stuff was kicking in big-time, and Eleanora couldn't stop herself from yawning.

"I said to sit down," she growled, blinking furiously.

The man began to advance toward her, and she tightened her grip on the gun's trigger. He took another step forward, and then the room slid out of focus, her brain reeling. She felt a hand on her wrist . . .

. . . *and she screamed.*

The pain was so intense, she could hardly breathe.

"Make it stop," she pleaded with Hessika, squeezing the other woman's fingers until both their hands were bloodless.

"We're close," Hilda said, a look of complete concentration on her face.

She was older than Hessika and Eleanora, in her late fifties, and extremely competent. As the coven herbalist and a practicing midwife, she was the only person Hessika trusted to deliver Eleanora's baby . . .

"No," Eleanora said, dragging herself back to the present.

The man was staring at her as he gripped her wrist . . .

. . . *"It's coming," Hilda said. "I can see the head."*

Eleanora was sobbing.

It was so close to being over that she could taste it.

"One more push, Eleanora," Hilda said, her forehead slick with sweat. "We're almost there."

She gritted her teeth and pushed so hard it felt like her womb was being expelled along with the baby. There was a loud, mewling cry, and everyone in the room began to smile.

"It's a boy," Hilda said, holding the tiny, squirming thing up to Eleanora. "A healthy baby boy."

All Eleanora could see was the blood and viscera, the utter alienness of the creature screeching in Hilda's hands.

"Wait, we have another one," Hilda said abruptly, handing off the first baby to Hessika, who swaddled the tiny thing in a soft, woolen blanket that Donna, the coven's diviner, had knitted especially for the occasion.

Pain ripped through Eleanora's belly, and she began to sob.

"Push, Eleanora," Hilda said. "Push now!"

There was a soft cry, not as strong as the first baby's yowls, but still full of life.

"A girl," Hilda said, looking as exhausted as Eleanora felt. "She's a lot smaller, but everything looks like it's in the right place."

The second baby was shivering in Hilda's arms—they'd been unprepared, had expected only one child, not two. There wasn't another blanket.

"I'll go fetch something," Hessika said, and held out the first baby to Eleanora, offering her his tiny, squirming body. "You wanna hold him, ma belle?*"*

She knew she should feel something for it. It'd come out of her, was part of her, had been carried around inside her for nine months . . . but no matter how deeply she probed, searching for the maternal love that was supposed to already be there inside her, she could not find an ounce of feeling for the newborn creature.

"No," Eleanora said, turning her head away, hiding the newborn baby from her view. "I don't want to hold it."

She could sense Hilda's shock. Even Hessika seemed disappointed by her lack of maternal feeling. Eleanora knew they were

*thinking that she was cruel and inhuman—and maybe she was.
But she just couldn't face holding them if she was only going to
have to give them away.*

She closed her eyes as the hot tears slid down her cheeks . . .

. . . and when she opened her eyes again, the man in
Daniela's living room was gone.

"How do you feel?" Eleanora asked when Daniela came to.

"Okay."

Eleanora made a quick phone call to Arrabelle. The herbalist arrived minutes after the EMTs and persuaded them—
once they checked Daniela's vitals, which were normal—to
let them take her to Eleanora's house to recuperate.

So while the police skulked around looking for clues to
the break-in, Eleanora and Arrabelle sat in Eleanora's bedroom with Daniela and the two cats, both of whom refused
to be separated from their mistress.

"Seizure," Arrabelle said, from her perch on the end of
Eleanora's bed. "Your throat's gonna be pretty sore, too."

"Yeah," Daniela said, her voice hoarse. "I figured as much."

"So, why was this man in your house? Any ideas?" Arrabelle asked.

Daniela shook her head.

"You know if Eleanora hadn't come storming in like
Rambo, you'd probably be dead."

Daniela caught Eleanora's eye.

"Thank you," she said. "I heard you come in and start
yelling at the guy."

"Actually, I think he was more scared of the cats than
my gun," Eleanora said.

Daniela sat up, displacing the cats, who stretched and
jumped off the bed to go explore the rest of Eleanora's house.

"They're so fickle," Daniela murmured. "Just as long as I
feed them—"

She stopped and looked distressed.

"Don't worry," Eleanora said. "Arrabelle and I took care of them."

Daniela nodded and closed her eyes.

"I know you're exhausted," Arrabelle said to Daniela, "but this break-in? I have a hard time believing it's just a coincidence."

Daniela opened her eyes and shot Eleanora a look that said she was resigned to telling Arrabelle the truth.

"I think it's time to tell the others why I'm here."

Arrabelle didn't look surprised by this revelation—not that Eleanora expected her to. Arrabelle was sharp as a tack, and too quick on the uptake to have the wool pulled over her eyes for very long.

"Obviously, I'm not happy about being left out of the loop. But I trust you, Eleanora, and I think you had your reasons for keeping us in the dark."

"Daniela is here at the behest of the Greater Council," Eleanora said, exhaustion stealing over her body.

She felt bad about keeping important information from Arrabelle, but the time to share had come only after Lyse's return home.

"That's not exactly the truth," Daniela said, correcting Eleanora. "More like a secret group inside the Council that, until her death, included my mother."

"I don't understand," Arrabelle said, confused. "Why does the Greater Council care about us?"

"Daniela is here to protect someone," Eleanora said. "Someone very important."

"What the hell are you talking about?" Arrabelle asked, looking from Eleanora to Daniela. "I thought she was like quality control, here to check in on our coven, make sure we were doing what we were supposed to be doing—"

"What're *you* talking about?" Daniela asked, rolling her eyes. "The Greater Council doesn't do check-ins on its members, crazy person."

Arrabelle flushed, embarrassed.

"I don't know. It's all I could think of."

"Arrabelle, for a long time, I and a few others have known something important . . ." Eleanora said, trying to find the right words to explain.

Arrabelle nodded.

"Go on."

"Well . . ."

"Just spit it out," Daniela said, exasperated.

Eleanora opened her mouth to protest, but Daniela waved her away:

"You have a Dream Keeper in your coven."

Arrabelle frowned at Daniela and shook her head.

"No, we *had* a Dream Keeper, but Hessika died a long time ago."

"Not before her dreams predicted the arrival of someone special," Eleanora said. "Someone who would be the last of Hessika's kind . . ."

"The final Dream Keeper born to our world," Daniela finished for her. "And this girl is so important that a secret cabal was formed to figure out the best way to look after and protect her."

"And you're only here to protect this Dream Keeper?" Arrabelle asked Daniela. "Not spy on us?"

"I am only here to protect the girl," Daniela said, as she grabbed another of Eleanora's pillows and put it behind her head. "My mother knew she was coming, and she and Hessika both dreamed that Eleanora would be the one to find her."

"And you didn't tell me or Dev or Lizbeth this because . . . ?" Arrabelle asked—and there was no anger in her words, just confusion.

Daniela continued to answer for Eleanora.

"Dev already knows"—Arrabelle's mouth dropped open in surprise—"and that wasn't Eleanora's call. Things were becoming difficult in our world. It's hard to know who to trust these days. There've been disappearances, and murders . . . I'm sorry that I didn't trust you, Arrabelle. Forgive me."

Daniela's eyes were filled with a sadness that only Eleanora understood.

"Yeah, you not trusting me stings, obviously, and I know you will both apologize more fully to me later," Arrabelle said. "But ego aside . . . how is this not common knowledge? There's been no word about any of this from the Greater Council—"

"Because they don't want to believe it's really happening," Daniela said. "The Flood is coming and the idiots are just ignoring it—or worse."

"It's not bad here yet," Daniela continued, "but in other places, less civilized countries, covens are being uprooted or destroyed."

"By whom? Who's doing it?" Arrabelle asked.

"They call themselves The Flood, but no one has any idea who they are," Daniela said.

Arrabelle looked dazed as she tried to take in everything Daniela was saying.

"Okay, The Flood, fine." Arrabelle nodded. "And you're here to protect the last Dream Keeper?"

"Yes," Daniela said, exasperated, her voice raspy from too much talking. "And I'm not saying it again."

"Well, at least I understand why you've been so hellbent on getting Lyse into the coven," Arrabelle said, turning back to Eleanora. "If she's the last Dream Keeper—"

"Lyse *isn't* the last Dream Keeper, Arrabelle," Daniela said, interrupting her.

"Lizbeth is," Eleanora said.

Eleanora thought Arrabelle took the news well. At least, as well as could be expected given the situation. After she'd gone, Eleanora sat with Daniela in the bedroom, the two of them watching through the window as the sun crested the hillside and morning broke open like the yolk of an egg. She wished she could hold Daniela's hand—as much to comfort herself as the girl—but without the leather gloves to protect her, Eleanora was too scared to try.

"You look terrible, you know," Daniela said, after a long silence. "You should really slow the hell down."

"I'm fine—" Eleanora protested, but Daniela held up a hand.

"No response requested. It was just a piece of advice. But you should go and get some sleep. It's almost six."

Eleanora shrugged, though she couldn't argue with Daniela's assessment. She felt nauseated and was so damn tired she could barely keep her eyes open.

"I will go get some sleep," Eleanora said, dragging her chair even closer to the side of the bed. "I promise, but first, tell me what you felt when you touched your attacker."

Daniela let her head flop back onto the pillows.

"Of course, you would pick up on that, wouldn't you?" Daniela said, and sighed. Then she changed the subject. "There's so much more going on than you even know. What I told Arrabelle tonight is just the tip of the iceberg. I don't want to frighten you, but there have been rumors . . . of modern-day witch hunts. Stuff not unlike what we know happened in the Dark Ages, or in the Americas with the Puritans."

This was news to Eleanora. There hadn't been anything like what Daniela was describing in more than a hundred years.

"Arrabelle's right. Why haven't the covens been warned about this?" Eleanora asked. Daniela shook her head.

"My mother tried, but you know how that ended."

Eleanora watched as silent tears fell down Daniela's cheeks.

"Eleanora?" Daniela asked, her voice cracking with emotion.

"Yes?"

"I felt nothing."

"Nothing?" Eleanora repeated, not sure what Daniela meant.

"The man who attacked me," she whispered. "I looked into his soul."

She paused, and for the first time Eleanora felt real fear behind Daniela's words.

"There was nothing there."

Eleanora slept fitfully and woke up too early, the sunlight streaming through the living room windows almost as bad as an alarm clock. She rolled over, aching with the hot/cold, pins/needles sensation you get when your foot "falls asleep"—only the feeling had taken over her entire body.

"My God," she moaned, trying to sit up but not having the energy to make it happen.

She fell back onto the couch, the pillow she'd borrowed from Lyse's empty bed a soft cloud she couldn't seem to escape. After exerting so much effort to sit up, and then failing, it felt heavenly to just lie there, unmoving, eyes closed against the dappled, morning light.

I have to get up, she thought. *It's not an option to lie here all day.*

She took a deep breath and reached out with a trembling hand, grabbing hold of the back of the couch and using it to leverage herself into a sitting position. Just this small effort caused her to break out in a cold sweat. She wiped her face with the inside of her nightgown, then let the neckline drop back into place, the wet fabric chilling the heated flesh of her chest.

The triumph of getting herself into a sitting position gave her a little energy, and she used it to scoot herself forward on the seat of the couch. She looked over at the alarm clock she'd brought with her from the bedroom and sighed.

Not even ten yet, she thought. *Too damn early.*

She felt her forehead with the back of her hand.

And I have a goddamned fever, to boot.

She needed to get up, have some pot tincture and a few of Arrabelle's potions, and then take a shower.

Act like everything is normal and it will be, she thought. *It's as simple as telling your body to move.*

She was struck by a flash from the night before, the cry of a newborn infant echoing in her subconscious. The pain of remembering her children's births knocked against her heart, begging to be let in, but she pushed it away. Ignoring it as best she could, she took a deep breath and told her body to move its ass. She hoisted herself onto her feet and swayed a little, her body like jelly, but strength of will kept her from sitting back down.

One foot in front of the other.

One small step for man.

One giant leap for mankind.

These were the odd phrases filtering through her head as she forced her feet to move. It was slow going at first, but with each subsequent step, she regained a little more energy—and when she got to the kitchen, she almost felt human. Almost.

She dug through the cabinet and found the bottles she wanted, setting them up in a row on the kitchen counter. Their glass containers reflected back the sunlight shining in through the kitchen window.

It was going to be a beautiful day.

She poured herself a glass of water from the tap and added it to the lineup.

She didn't know if Lyse was home yet, and frankly it was none of her business. She just hoped Lyse had had a good time. She deserved to be happy in love, and Eleanora wasn't going to tease her about Weir or ask for any details. Not unless Lyse *wanted* to share.

"Hello, lovely," she said as she picked up the pot tincture and unscrewed the top.

She placed a few drops under her tongue and didn't have to wait long for the nausea to dissipate. She followed this with two of Arrabelle's potions—made especially for her—then washed the lot down with the glass of tap water.

She heard the back door open as she put the empty glass in the sink. She looked up to find Lyse in the doorway, limping on her right foot.

"Good night?" Eleanora asked.

Lyse got a sheepish look on her face and blushed.

"Yeah, sorry about that," she said. "I mean, about staying out all night."

"None of my business," Eleanora said, amused at seeing Lyse so embarrassed.

"I fell," Lyse said, looking down at her leg. "And I needed a bandage, and there was this guy. Who kind of helped . . ."

She seemed to realize she was babbling and clammed up.

"Interesting," Eleanora said, nodding.

"Okay, this is embarrassing. I'm just gonna stop talking," Lyse growled, and blushed even more.

"Well, I'm going to take a shower." Eleanora put the glass bottles back in the cabinet and closed the door.

"Okay," Lyse said, leaning against the kitchen counter that separated them. "So, uh, I think you might know this guy? His name's Weir?"

"Lizbeth's brother?" Eleanora asked, quirking an eyebrow.

"Uhm, yeah," Lyse said, drumming her fingertips against the Formica countertop. "You like him? I mean, you think he's all right?"

Eleanora thought about her answer for a long moment, then nodded.

"I think he's great."

"Me, too." Lyse grinned. "And I know what you're thinking

in that naughty mind of yours, but we didn't . . . *you know*. We could've, but I didn't want to."

"You don't have to explain yourself—"

Lyse waved the words away.

"We just talked all night. And it was nice. To feel like someone—a guy—was really listening to me."

Eleanora nodded—and though she hadn't given much thought to male/female relationships in the last few years, she recognized Lyse's need to be understood. It was a thing every human being craved and very few ever found.

Eleanora included.

She smiled at Lyse.

"I'm glad, Bear. You deserve the best. No matter what— you must always remember that."

Then Eleanora turned and walked down the hallway, leaving Lyse alone in the kitchen to bask in the warming glow of newfound love.

Lyse

Lyse was slipping a clean shirt on when she heard a voice calling to her.

"Hello? Anyone up?"

She poked her head out the bedroom door but didn't see anyone in the hallway.

"Yes, hello?" Lyse said. "I'm up. Who's there?"

She walked down the hall, peering through the doorway that led to Eleanora's room, and found Daniela sitting up in the bed, her bright pink head propped on a mound of pillows.

"Hi," Lyse said, uncertainly.

But in her head, she thought: *Why is Daniela in Eleanora's bed?*

"You have the funniest look on your face."

"I'm just . . ." Lyse stopped herself from adding the word *surprised.* "Well, it's been kind of a strange twenty-four hours."

"You're blushing," Daniela said.

"Oh, yeah, well, I don't know," Lyse said, looking away to hide her embarrassment.

Daniela raised an eyebrow.

"From the look on your face, I'd say it was a *very* interesting night." Daniela laughed. "Hey, is Eleanora awake? I thought I heard her moving around."

"She's up. I ran into her earlier puttering around the kitchen. I think she was getting stoned."

"Ha!" Daniela laughed again. "Sounds about right. She acts like she's only been doing it since the doc prescribed her that medical marijuana card, but I hear tell she and my mom used to be total hippies in the sixties."

"Wait, where did you hear that?"

"My mom. And, I mean, they lived here. In hippie-dippie Los Angeles. In this place." Daniela raised her arms to indicate the house. "My mother and Eleanora were blood sisters together in the Echo Park coven."

Lyse frowned.

"I had no idea."

"How could you?" Daniela replied. "Eleanora wouldn't have said anything. She hardly ever talks about the past."

"I can imagine why," Lyse said. "I think she had a pretty shitty one."

"But then she found the coven. And from what my mother said, the time they spent with Hessika in Echo Park were some of the best years of both of their lives."

"I wish she'd told me some of this stuff before," Lyse said.

"Well, do you believe it now?" Daniela asked. "Because if you don't believe any of this now, as an adult, do you really think you would've been open to it as a teenager?"

This was food for thought.

"I'm right, aren't I?" Daniela continued. "You're still not sure if any of this is real."

"I don't know what I believe," Lyse said, leaning against the doorjamb.

"I think you have to follow your heart," Daniela replied. "Do what feels right."

Lyse turned at the sound of the back door slamming shut.

"Hold on. I think I'm gonna go see if I can catch her."

Lyse took off, giving Daniela a wave as she jogged down the hallway.

But she found the kitchen empty save for Eleanora's water glass, which was drying in the sink.

Lyse opened the back door and looked outside.

"Eleanora?"

She stepped out onto the deck and called Eleanora's name again—with no response. She walked to the front of the house, but Eleanora wasn't there, either. Nor was she on the arched bridge, or the stairs leading to the street. Lyse followed the deck around to the far side of the house where Eleanora's garden was planted. The neat rows of beets, endive, carrots, artichokes, and cauliflower were bursting with color from yesterday's rain—but there was no sign of her great-aunt.

Lyse jogged down to the street, and even though it was late on a Saturday morning, she found no signs of human life, just empty asphalt and sidewalks wet with dew.

"Eleanora!?" she called, though she knew it was pointless. *"Eleanora!"*

After a few minutes of standing on the sidewalk, she gave up and went back inside. There was no reason to wait for someone who wasn't there.

"I'm heading over to Dev's," Daniela said when she came into the kitchen. "Join me? If you feel like going out, that is."

Lyse was sitting at the round oak table, in the middle of her second cup of coffee. She'd used the stovetop espresso maker, and the influx of caffeine had helped to shake off her exhaustion—at least temporarily.

"Yeah?" Lyse said, looking up from the magazine she was reading. An old copy of *Scientific American* that she'd foraged from Eleanora's bathroom. "You think Eleanora will be there?"

Daniela poured herself some espresso and took the seat across from Lyse.

"Maybe. Though after the rough night we had, I'm surprised she's not still sleeping," Daniela said, taking a sip from her mug, and making a face. "Needs cream."

She went over to the refrigerator and pulled out a carton of half-and-half.

"Rough night?"

"A little trouble at my house," Daniela said. "I don't want to talk about it right now."

"So, what's happening at Dev's house, then?" Lyse asked, deciding not to press Daniela on the other subject.

"Well, Dev's an amazing cook, and she and her partner, Freddy, do this brunch thing at their Echo Park Weekend Bar. The whole neighborhood is usually there. Free food," Daniela said, trying to get a peek at the cover of the magazine Lyse was reading. She held it up so Daniela could see. "*Scientific American*, eh?"

"Eleanora's 'light' bathroom reading," Lyse said. "Hey, no gloves today?"

"Yeah, that's part of the whole 'rough night' thing," Daniela said, looking at her bare hands. "I gotta make a pit stop at my place to get another pair."

"Cool," Lyse said, nodding.

"I can totally see it in your eyes—"

"My eyes?" Lyse said.

"You're *so* curious, and you can barely restrain yourself from asking—"

"Asking about what?"

Daniela waggled her fingers at Lyse.

"The story of the gloves," Daniela said, reaching for the creamer and pouring half the carton into her mug before taking a sip. "Much better."

"I'm a coffee addict, and I spend a lot of time in coffee shops," Lyse said, resting her elbows on the tabletop and staring at Daniela. "But I've never seen anyone use that much creamer. Ever."

Daniela laughed.

"Love the caffeine buzz, hate the actual coffee."

"So, why the gloves, then?" Lyse asked, taking the bait.

"More fun magic-related stuff," Daniela said. "Can you handle it?"

"Sure. Hit me."

"Well, I'm an empath," Daniela said. She waited for a response. "Okay, you don't have a problem with that. Good. Because what I do is a little bit like seeing into someone's soul."

She laughed as Lyse leaned back in her chair, putting space between them.

"Don't worry, I'm not an outright mind reader. I need to be touching you with my bare hands in order to see what you're thinking and feeling."

Lyse sat back up in her chair.

"Sorry."

"No worries, I totally get it," Daniela said. "It freaks me out and I'm the one who can do it."

"So the gloves protect people from you?" Lyse asked, and Daniela shook her head.

"Other way around, actually. My brain overloads when I use my gift, and I have a seizure—too many of them and my brain gets fried. Permanently."

"Holy shit," Lyse said, frowning.

"So I try to wear the gloves at all times."

"If I see someone wearing leather gloves on a hot summer day, that equals empath?" Lyse asked, but Daniela shook her head.

"Not always," Daniela said. "There aren't that many of us out there. And there are even fewer ones like me."

"And what makes you so special?" Lyse asked.

"I'm a little . . . unusual. Where most empaths might just *feel* another person's emotions and thoughts, I can change them."

Lyse stared at her.

"You're full of shit."

"I'm not," Daniela said. "I can touch you and you can see for yourself—"

"No, that's okay," Lyse said—not wanting to risk the slight chance that Daniela might actually be telling the truth.

"I don't change things in people's minds anymore," Daniela said.

"Anymore?" Lyse said, looking concerned. "Not sure that makes me feel any better."

"I promise that you're safe with me—"

"If any of this is even real," Lyse said, flipping the magazine over and staring at a random page. "Which I still doubt."

"Believe in it or not," Daniela said, cupping her coffee mug between her palms. "It almost doesn't matter."

"I think we should get out of here," Lyse said. "See if we can find Eleanora."

"Sure," Daniela agreed, getting up and setting her mug in the sink. "But pit stop at my house first."

"I just need to stop, grab some gloves, and feed the girls," Daniela said, crossing the street to her house. "Then we can go."

"The girls?" Lyse asked, slipping the shawl's hood over her head to keep the chilly morning air at bay.

"Verity and Veracity," Daniela said, opening the gate. "My cats."

As if on cue, two large black felines appeared out of nowhere, skulking onto the porch.

"They're gorgeous," Lyse said, unconsciously moving toward them. "Are they friendly?"

"They're whores," Daniela said, laughing. "And their fee is cat food and heavy petting."

The two cats made a beeline for Lyse as she knelt by the porch steps, their sleek bodies sharklike as they circled her for attention. She was surprised by their strangely human faces: elongated noses, pursed mouths, and oddly round eyes that seemed to see right into Lyse's soul. She found herself relaxing as she petted them, something about their mellow vibe rubbing off on her.

"They're so alike. How would you tell them apart if their tails weren't different?" Lyse asked, turning to Daniela.

"They're like night and day to me. I could never mix them up—tails or no tails," she said, shrugging. "Let me go in and get their food. I'm sure they're starving as usual."

She left Lyse with the cats and went into the house. As the door swung inward on its hinges, Lyse gasped.

"Oh my God," she said, immediately climbing to her feet. "What the hell happened?"

"This is the craziness from last night," Daniela said, hesitating just inside the doorway. "Someone took my place apart and was still here when I got home. If Eleanora hadn't intervened—"

"You're kidding," Lyse said, shocked.

"I only wish I were," Daniela replied as she picked her way through the mess, Lyse right behind her.

At least now Lyse knew why Daniela had slept at Eleanora's the night before. No one could get any rest in this chaos.

When they got to the kitchen, Daniela righted a step stool that was lying on its side and climbed up so she could reach the top of the refrigerator.

"Do you mind keeping a lookout?" she said. "This is where the asshole attacked me last night and I feel kinda weird about turning my back to the door."

"Of course," Lyse said, hands on hips as she kept watch. "How much of this mess was caused by the guy trashing your place versus him trashing you?"

Daniela plucked her turquoise gloves off the top of the fridge and slipped them over her hands.

"Don't think he got off scot-free. I gave as good as I got," Daniela said, retrieving a large plastic tub of cat food from the cabinet and handing it down to Lyse. "And here's the most important stuff."

Daniela jumped down from the step stool.

"Hmm." She looked at the tub of cat food. "What did Arrabelle and Eleanora feed them last night? This hasn't been touched."

"Maybe these?" Lyse said, and pointed to two empty cans of smoked oysters lying in the sink.

"They did *not*," Daniela said, exasperated.

"Oh, yes, they did," Lyse said, looking down at the uneaten bowl of oysters on the floor. She kicked it with the toe of her sneaker. "And I don't think the cats liked them very much."

"You guys must be starving," Daniela said, uncapping the tub of cat food for the two felines twining around her ankles. She set their bowls—filled to the brim now—on the messy floor, and Lyse watched the cats attack, devouring the food.

"You'd think they hadn't eaten in weeks," Daniela said, shaking her head. "Let's get out of here."

Lyse followed Daniela through the house and out onto the front porch. Daniela took the steps at a jog, pushing through the gate and hitting the sidewalk in two seconds flat. Not knowing Devandra's address, Lyse was forced to follow at Daniela's pace.

"It's not too far," Daniela said.

"You're in better shape than me," Lyse said, breathing hard and trying to ignore the ache in her calf. "And you just got beaten up."

"I made a decision a long time ago not to let anything slow me down. So, I just don't."

Lyse couldn't argue with that.

They walked in companionable silence, Daniela slowing down once she noticed Lyse's limp.

"You should've said your leg was hurting."

Lyse shrugged.

"It's your funeral," Daniela said, but continued to maintain the slower pace. "I'm like a hummingbird. I never stop moving."

"I'll try to remember that for the future," Lyse said, but secretly she was pleased they were now taking a more leisurely stroll. This way she could once again marvel at how little the old neighborhood had changed since she'd lived there.

As they walked, the sun came out from behind the clouds and started to burn off the morning smog, lifting Lyse's spirits. Bright sheets of light, cut into impressionistic shapes by the canopy of trees above their heads, melted down around them, and Lyse felt like she was walking in a glorious daydream. The change in mood seemed to wake the neighborhood from its Saturday morning slumber, and people began to appear on the street: joggers, bicyclists, new parents pushing strollers, families trundling along with small children in hand.

The sense of community experienced by so many people from so many different ethnic, religious, and socioeconomic backgrounds was one of the things Lyse loved best about the neighborhood. Echo Park's disparate inhabitants lived together in a multicultural microcosm—dressing, eating, and communicating in their own styles—with only minor discord.

Lyse was happy to note that the Eastside of Los Angeles was still keeping it real.

"So, I've been thinking about something," Lyse said, giving Daniela a sideways glance. "And I don't know if it has any bearing on anything, but apparently somebody broke into my place in Athens yesterday after I left."

"You're kidding," Daniela said.

"I talked to my friend Carole. Nothing big was taken, just my computer."

Daniela stopped in her tracks.

"Shit. That's not good. I bet more stuff's missing, stuff your friend doesn't know to look for."

"Like what?" Lyse asked, not sure what kind of stuff Daniela was talking about.

"Birth certificate, social security card . . . info like that."

"But why?"

"To verify who you really are," Daniela said—and then she realized she might've overstepped her bounds, and she backed off the topic. "Look, just . . . talk to Eleanora about this. I'm making educated guesses and I don't know what I'm talking about."

"No, tell me what you mean," Lyse said, reaching for Daniela's arm—but the other woman quickly moved away from her grasp.

"Unh-unh," Daniela said. "Now is not the time to touch me. Shit's been weird lately and I don't want anyone touching me, period."

"Fine," Lyse said, and headed off down the street, annoyed by the whole situation. It only took her a second to realize she had no idea where she was going, and, chagrined, she was forced to retrace her steps back to Daniela.

"Okay," Lyse said, throwing up her hands in surrender. "You win. Suppose, for the sake of argument, someone wanted info about me and that's why they broke into my place— what's the deal with you? Does someone want to verify who you are, too? What's the connection?"

Daniela scratched the tip of her nose with a gloved finger, thinking.

"The obvious answer is someone is looking for something—and maybe it's more than *one* thing. Like they want personal info on you. And they think I'm hiding something important, and they want it."

"Are you?"

"Hiding something important?" Daniela asked. "Maybe." She grinned at Lyse.

"But if I were, I wouldn't tell you . . . or anyone else."

"And who is this mysterious 'they' you keep mentioning?" Lyse asked.

"That," Daniela said, holding up her hand to block the sunlight streaming in through the trees, "I don't know yet."

"And do you have any ideas that don't sound like conspiracy theories?" Lyse asked.

She was surprised by Daniela's ready answer.

"Oh, that's an easy one," she said, continuing down the sidewalk. "Someone's just trying to scare the shit out of both of us."

There was only one word for Dev's house, and that word was *gorgeous*.

A lovingly maintained Victorian with intricate, cream-colored woodwork that resembled the delicate lace of a wedding gown, it boasted a wraparound porch studded by white wicker patio furniture and a glorious front garden full of Queen Anne's lace, daisies, red and orange poppies, and blue cornflowers.

"I keep expecting Snow White to come out and greet us," Lyse said, shaking her head in wonder.

"It's just as unbelievable on the inside," Daniela said as they walked up the driveway, passing through a wide-open gate leading into a large, grassy backyard whose centerpiece was a rusted iron table encircled by wrought-iron chairs.

Weeds grew thick and luxuriant around the table, giving

the yard a wild, overgrown quality that made Lyse feel like she'd been transported into a magical fairyland. Adding to the overall effect was a Medusa-headed brass chandelier—almost the circumference of the table—hanging from the bough of a large silk floss tree that shaded the yard, each of its snakelike arms holding a tiny tea light underneath a delicate glass globe.

Lyse could imagine the backyard at night, the lit chandelier giving off an eerie, ghostly glow.

"The place has been in Dev's family for over a hundred years," Daniela added, leading Lyse around the table and chandelier and toward a small garage/studio in the back that already had people milling around its door. A mix of both men and women, mostly in their twenties and thirties; they were loud and fraternal, red plastic cups filled with alcohol driving the chaotic, partylike atmosphere.

"What's going on?" Lyse asked. "I thought you said we were going to brunch."

"It *is* brunch—but for the whole neighborhood. Dev and Freddy call it the Echo Park Weekend Bar," Daniela said, "and we made it just in time for mimosas."

As if Daniela's words had summoned them into being, Dev and a short guy with a hipster mustache and wavy black hair came out the back door of the main house, carrying aluminum trays loaded down with homemade French toast. The already assembled group of neighbors fell into an impromptu second line, following the duo across the yard to where a long, rectangular folding table was already set up against the garage, its top loaded down with plates, napkins, and cutlery.

"This is amazing," Lyse said, as she and Daniela were caught up in the food procession.

When they finally reached the table, they found Dev putting a pair of metal tongs into each of the aluminum trays. She saw them and her eyes lit up.

"Hey, you guys!" she said, sounding tickled to see them. "Wanna come in and help with the syrup and fruit?"

"Sure," Daniela said, and Lyse nodded.

The two of them followed Dev up the back stairs into the mudroom.

"This is incredible," Lyse said.

"We've been doing this for a while and it just seems to grow and grow!"

They hit the kitchen, and Lyse realized Daniela was right. The place was just as incredible on the inside as it was on the outside. With its delicate wood floors, vintage O'Keefe and Merritt stove, and ceiling rack loaded down with copper pots, pans, and other cookware, the house was an architectural magazine spread come to life.

"Here, take this," Dev said, handing Lyse a large metal container with the words *Real Maple Syrup* stenciled across its front.

"I love your house," Lyse said, watching as Dev placed handfuls of plump strawberries into a large ceramic bowl.

"I grew up here," Dev replied, and added raspberries to the already-overflowing bowl before foisting it into Daniela's hands. "It's been in my family for ages."

"That's what Daniela was telling me," Lyse said, keeping the container of syrup at arm's length, so Eleanora's shawl wouldn't get sticky.

"Want me to take anything else?" Daniela asked, her arms now full of berries.

"No, I think this'll do it," Dev said, surveying her handiwork. "Time to finish feeding the masses."

She picked up a shaker full of powdered sugar and indicated that they should accompany her back outside. Lyse followed Daniela, keeping her friend's back in view as they weaved through the crowd. Everyone seemed to sense that more food was arriving and parted so the women could place their offerings on the table.

She felt a tap on her shoulder and turned to find the short guy with the hipster mustache—she had about an inch or two on him—standing behind her, holding out his hand. Up close, she saw how wickedly handsome he was. Smooth tan skin, soulful dark brown eyes, and expressive eyebrows that moved up and down when he talked.

"You must be Lyse," he said, watching her wipe the syrup from her hands onto the front of her jeans. "I'm Freddy Cardoza, Dev's partner."

Lyse grinned and shook his hand. "I'm sorry. I'm covered in syrup!"

"Don't worry about it," he said, smiling back at her and holding her hand for a beat too long. "I like my ladies sticky-sweet."

Okay, the man has more than just looks, Lyse thought. *He has charisma, too.*

He pulled her to him and gave her a kiss on both cheeks.

"Oh," Lyse said, surprised by the kisses but deciding to go with it.

"You smell delicious," he whispered in her ear before releasing her.

"Thank you . . . ?" she said, not sure how to reply to the flirtatious compliment. "I love your place. I'm really jealous of you guys."

"Oh, please, you and Auntie E have the house my daughters adore," he laughed, shaking his head.

"It's the koi pond," Lyse said. "Sucks the kids in every time."

"Well, it's really nice having you in the neighborhood," he said, patting her shoulder. "Can I get you a mimosa?"

"Sure, I'd love one."

"I'll be right back," he said, and winked at her, tipping his porkpie hat.

She watched him go, wondering how Dev handled being with a man who was such a flirt. If Freddy had belonged to her, his behavior would've driven her mad with jealousy.

While she waited for him to return with the drink, she looked around the crush of bodies, amazed so many people could fit into one backyard. Everywhere she saw men and women talking over one another, passing food around, laughing. She didn't feel like joining in, and besides, she didn't really know anyone *to* talk to, so she just smiled and listened to the conversations swirling around her.

"I was thinking of reviving an old tradition, throw a little salon like the ones the illustrious Zeke Title used to have in the 1920s," Daniela was saying to some man Lyse didn't know. "Seems like it would be lots of fun—Dev has to cater it, of course, and we can set up a little photo studio in the back. And I was thinking Aleister Crowley's birthday would be the perfect kickoff for the first one. He'd have adored something like that in his honor."

Daniela caught Lyse listening and gave her a wink before returning to her conversation.

"Lyse?"

She turned at the sound of her name.

"Hey! Is Eleanora with you—" she started to ask.

But the question died on her lips when she saw Arrabelle's face.

Eleanora

Eleanora had always spent more time in the clearing than any of the others. She felt connected to it in a way that transcended its ties to the coven, as if there were something here in this sacred grove that called out to her secret soul. It was why she'd come this morning, to ground herself after a long and exhausting night.

The wind whipped at her hair, making her shiver, and Eleanora pulled the thick black jacket even tighter around her middle. She'd grabbed one of her heavier coats from the hall closet when she'd gone out, and she was glad of it as she stood in the open air with the cold biting into her skin, yanking at her coat as if it could tear the thing from her body.

She had no fight left in her to push back against Mother Nature. Her exhaustion made her feel old and used up, and it was in these raw moments that she longed to flee responsibility. To crawl under her house, make a little nest in the dirt, and curl up and die like one of Dev's old, toothless tomcats.

She was tired, and she wanted someone else to take the reins.

She wanted Lyse.

We trust only our own flesh and blood to look after the last Dream Keeper, Eleanora thought, as the wind danced through the eucalyptus leaves, ruffling her hair.

When so many pretend there is no threat, our children and children's children are left to fight the battle for us all.

She and Marie-Faith had both called on the efforts of the ones they loved best.

"Keep them safe," she said out loud, the trees her only witness. "If I could sacrifice myself twice for them and for Lizbeth, you know I would."

Eleanora didn't hear the man approach. To her credit, though, he was silent as death as he wound his way through the underbrush. He moved with the calculated grace of someone who planned everything, leaving nothing to chance, and so he was only a few feet away from her, but outside the circle of protection, when some sixth sense told her she was not alone.

Before she could turn around, the voice was in her head. It was tarnished now by time and age, but the sound of it, the familiar New England cadence, transported her back more than forty years into the past . . .

". . . Eleanora?"

She would not turn around. There were enough people in the train station; she could make a run for it and lose herself in the crowd if she needed to.

"Eleanora, please," Mitchell called out to her, and the pleading quality of his voice broke her resolve.

The cacophonous stampede of travelers moving through South Station gave her a false sense of safety, drowning out her reservations, and she stopped in the middle of the crowded room and waited for him to catch up.

"Eleanora," he said as he closed the distance between them, gently grasping her upper arm and turning her to face him.

He was thinner than she remembered, his face drawn with worry.

"Can we talk? Please . . . ?"

He was already guiding her away from the masses, pulling her toward a quiet corner.

"How did you find me?" she asked.

"They wouldn't let me into the hospital to see you, so I've been watching your grandmother's place. I was hoping you'd come by."

Even though he's been outside that house for days, *Eleanora realized*, he has no idea Mimi is laid out on the bed, waiting for someone to discover her body.

It was a gruesome thought.

"—I tried to stop them." Mitchell was still talking. "You have to believe me. I wouldn't have let them hurt you—"

He was holding on to her arm, grasping at her skin with frantic fingers—but he dropped his hand, flexing his fingers nervously when he realized it was making her uncomfortable. She set her traveling case on the shiny tile floor—its contents the last remnants of her former life—and reached for her arm, rubbing the place he'd just touched. The skin felt hot beneath her fingertips and she shuddered, terrified that he would guess what she was carrying inside her belly just by touching her.

"I have no ill will toward you, Mitchell," she heard herself saying in a calm voice. "I believe you didn't want to hurt me."

He was nodding in agreement.

"Yes, truly. I would never hurt you."

He reached for her hand, and she had to stop herself from yanking it away. She squirmed inside as he brought her fingers to his lips, kissing the delicate skin of her knuckles.

"I have to go," she said; the feverish way he was looking at her, holding on to her, made her want to bolt.

She didn't know how she'd ever thought he was attractive. There was something wild and desperate in his eyes, and it repulsed her.

"I don't want you to go," he said, using his grip on her hand to pull her even closer to him. "When we made love—"

She didn't want to hear it, hated that he'd ever touched her. Just the thought made her nauseated.

"Don't. Not here, please."

He stopped, swallowing back a torrent of words.

"You belong to me now, Eleanora," he said. "You lay down with me, and, in God's eyes, I believe we're joined forever."

She wanted to scream, to claw at his eyes and drive him away. She knew the road he envisioned for her, had lived there the whole of her life, been subjugated to another's will and religion and cruelty—and she was determined that this son of a bitch would not do the same thing to her.

"I don't give a damn what you want," she said, the rage she felt driving her words. "You don't own me, no matter how many times you lie with me."

He was aghast, shocked by her tone of voice and choice of words.

"I don't understand," he said. "I told you that I love you. What else do you want?"

For a moment, she was rendered mute by the question—but suddenly the answer was on her lips, fighting with a raw viciousness to rip its way out of her.

"I want to be left alone," she said. "I want you small-minded, narrow-thinking people to leave me be. I don't belong to you, just like I didn't belong to my grandmother. I want the freedom to do what I like, the way I like, and I don't want to ever be judged again. Not by you. Not by anyone."

The words came out in a rush, uncensored, and, even if she'd had a thousand years to fashion them, she would not have changed a single one. The truth spoke louder than anything she could ever contrive.

Mitchell took his hat off, running the brim through his fingers—something she remembered him doing the very first time she met him.

"I don't want to do any of that to you, Eleanora," he said, looking down at his hands. "I just want to marry you."

To her shock, he dug into the pocket of his suit coat and produced a small white plastic ring box. Holding it in the palm of his hand, he sank onto one knee and smiled up at her. She thought he resembled a hungry wolf, all sharp teeth and desperate eyes.

"*Eleanora Eames,*" *he said, his shaking fingers flipping open the top of the ring box,* "*will you do me the honor of taking my hand in marriage?*"

Eleanora looked around the waiting area and realized they were attracting attention. Two middle-aged women who were seated together on one of the nearby benches were watching them like hawks. An older couple, cheap suitcases at their feet, whispered together, throwing the occasional glance in their direction.

She decided she hated Mitchell even more for turning this into a public spectacle.

"*No,*" *she whispered, shaking her head, not even looking at the ring.* "*I won't do this with you. Not here.*"

She grabbed his arm, trying to lift him to his feet, but he was so much heavier than her and wouldn't budge.

"*Well, where then?*" *he asked, misinterpreting her words.*

"*Not where. Not when,*" *Eleanora said, finally losing her temper.* "*I am not going to do this with you* anywhere!"

She was getting too loud. Rage that someone like Mitchell could just waltz into her new life and try to destroy it before it'd even begun filled every molecule of her being.

"*Please, Eleanora, be reasonable—*" *he was saying, but she ignored him.*

"*You're the unreasonable one! Watching my house, then waylaying me at the train station—*"

They were getting more looks now, strangers' eyes riveted to the drama playing out in front of them.

"*I don't understand,*" *Mitchell said, brow furrowing.* "*What do you want me to do?*"

She rolled her eyes heavenward, hoping for some divine intervention, though she knew none would be forthcoming.

"*I want you to go away,*" *she cried in frustration.* "*I want you to go away and leave me alone. Forever.*"

He closed the ring box with a snap, eyes on something just over her right shoulder. She turned and saw a policeman heading their way—someone must've alerted him when they'd started yelling.

Mitchell's eyes flashed like a cornered animal's, and he scrambled to his feet.

"This isn't the last you'll see of me," he growled, spittle flying from his lips.

And then he was gone.

She was trembling when the policeman arrived at her side, his bulky presence the most reassuring thing she'd seen in days.

"Ma'am, are you all right?" he asked, concern weighing down his doughy features.

She nodded and picked up her traveling case.

"Yes, sir," she said, forcing a smile onto her lips. "Just a boy from my hometown who has trouble with the word no.*"*

The policeman nodded.

"Well, if there's any further trouble, just come look for me," he said, patting her arm.

She watched him go, feeling unsettled and very much alone as she looked around the waiting area and . . .

. . . she was in the middle of the clearing again, shivering. She wondered how long she'd been gone.

Long enough for him to sneak up on me, she realized. He was so close she could almost taste him.

"I hear you're dying," he said, his words a whisper inside the coil of her ear—even though he could not cross the magical barrier at the tree line.

"I don't know what you're talking about," she said, and an anger she hadn't felt in years circulated through her veins like poison.

She turned her head to find he was not just close to her; he was beside her.

"How are you inside . . . No, you, you can't be—" she stuttered, but he only smiled.

"Your magic only works on someone who wishes you ill, and I love you," he said. His right hand clutched a walking stick as he leaned toward her, its silvery tip forged into the shape of a lion's head. "I've always loved you, Eleanora."

His voice was not the only thing that was the same about him. His eyes still glinted at her with the same feral intensity—only this time they were not filled with desperate hunger but the cold blue flame of power.

She took a few steps back, moving herself out of his orbit. *Why, after over forty years, is he here?* she wondered. She had neither seen nor heard from him in all these intervening years—what did he hope to accomplish by confronting her now?

"What do you want?" she asked. "I don't believe for a second you just happened upon me out here."

Too many cigarettes had turned his laugh into a rasp.

"Of course not," he said, laughter turning into a hacking cough. "I'm here, really . . . at the behest of someone else."

She didn't have a clue what he was talking about.

"Aren't you at all curious who I've brought to see you?" he asked, goading her.

She didn't care one iota who or what he'd brought with him—and she said as much.

"I don't give a pig's fart what you're doing here, Mitchell," she said, and turned to go—but he caught her arm, refusing to let her leave.

He was strong for an old man, and this surprised Eleanora. But she had a few tricks up her sleeve, too, and wasn't afraid to use them.

"Let me go," she said, calmly.

He grinned at her, squeezing the delicate flesh of her upper arm in almost an exact repetition of what he'd done at the train station all those years before.

"Let me go," she said, glaring at him. "If you don't let me go—"

"You'll do what?" he purred into her ear. "Call the police?"

He cackled, enjoying his little joke—but she'd had enough.

"I warned you," she said, and smashed the heel of her shoe into his foot, digging into his suede loafer.

He yowled, releasing his hold on her just long enough for her to get away, and she didn't waste the opportunity. She took off, an old woman pursued by a past that had become real once more.

She hadn't physically exerted herself like this in months, and at first it was exhilarating, but after a few minutes of scrambling through the underbrush, she was exhausted. She hadn't slept well, hadn't taken care of herself . . . hadn't relaxed once since Lyse's arrival, and now she was paying for it.

She gulped air as she ran, a stitch lacing through her right side, making it hard to keep going. She slowed down to a fast walk, listening for sounds that told her she was being pursued, but all she could hear was the rush of her own breath and the drone of an airplane passing overhead.

Her heart was beating too quickly. She could feel it in her chest, her throat, and at the pulse points on both wrists.

Slow down, she thought. *Take a breath. It's just an old man with obsessive love in his heart. He can't hurt you. Not if you don't let him.*

She reduced her speed, taking her time as she navigated through the trees until one of the hiking trails appeared ahead of her. There was no one on the path, no hikers or joggers to blend into, but she didn't care. She moved more quickly, sensing she wasn't far from one of the main roads that crisscrossed the park.

She hit the hiking trail and started jogging, a sense of urgency driving her forward. The path took her over a small hill and then, as it leveled out, she saw the exit to the park just a straight shot ahead of her. Breathing hard, she almost laughed with joy as she reached the end of the trail and saw a suburban street full of parked cars.

Thank God, she thought as she stepped onto the asphalt,

wiping away the sweat from her face with the back of her hand.

She didn't think she could make it to her house. Her heartbeat was erratic, and she was incapable of drawing a full breath. She leaned forward, resting her hands on her thighs, trying not to pass out. Little black dots swam in front of her eyes, and nausea took hold of her belly. She'd overdone it. She'd passed the point of no return, and her body was telling her that this was it.

Hessika's gift had been depleted.

Not yet, she pleaded. *It's not time yet.*

She wrestled with inertia, forcing her body to drag itself into a standing position—to take one step after another toward the row of parked cars. If she could find someone inside one of them, get the person to call an ambulance, then maybe everything would be all right.

Just ahead of her, a man opened the driver's-side door of his Lincoln Town Car and climbed out. He was tall and well dressed and had a silver buzz cut. Happily, she saw that he was moving in her direction, arms outstretched as he ran toward her—which didn't make any sense until she realized he was trying to catch her before she collapsed onto the asphalt road.

"Eleanora," the man said, managing to reach her before she hit the ground.

She raised her eyes to his face and tried to lift her hand, to touch the man's cheek in gratitude, but her body would not do what she wanted.

She stared at him. He looked so familiar, as though he were someone she'd known all her life—but his name would not come to her.

Who are you? she said, the words forming in her brain but never making it past her lips. *How do I know you?*

The man eased her to the ground, cradling Eleanora's head to his chest, as the life began to ebb from her body. He lovingly stroked her hair, his long fingers tracing the curve of her cheek, coming back wet from the tears trickling down the sides of her face.

Tears she could not feel or control.

Who are you? she wondered, searching his face for the answer—pale green eyes, pink lips, a webbing of lines around his mouth.

He leaned down and kissed her on the forehead. It was a simple gesture, sweet and heartbreakingly sad, a *hello* and a *good-bye.* He looked up, scanning the area for help, she assumed—but then she noticed the gloves he was wearing, and with a dawning sense of horror, she understood what was about to happen.

No, she thought as he placed his gloved hand over her nose and mouth. *No, not like this.*

She was already dying—would be dead soon, even, without his help. But he kept his hand in place and stared into her eyes, watching her struggle ever so slightly to draw breath.

"Godspeed, Mother," he said.

Of course, she thought.

She wanted to say something, anything, to this man— this murderer—whom she'd borne and given away. She wanted to tell him she'd always watched over him, always kept him close—even if he had not known it—until he'd disappeared without a trace as a teenager, and even then she'd looked for him . . . but she could not speak, could not tell him any of this.

Instead, she obliged his last wish.

Her heart pulsed one final time, then forever ceased its beat.

Lyse

The concrete and glass waiting room of the hospital; the ebb and flow of people going in and out its front doors. All went unobserved because Lyse had no awareness of her surroundings: not the sharp edge of the metal bench cutting into the backs of her thighs, or the deep gouge she'd made in the nail bed of her right thumb, or the bloody sting where she'd bitten the skin of her bottom lip ragged.

She didn't notice any of this, felt none of the physical wounds because the emotional ones were so great. They took up too much space, were all-consuming, and left no room for anything else.

No, that wasn't quite true. There was the numbness . . . the only thing that made it possible to keep breathing. It sat on her chest like a heavy blanket, smothering the fiery cascade of emotions—anger, grief, and anguish—beating at her door. The numbness rooted her in place and would not allow her to answer their pounding calls to be let in.

When she looked back over this time in her life, it would be hard to process it as anything other than a dream.

If she hadn't been hit with the reality of a memorial and an empty house, she would've chalked the whole experience up to a terrible nightmare and left it at that. There was a surreal quality to it, as though it'd occurred underwater, the fabric of the memory a rippling, blue blur.

"Lyse?"

She turned her head toward the sound. She knew she was being spoken to, but she couldn't think what the words might mean.

"It's time to go."

Then a hand was grasping her under the armpit and helping her to stand. Her legs were rubbery, but they managed to hold her up. The hand slid around her rib cage, letting her lean her weight against its owner.

"Do you want another tissue?"

She shook her head. At some point, someone had given her a Kleenex, and she clutched at this flimsy piece of tissue as though her life depended on it, gripping it in her fist until it had become a sodden, sweaty mess.

"That one's done—"

But like a small child, Lyse snatched her fist away, keeping the tissue safely out of reach.

"It's okay. You just hold on to it, if you want."

They began to walk, and it felt strange to move without thought, without looking where you were going. To give over so completely to another human being that they could walk you off a cliff, and you'd be helpless to do anything about it.

"The car's right outside. Do you think you can make it?"

She felt herself nodding, the weight of her head dragging her chin down almost to her chest, and then back up.

"Good."

Despite all the windows, it had been dark inside the hospital. But now, as they passed through the sliding glass doors, sunlight cold-cocked her in the face, so bright she had to close her eyes against it or go blind. For the first time, she felt the wetness on her cheeks, the cold air chilling the tears and stealing the heat from her skin. With her balled fist, she reached up and wiped at her nose, disgorging bits of tissue that stuck to her skin like snowflakes.

"It's right here."

She was led to the car. The passenger door was opened for her, and she was placed inside. There were dirty spots on the windshield. Oddly shaped white mineral deposits left behind where rainwater had evaporated.

She wanted the windows washed clean, wanted all the dirty spots gone—*I don't know what I want,* she cried. But she did, she did know what she wanted. She wanted things the way they were before. She wanted to curl up in a ball and disappear.

She heard the key slide into the ignition, felt the thrum of the engine coming to life, the idle shaking in her seat. She let her head fall to the side, and the plastic casing that covered the strap of the seat belt pressed into her temple. Then, as the car backed up and began to pull away from the hospital, the numbness cracked in two, and Lyse began to sob.

Arrabelle reached over and rested her hand on Lyse's shoulder.

"This too shall pass. I promise, Mama."

Yes, that is a truth, Lyse thought, but it did nothing to ease her broken heart.

The memorial was a simple affair, but there were so many people, well-wishers from far-flung places like Tibet, New Zealand, and Ukraine—places she didn't know Eleanora had ever visited.

Who was Eleanora Eames really?

The question haunted Lyse.

"Why don't you go inside, speak to some of these people?"

Dev said, as Lyse sat in an old Adirondack chair on the deck, staring out at the koi pond. "They've all come from so far away."

Like Lyse, she was dressed in black, her strawberry-blond hair pulled into a tight bun at the nape of her neck. She was paler and more subdued, a testament to how rough Eleanora's death had been on all of them.

"I don't think so," Lyse said, giving Dev a wry smile. "I don't think I have what it takes to make small talk with a bunch of people I don't know. I really just want to be alone. Thanks."

She was alone by choice. Carole had offered to come out for the memorial, but Lyse had politely declined. She knew that as a single mom and co–business owner, Carole was always strapped for cash. She had no intention of letting her friend waste what little she had on a ticket to California. Besides, she didn't need anyone to sit there and hold her hand.

"Well, is it all right if the girls come out?" Dev asked. "They wanted to say hi to the fish."

"Sure," Lyse said. "Of course."

Dev came over and patted her on the back.

"I know you don't want to hear this," Dev said, "but I think it was for the best. She'd already suffered so much."

No, I don't want to hear that, Lyse thought, but she held her tongue.

"Okay," Dev continued, "if you're sure you don't mind?"

"I really don't."

Dev motioned toward the sliding glass doors, and two dark-haired urchins scampered out onto the deck.

"This is Marji," Dev said, as the older girl came over and stood in front of her mother. "She's eleven, and she's my shy one. The other weasel, the one invading your personal space right now . . . that's Ginny."

Ginny was, indeed, standing almost on top of Lyse, staring down at her with a look of intense curiosity.

"I'm seven," she said proudly, pointing to her own chest. "And you're pretty like Daddy said."

Lyse shot Dev a surprised look.

"Yes, of course, she's pretty," Dev said to Ginny, ruffling her daughter's hair. "Now, girls, please be respectful of Lyse. She's had a hard few days, and you not asking her too many questions would be appreciated."

She gave Marji's shoulders a squeeze, then left the three of them alone on the deck.

"Great-Auntie E died," Ginny said to Lyse.

Lyse nodded.

"Yeah, I know she did."

"Will she ever go to heaven?" Ginny asked.

"I don't know," Lyse replied. "Maybe."

Marji moved closer to Lyse and Ginny, sitting down on the edge of the deck, not far from Lyse's feet.

"Great-Auntie E's not dead," Marji said quietly, joining their conversation. "Well, part of her is . . . but not her spirit."

It was strange to be having such an esoteric conversation with a couple of elementary school kids, but Lyse found she was enjoying the girls' company.

"What makes you say that?" Lyse asked, curious.

"I talked to her about it and that's what she said."

The hair on the back of Lyse's neck prickled to life, and she sat up in her chair.

"What did you say?"

Marji looked up at her with liquid brown eyes—and Lyse realized the kid had no idea how incredibly spooky she was being right then.

"Marji talked to Great-Auntie E," Ginny said. "I heard her."

"She talks to me at night," Marji said. "She likes to whisper."

Ginny nodded in agreement.

Lyse wasn't sure what she was supposed to say to this. Obviously, the girls were sad and had imagined Eleanora visiting them in order to feel better about her death. She didn't want to be nasty, but she also didn't think it was a good idea to let them think things that weren't actually true.

"*I* believe that *you* believe Great-Auntie E comes to talk to you," Lyse began, trying to be judicious.

"She said you'd say that," Marji said, kicking her feet back and forth over the edge of the deck.

"Great-Auntie E said I'd say that?"

Marji stopped kicking and fixed Lyse with a long stare.

"She said you were in denial. That if you didn't believe me, then you should go look at the Bible."

"The Bible?" Lyse asked, trying not to sound too incredulous.

"Ginny will show you," Marji said, and went back to swinging her feet.

Ginny reached over and took Lyse's hand, smiling up at her—a big gap where her right eyetooth should've been.

"Wanna see?" she asked Lyse.

"Sure," Lyse said, uncertainly. Then: "Why not?"

She climbed to her feet and followed Ginny back into the house. She found she was curious to see what kind of mischief the girls had worked out between them.

They stepped into the loud, bustling living room, and Lyse closed the sliding glass door behind them. There were people everywhere, and a few of them stopped what they were doing to follow Lyse's movements.

"It's over here," Ginny said, still holding her hand as she led Lyse across the room. "In here."

The little girl knelt in front of a tall brown bookcase and pointed to a book wedged in between a copy of the *Larousse Encyclopedia of Mythology* and some World Books. Lyse sat down on the floor next to her, staring at the mysterious leather-bound thing . . . until something else caught her eye.

It was an old Kodachrome snapshot set inside a simple silver frame. She realized it'd probably been there, sitting on the shelf with a bunch of other photos, the whole time she'd lived with Eleanora. She didn't know why she'd never noticed it before, but now she was transfixed by its contents.

It was a candid of Eleanora taken when she was in her late twenties, surrounded by four other women, all but one much older than her. Her great-aunt was easily recognizable among the others, all dewy youth and excited smile, but that wasn't what caught Lyse's attention. The woman in the far left of the photo drew her eye. She was so tall she had to hunch down in order to fit into the shot with the others.

It's the giant woman from my dream, Lyse thought. *She's real. I didn't just imagine her.*

"That lady is tall," Ginny said, following Lyse's gaze.

"Yes, she is," Lyse agreed, her eyes finally leaving the photo and returning to the leather book Ginny had originally brought her to see.

"Marji says you need to read it," Ginny urged. "You should open it."

Lyse did as the little girl said, sliding the book out of the bookshelf. She turned it over, running her fingers along the gold leaf title stamped into the dark leather.

"You weren't kidding," Lyse said. "It really is a Bible."

Ginny cocked her head, making a funny face at Lyse.

"Of course it is, silly," she said, and grinned.

Lyse looked at the book in her lap and, not sure what to expect, opened it, flipping to a random page in the middle.

"It just looks like a regular old Bible to me," Lyse said, closing it up.

Ginny gave Lyse an exasperated look that said, *You're kind of slow, aren't you?*

"Marji said to look inside the cover."

"Well, you should've just said that."

Lyse opened the book again, this time flipping to the inside front cover.

"Oh," she said, shocked that there was actually something to see: a series of handwritten names and dates.

The first two entries were in a looping cursive she didn't recognize:

May Louella Eames—b. June 30th, 1922
Eleanora Davenport Eames—b. January 9th, 1944

The next three entries were in Eleanora's strong, block printing:

My Twins:
Sonya May Eames—b. October 12th, 1967
&
David Davenport Eames—b. October 12th, 1967
Lyse Eames MacAllister—b. August 8th, 1988

Lyse stared at the page in disbelief.

"Everything all right?"

It was Arrabelle, her black skirts swirling like raven's wings as she came up behind them.

"Fine," Lyse said, snapping the Bible shut.

Arrabelle had no compunction about wading in where she wasn't wanted. She hunkered down on the floor beside Lyse.

"Ginny, go outside with your sister."

Lyse was amused by the little girl's reaction. Ginny gave an exaggerated nod of her head and took off like a shot. Obviously, Lyse wasn't the only one Arrabelle intimidated.

"What've you found?" Arrabelle asked, now that they were alone.

"Nothing," Lyse said, holding the book protectively in her lap.

Arrabelle and Dev had both been great, arranging everything—and she meant *everything*—for the memorial, and Lyse would always be grateful to them. But right now she just didn't want to share this new information with anyone.

She wanted to hold it close. To treat it like something shiny and new that needed her protection.

"Okay, I won't press you," Arrabelle said. "But if you want to talk, my door is always open."

After what seemed like an eternity, Arrabelle crawled to her feet and gave Lyse's shoulder a quick squeeze before she disappeared into the crowd. When she was gone, Lyse stuffed the Bible back into the bookcase.

She needed to get the hell out of there.

Lyse had arrived in Los Angeles during the coldest days of October—but after Eleanora's death, the cold spell broke and a fierce Indian summer sent daytime temperatures soaring into the eighties. She hardly noticed the heat as she ran, feet pounding across the wooden bridge and down the stairs that led to the road.

She didn't know where she was going or what she was doing, but three little words echoed in her brain: *Sonya May Eames.*

Sonya May Eames was Lyse's mother—*My Twins*, Eleanora had written—which meant Eleanora was not Lyse's distant relative; she was Lyse's *grandmother.*

"Hey, where are you headed in such a hurry? I only just got here."

The voice was teasing.

"Huh?" she replied, her mind blank as she looked up and saw Weir standing in the street beside his car, staring at her. He looked incredible in his black suit and skinny tie, dark blond hair pleasantly mussed. There were dark circles under his eyes, but Lyse knew hers were worse.

"Are you okay?" he asked, crossing to her. His long

fingers brushed her bangs out of her eyes. "You look awful. What's wrong?"

"I don't. I—" she said, not making sense even to herself. "A walk. I—I had to get out of there."

There was no judgment in his eyes. He seemed to understand her need to flee.

"How about some company?" he asked, taking her hand and slipping it inside his own.

She didn't know if she wanted company. There was so much information to think over, so many thoughts she wanted to take out and look at without anyone keeping tabs, or looking over her shoulder, or inserting themselves into the process. She almost said as much to Weir, but then something about his tranquil gaze disarmed her.

She wasn't sure what had changed, or why she felt so different—and then it hit her: All of her frantic, out-of-control feelings were gone. She didn't know what part of him was responsible, but something in the very essence of who he was had calmed her down. Maybe it was his unobtrusive presence, the way he didn't need anything from her, just wanted to hold her and love her.

She'd never had that in a lover before, and suddenly she understood that being with him was, for her, no different from being alone. He didn't take anything away, only added to the equation.

She hadn't noticed it before, but when she thought back over their interactions, she could see that he brought a sense of peace wherever he went.

"I've tried to give you a little space," he said, squeezing her fingers. "I know it's been rough and I didn't want you to think I needed anything from you. I'm just . . . here. If you want me."

She returned his squeeze.

"I appreciate it. I'd like you to stay. Maybe take a walk with me?"

He nodded, and they began to stroll. They didn't need words, each unconsciously choosing to head away from Echo Park Avenue, toward the set of stairs that rose up out of the hills where Curran came to a dead end.

"I wanted to see you," he said. "Of course, I wanted to see you, but I knew—I could feel—that you needed some time alone to process things before I started bugging you."

He followed her down the slanted steps, leaving Curran Street and Eleanora's memorial far behind them.

"Yeah?" she said.

"Yeah," he said, softly, bringing them to a stop just below the top of the stairs, so they could see Elysian Park laid out before them like an oil painting.

"I appreciate that," Lyse said. "My brain's been a little foggy the last few days."

"Sit down," he said, taking her by the shoulders and gently easing her onto one of the steps.

He sat beside her.

"Now look at the view."

She did as he said. It was so beautiful here on the stairs. Like that old Carole King song her mom had liked to sing when Lyse was a kid . . . "Up on the Roof"—only sitting here was like sitting up on the roof of the world with only the deep blue sky to keep you from floating into outer space.

"I used to hide out here when I was a teenager," Lyse said, lacing her fingers in between his. "When I was mad at Eleanora, I'd sit out on the stairs and watch the sunset. It reminded me, no matter how angry, or lonely, or frustrated I felt, there was so much more out there to see. That sooner or later things would get better."

Weir nodded.

"But right now, I don't know. I'm not a kid anymore. I'm not supposed to believe things will get better—I'm supposed to *make* them better."

Weir wrapped his arm around Lyse's shoulders and

pulled her close. She wanted to tell him about Eleanora, but she didn't even know how to begin. Instead, she let her brain go, focusing on his nearness, the way he smelled and tasted . . . the beat of his heart against her cheek.

"You smell so good," she said, lifting her chin, so she could nuzzle her face against his neck.

He stroked her hair and kissed the top of her head.

"So do you."

He held her chin in his hand, lifting her face, so he could look into her eyes before he leaned in and took her mouth. He tasted so sweet. She turned, wrapping her arms around his waist and squeezing him tight as they kissed. The connection between them was delicious.

She wanted more, wanted to crawl inside him and wear him like a second skin. Her kisses became more urgent as she felt herself give over to the burning attraction, tiny guttural moans escaping her lips. He grabbed her by the back of the head, gently tugging at her hair to expose her throat, trailing kisses down her skin and nibbling at her neck, leaving delicate love bites in his wake.

He put his callused hands on either side of her face, his fingers pressing into the hollows of her cheeks. His pupils were dilated, large black windows giving her a view into his soul— and she could see that his need was as desperate as her own.

"I want you," he said, kissing her full on the mouth, sucking on her lower lip until it felt heavy and bruised.

She felt lazy with lust, the smell of hormones and sex so overpowering and undeniable it took her breath away. She couldn't speak, so she just nodded.

"You're the most glorious thing I've ever seen," he whispered in her ear, his moist breath tickling her earlobe. "So beautiful. Your face, your body . . . I get hard just imagining you."

She ached for him, his words as much of an aphrodisiac as the hard thing between his legs.

"I feel like I already know you, know what you like, what turns you on," he said, kissing down the length of her jawline. "Like I've already made love to you—"

His words doused her ardor like a bucket of cold water. Weir sensed the change in her mood and immediately stopped kissing her.

"Lyse? What's wrong?"

She could see she'd confused him but that he was trying to be gentle with her.

"Those things you said . . ." She trailed off.

"That you're glorious, that I get hard just thinking about you?" he repeated, teasing. "Too sexy?"

She shook her head, not looking him in the eye.

"No, I liked all that stuff. That stuff was amazing."

"What did I say that upset you, then?" he asked, taking her fingers and rubbing them in between his hands.

She wasn't sure how to respond. She just knew she felt incredibly raw and vulnerable—and she wasn't one hundred percent sure why.

"Lyse?" Weir said, encouraging her to tell him what was wrong.

She shrugged, eyes focusing on the view—not him.

"The familiar part," she began. "You said you feel like we've already been together—"

"*That's* what's bothering you?" he asked, a teasing lilt to his words.

"It's just that . . . something happened to me."

"Oh, Lyse," he said. "I want you to know that you're safe with me. Always . . ."

She realized he'd misinterpreted her words.

"No, it's nothing like that," she said, feeling frazzled. "I've never . . . I've been lucky on that front."

He squeezed her hand.

"You can tell me anything, Lyse."

She shook her head, unwilling to meet his gaze.

"I—"

She stopped, deciding to approach the subject from another direction.

"Do you believe in magic?" she asked.

"What do you mean? Like fairies, witches, and ghosts? That kind of magic? Or Magic Castle, card tricks, and sawing-a-lady-in-half magic?"

She shook her head—not feeling like this was the right way to broach the subject, after all.

"I don't know. Let's just drop it."

She leaned into him, rubbing her cheek against his neck, and tried to erase the awkwardness with butterfly kisses— but he put his hands on her shoulders and pushed her away.

"I know what you're doing," he said, with a crooked smile. "And as much as I want to kiss you and touch you, I don't want to be placated with sex because you're too scared to talk to me about something."

"I'm not scared—" she protested.

"You feel vulnerable talking about whatever it is you want to talk about," he said. "And I get that—but you need to understand something, Lyse. This isn't just gonna be about sex. When I say that I want you, I mean *all* of you. I want your body and your mouth and your brain and your heart. Everything that makes you *you*. I'm the guy you come with and the guy you come *to* when you need to talk. And if you can't handle that, then we shouldn't be doing this."

Lyse was shocked. No man had ever spoken to her so bluntly. Weir had laid it all out there, being as honest as possible with her, wanting her to know exactly what he was thinking and where he stood. Obviously, the man meant what he said, and said what he meant—and this was both intoxicating and utterly terrifying to her.

"I don't know," she said, after a few seconds of silence on her part. "It's a lot to think about. What you just said."

What are you doing? her brain was screaming at her. *Shut up! Don't ruin this because you're a coward! Just tell him that you understand!*

Weir stared at her face for a long moment, then nodded. Was she mistaken, or did he look disappointed by her response?

"Sure," he said. "Yes, it is a lot to think about. Maybe you should go think about it for a while and get back to me."

He would never say it out loud, but she knew she'd dealt with his feelings badly.

"I'm sorry," she said, fumbling for words. "I just . . . Eleanora . . . and I'm confused. I don't know if I'm ready to jump into something super-serious with you right now."

"I'm not asking you to jump into anything," he said, not arguing with her, but trying to clarify. "I'm telling you that I don't want to just fuck you. I want to be your friend, too. That means being honest with each other. It means that this is a no-bullshit zone."

She sighed, the sun beating down on top of her head and making her feel cranky. She hated the long tank dress she was wearing, the only piece of black clothing she'd been able to find in her closet—since she'd obviously brought nothing appropriate for a funeral with her from Athens. The dress made her feel constrained, frustrated, and she wanted to rip it off and shred it into pieces—even if it meant she had to sit on the steps in her bra and underwear.

"Don't be mad at me," he said, reaching for her hand. "I'm not trying to force you into anything. Take your time. Think about it. I'm not going anywhere."

He began to stroke her inner wrist, drawing concentric circles on her skin with his thumb. It was distracting and made it hard for her to think straight.

"I need to get out of here," she said, standing up and pulling her hand from his grasp.

"Lyse—" he began, but she was already moving, her feet slapping loudly against the concrete stairs as she took them two at a time.

She didn't slow down when she reached the top, only picked up speed, running down the middle of the street as a flood of tears blinded her. She didn't see the man in front of her. She slammed into him, and her legs flew out from under her. She landed on the ground, fingers clutching at the dirty asphalt. She didn't try to get up, but sat in the street, blood smeared across her abraded palms.

"Are you all right?"

The man was beside her, worry pinching his handsome face into a grimace. She looked at him, and shook her head.

"No," she said, as a sob escaped her lips.

He nodded, pursing his lips into a straight line. Something about this gesture reminded her of Eleanora, and she stopped crying. There was something familiar about this man with the steel-gray buzz cut and intelligent green eyes. She couldn't stop herself from thinking that she knew him—or, at least, felt like she did.

"Well, I don't know if this is gonna make you feel any better," he said, giving her a quizzical smile, "but I think I might be your uncle."

Arrabelle

The Bible sat between them on the round oak kitchen table, open to the front cover, so that everyone could see the names written inside. There was no mistaking Eleanora's handwriting, her neat block letters straight and precise.

This was the real deal, Arrabelle realized.

"See? There's my name and my mom's name—" Lyse said, as she pointed to each entry. Then she turned her gaze to the man sitting beside her. "And that's your name, isn't it? David Davenport Eames."

"Yes, I think that's me," the man—David, as he'd introduced himself—said. "I've never seen my actual birth certificate, but I know David was my birth name and Eleanora Eames was my mother."

Arrabelle had to admit the whole thing was a bit of a shock. She'd been completely unaware of Eleanora's secret life—but now that everything was out in the open, the pieces of the puzzle were starting to fall into place.

No wonder you wanted Lyse to join us, to take your place even, Eleanora, she thought. *She was your granddaughter.*

Arrabelle did not often bow to emotion. Emotion was vulnerability, a weakness that others could exploit—but the idea of Eleanora living such a horrific lie, and dying before she had a chance to tell her granddaughter the truth . . . well, it broke Arrabelle's heart.

And now here was this man. Purporting to be Eleanora's son and Lyse's uncle—and there was just something not right about him.

Even his name felt wrong.

This David didn't seem like the kind of man who fought Goliath for a living. He reminded Arrabelle more of a machine, all crew cut and unwavering gaze, green eyes that cut through to the heart of things, mining the delicate innards of his prey for information and profit—and she didn't believe he'd made his presence known to Lyse out of any filial concern.

No, he wanted something from her—and it was Arrabelle's job (she owed this much to Eleanora) to stop him from collecting whatever prize he'd come for.

"How did you find us?" Arrabelle asked. "I mean, find Eleanora and Lyse?"

She tried to appear nonchalant as she sipped from her chipped mug of green tea, but she was nervous. There was something about David, the way he held himself and moved his body, that reminded her of an ex-military man she'd dated—a relationship that hadn't gone anywhere because she couldn't stand his moral inflexibility. To men like her ex and David, there were no gradations of gray—only the fierce black and white of a German Expressionist print.

"I've actually been searching for my birth mother for a long time," David said, an earnest quality to his voice that made Arrabelle suddenly doubt her first impression of the man. "In 1974, a fire destroyed the agency that handled our adoption, along with all their records, so this made finding information difficult—"

He seemed to have an easy answer for every question put to him—not that the others had asked him anything more pressing than, "Do you want more coffee?" or "Can I get you some quiche?"

"You look unhappy with me," he continued, giving Arrabelle an apologetic smile. "Because that's not really what you wanted to know. You want to know why *now*? Why choose the day of my mother's memorial service?"

Arrabelle leaned forward in her chair, elbows pressing into the top of Eleanora's round oak table.

Yes, why didn't you come sooner? Why didn't you want to meet the woman who bore you? Arrabelle thought. *It would've been the top priority on my list.*

"Well, to be honest, the answer is . . . I don't know. I don't know why I waited to confront her. I think it was because I was scared"—he turned to Lyse, who was curled in her seat, knees against her chest—"and now I realize I don't want to make that same mistake with you, Lyse."

Lyse nodded, eyes red and puffy from crying.

"I wish you'd known her," Lyse said, swallowing hard to dislodge the growing lump in her throat. "She was . . . wonderful and tough and I miss her so much already."

"I can only imagine how much," David said, covering her hand with his own and giving it a gentle squeeze. "But I hope we can be there for each other during this painful time."

The words sounded false coming out of his mouth—like he was a funeral director parroting what the mourners wanted to hear. Arrabelle wondered if Lyse had picked up on the discrepancy—but she couldn't tell.

As they'd been talking, Dev had quietly slipped into the seat next to Arrabelle. Now Arrabelle caught her casting worried glances in Lyse's direction.

"Yeah, it's been really tough," Lyse said, gently removing her hand from David's grasp, so she could wrap her arms around her knees again. "She was sick, was dying, really, but I just . . . I didn't expect it to happen so quickly."

"I understand," he said, nodding. "Nothing really happens until it *happens*."

"Yes, something like that," Lyse agreed, then said, "But if there was a fire? How did you find Eleanora when all the information was destroyed?"

"Everyone loves a good story without a happy ending," Daniela said, from her perch on the kitchen counter. Until that moment she'd been watching the proceedings with half-closed cat's eyes, but now she jumped into the conversation.

"Excuse me?" David said, turning in his seat to look at her.

Daniela—black leather gloves her only nod to the somber occasion—hopped off the kitchen counter.

"Well," she said, extracting a silver flask from her back pocket and taking a long swallow. "Your timing was pretty shitty."

She wiped her mouth with the back of her gloved hand and leaned against the kitchen sink, glaring at him.

"Don't you think?"

Arrabelle wished that whatever was in the flask, Daniela would pass it her way. She could use a stiff drink.

"No, you're right," David said, without hesitation, looking first at Daniela and then at each of the others in turn. "You're *all* right. I should've been here. Should've made my peace with my mother before she died. It was stupid of me. But you can't fault a man for being human, can you? For making a mistake."

He was good. Very, very good. Was she actually judging an honest man to be false—and declaring him guilty because she could?

"In the end, *I* didn't actually find anyone. They found me."

"Who found you?" Lyse wanted to know.

"My father. Your grandfather."

"Why isn't he here now?" Lyse asked, brows knit together as she frowned. "Why didn't he come with you? I don't understand."

"He and Eleanora were . . . I think *estranged* is the right word," David said. "When she found out she was pregnant, she wanted to get rid of the babies, but our father said no. So she ran away, and put us up for adoption as soon as we were born. That way she could be free, *and* could also punish our father at the same time. I hate to think of the woman who gave birth to me being so deceitful, but, well, you can imagine how betrayed he felt. The loss of his family almost destroyed him . . ."

"I don't think Eleanora would do that," Lyse said. "I think there has to be some kind of misunderstanding."

"That doesn't sound like Eleanora," Arrabelle agreed. "She may have had secrets, but she wasn't a cruel person—"

"She destroyed three—no, four—people's lives, and never did anything to make it right," David said, his voice rising in anger. "Her whole life was a lie!"

"You didn't know her. She wouldn't have—" Lyse began.

"I'm glad I didn't," David spat back at Lyse. "She wasn't capable of love. She was empty."

"That's not true," Arrabelle said, slamming her fists down on the tabletop. "Eleanora loved you, Lyse. I believe she had reasons for not being completely honest—"

"She lied to us. She selfishly kept you from me, and your grandfather," David whispered, compelling Lyse to listen to him. "Prevented me from ever knowing your mother, my own twin—"

Lyse stood up.

"I need a refill. Arrabelle? Would you get the tea for me, please?"

"Of course."

But when Arrabelle began to open the drawer where they both knew Eleanora kept her tea, Lyse shook her head.

"No, not that drawer. The one back there."

Arrabelle followed Lyse's gaze over to the cabinet where Eleanora kept her drugs, her eyes widening in surprise. Lyse gave another subtle nod, and Arrabelle understood: Lyse wanted Arrabelle to dose her uncle.

While Arrabelle began to put their plan into action, David continued to wheedle Lyse:

"I'm not looking to start a fight with anyone here," he was saying, "but you should know that your grandfather would love to meet you. In fact, I told him I'd bring you straight to see him once we'd talked."

"Oh?" Lyse said, filling the kettle with water and setting it on the stove. "You did?"

Behind her, blocked from his view, Arrabelle was uncorking one of Eleanora's pot tinctures. She measured out a dosage that wouldn't kill him—but would make him *wish* he were dead—and poured it into a nondescript brown mug.

The kettle whistled, and Lyse poured hot water into the waiting mugs, including the one laced with marijuana.

"We can go this afternoon," David said, taking out his cell phone. "I can arrange it right now."

Lyse indicated that Arrabelle should carry the mugs back to the table—except for the one reserved for her uncle. That one Lyse delivered herself, setting it down directly in front of him.

"Have some tea with me, Uncle David," Lyse said, retaking her chair.

David stared down at the mug and made a face—but Arrabelle could see that he didn't want to offend Lyse.

"Cheers," Lyse said, tapping the side of her mug against his own. "Drink up."

David picked up the tea and took a tentative sip.

"So where is he?" Lyse asked.

Impatient for David to drink his tea, Arrabelle took a sip from her own steaming mug, and burned her mouth.

"He's in San Francisco right now," David said, sipping his drink. "He travels a lot for work."

"Oh," Lyse said. "I thought you meant he was nearby. That he was itching to meet me."

"That *was* the plan," David assured her, "but at the last minute he was called away on business. Trust me when I say he's dying to see you."

Just to be done with it, David raised his mug to his lips and, making a face, downed the whole thing in one swallow. Arrabelle sat back in her chair and smiled.

"We can leave right now, if you want to," David said. "Once you've finished your tea."

Lyse considered her uncle's offer.

"Well, we're scattering Eleanora's ashes tomorrow afternoon—"

David nodded, schooling his features into something resembling thoughtfulness.

"Of course. I understand. But, in full disclosure, your grandfather is leaving for Chile in the morning, and I'm not sure when he'll be back."

Arrabelle opened her mouth, but Lyse caught her eye and slowly shook her head.

"I don't know," Lyse said, as if she were a small child who couldn't make a decision between cupcakes or ice cream. "It's such a difficult decision . . ."

David began to rub his eyes.

"Lyse, I really must insist you come with me." He stood up and grabbed hold of her arm, trying to drag her to her feet—but the tincture was finally starting to take effect, and he began to sway woozily.

"I don't feel well," he murmured, dropping Lyse's arm and resting his forehead on the back of his chair.

Dev stared at David, confused by his odd behavior—
and then her eyes flew to Arrabelle's face.

What did you do? she mouthed. Arrabelle shook her head
and pointed at Lyse.

"Are you all right?" Arrabelle asked David.

He looked up at her and shook his head.

"What . . . did you . . . do?" he moaned, and lunged for
Arrabelle.

She sidestepped his uncoordinated attack, and he
slammed into the table, overturning cups and sending hot
tea spilling onto the floor.

"I'm gonna kill you," he said, picking himself up and
glaring at Arrabelle.

He began to lurch toward Arrabelle again, but Daniela
stepped in.

"I've got this," she said—and shoved a kitchen chair in
his path.

His reaction time was too slow, and he couldn't get out
of the way in time. His legs hit the solid wood seat, knock-
ing him off his feet. He landed on his ass, his legs sprawled
across the floor—but he didn't stay down for long. He
grabbed for the chair and dragged himself back onto his
feet, eyes pinwheeling in their sockets as he lunged for
Daniela, who easily danced out of his reach.

"I don't think you ladies like me very much," David
slurred. "I can't imagine why. You hardly know me."

"I don't care who you are," Lyse said, shaking with anger.
"I want you to leave!"

David shook his head no, his movements as jerky as a
marionette's.

"I assure you," he bellowed, swaying back and forth,
"that I have just as much of a right to be here as you do!"

"And what makes you say that?" Arrabelle yelled back
at him.

"I'm Eleanora's son. This was her house, so now it's mine."

"Nope, I don't think so," Arrabelle said, almost laughing with the joy of getting to stick it to him. "This house belongs to all of us."

"So when Lyse tells you to get the hell out of her house," Daniela said, grinning, "she means it."

"Then I'll be back for you," David growled, pointing his finger at Lyse.

"Like hell you will," Lyse shot back, glaring at him.

"Oh, I will." He grinned, his eyes wild. "And when I do, none of you *witches* will be able to stop me."

He turned to go, but Daniela called after him:

"She's already been inducted, asshole."

He stopped, his shoulders drooping. Then he whirled around, his face twisted with rage.

"Liar," he hissed, grasping the back of the chair with his hands. "I don't believe you."

"I assure you that it's the truth," Dev said, primly. "She consummated her relationship with the Horned God."

David gripped the back of the chair so hard his knuckles turned white.

"These things can be undone—"

"Yeah, have fun with that," Daniela said, and cackled. "But if you know anything about us, then you know how tricky it is to unbind someone from their coven once they've given themselves freely to the Horned God."

"You think you're so smart," he spat at them, slamming the chair down in his anger, causing one of its legs to snap in two. "But The Flood is coming and it will rip you apart."

He released his hold on the back of the chair, and it tipped over onto the floor.

"See?" he said. "All broken."

Then he weaved his way toward the back door, fumbled drunkenly with the lock, and let himself out.

The four of them stayed frozen in place until the door

slammed shut, and then Daniela sat down at the table and picked up David's empty mug, rolling it between her hands.

"Just FYI, you guys, but Lyse's uncle or not, I'm pretty sure that was the bastard who broke into my house. I didn't get a good look at him until you dosed him—but the eyes . . . they were the same."

"We should call the police—" Dev started to say, but Daniela shook her head.

"No, there's nothing they can do." She turned to look at Lyse. "And you, who the hell knew you had it in you?"

Lyse blushed.

"That was genius," Dev said, hugging first Lyse and then Arrabelle. "What made you think of it?"

"I don't know," Lyse said. "But what that man said about Eleanora . . . It was wrong. She was abused, was forced to do things she didn't want to do. She gave up the babies for a reason. I know it."

"Poor Eleanora," Dev said. "And none of us had any idea."

Lyse's gaze settled on Daniela.

"You did."

"Eleanora and my mother were best friends," Daniela replied. "Of course, I had an inkling that there was more to the story. But all of this is beside the point right now."

"What do you mean?" Arrabelle asked.

"I'm sorry to be the one to say this . . ." She paused, looking around at the worried faces of her fellow blood sisters. "But no one is safe here."

Lizbeth

Lizbeth sat on the edge of the deck with Marji and Ginny, watching the carp in Eleanora's koi pond break the surface of the water and collect bits of bread the girls threw down for them. She was glad the sunset fell so early in October, enfolding this side of the house in its protective shadow. She'd been unsettled by the arrival of the strange man with the gray hair and green eyes, and she wanted to hide away from him.

That was why she'd volunteered to watch Dev's girls after the reception was over.

To keep them occupied, Lizbeth had stolen some bread from the long table of food in the living room, helping the girls roll tiny bread pellets between their fingers and lob them into the water.

"LB?" Marji said, as she reached for Lizbeth's hand.

Dev's girls were sweethearts, always wanting to hold your hand or tell you a funny little story.

"LB?" Marji said again.

Lizbeth nodded, so Marji would know she'd heard her.

"LB, do you ever talk to ghosts?" Marji asked, their entwined hands swinging over the wooden decking.

Lizbeth picked up her sketch pad and began to write. It was hard to get so many thoughts down at once, but over the years she'd learned to be succinct. When she was done, she let the sketch pad drop onto her lap, so both girls could read it:

There are spirits around us always.

"I know that, silly," Marji said, playfully slapping at Lizbeth's arm. "But do *you* talk to them?"

Ginny was becoming more interested in the conversation. Ignoring the fish and the hunk of bread in her hand, she got up from her spot next to Marji and came over to Lizbeth, moving the sketch pad so she could plop down in Lizbeth's lap.

"Braid my hair?" she asked, leaning back into Lizbeth's chest.

Lizbeth took a handful of brown hair from the crown of Ginny's head and began to weave it together, twisting the pieces until every last strand had been pulled into a French braid.

"Ginny!" Marji cried, annoyed with her little sister for hogging Lizbeth's hands. "How can she talk when you're making her do that?"

"She can talk to you later," Ginny said—as if this solved everything.

"Not fair," Marji said, sulking. "I was talking to her first."

"She's fast. She's almost done."

What Ginny said was true. Lizbeth had nimble fingers, and she was already securing the braid in place with a rubber band she kept wound around her wrist for just such occasions.

"But I need to ask her this stuff *now*," Marji whined, then threw up her hands in defeat. "Fine. I quit."

Ginny, having won that round, smiled broadly.

"You're faster than Mommy and you don't pull too hard," she said, and patted Lizbeth's arm.

Lizbeth smiled, pleased such a simple task could make them both happy.

"And you always make it straight—"

They heard the back door slam, and then a moment later the green-eyed stranger was walking toward them, his steps slow and uncertain. He stopped a few feet away from the girls, one foot on the curved arch of the bridge, and gave them a strange, dark smile.

"Be careful, girls," he said, his slurred speech belying the threat behind his words. "Wouldn't want one of you to fall in. It's an old wives' tale that witches float."

Ginny stiffened in Lizbeth's lap, her face scrunching up in anger.

"The Flood is coming. Remember that, girls."

Chilling words, from a chilling man. He made a move to go, but his knees seemed to crumple beneath him. He grabbed the handrail and righted himself. He didn't wait for a reaction. Just continued over the bridge—weaving back and forth with that slow, awkward gait—and then he was gone.

"He was mean, LB," Ginny said, wrapping her arms around Lizbeth's neck.

Lizbeth looked over at Marji, who sat in silence, chewing at her bottom lip.

"We're not witches," Marji whispered, and Lizbeth snaked an arm around her thin shoulders, pulling her close.

No, not witches, Lizbeth thought. *At least, not yet.*

Weir's old Volvo station wagon idled on the street in front of Eleanora's house, tailpipe exuding white smoke. Lizbeth was intimidated by the car, and no matter how many times Weir tried to teach her how to drive it, she just couldn't get comfortable behind its wheel.

She didn't have a license—she doubted she ever would—but Weir encouraged her to be self-sufficient, which included at least knowing how to drive, so if there was ever an emergency, she wouldn't be stuck. He'd also made sure she knew how to use the ATM. He wanted her to be able to have access to money if he wasn't around.

She dutifully learned how to make the bank machines work, but that didn't mean she liked them. To her, they were like giant, all-seeing eyes, recording everything she did. She hated that some unknown person might be watching her fidgeting as she entered her passcode, or that they knew she was wearing a particular outfit on a particular date, or that she'd worn her hair down, or brought a purse, or . . . Well, the list was endless.

She'd read in one of Weir's old *National Geographic*s that some native tribes believed that taking a person's picture was tantamount to stealing their soul—and she believed it.

Though she didn't think it was possible to live in a modern world and not be photographed—there were just too many cameras.

"All right, kiddo," Weir said, as he climbed out of the driver's seat and walked around to open the passenger door for her.

She held up her sketch pad as he approached, and he froze when he saw what she'd written:

Are you dating Lyse now?

"No," he said, shifting his eyes away—a sure sign he wasn't being completely honest. "Not dating. Just spending time together. Maybe. Maybe not. I don't know."

She found it very endearing, this need of his to blur the meaning of things and soften the rough edges of the truth.

Lizbeth had heard him and Lyse the other night, in his

bedroom, talking and laughing. It made her happy to hear Weir laugh. He didn't do it enough.

"No more third degree. Get in the car," Weir said, giving her a brotherly push toward her seat.

She grinned back at him and climbed into the car, watching as he shut the door behind her. She wanted him to confide in her, to tell her about him and Lyse—but then she realized he might not want to say anything out loud. Just in case he jinxed it. She understood wanting to keep some things private. There were many special things in her life. Things she didn't share with anyone. Not Weir, not her sketch pad . . . They were for her mind only.

Before her brother could even begin to get around to the driver's side of the car, she was pulling out her pen and writing something new. She held the sketch pad up for him to see:

Take me to the Dragon?

"Right now?" he said, as he fastened his seat belt. "It's gonna be dark soon."

She knew the night was lying in wait for her, but she wanted to go to the clearing. The tall lady from her dreams had told Lizbeth something was hidden there. She didn't tell Lizbeth what it was, but she encouraged the girl to go soon, before somebody else found it.

Before something really bad happened.

Since Eleanora's death, Lizbeth hadn't felt safe. Dev had told her that Eleanora died because she was sick. That her old heart hadn't been able to take all the chemotherapy and stress—but Lizbeth didn't believe this.

In her dream the night before, she'd tried to ask the tall lady about it, but Lizbeth had woken up before she could give an answer.

Lizbeth wrote a word on the sketch pad and turned it in Weir's direction:

Please?

Her older brother could deny her nothing.

He sighed and put the car in gear.

"We're not going for long," he said, eyes on the road ahead. "I know you like it in Elysian Park, but there are all kinds of weirdos out there. Dudes who would take advantage of you in a millisecond."

Lizbeth tried to imagine what kind of a man had the musculature to overpower her. She was a monster, tall and ungainly, and much stronger than she looked. It would take a man her equal to best her—and she hadn't come across many of those.

Her brother was one. Taller than Lizbeth, he could beat her up if he wanted to, but that wasn't his way. Weir was the sweetest, kindest human being she'd ever known, and he wouldn't hurt a fly unless he was protecting someone he loved.

"You're young. You think you're invincible," Weir was saying. "That's just not true. You have to be smart and keep your eyes open."

Weir was overprotective, but not usually *this* bad. Lizbeth wondered if the circumstances of Eleanora's death had unsettled him, too.

She wrote something on her sketch pad, but waited until he slowed down for a stop sign to show it to him:

Bad juju in the air.

Weir gave it a cursory glance, then took his foot off the brake.

"Yup," he said, catching her eye in the rearview mirror. "You feel it, too?"

She nodded. Of course, she felt it.

"This thing with Eleanora . . . and Lyse . . . I don't know," he said. "Something weird is going on."

Again, Lizbeth nodded. Weir was speaking her language.

"You've always been sensitive. Even as a baby . . ." He trailed off, then stopped speaking completely when he noticed how tense the conversation was making her.

Lizbeth could not talk about the past. Weir understood this about her and was usually vigilant about not saying anything that would set her off.

"I'm sorry," he said, gripping the steering wheel so hard his knuckles went white. "I wasn't thinking."

She began to rock back and forth in her seat, the trip to the park forgotten. She closed her eyes, shutting him out as she retreated into her own private world where none of the bad stuff could touch her.

When it happened, it was like she became split into two distinct entities: There was the terrified child, who couldn't speak but could shut Lizbeth down with a snap of its fingers. The cognizant part of Lizbeth was aware, knew the terrified child was hiding, locking them both away inside Lizbeth's brain for protection, but it possessed zero power to stop it once it started.

This was how it went, time and time again, the irrational child in her brain dominating the logical adult part until some arbitrary switch was flipped and the lockdown was rescinded. She hated that she couldn't control it. She didn't want to retreat, didn't want to wall herself up in her own mind. Thankfully, the episodes happened far less frequently than when she was in the institution.

But still, she longed for them to stop altogether.

"Lizbeth?" She heard Weir's voice trying desperately to reach her, but it was no use.

Don't waste your breath, sweet brother, she thought. *I'm locked up tight in here.*

She wished he could hear her.

Devandra

"Sleep tight, don't let the bed bugs bite," Dev said as she tucked the girls into bed. It was her turn tonight. Freddy had done it the evening before, and they liked to share the sweeter tasks of parenthood between them.

"Mommy," Ginny said, rubbing her eyes with the backs of her fists. She was still young enough that exhaustion manifested itself in these adorable little quirks. "Will you sleep in here with us tonight?"

The room was lit by the glow of the bedside lamp, and in the semidarkness the girls seemed dwarfed by the shadowy overhang of Marji's canopy princess bed, making Dev want to scoop her babies up and hug them to her.

Not that they wouldn't have protested. Marji was already too old to be held or covered in kisses—and Ginny was just on the cusp.

Instead of smothering them with her mama bear love, she sat down primly on the edge of Marji's Little Mermaid comforter, her butt accidentally smushing the section that contained Ariel's tail. She quickly switched positions, but to her surprise, neither of the girls commented on this blasphemy. Usually, they were hard-core about Dev not sitting on any of the important parts of the Little Mermaid or her fish friends, but tonight her daughters were unusually subdued.

After the strangeness of the day, she didn't blame them. They were upset about Eleanora—not that she really thought either girl wholly grasped the concept of death yet—but she knew that only time could heal their wounds.

"If I sleep in here with you guys, who's gonna protect your daddy from the monsters under my bed?" Dev asked them, appealing to their sense of fair play. "You guys already have each other. Daddy would be all alone."

Marji made a sour face.

"There aren't any monsters under the bed," Ginny cried.

Dev sighed, realizing the girls were getting too old for her silly made-up stories—her babies weren't gonna be babies for much longer.

"Mama, please," Ginny said, whining.

"Isn't having your sister enough for you?" Dev asked, in all seriousness.

Dev didn't mind the girls sleeping together in each other's rooms. They did it with some regularity, and she encouraged it, wanting them to be close. Like Dev was with her own sisters.

"No, Marji talks to the ghosts. It's scary sometimes," Ginny said, shaking her head back and forth, her hair bunching around the pillow.

"Marji," Dev said, teasing. "Please don't talk to ghosts while your sister's sleeping in here."

Marji rolled her eyes at her mom and crossed her arms over her chest.

"They talk to me. I don't talk to them."

"Well, just don't listen to them," Dev said, enjoying their make-believe game. "Tell 'em to knock it off."

Marji bit her lower lip, a habit she'd had since she was

itsy-bitsy, and Dev realized that maybe this wasn't a game. That Marji and Ginny were being serious about the ghost talk.

"*You* tell them for her, Mommy," Ginny said. Even though she was younger, Ginny was tougher than Marji, and it'd become a habit, her sticking up for her older sister.

Dev looked over at Marji.

"Is that what you want?" she asked, and Marji nodded.

Hauling herself to her feet, Dev stood in the middle of the room and lifted her arms in the air. She thought about what she could say to force make-believe ghosts to go away. She settled on something simple.

"Get thee gone, spirits, who are haunting this house!" she bellowed in a deep voice, turning clockwise in place, her hair flying in her eyes. "Be gone, I say—"

Both girls screamed.

"What in the world?" Dev cried as she stopped spinning and pushed her hair out of her eyes so she could see what had spooked the girls.

"What is it?" Dev asked, looking around the room.

The girls were cowering together in the bed, covers pulled up to their chins, two sets of saucer-wide eyes staring back at her.

"Mommy," Marji whispered.

With a shaking finger, she pointed to a spot behind Dev's head.

"*Hair* is in my room."

Dev noticed that the temperature in the room had dropped considerably. She began to shiver, the air around her heavier, too, somehow. Almost like it was pressing down on her, trying to grind her into the ground.

"Hair?" Dev said, her voice sounding foreign even to her own ears.

She slowly turned around.

"Oh, Lord."

Her great-great-grandmother Lucretia's mourning hair

wreath was leaning on the mantelpiece above Marji's fire-place. The memento mori was spooky enough downstairs above the living room fireplace, but up here in one of the girls' rooms, with no logical explanation for its presence, it was downright terrifying.

"Make it go away," Marji cried, her eyes welling with tears.

Dev hurried over to the fireplace, plucking the frame from the mantel. She gasped. It was like touching something that'd just come out of a deep freeze. The cold bit into Dev's fingers with a burning sensation, and she dropped the frame. It crashed to the floor, one of the corners hitting the hard-wood floor with enough force to split the frame into pieces.

The *crash* of breaking wood and glass made the girls shriek.

"Sweetheart," Dev said to Marji, as she knelt next to the ruined memento mori. "Could you go get me the broom and dustpan from the kitchen, please?"

Marji looked uncertain, but the need to please her mother outweighed her fear, and she crawled out of the warm bed, leaving Ginny alone under the covers.

"And put your shoes on," Dev added, pointing to a pair of Pepto-Bismol-pink Crocs someone had kicked haphaz-ardly onto the floor beside the bed.

Marji did a little hop and slipped her feet into the shoes. Then she took off for the kitchen. Dev watched her eldest go, a fleet-footed *almost* adolescent.

"Mommy," Ginny said, climbing out from under the covers so she could crawl over to the end of the bed. "Will they do that to my hair when I die?"

"Probably not, sweetie," Dev said as she collected some of the bigger pieces of glass into a pile. "This was some-thing people did a long time ago."

Ginny nodded, splaying out on her stomach. She didn't seem the least bit scared now that Marji was out of the room. Instead, she rested her chin in her hands and watched Dev work.

"You were spinning, Mommy," Ginny said, kicking her feet in the air. "And the tall lady brought it."

Dev froze, a long shard of glass in her hand.

"What?"

Ginny started kicking her feet even faster, sensing she'd unsettled her mother.

"The tall lady, Mommy," she said. "She was in the picture at Auntie E's house."

Dev racked her brain, trying to think of what picture Ginny was referring to—and then suddenly she knew. Knew like the knowledge had always been there, nestled inside her brain.

Hessika.

"Not a drawing or a picture, Ginny," Dev said, "but a photo? In the bookcase?"

Ginny nodded, enjoying the guessing game.

"The tall lady from the picture. She brought it."

Dev felt a trickle of wetness on her wrist, and she looked down—she'd forgotten about the glass she'd been holding. She opened her palm, and the glass dropped to the floor, one of its razor-sharp edges smeared with her blood.

"Damn," Dev said, staring at the line of scarlet standing out on the plane of her palm. She gently made a fist, and the gash split apart like a hungry mouth, more blood flowing down her wrist.

"Stay right there. Don't get off the bed," she said to Ginny as she stood up and, holding her hand at waist level, headed to the door.

She almost collided with an out-of-breath Marji, who was carrying a broom and dustpan in one hand and a brown paper bag in the other.

"Don't try to clean it up," Dev said to Marji, scooting past her daughter in the doorway. "I'll do it when I get back."

Marji stood at the threshold to her room, grinding her jaw with tension, but she nodded.

"Okay, Mama," she said, taking a step back into the hallway, leaving Ginny as the sole occupant of the bedroom.

"I'll be right back," Dev called over her shoulder as she moved down the darkened passageway.

At the end of the hall, the bathroom door stood wide open as if it were waiting for her. She slipped inside, flipping on the overhead light.

"Shit," she whispered when she saw how deep the cut was—deep enough she almost thought she might need stitches. Instead, she grabbed a hand towel from the cupboard and wrapped it around her palm.

Immediately, the blood soaked through the fabric, leaving a line of dark red in the material. She cinched the towel even more tightly around her hand, hoping this would staunch the flow.

"Okay, on my way back!" Dev yelled as she left the bathroom, turning the light off and shutting the door behind her.

She shuffled down the hallway, her woolen house shoes making *shushing* sounds on the polished hardwood floor. She could already see now that Marji hadn't waited in the hall like she'd asked.

"Marji!" Dev said as she rounded the doorjamb and found her older daughter kneeling over the broken glass. "What're you doing? I said not to touch it!"

Marji looked up, caught by the sharpness in her mother's voice.

"I found something," she said, holding up a square of faded brown paper for Dev to see. "It's for you."

Dev crossed the room and knelt beside her daughter, taking the folded paper from Marji's fingers. Its fragility and age were only noticeable once she had the note in her hands.

"Open it, Mama," Ginny said from her perch on the edge of the canopy bed.

Dev turned the note over and was shocked to see her own name scrawled across its back in a flowing, calligraphic hand.

Dev looked over at Marji, who was trembling.

"What's wrong, Marji?" she said, slipping an arm around her daughter and pulling her close.

"I don't know," Marji said, her brown eyes large with fear.

"Does this note upset you?"

Marji shook her head.

"I don't know," she said, still trembling.

Dev slipped the paper into her housedress pocket, and Marji seemed to relax a little.

"Go get in bed with your sister," Dev said, helping Marji stand.

"Sleep with us, Mama," Ginny said as she crawled back up to the top of the mattress and slid under the covers, waiting for her sister to join her.

Dev guided Marji to the bed, and once she was tucked safely inside, Ginny was there, clinging to her older sister like a limpet. At first Dev mistook the action, thinking Ginny was holding on to her sister out of fear, but then she realized her mistake.

Ginny wasn't scared.

She was protecting Marji.

From the time they were infants, she'd instinctively known this about her girls: that Marji was her sensitive one, and Ginny was her scrapper. Still, it always surprised her how this disparateness manifested itself more and more as the girls grew older.

She knew it was both a blessing and a curse—as glad as she was that the girls could rely on each other, their strengths and weaknesses jibing so perfectly, she also knew that at some point, their relationship could become *too* symbiotic.

It was her job to make sure they were each their own person

and they could survive without each other, creating their own separate lives . . . because one day the house, and possibly a role in the coven, would go to Marji, and she would need to be strong enough to handle it without her little sister's protection.

"How about we compromise?" Dev said as she picked up the broom and dustpan from the floor and began to sweep up the broken glass. "I'll take everything down to the garbage and make myself some tea. Then I'll come back up here and sit in the rocking chair until you guys fall asleep."

Ginny and Marji conferred, whispering together.

"Okay, Mom," Marji said, speaking for both of them. "But don't be gone too long."

"I'll be back up here in a few minutes," she said, picking up the bag, the broom, the dustpan, and the larger pieces of the broken frame. "Can I turn off the lamp for you guys?"

"Can we sleep with it on?" Ginny asked.

"As long as when I come back up here all eyes are closed." Both girls nodded vigorously.

"Okay, okay, I believe you," Dev said, laughing. "Now close your eyes and I'll be back before you know it."

When she left them, they were all snuggled up together like two bugs in a rug, the light from the bedside lamp casting a pale yellow glow over their entwined bodies.

She set the water to boil on the eye of the stove, a mug filled with chamomile tea ready to go on the counter. Then she pulled the piece of paper from her pocket and sat down at the kitchen table. Still feeling unsettled by the episode in the girls' room, she'd turned on all the lights in the kitchen—but now she felt vulnerable and exposed to whatever was lurking in the darkness outside the windows.

She set the folded note down on the tabletop and stared at her own name, written on the back. It was freaky. So freaky she'd almost woken Freddy up, but she'd stopped herself. He was out of the house for work at six, and he didn't need his sleep interrupted for something as silly as a ghostly piece of paper.

As much as she and Eleanora had their differences, she'd come to rely on the older woman's strength and force of will, and Dev dearly wished she could pick up the phone and call her now.

She knew Eleanora would tell her there was nothing to be scared of—*Just open the damn thing, for God's sake*—and as she thought these words, she could hear Eleanora's voice in them, and even this small remembrance was a consolation.

"Okay," Dev said out loud. "I'm just gonna open it."

She carefully unfolded the square, but even with her delicate fingers, bits of paper still flaked off onto the table.

"Damn," she said as a chunk of the paper tore away in her hand.

She finished unfolding it and set the note on the table, putting the torn bit back in its place. Her eyes scanned the spidery cursive, the looping letters dancing across the page. Age had blurred some of the words, making the note hard to decipher in places, but, with context, she was finally able to piece it together:

My Dearest Devandra—

When you read these lines I will be dead, my corporeal body no more than dust. It is with a heavy heart that I have asked my daughter, Purity, to entomb this letter with the mourning wreath they will create upon my death. It will then be passed down from eldest to eldest, always in the keeping of the Montrose women, until, one day, it will come into your hands.

I wish the news were not so grave, but time and time again, as I draw the cards, the spread is always the same: Terrible things await you, my darling. A great evil is upon our world, waiting and biding its time. It will reach its zenith during your lifetime—and only you and yours will have the power to stop it.

But you must choose the right path: The World, The Magician, The Hierophant, The Devil, and The Fool.

Trust in the spread. It will guide you.

All my love,
Lucretia

The letter made Dev's blood run cold. It was Eleanora's spread—and it concerned the last Dream Keeper.

Daniela

Daniela enjoyed the feel of the wind on her cheeks as she walked through the silent neighborhood. She pulled up the collar of her jacket and picked up her pace, so that she was almost jogging, the syncopated *tap* of her feet on the asphalt calming her frenetic mind.

Sometimes she just needed to move—and the time she spent walking around her neighborhood was like a balm for her soul.

When she was a kid, she'd been incapable of sitting still for longer than a few minutes at a time. There was just so much to think about, so much to do . . . her brain was always running in fifth gear. Unless she was passionate about something—like painting—she just couldn't focus for very long.

Even as a kid, if she was bored by something the teacher was saying in class, she'd just get up and roam around the room, looking at stuff. Add in the strange seizures and then, later, the odd leather gloves she was forced to wear, and she knew she must've driven the already stressed-out and time-strapped public schoolteachers crazy.

The last Dream Keeper. Under my protection.

These words haunted Daniela.

Until the last few days, she'd felt torn. Her mother, Hessika, Eleanora . . . they'd all believed the girl would come. Daniela, on the other hand, hadn't known what to believe. Not until she'd come to Echo Park, and Eleanora had introduced her to Lizbeth. That was when she'd felt the first glimmers of possibility, a thing she'd long thought extinguished inside her.

Now there was actually something to hold on to. Someone real to believe in, so that the promise she'd made to her mother could be kept in good faith.

The sound of a car idling up ahead caught her attention, and she slowed down, instinct warning her to be cautious. It was a Lincoln Town Car with black-tinted windows, and the exhaust from its tailpipe curled around its metal body, creating a ghostly fog that caught the glow from the streetlights and reflected it.

As she came even with the car, the back passenger window rolled down, and, against her better judgment, Daniela stopped, curiosity getting the better of her. A pale white head appeared in the frame of the window, and Daniela let out a low whistle, her nervousness giving over to relief as she realized that she knew the man.

"You scared me," Daniela said leaning into the window. "What're you even doing here? I thought you were in New York?"

The man shook his head, his wrinkled face breaking into a smile.

"We heard things were afoot here, and the Greater Council decided it was time to send in the big dogs," the man said, shrugging.

"And by big dogs, they mean you," Daniela said, grinning back at him.

Other than Eleanora, Desmond Delay had been her

mother's closest confidant, and Daniela trusted him implicitly. Though he wasn't a blood relative, he'd always treated Daniela and Marie-Faith like they were family—and Daniela often wondered if he'd been in love with her mother.

"Get in the car," he said, gesturing for her to join him. "You must be freezing out there."

He opened the door and scooted over so she could climb in beside him. He was right. It was much warmer in the car—especially after he shut the door and rolled up the window.

"Shall we take you home?" he asked.

"I'd appreciate that," she said, and then leaned over and gave him a hug.

He felt fragile in her arms, and she realized it'd been six months since she'd last seen him.

At her mother's funeral.

And the intervening months had not been good to him.

"I've missed you," she said as she pulled away from him.

"I've missed you, too," he replied, and there was a rheumy redness to his sad gray eyes. One that hadn't been there before.

To her pleasure and surprise, she saw he still carried the walking stick she'd had made for his sixtieth birthday. She'd chosen the silvery lion's head because to her, he would always be her lion, doing whatever was necessary to look after and protect her family.

The gift had been in recognition of this.

"You still use it," she said, pleased.

"Of course," he said, hoisting the cane in the air for her to see. "*You* gave it to me."

Her heart was filled with love for the wily old man sitting beside her, and she took his hand, squeezing it in her own gloved one.

"There's so much to tell you, Desmond," she said, finding herself, as always, intoxicated by his presence.

"Yes," he said, pleasantly. "Tell me everything."

Lyse

Stay busy, so you don't have to think.

This phrase repeated itself on a loop inside her head, her lips mindlessly reconstituting the hard consonants over and over again until the words ceased to have any meaning and only the intent of their message remained.

This was how she'd ended up in Eleanora's garden, elbow deep in soil, her black dress covered in mud. As the dusk had settled into night, she'd been forced to turn on all the outdoor lights to continue her work—and even when the moon had risen to its zenith, she was still out there in the dirt, lost in the thrill of physical labor.

Pausing for a moment to rub the gritty soil in between her fingers, she took a deep breath and pushed away any conscious thought before it could absorb her. She was in the middle of repotting some mint she'd found on Eleanora's deck. The springy green plant had outgrown its original clay pot, and Lyse had decided to place it into a larger container.

She held the plant's body in her hands, feeling its lifeblood— the soil—thick under her nails, the veinlike roots delicate and fragile between her fingers. If she dropped the plant or potted it incorrectly, it would die of shock, something her experience working in plant nurseries had taught her to avoid.

After a few minutes, mint plant tucked safely into its new home, she brushed a loose strand of black hair from her cheek and, ignoring the smudge of dirt on her nose, sat back on her heels. She rolled her neck in circles, the small motion releasing the tension in her shoulders built up after long hours of hunching over the dirt.

Hands still covered in humus, she stood up and stretched, exhaustion curling like a weed inside her. Her brain had been right. Going back to the earth had been exactly what she needed. She yawned and wished she were already in bed, covers up to her chin, a warm glass of milk on the side table—

Her thoughts were interrupted by the soft *thwack* of something firm slamming into the base of her skull. She fell forward onto her knees, pain blossoming in her head. Without her even having to shut her eyes, a growing blackness stretched out before her, and she skipped off into inky black oblivion.

Wake up, I said. Wake up now.

The sound was like a sawmill chipping away at her skull. She realized the voice had been goading her awake for a while now, pushing her back to consciousness with the persistence of its words. She tried to open her eyes—and realized they were already open. There was just nothing to see because she was somewhere dark.

Get up, Lyse. Push at the door with your back. It's time to get yourself out of here.

The voice was insistent—would not take no for an answer, even when she nodded her head and the motion jarred her brain, causing her to gasp out in pain.

"Leave me alone," she said, as nausea roiled her stomach in waves. "I don't wanna."

Get the hell up, or you're going to die.

The panic in the voice brought Lyse around, and she swallowed hard, her mouth sandpaper dry. She lifted her arms—or tried to lift them, rather—and unwittingly discovered how narrow her prison was.

Coffin narrow, she thought as fat teardrops coursed down her cheeks, slipping off the slope of her chin and pooling in the dip of her collarbone. At least she knew she was standing upright, or the tears would've been switchbacking toward her ears—

Tears . . . ? Her conscious brain had finally processed the fact she was crying—and not just tears, but sobs that came from deep in her belly, shaking her body like earthquakes.

Why am I crying? she asked herself.

She had no ready answer. Her head hurt, a dark ache that throbbed with every pulse of her heart, but it was more than just physical pain. Something had sliced through the flesh and sinew of her chest to pierce the quick of her heart.

The voice.

It couldn't be real. It was a figment of her distressed mind, an old-school survival instinct from her primitive lizard brain.

Get out, Lyse. Save yourself.

She knew Eleanora's voice like she knew her own. She wasn't sure how it was possible, but somehow Eleanora was speaking to her from beyond the grave.

"Eleanora?" Lyse whispered.

No time for chitchat, Eleanora said. *Time is slipping away from us. You have to hurry.*

It was like a punch to her solar plexus.

"Where are you? Are you alive or dead? Eleanora . . . ?" The words came out in a rush.

They went unanswered.

Instead, it felt as though a blanket of calming warmth settled across the top of her skull, its arrival extinguishing the pain in her head. But the warmth didn't stop there. It trickled down to the rest of her body, enveloping Lyse and giving her back energy she hadn't realized she'd lost.

Time to go.

The voice was inside her head now, a part of her.

She raised her hands to her waist and gently turned them over, so her palms were pressing against the cold metal in front of her.

Push.

She did as the voice asked, taking all her new energy and channeling it toward escape. She pushed with her hands, pressing her back against the other side, using the wall in front of her for leverage. She strained, gritting her teeth, and heard a faint *pop* as the metal behind her gave way. She fell backward, arms pinwheeling as she tried to keep her balance. She did not succeed. Her head slammed into the concrete, stars blooming like daisies in front of her eyes.

She rolled over, hands scrabbling at the chilly cement floor as she raised herself onto her knees. She gave thanks for the ice-blue emergency light above the door in front of her—otherwise, she would've been entirely in darkness—and looked around the room, her eyes adjusting to the low light.

The room was small and square, no bigger than the interior of a car. There were three rusted metal lockers on the wall behind her, and up until a few seconds earlier, she'd been trapped inside the middle one. There was only one exit: the riveted metal door sitting below the emergency light.

"I'm gonna try the door," Lyse said out loud—even though she had no idea if Eleanora was really there or just a figment of her imagination.

She dragged herself to her feet, her head beginning to throb again. The original warmth she'd felt inside the locker was dissipating fast. She grasped the door handle and pulled, the heavy door gliding silently on its tracks, and she shivered, her black sheath dress providing zero protection from the cold.

She stepped through the doorway, the stink of dank rot filling her nostrils, and found herself in the middle of a long, abandoned tunnel. Up ahead, she could see another door, and she headed toward it, moving quickly to fight off the cold.

Hurry, he's coming.

The voice again, but this time it was not inside her head.

"Eleanora?" Lyse said.

Just hurry!

It was darker at this end of the tunnel, away from the blue light spilling out of the tiny room, and it took Lyse a few seconds of frantic search for her hands to find the door handle.

Go, Lyse. Go!

She pulled on the handle, throwing all her strength into the action, and the door slid back with a *creak*. A burst of fresh air hit her in the face, and she was outside in the middle of a stand of trees, scrambling up an incline leading away from the door.

She hit the top of the hill and began to run—though she had no idea where she was going—the urgency in Eleanora's voice driving her forward. She cut through a dense swath of trees, the moon lighting her way, but came to an abrupt stop just before she stepped off the edge of a short cliff, one that would've dropped her out onto a massive freeway. Out of breath, she stood there uncertainly, listening to the rush of cars speeding below her.

She didn't know where she was or where she was supposed to go. She stared down at the cars, her nose itching from the stench of car exhaust, and was amazed that even at this late hour, so many travelers were making their way through Los Angeles. At least, she hoped she was still in Los Angeles.

"Shit," she said, beginning to feel overwhelmed—and then, like a beacon in the night, she saw a forest-green road sign sitting high above the 101 freeway, an arrow pointing down to the Echo Park exit ramp.

She relaxed when she realized she was less than a ten-minute walk from Eleanora's house.

Leaving the roar of the freeway behind her, she headed back the way she'd come, jogging through the trees. She passed the door she'd just escaped through and paused. From the abandoned air of the place, she doubted anyone—not even the highway maintenance crews—used the tunnel anymore, and unless you knew to look for it, it was so well hidden within the underbrush that once closed, it would be almost invisible to the human eye.

No one would've ever found my body, she realized. *Not once whoever put me there came back to finish the job.*

Hurry, hurry, the voice—Eleanora's voice—cried.

Lyse took off running again. It didn't take her long to hit the chin-high chain-link fence that separated the sidewalk of Bellevue Avenue from the wooded area bordering the freeway. She grabbed the metal top rail and pulled herself over the fence, adrenaline coursing through her body as she hit the sidewalk and kept going.

The street was empty. She could still hear the freeway traffic behind her, but it was getting fainter. Up ahead, she could see the bright lights of Echo Park Lake. She crossed the street, ignoring the *Don't Walk* sign, and jogged toward the park. From there, it would be a straight shot up Echo Park Avenue to Eleanora's bungalow.

Maybe I shouldn't go home, she thought. Whoever had kidnapped her was bold. They'd plucked her right out of Eleanora's front yard, so maybe going to Dev's place, where there'd be lots of people, would be the better choice. Besides, it was close to the lake and would be easiest to get to.

Run, Lyse!

Eleanora's voice cut through her thoughts—and Lyse looked up just in time to see a figure in a dark hooded sweatshirt walking determinedly in her direction. She froze, not sure which way to turn. The figure was getting closer, speeding up now that it realized she was aware of it.

Go to the Lady of the Lake!

Lyse did as she was told, veering off the sidewalk and cutting across the grassy slope leading down to the water. Picking up speed, she circumvented a garbage can that was in her way, but before she could commend herself on her fast reaction time, the thick grass under her feet abruptly gave way to asphalt, and she almost went flying. Luckily, she managed to stay upright, and without missing a beat, she turned toward the path that would take her to the Lady of the Lake, the art deco statue that held court over the east end of Echo Park Lake.

She followed the curve of the walking path, able to run much faster now that she was on level ground. She glanced over her shoulder and was surprised to discover that the hooded figure was not following her. She eased up on her speed, slowing down to a jog in order to catch her breath.

To her left, she passed the darkened boathouse. Adorable in daylight, the little squat building with the red-tiled roof gave off an eerie vibe now that it was empty for the night. She increased her speed again, not wanting to linger in its shadow.

Lyse!

Eleanora's anguished voice filled her head, but not before she felt two gloved hands wrap themselves around her neck.

"No!" Lyse cried as her legs were kicked out from underneath her, and she collapsed onto her knees in the middle of the walking path.

In the darkness, she couldn't see the man's face, but she knew it was the hooded figure she'd seen up on the sidewalk—and there was something familiar about him, too. A smell, a feeling, a sense . . . She wasn't sure what gave him away, but she knew she'd met him before.

Not wanting to get trapped here under his control, she did the only thing she could think of that might set her free. She balled her left hand into a fist and punched her attacker in the crotch as hard as she could manage.

Bull's-eye. The man howled, enraged, and released her. Lyse didn't squander the opportunity. She crawled to her feet and took off, racing into the darkness. Pushing aside the mortal pain she'd inflicted on him, the man went charging after her.

He was faster than Lyse, and she had to zigzag back toward the east end of the lake to steer clear of his grasp. But he was dogged, matching her every move until, finally, he was close enough to shove her from the side and knock her to the ground. She rolled out of his reach and belly-crawled away, but he got hold of her ankle and yanked her back toward him.

"Leave me alone," Lyse cried, kicking out at his face with her other foot.

Luck was with her, and she heard a *crunch* as her shoe connected with the soft cartilage of her attacker's nose. He yelped but didn't release her.

"What do you want?" Lyse asked, kicking at his face again.

But this time he knew what she going to do, and grabbed her other ankle, stopping her from making contact with his face.

"I don't understand," she added, struggling to free her legs. "Why are you doing this?"

The man's grip was like iron, and she knew she wouldn't get away from him this time if he got his fingers around her throat.

Go to the Lady.

Eleanora's voice was more than a whisper in her ear—Lyse could actually feel hot breath fluttering against her cheek. She turned her head, expecting to find Eleanora there beside her, but she was alone. Only empty space—and the man in the hoodie, whose hands were moving slowly, inexorably toward her throat.

"No!" Lyse screamed, a shot of adrenaline ratcheting through her body.

She wasn't going to die like this—not here in Echo Park Lake, murdered by someone she knew but could not see.

"Who the hell are you!?" she cried. Then she reached down and yanked the man's hood away from his face.

Shock rendered her unable to speak. She knew the identity of her attacker, but she didn't want to believe it.

"Surprise," the man said, grinning up at her, the moonlight casting strange shadows across his face.

"But . . . but . . . *why?*" Lyse murmured when she could finally manage to speak again.

Her uncle David laughed—and she understood now that she'd unmasked him, he wasn't as eager to end her. Not because he didn't want to kill her—oh, she had no doubts that this was his endgame—but because he wanted to share something with her. Wanted to tell her why she was going to die, wanted her to understand.

"It's nothing personal," he said, grabbing Lyse's arm and pulling her into his lap, his gloved fingers gently running along the hollow at her throat. "The Flood is coming and we have to clear the path."

Lyse nodded, encouraging him to keep talking.

"The Flood," she said. "What is it exactly?"

Her uncle laughed in her ear, and she wished she could see his face, but he'd turned her away from him, his arm trapping her against him.

"I longed to tell you about it under different circumstances," he said. "I'd hoped you'd come with me willingly, but that wasn't to be."

"I'm sorry," Lyse said, stalling for more time in the hopes that some late-night dog walker or jogger would pass by to interrupt their messed-up little family reunion. "But tell me now. Explain it to me."

He thought about her request, mulling it over in his mind.

"Get up," he said. "I don't want anyone to see us and call the police."

She did as he said, allowing him to help her to her

feet—and that was when she saw the knife in his hand. Though she got the sense he'd rather strangle than stab, one puncture from the long, thin blade he was holding and that would be the end of her.

"Will you tell me?" Lyse asked again, letting him guide her away from the boathouse. "What does it mean when you say that you need to clear the path?"

To her surprise, she realized her uncle wasn't heading out of the park but was continuing around the path, toward the east end of the lake where the Lady resided.

Where Eleanora wants me to go, she thought. *I just need to keep him talking.*

"Uncle David?" she asked, after her last question received no answer.

"I was just thinking what a shame it was not to get to really know you, Lyse," he said. "Especially because you're the only family I have left now."

Lyse went with this train of thought.

"I wish you'd known my mom. She was magical. And Eleanora, too—"

"Oh, I met Mother. Only for a few moments, but I was there with her at the end."

"Wait, what do you mean?" Lyse asked, confused, and then she felt the tip of the blade pressing into her side. It seemed as though just the mention of Eleanora's name was enough to put him on edge.

"I was there," he whispered in her ear. "I helped her out. She wanted me to."

This statement froze the blood in Lyse's veins—and now she didn't want to know any more.

"But don't you want me to tell you what it was like?" he asked, his breath hot and foul against the side of her cheek. "What it felt like to put my hand over her mouth and nose. To watch the life flicker out of her eyes—all at my own personal whim."

Lyse began to cry. She tried to hold it in, to do what she could to not give her uncle cause to kill her, but she couldn't help herself. The image of Eleanora alone with this man—her own flesh and blood—as he smothered the life out of her made Lyse sick to her stomach.

"How?" she said, her voice thick with emotion. "How could you do that?"

He shrugged, still easing her down the path toward the Lady, the knife pressed against her side, making her wince as its tip dug into her skin through the flimsy material of her dress.

"I never knew the woman. She was nothing to me."

"Am I nothing to you?" Lyse asked.

He stopped walking, holding her in place. She didn't think he was going to answer her, but finally he spoke:

"She gave me away, Lyse. She did the same to your mother, and to you, even. She never wanted any of us. She was cold as ice."

Lyse shook her head.

"I don't think that's true. I know she had reasons for what she did—"

He shook her roughly.

"Shut up, or I'll stick this blade into you," he growled. "You don't know what you're talking about."

Lyse kept her mouth shut, taking him at his word.

"Start walking," he said. "My car is just across the way. You're going to be a good girl and get inside without a word—and then we'll go somewhere a little more private. Where we can conclude our business in peace."

Lyse could imagine where he would take her. Probably back to the abandoned tunnel. He could strangle her there at his leisure and no one would ever be the wiser.

You're almost there.

Eleanora sounded as though she were standing beside them. Lyse crooked her neck, trying to see if her uncle had heard the voice, too, but his rugged face was like granite, impassive in the moonlight.

"I'll go with you," Lyse said. "I'll do whatever you want. Just don't hold that knife so close to my side."

He laughed and let the blade drift away from her skin.

"Your wish is my command."

Run, Lyse!

Lyse did as Eleanora said, breaking free from her uncle's grasp. She heard him inhale sharply, felt his anger reaching out for her, but she didn't look back, just ran as fast as she could toward the Lady of the Lake.

"Help me!" she cried.

Where there had only been calm skies above her, now a flash of lightning shot across the inky night. She could feel her uncle gaining on her, the blade of his knife itching to find the softness of her belly.

Thunder boomed, shaking the ground. Another flash of lightning lit up the sky, the atmosphere thrumming with electricity.

"Eleanora!" Lyse yelled. "Help me, please!"

Lyse reached the statue the very moment the third and final bolt of lightning raced across the heavens and embedded itself into the base of the statue. The stone exploded with an earsplitting *crack*, and the Lady of the Lake toppled forward. Lyse watched in horror as it fell on top of her uncle, crushing him into the ground.

"Oh my God," Lyse whispered, falling to her knees, eyes glued to the ghostly white hand protruding from underneath the Lady of the Lake.

"Lyse?"

Lyse dragged her gaze away from the ghastly sight of her uncle's body and stared at the ghostly young woman who stood before her.

"Eleanora?" she whispered, incredulous.

The young Eleanora looked so much like the image on

the Saint Anne candle that the woman in the bodega had given her that Lyse could hardly believe it.

"You're so beautiful," Lyse said. "So young."

"I'm here, Lyse," she said, smiling as she knelt beside her granddaughter. *"I'll be with you whenever you need me."*

"I miss you," Lyse said, trying not to cry.

"Don't," Eleanora said—but Lyse couldn't help it. It'd been an overwhelming night, and she was beaten.

She covered her face with her hands, wanting to curl into a ball and sob herself to sleep, but Eleanora's next few words washed over her like a tidal wave.

"The Flood is coming, Lyse. Prepare yourself."

The silence that followed Eleanora's last words was long and unbroken. When Lyse finally found the courage to open her eyes again, her grandmother's ghost was gone.

"Eleanora?" Lyse whispered—but there was no reply.

Finally Lyse crawled to her feet, her body aching with exhaustion. With an unsteady gait, she began the long, lonely walk back to the empty bungalow on Curran Street.

Lyse sat up in bed, her entire body drenched in sweat. She looked around the room, frantic. She wasn't sure where she was and it scared her. But slowly, the darkness bled away, and the space came into focus. She was in Eleanora's house, tucked away in her childhood bed.

Alone.

Outside the bedroom windows, the wind whistled and skittered like buckshot. Lyse lay in her bed thinking as she listened to the outdoor sounds.

Was it a dream? Her aching body and stiff limbs told her it was not. The Lady of the Lake was gone—and she and Eleanora had murdered a man. Albeit one who would have killed her had she not gotten him first.

She put away the image of her uncle's ruined body, filing

it in a part of her brain she naïvely hoped she would never have to access again. It was all just too much to process—though she knew it was only the beginning. That, like a tidal wave, Eleanora's secret life was about to swallow her up.

After what seemed like ages, Lyse threw off the blankets and got up. She realized she was still in the black sheath dress from the memorial, and she yanked at its hem, ripping and tearing it as she pulled the fabric over her head, then threw it on the floor. In her bra and panties, she ran to the closest window and opened it wide, daring the storm outside to spirit her away. When this didn't happen—and she got tired of the rain lashing at her face—she sat in the middle of the bedroom floor and wrapped her arms around her naked knees. Her fingers played with the bandage on her calf, yanking at the gauze until she'd torn it away from her skin.

I am alone in Eleanora's house, she thought—and she started to cry.

She thought about Eleanora and the twin babies she'd given up, thought about her uncle crushed underneath the stone Lady of the Lake, thought about where she, Lyse, fit into the unfolding story. She sat within the feathery tendrils of the wind as it blew in through the windows, reaching out for her with grasping fingers. She sat in darkness, rocking back and forth, hands clutching at her ankles.

It wasn't until close to dawn that she finally fell asleep, curled in the fetal position on the rag rug, the rain singing against the roof of the house as it lulled her into unconsciousness—her decision finally made.

Sitting on the side table next to her bed, the Saint Anne candle flared to life, its flame flickering like a signal fire in the night.

Eleanora was pleased her granddaughter had decided to stay in Echo Park.